U0165599

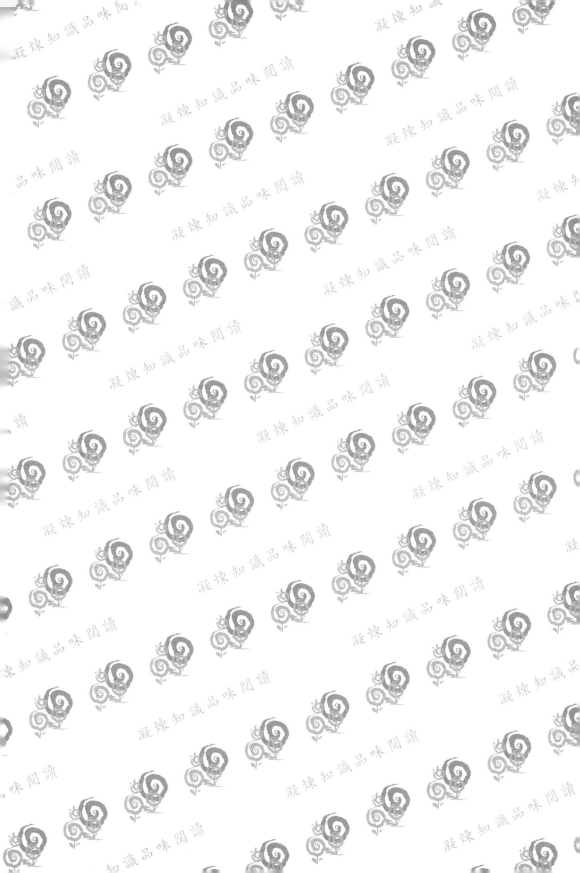

應用外語
43

談笑用兵
英文句型全攻略

逢甲大學 林羨峯 博士 著

五南圖書出版公司 印行

ENGLISH

Thank You! 致謝 ｜

感謝先嚴林德寬先生與先慈林吳月珠女士的寬容與養育栽培之恩！

感謝賜給我充滿希望動力新生命的上帝！

感謝妻子洪曉莉的默默支持與鼓勵！

感謝中山大學外文系語言學專家黃舒屏教授、逢甲大學外文系翻譯專家蔡明秀教授、以及逢甲大學外文系翻譯專家王大維教授費心協助審稿，提供寶貴的專業意見！

感謝前國立師範大學英語系教授現任逢甲大學外文系特聘教授何文敬博士為本書撰寫推薦序文！

感謝臺灣大學語文中心主任宋麗梅博士推薦本書！

感謝所有曾經敦促幫助我英文不斷進步的所有老師、好友、學生！

感謝五南圖書出版公司超強編輯群鉅細靡遺地審稿修訂，本書始得以順利出版！

推薦序 | Foreword

　　在「雙語教育」幾乎成為全民運動的今天，眾人皆知英語能力的培養與訓練日益重要，然而「如何學好英文」或「學英文需不需要學文法呢」？鑑於英文並非我們的母語，而且我們不是從小即生活在說英文的日常環境與文化中，所以熟習文法規則乃是學好英文之奠基過程。而挑選優良的文法教材，則可節省學習時間和精力，坐收事半功倍之效。

　　《談笑用兵　英文句型全攻略》乃是當今極為出色的文法兼寫作教材，非常適合當前的高中生和大學生，甚至社會人士。作者林羨峯博士早年任教於僑光商專（現改制為僑光科技大學），十年前轉至逢甲大學外文系，十多年來一直任教「文法與修辭」與「英文作文」等課程，教學經驗與專業學養豐富，本書即為林博士積年累月之心血結晶。

　　本書最大的特色，乃是它著重於句型的解說、練習與靈活運用，也是它有別於坊間大多數文法教材之處，這也是為什麼要強調句型呢？這可以從「英文單字如何組成有意義的句子？」這個問題窺出端倪，答案是依照句型的排列組合；換言之，句型乃是句子組合的方式，熟悉英語的各種句型，確實可以改善英語表述技巧，進而有效提升造句、寫作和口語表達等能力。其次，本書在結構、內容與作業上，都是以循序漸進、由淺入深的方式安排，章節段落條理分明。第三個特色乃是該書範例和練習題較多，而且強調完整句子的練習，亦適合當作初階的寫作教材。最後，本書所有習題皆附有解答或參考答案，堪供社會人士自習之用。

何文敬
逢甲大學外國語文學系特聘教授
中央研究院歐美研究所兼任研究員

自序 | Preface

　　能夠完成這本英文教材，首先要感謝兩位恩師：一位是帶我進入英文世界的陳學華老師，另一位是帶我認識耶穌信仰的 Brian Short 老師。

　　距離生平頭一次接觸英文已經整整五十年了！猶清楚記得小學畢業的暑假，我讀臺中女中的姊姊帶我報名英文暑期先修班，由當時已頗有名氣的臺中一中英文老師陳學華授課。有趣的是，我們上課的地方竟然是一家幼稚園的教室。教室很大，可以容納六、七十位學生，勉強擠在狹窄的課桌椅上課，絲毫不影響我初次接觸英文的興奮。陳老師的教學幽默流暢，條理清晰。雖然是在悶熱的午後上課，卻是聽得津津有味，根本無暇打瞌睡。在陳老師的引導下，英文漸漸在我心底萌芽。

　　當時每次上課，都先小考，下課前也都會交代作業。小時候我其實很貪玩，並不是勤快讀書的孩子。奇怪的是，陳老師的作業我是一回到家立刻寫好，每次上課都很期待考試，下課時更想知道當天的考試成績，天天興致高昂的讀英文。

　　很快地，暑期英文班即將結束，進行最後一次總測驗，驗收學習成果，前三名學生將獲頒獎品。考試結果出爐，一共有三位同學考滿分 100 分，我是其中一位。陳老師準備了三份不一樣的獎品，第一名的獎品是一枝價值不斐的名牌鋼筆，以抽籤的方式來決定誰是第一名。也許是命中注定，第一獎竟然由我僥倖獲得！

陳學華老師是我的英文啟蒙老師，引導我開心地踏入英文的世界，從此與英文結下不解之緣，而英文居然也成為我一生的工作。

國中三年，英文都在班上名列前茅，畢業後考上臺中一中，卻漸漸荒廢功課，成天與狐群狗黨到處鬼混，成績一落千丈，雖然英文仍然維持高分，但終致大學聯考連連落榜，沉淪社會底層，無力自拔。父母對我從滿懷期待，逐漸失望，最後澈底絕望。就在人生最低谷的時候，上帝伸出援手，透過中古機車的買賣，我認識了甫自美國堪薩斯來東海大學教英文的 Brian Short 老師。我學習英文多年，可是從來沒遇見說英語的外國人，我心想這可是磨練口說英語的大好機會。而這位比我年輕一歲的帥哥雖然買了我那部很破的中古機車而損失慘重，卻因為身負使命，來臺灣分享耶穌的福音，仍然願意與我這個壞人交朋友。就這樣，我混進了東海大學導航會的大學生團契，卻意外地感受到濃濃的溫暖與關心，發現他們身上有積極生命的特質，我也渴望活出那樣的生命，寄望掙脫困縛，找到人生出路。不久之後，我接受耶穌十字架的福音，在教會受洗，從此舊事已過，都變成新的了！新生命神奇的力量澈底翻轉了我的人生。

上帝透過 Brian Short 的關懷與教導，讓我得到人生第二個機會，終於在高中畢業七年後考上臺大哲學系，大二轉讀法律系，畢業兩年後前往 Brian 家鄉堪薩斯州，於 University of Kansas 取得英語教學碩士學位，返國後僥倖獲得當時僑光商專陳伯濤校長聘任為講師，開始夢寐以求的英文教學生涯。

　　在僑光商專任教十年，學校已升格改制為技術學院，深感學識能力不足，於是再度赴美，於 University of Delaware 進修，順利取得博士學位，旋即返回僑光復職，並升等為副教授，前後兼任多媒體中心主任與應用外語系系主任。隔年，行政院研考會招募翻譯人員參與營造英語環境計畫，我僥倖通過測驗，獲聘為兼職的特約英文翻譯，負責中翻英與審稿。同時，亦獲聘為外語替代役專業英文筆譯授課講座，指導學員中翻英技巧。之後於 2008 年，感謝時任外文系主任彭芳美教授引薦，幸運獲聘進入逢甲大學外文系，任職至今。期間主要授課科目為語言學概論、英文文法與修辭、以及英文作文。

　　在長年的教學過程中，深覺臺灣學生在英文寫作上受到中文母語根深柢固的影響，往往以不一定正確的英文詞彙套用在中文句型結構上，因此所寫出來的英文句子總會出現文法上的瑕疵與文義上的不明。這樣的英文句子，對於不諳中文的外籍教師而言難以理解，反倒是本國教師能夠推敲出學生所要表達的涵義。究其原因，主要在於中英文兩種語言彼此差距甚大，不但兩者詞彙之間並非一對一的簡單對應，而在句子結構上更是南轅北轍，從而形成臺灣學生在學習英文寫作上高牆障礙，難以攀越。學生一方面要學習英文詞彙的正確涵義與用法，而很多英文詞彙又是一字多義或多字同義；另一方面又需努力認識極為陌生的英文句型結構，再將這兩大方面的語文知識應用在英文寫作上，其經歷的困難可想而知。

　　緣此，該如何幫助學生突破英文寫作的困難，簡化學習過程並縮短學習時間，有效強化學生對英文句型結構的瞭解與運用，寫出正確合乎文法的英文句子，並進而善用各種英文句型變化，寫出流暢又富變化的英文文章，而有了本書的發想。本書針對英文句型結構，由淺入深，從英文單字、片語、動狀詞的種類與運用以及各類型動詞所適用的簡單句句型，進入獨立子句與從屬子句句型以及其相互結合所形成的合句、複句、複合句，並其簡化後的分詞構句，最後介紹英文的特殊句型，包括假設語氣、比較句型、倒裝句等等。透過一系列的句型講解與由易而難的各式練習題，有效地引導學生充分掌握英文句型的結構與變化，而得以談笑用兵，輕鬆寫出正確又富變化的英文句子！

前言 | Preface

在英語對話中，單獨一個英文單字即可以用來表達說話者的意思。例如，亞當初次看到夏娃的那一刻，他有可能直接說出 "Wow!" 來表達他的驚喜；或是小孩子看到不喜歡的食物脫口而出 "Yuck!"；或是遇有緊急危險狀況，會有人大喊 "Run!"；或是老師面對一群吵鬧不休的學生，會說出 "Quiet!" 要學生安靜；或是當我們目睹大自然的奇景或藝術家出神入化的表演，我們會驚嘆地說出 "Awesome!"，"Marvelous!"，"Amazing!"，"Spectacular!" 等等字眼；或甚至不發一語，保持沉默也可以表達抗議或冷漠。另外，我們也常常使用單獨一個片語來傳達訊息，例如當被問到所在位置時，可以回答 "In the kitchen."；或是被問到交通工具時，可以回答 "By car."；或是被問到哪一年時，可以回答 "In 2012."

然而，在正式英文寫作，則是運用完整的句子 (complete sentence) 來傳遞較複雜的訊息和涵義。英文的句子依其結構分為四種類型，而且僅有這四種類型：簡單句 (simple sentence)，複句 (complex sentence)，合句 (compound sentence)，及複合句 (compound complex sentence)。每一種類型的句子各有其不可或缺的要件與結構，絲毫不得馬虎。

英文句子的創作就像是在組裝一部汽車，需要先把各式各樣的零件準備好，再加以裝配，而其中最重要的部分當然不是汽車的外殼，也不是輪胎或是導航系統，而是汽車的引擎，因為缺了引擎，汽車完全無法發揮功能。單字和片語就是用來組合句子的零件，其中最關鍵的則是動詞，動詞就是句子的核心，而主詞則是方向盤，也是不可或缺的零件。要特別瞭解的是，英文不同類型的動詞會決定還有哪些零件是必需的配備，而哪些配備則是選配。最陽春的英文句子只需要動詞搭配主詞即可組裝完成，其餘的修飾語則是選配，例如：*The baby is talking.* 這個句子的動詞 is talking 搭配主詞 the baby 即可構成一個完整的句子。若是加上選配的修飾語，則句子可以變成 *The bright baby is talking to her sister fluently.* 句子中的 bright（形容詞）、to her sister（介系詞片語）、以及 fluently（副詞）都是選配的零件。

有的動詞除了主詞，還必須搭配其他必要的零件，例如受詞、主詞補語、受詞補語等等，才能組成完整的英文句子，例如：*The baby loves music.*（music 為受詞）；或是 *The baby is cute.*（cute 為主詞補語）；或是 *The baby calls the cat tiger.*（tiger 為受詞補語）。少了這些必要的配件，即使具備了動詞和主詞，仍然無法表達完整的涵義，而不足以構成句子，就像是汽車少了必要的組件，不能出廠上路。

英文句子中最基本的類型為簡單句（simple sentences），由一個獨立子句（independent clauses）所構成，其結構包含主部（subject）與述部（predicate），主部由名詞片語（noun phrases）或與名詞片語相同功能的片語所構成，而述部則由動詞片語（verb phrases）所構成。例如：

| People | learn English | . = | 主部／名詞片語 | + | 述部／動詞片語 |

所謂的簡單句，指的是句子的結構單純，而非表達的內容簡單。英文的簡單句也運用動詞的時態來表達時間，或是加上各類型的片語（phrase），進行句子的**內部擴充**，仍然維持簡單句的結構，以傳達更多的訊息。例如：

| People of all ages | are learning English to connect with those in other countries | .
= | 主部／名詞片語 | + | 述部／動詞片語 |

除了內部擴充，簡單句也可以與簡單句或從屬子句（dependent clause）結合，進行**外部的延伸**，以合句、複句、或複合句的結構來表達更豐富的涵義。例如：

合句（簡單句 + 對等連接詞 + 簡單句）：
English is the most common language in the world, **so** people of all ages are learning it to connect with those in other countries.

複句（從屬子句 + 簡單句）：
Because English is the most common language in the world, people of all ages are learning it to connect with those in other countries.

複合句（合句 + 從屬子句）：
English is the most common language in the world, **so** peo-

ple of all ages **whose native language is not English** are learning it to connect with those in other countries.

英文句型的變化除了以上呈現的四種結構的變動，尚有許多特殊的句式，包括：主動語態與被動語態的互換、分詞構句、連接副詞的運用、假設語氣、比較、直接引述與間接引述、分裂句、與倒裝句。英文句子可以依不同的情境和所強調的重點，使用不同的句型，在**正確中求變化，變化中求正確**，而不致流於單調。

英文的單字儘管很多，卻也是有限的，然而以有限的單字所能夠造出來的英文句子卻是無限多。道理很簡單，就像是各種料理的大廚能夠以有限的食材創造出無限多的佳餚，靠的是紮實的基本料理功夫與精進的手藝。英文寫作也是要借助紮實的基本造句能力，加上不斷練習各種英文句型變化的技巧，便能如行雲流水的寫出**正確又富於變化**的好句子、好段落、好文章了。

本書分成四大篇，包括基本概念篇、動詞進階篇、句型變化篇、以及特殊句式篇。基本概念篇包含了英文句子的構成與擴充、英文單字的種類、動狀詞、片語；動詞進階篇介紹英文五種基本動詞類型之外的其他類型的動詞以及被動語態；句型變化篇篇幅最長，內容包含獨立子句與名詞子句、副詞子句、形容詞子句等三種從屬子句、複句、複合句、副詞子句與形容詞子句的簡化、分詞構句、數個簡單句的結合，連接副詞的運用，以及誤置與脫節修飾語；特殊句式篇是說明英文的特殊句型，包括條件句與假設語氣、比較句型、直接引述與間接引述、代名詞 it 的用法，以及倒裝句。

整本教材由淺顯簡單逐漸深入複雜，而每個章節的練習題也包括：最基本的「小試身手」、稍微難一點的「打通關」，以及最難的「挑戰題中翻英」。本書附有習題解答，其中中翻英的答案可能會因為使用不同的用詞或句型結構而有所不同，因此習題解答所提供的英譯為參考答案，若有疑問，可以請教授課老師，或是來信與作者討論指正。

目錄 | Contents

基本概念篇 |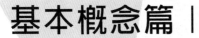

英文句子的構成元素

一句話說得合宜，就如金蘋果在銀網子裡。

（聖經 箴言 25:11）

A wod aptly spoken is like apples of gold in settings of silver.

(Proverbs 25:11)

第一章 英文句子的構成

英文句子的構成是由單字構成片語，再由數個片語構成句子。

英文單字有多少呢？
事實：很多，很多，非常多！（儘管非常多，卻還是有限的！）
英文的句子又有多少呢？
事實：跟天上的星星一樣多！跟海灘的細沙一樣多！無限多！

請問：**你會使用的英文單字有多少？** 回答：很多，不少，還可以，不太夠…，反正是有限的！

請問：**你認為你用有限的單字可以寫出多少不同的英文句子？**
回答：不多，還不少，很多，非常多，無限多？
事實：跟天上的星星一樣多！跟海灘的細沙一樣多！無限多！

真的假的？騙我！

嚇到了嗎？事實上，你真的可以用**有限的英文單字**寫出**無限多的英文句子**！

怎麼可能？係金ㄟ嗎？

千真萬確，一點都不假！道理很簡單，就像世界上的食材也是有限的，技巧高超的廚師卻能變化出千萬種不同的菜餚；同樣地，我們也可以使用有限的英文單字，巧妙運用句型的變化，而寫出無限多的英文句子。

底下的幾個例句顯示如何以簡單易懂的單字，建構出各種不同句型的英文句子。

Sam 熱愛漢堡。
Sam loves hamburgers.
（由獨立子句構成的**簡單句**）

Sam 是英文老師，熱愛漢堡。
Sam, **who is an English teacher**, loves hamburgers.
（簡單句中含有一個**非限定形容詞子句**而構成**複句**）

Sam 是英文老師，受到美國文化影響，熱愛漢堡。
Influenced by American culture, Sam, **an English teacher**, loves hamburgers.
（句首加了過去分詞片語 **Influenced by American culture**，形成**分詞構句**的句型，而原來的非限定形容詞子句已經**簡化為名詞片語 an English teacher**，作為 Sam 的同位語。句子的結構又轉變成**簡單句**。）

Sam 是英文老師，受到美國文化影響，熱愛漢堡，並且他打算開一家漢堡餐廳。
Influenced by American culture, Sam, an English teacher, loves hamburgers, **and** he plans to open a hamburger restaurant.
（兩個簡單句由對等連接詞 **and** 結合成為**合句**）

Sam 是英文老師，受到美國文化影響，熱愛漢堡，並且他打算退休之後開一家漢堡餐廳。

Influenced by American culture, Sam, an Enlgish teacher, loves hamburgers, **and** he plans to open a hamburger restaurant **after he retires**.

（合句的結構中加入副詞子句 **after he retires**，句子結構成為**複合句**。）

　　以上的例句所使用的單字同學們一定都會，差別在於句子結構的變化，從簡單句到複句，到合句，再到複合句，以及分詞的運用與從屬子句的簡化。這本書的目的就是要讓同學澈底瞭解各種英文句型的變化，經過不斷練習，最終可以熟練地運用這些句型變化的技巧，寫出變化多端又合乎文法的英文句子。就像學做料理、練武功、或是變魔術，都是先把基本功練好，再進而鑽研更高超的技巧，而能隨心所欲，如行雲流水的出手。

　　英文的句子由單字組成片語，片語再結合成為獨立子句，進而構成簡單句。這就是英文寫作的基本功。我們可以使用對等連接詞把兩個獨立子句結合成為合句；或是獨立子句也可以搖身一變，成為從屬子句，再嵌入或附屬於單一的獨立子句而構成複句；或是從屬子句嵌入或依附於合句中而構成複合句，這些屬於進階的句型，也是英文寫作不可或缺的變化技巧。

　　正確中求變化，變化中求正確。正是英文句型變化的最高指導原則！

1.1 簡單句的基本結構

　　英文的簡單句由獨立子句所構成,而獨立子句由單字與片語所搭配而成,其結構**所需要的元素是由動詞的類型所決定,不同類型的動詞需要搭配不同的必要元素**,才能構成一個完整的獨立子句,進而形成簡單句。我們首先來認識簡單句的結構:

　　語言學中的句構學分析簡單句的結構為:**名詞片語結合動詞片語構成簡單句。**

句子 (S) = 名詞片語 (NP) + 動詞片語 (VP)

名詞片語 (NP)	動詞片語 (VP)
The smartphone	is a useful tool.

　　也就是文法書所說的:**主部(名詞片語)結合述部(動詞片語)**構成簡單句。

句子 (Sentence) = 主部 (Subject) + 述部 (Predicate)

主部 (Subject)	述部 (Predicate)
The smartphone	is a useful tool.

1.2 構成主部的名詞片語

　　名詞片語(主部)包括 (1) 由名詞帶頭所構成的**名詞片語**,以及作用與名詞片語功能相同的(2) **動名詞片語**與 (3) **不定詞片語**（若是複句的結構，名詞子句也可以作為主詞）；名詞片語可長可短，可以只是單一名詞、動名詞、或不定詞；也可以再加上其他的片語而擴充其涵義，例如：

dogs, honesty, the secret **project**, his parking **spot**, a stunning **miracle**, **a father** of two children, the **reputation** of the company, **a courageous act** witnessed by many people 等等屬於**由名詞帶頭的名詞片語**

cooking, owning a scooter, accidently **breaking the vase** in the gallery 等等屬於**動名詞片語**

to succeed, to purchase merchandise online, **to** gratefully **accept the** generous **gift** 等等則屬於不定詞片語。

說明

帶頭的名詞、或是**動名詞**、或是**不定詞**就是文法書所稱的句子的**主詞**，其單複數決定動詞的單複數，上述名詞片語中的粗體字即是決定單複數的主詞，其中**動名詞片語**與**不定詞片語**都是**單數的主詞**。

1.3 構成述部的動詞片語

動詞片語（述部）則是**由動詞所帶頭的動詞片語**，而動詞片語所需具備的必要元素依動詞類型有所不同。動詞片語也是可長可短，可以是 (1) 單一的動詞加上其他必要的元素，或是 (2) 再加上其他片語擴充其涵義，例如：

talk, **can swim**, **is fun**, **cost the tourist a fortune** to compensate, **is happening** to them right now, **requires hard work and a little luck**, **has allowed him** to move around the city freely, **promises them** to take the family to Hawaii for a one-week vacation in the summer 等等。（**粗體字部分爲動詞以及依動詞類型所必要的元素**）

我們現在試著使用剛剛列出來的名詞片語和動詞片語寫出簡單句，例如：

Dogs can swim .
NP／主部 + VP／述部
= 名詞 + 完全不及物動詞

Cooking is fun .
NP／主部 + VP／述部
= 動名詞 + 不完全不及物動詞 + 主詞補語

To succeed requires hard work and a little luck .
NP／主部 + VP／述部
= 不定詞 + 完全及物動詞 + 受詞

A stunning **miracle** **is happening** to them right now .
NP／主部 + VP／述部
= 名詞片語 + 完全不及物動詞 + 介系詞片語

Owning a scooter **has allowed him** to move around the city freely .

NP／主部 + VP／述部

= 動名詞片語 + 完全及物動詞 + 受詞 + 不定詞片語

Accidently **breaking the antique vase** in the gallery **cost the tourist a fortune** to compensate .

NP／主部 + VP／述部

= 動名詞片語 + 不完全及物動詞 + 受詞 + 受詞補語 + 不定詞

（有關片語的分類與功能將在第四章詳細說明）

1.4 英文五種基本動詞句型

　　英文句子的核心元素為主詞和動詞，但是句子的句型並非由主詞所左右，而是由動詞所決定。我們來看以下的例子：

　　起初，上帝創造了天地萬物，接著又造了亞當，上帝覺得亞當一個人太孤單，於是又取了亞當的一條肋骨，造了夏娃。亞當第一眼看見夏娃時，睜大了眼睛說：

Wow! You are ....

夏娃等了數十秒，忍不住催促亞當把話說完：

亞當趕緊補上：

You are .... **gorgeous!**

接著，亞當又對夏娃說：

Will you marry ....

夏娃又等了好一會兒，於是又催促亞當把話說完，亞當趕緊回答：

Will you marry .... **me**?

於是，夏娃嫁給了亞當，成為夫妻。

後來，夏娃生下他們的第一個男孩，夏娃說：

We will name our baby ....
這次換亞當等了半天，終於忍不住催促夏娃把話說完，夏娃回答說：

We will name our baby .... **Cain**.

於是亞當對夏娃說：

I will give Cain ....
夏娃又等的不耐煩，再度催促亞當：你到底要給兒子什麼？
亞當回答說：

I will give Cain .... **my blessing**.

前述亞當或夏娃的話之所以沒說完，正是因為句子少了某種不可或缺的元素，以致無法表達完整的涵義，如以下說明：

You are **gorgeous**!
（are 是不完全不及物動詞，除了主詞與動詞，還需要有**主詞補語 gorgeous** 來完成句子的結構。）

Will you marry **me**?
（marry 是完全及物動詞，除了主詞與動詞，還需要有**受詞**

<u>me</u> 來完成句子的結構。）

We will name our baby **Cain**.
（name 是不完全及物動詞，除了主詞、動詞、與受詞，還需要有**受詞補語 Cain** 來完成句子的結構。）

I will give Cain **my blessing**.
（give 是授與動詞，除了主詞、動詞、間接受詞，還需要有**直接受詞 my blessing** 來完成句子的結構。）

　　從以上亞當與夏娃的對話，我們瞭解到：要寫出正確的英文句子，首先要認識英文動詞所扮演的角色。英文的句子由主部與述部所構成，述部就是動詞片語，而構成動詞片語的必要元素則取決於動詞所屬的類型，換言之，不同類型的動詞構成動詞片語時所需要的必要元素也有所不同。不同類型的英文動詞必須搭配不同的要素形成動詞片語，進而決定子句（clause）及句子（sentence）的句型。換言之，英文句子構成的核心樞紐並不是主詞，而是動詞。

　　使用英文動詞來創造句子時，必須分辨其屬於哪一種類型，需要具備哪些必要的元素，以組成句子的完整結構，否則句子的結構一旦缺少任一必要元素，就形成不合文法、殘缺的句子了。因此，若要英文寫作進步，寫出完整正確的句子，要勤快使用紙本或線上字典，參考字典所提供的例句，或是上網搜尋該動詞的相關句子，方能澈底瞭解每一個動詞的屬性與適用的句型，以避免誤用犯錯。

　　值得注意的是，許多英文動詞不僅限於一種適用的句型，而是具備兩種或更多的屬性，依照其不同的涵義適用不同的句型。例如：

Can the eyewitness **identify** the suspect?（指認／及物動詞）
目擊證人能不能指認出嫌犯呢？
We **identify with** people with the same interests.（認同／不及物動詞）
我們會認同有相同興趣的人。

英文動詞句型繁多，本章僅先介紹五種常用的英文的動詞句型，包括：

(1) 完全不及物動詞
(2) 不完全不及物動詞
(3) 完全及物動詞
(4) 不完全及物動詞
(5) 授與動詞

其他的動詞句型則在第六章進階動詞再詳細解說。

▶▶ 1.4.1 不及物動詞句型

不及物動詞，顧名思義，就是這一類的動詞不需要搭配受詞，即可成句。不及物動詞又可分為三類，第一類是動詞本身搭配主詞 (S. + Vi.) 即可組成主部與述部的結構，表達完整的涵義，稱為完全不及物動詞 (complete intransitive verbs)。第二類則是動詞之後必須加上主詞補語 (Vi. + S.C.)，才能組成完整的動詞片語／述部，再結合主部構成句子，表達完整的涵義，稱為不完全不及物動詞 (incomplete intransitive verbs)。而第三類的不及物動詞則是先接介系詞後，再接受詞 (Vi. + Prep. + O.)，從而組成完整的動詞片語／述部，再與主部構成句子，表達完整的涵義。本節先只介紹完全不及物動詞與不完全不及物動詞這兩類不及物動詞，而不及物動詞接介系詞再接受詞的句型則留待第六章動詞進階句型中介紹。

1.4.2 完全不及物動詞 (complete intransitive verbs)

完全不及物動詞不需搭配受詞，只要與主部結合即可表達完整的涵義，構成一個完整的句子，這是英文當中最簡單的句子結構。

完全不及物動詞的句型為：

主部 S. ＋ 述部 / 完全不及物動詞 Vi.

The small boat floats .（浮著）　　　　　　　　(S. + Vi.)

The jet fighter flies really fast .（飛行）　　　　(S. + Vi.)

My happy daughter is singing in the bathroom .（唱歌）

(S. + Vi.)

The pressure cooker suddenly exploded .（爆炸）　(S. + Vi.)

My lease of the apartment will expire next month .（到期）

(S. + Vi.)

1.4.3 不完全不及物動詞 (incomplete intransitive verbs)

不完全不及物動詞雖然不需要搭配受詞，但僅僅結合主部不足以表達完整的涵義，此類動詞必須要搭配主詞補語 (subject complements)，才能形成一個完整的動詞片語，進而與主部構成完整的句子。主詞補語可以是**名詞片語**、**動名詞片語**、**不定詞片**

語、形容詞片語、現在分詞片語、過去分詞片語。

不完全不及物動詞又稱爲連綴動詞 (linking verbs)，常用的有 **appear, be, become, feel, get, grow, lie, remain, seem, stay, stand, sound, look, smell, taste**。

不完全不及物動詞句型爲：

主部 S. + 述部 / 不完全不及物動詞 Vi. + 主詞補語 S.C.

The lawyer **became a** famous **writer** .（成爲…）

(S. + Vi. + S.C.)

（名詞片語 a famous writer 作爲主詞補語）

His brother **is an English professor** .（是…）(S. + Vi. + S.C.)

（名詞片語 an English professo 作爲主詞補語）

Her hobby **is painting pictures** in scenic places .（是…）

(S. + Vi. + S.C.)

（動名詞片語 painting pictures in scenic places 作爲主詞補語）

His ambition **is to become a successful entrepreneur** .（是…）

(S. + Vi. + S.C.)

（不定詞片語 to become a successful entrepreneur 作爲主詞補語）

The food on the table **looks** really **good** .（看起來…）

(S. + Vi. + S.C.)

（形容詞片語 really good 作爲主詞補語）

The new secretary **seems comfortable** with her job . (似乎是…)

(S. + Vi. + S.C.)

（形容詞片語 comfortable with her job 作為主詞補語）

The news story **sounds interesting** to me . (聽起來…)

(S. + Vi. + S.C.)

（現在分詞片語 interesting to me 作為主詞補語）

She **feels relaxed** listening to jazz music after work . (覺得…)

(S. + Vi. + S.C.)

（過去分詞片語 relaxed listening to jazz music after work 作為主詞補語）

▶▶ 1.4.4 小試身手

使用 完全不及物動詞 或 不完全不及物動詞 的句型將下列中文句子翻成英文。

1. 經過一天辛苦的工作，這個農夫**覺得**累壞了。(feel)

_____

2. 這幾道菜太**好吃**了！(taste)

_____

3. 垃圾食物**對**健康不好。(be)

_____

4. 他們**看起來似乎**不太高興。(seem)

_____

5. 其中一些客人一直到半夜才**離開**。(leave)

_____

6. 她在考試時**保持**冷靜。(stay)

_____

7. 鹿**消失**在樹林裡。(disappear)

_____

8. 他**已經成為**一位優秀的攝影師了。(become)

_____

9. 漢堡**一直是**我夏天最愛的餐點。(be)

_____

10. 東南亞國家由於國外的投資而**繁榮中**。(prosper)

_____

 ## 1.4.5 及物動詞句型 (transitive verbs)

及物動詞的句型必須具備的要素就是動詞之後一定要接受詞。及物動詞可分為兩類，其中一種只要搭配受詞即可組成完整的動詞片語，進而與主部構成句子，表達完整的涵義，這種動詞稱為**完全及物動詞** (complete transitive verbs)；另一種及物動詞則需要再搭配受詞補語 (object complements)，才能組成完整的動詞片語，再與主部結合，構成句子，表達完整涵義，這種動詞屬於**不完全及物動詞** (incomplete transitive verbs)。

1.4.6 完全及物動詞 (complete transitive verbs)

完全及物動詞 (complete transitive verbs) 與受詞組成完整的動詞片語，進而與主部構成一個完整的句子，表達完整的涵義。

完全及物動詞的句型為：

| 主部 S. | + | 述部／及物動詞 Vt. + 受詞 O. |

Belinda **is playing tennis** .（打…球） (S. + Vt. + O.)

The bright student **solved the math problem** .（解…題）

(S. + Vt. + O.)

Passing the test **takes a lot of practice** .（需要…）

(S. + Vt. + O.)

The congress **passed a new law** last week .（通過…）

(S. + Vt. + O.)

▶▶ 1.4.7 小試身手

　　使用 完全及物動詞 的句型將下列中文句子翻成英文。

1. 二十年前他成立了這家公司。(establish)

_____

2. 公司去年的營業額首次達到五億美金。(reach)

_____

3. 雇主感謝所有員工過去這一年的努力。(appreciate)

_____

4. 她今年已經從股票市場賺了超過三十萬美金了。(make)

_____

5. 這位教授正在進行一項有關網路購物的研究。(conduct)

_____

▶▶ 1.4.8 不完全及物動詞 (incomplete transitive verbs)

　　不完全及物動詞 (incomplete transitive verbs) 必須搭配兩個
要素，也就是受詞及受詞補語 (object complements)，才能構成完整的動詞片語，進而與主部結合構成句子，表達完整的涵義。

　　不完全及物動詞的句型爲：

主部 S. + 述部／及物動詞 Vt. + 受詞 O. + 受詞補語（名詞或形容詞）O.C.

例如：

They **named their baby Michael** .（爲…取名爲…）

　　　　　　　　　　　　　　　（S. + Vt. + O. + **名詞 O.C.** ）

（their baby 爲受詞，**Michael** 爲受詞補語）

The new watch **cost her US$3,000** .（使某人花費了…）

　　　　　　　　　　　　　　　（S. + Vt. + O. + **名詞 O.C.** ）

（her 爲受詞，**US$3,000** 爲受詞補語）

The movie **made the audience sad** .（使…感覺…）

　　　　　　　　　　　　　　　（S. + Vt. + O. + **形容詞 O.C.** ）

（the audience 爲受詞，**sad** 爲受詞補語）

People **consider swimming in the creek dangerous** .（認爲…是…的）　　　　　　　　　　（S. + Vt. + O. + **形容詞 O.C.** ）

（swimming in the creek 爲受詞，**dangerous** 爲受詞補語）

▶▶ 1.4.9 授與動詞／雙受詞動詞 (ditransitive verbs)

　　授與動詞／雙受詞動詞後面必須接兩個受詞，一個直接受詞（direct object O1，物），另一個間接受詞（indirect object

O2，人），如此才能組成完整的動詞片語，進而與主部構成完成的句子。間接受詞若是接在動詞之後則不需介系詞，但間接受詞若是接在直接受詞之後，則需要介系詞出現在間接受詞之前。

　　雙受詞動詞的句型為：

(1) 主部 S. + 及物動詞 Vt. + 間接受詞 O2 + 直接受詞 O1
(2) 主部 S. + 及物動詞 Vt. + 直接受詞 O1 + 介系詞 Prep. + 間接受詞 O2

他的女朋友送他一支新手機。

His girlfriend gave him a new cellphone . (S. + Vt. + O2 + O1)

His girlfriend gave a new cellphone to him .

(S. + Vt. + O1 + Prep. + O2)

（him 為間接受詞，a new cellphone 為直接受詞）

母親幫她女兒送來一把雨傘。

The mother brought her daughter an umbrella .

(S. + Vt. + O2 + O1)

The mother brought an umbrella for her daughter .

(S. + Vt. + O1 + Prep. + O2)

（her daughter 為間接受詞，an umbrella 為直接受詞）

他把他的舊車賣給一位外國學生。

He sold a foreign student his used car . (S. + Vt. + O2 + O1)

He sold his used car to a foreign student .

(S. + Vt. + O1 + Prep. + O2)

（a foreign student 為間接受詞，his used car 為直接受詞）

許多英文動詞具備不同的涵義,而且其屬性也並非一成不變,往往兼具不同的句型用法,例如:

survive

The victim of the accident survived .   (S. + Vi.)

意外的受害者**倖存了**。 （完全不及物動詞）

The little girl survived blood cancer .   (S. + Vt. + O.)

這個小女孩**勝過**血癌**活了下來**。 （完全及物動詞）

appear

An endangered Formosan black bear appeared in the high mountains .   (S. + Vi.)

瀕臨絕種的臺灣黑熊**出現**在高山裏。 （完全不及物動詞）

After a long flight, most of the passengers appeared tired .   (S. + Vi. + S.C.)

經過長程飛行之後,多數的旅客**顯得**疲累。 （**不完全不及物動詞**）

paint

She painted the walls of her room .   (S. + Vt. + O.)

她**粉刷**了她房間的牆壁。 （完全及物動詞）

She painted the walls of her room pink . (S. + Vt. + O. + O.C.)

她**把**她房間的牆壁**粉刷成**粉紅色。 （**不完全及物動詞**）

grow

The population of the migratory birds in Taiwan has **grown** .

臺灣候鳥的數量已經**增加**了。 （完全不及物動詞）   (S. + Vi.)

They $\boxed{\textbf{grow}}$ several kinds of vegetables in the garden .

他們在院子裡**種**了好幾種蔬菜。（**完全及物動詞**）(S. + Vt. + O.)

$\boxed{\text{Their relationship}}$ $\boxed{\text{has } \textbf{grown} \text{ better}}$. (S. + Vi. + S.C.)

他們的關係**漸漸變**好了。（**不完全不及物動詞**）

prove

$\boxed{\text{The new policy}}$ $\boxed{\textbf{proved} \text{ effective}}$. (S. + Vi. + S.C.)

這個新政策**證實**是有效的。（**不完全不及物動詞**）

$\boxed{\text{The police}}$ $\boxed{\text{could not } \textbf{prove} \text{ the guilt of the suspect}}$.

警察無法**證明**嫌犯的罪責。（**完全及物動詞**） (S. + Vt. + O.)

$\boxed{\text{The results of the experiment}}$ $\boxed{\textbf{proved} \text{ the theory wrong}}$.

(S. + Vt. + O. + O.C.)

實驗結果**證明**這個理論是錯的。（**不完全及物動詞**）

▶▶ 1.4.10 小試身手

　　使用 $\boxed{\text{不完全及物動詞}}$ 句型或 $\boxed{\text{雙受詞動詞}}$ 句型將下列中文句子翻成英文。

1. 做運動令人快樂。(make)

_____

2. 她把她的貓咪取名為老虎。(name)

_____

3. 這家律師事務所提供給她一份工作。(offer)

_____

4. 你有沒有把支票寄給他們了？(send)

_____

5. 他們之間的差異使得溝通很困難。(make)

_____

6. 大家視他為最有創意的領導人。(consider)

_____

7. 她把收據交給客人。(hand)

_____

8. 公司送我一張去西班牙的來回機票。(give)

_____

9. 他們任命她擔任新的執行長。(appoint)

_____

10. 這件意外事故使他付出臺幣五萬元的代價。(cost)

_____

1.5 英文句子的構成打通關

　　就下列句子 (1) 框出句子的主部與述部，(2) 並說明其屬於那一種動詞類型。

示範：*My aunt called my mother last night.*

→ My aunt called my mother last night . 完全及物動詞 + 受詞 (Vt. + O.)

1. The English teacher from Australia bought his girlfriend a new watch.

_____

2. To buy merchandise from online stores is more convenient and less time-consuming.

_____

3. Playing video games too much may harm one's eyes.

---

4. A man with a cellphone in his hand carelessly walked into a fountain.

---

5. Watching the funny skit made the kids sitting in front of the stage laugh wildly.

---

6. A lion escaping from the zoo looked hungry and angry.

---

7. Dora sent her friend in Paris a birthday present purchased in Italy.

---

8. Not getting sufficient exercise seems common among young people.

---

9. To win the championship takes a lot of painful training and endeavors.

---

10. Getting injured without health insurance can cost one a fortune.

---

11. People singing in the karaoke consider themselves the happiest in the world.

---

12. College students rarely borrow books from the library.

---

13. The woman in a purple dress hesitated in front of the ATM.

   _____

14. The jewelry displayed in the window seems expensive.

   _____

15. The bridge connecting the two cities suddenly collapsed last
    week.

   _____

第二章 英文單字的種類與功能

　　英文單字繁多，依其性質分為八大詞類：**動詞、名詞、代名詞、形容詞、副詞、介系詞、連接詞、感嘆詞**，在英文句子的結構中分別擔任不同的角色。其中動詞、名詞、代名詞、形容詞（作為主詞補語或受詞補語時）、疑問副詞，分別為構成不同類型簡單句不可或缺的要素，而副詞（除了疑問副詞）、介系詞、連接詞、與感嘆詞則非簡單句結構必要的元素。除此之外，還有**助動詞**，以及由動詞所衍生的**動狀詞**，包括**不定詞、動名詞、現在分詞、與過去分詞**，也都在句子的形成與自我內部擴充上扮演重要的角色。分別說明如下：

2.1 動詞 (verbs)

　　動詞為句子的核心，表達動作、行為、經驗、感受、想法、或狀態，句子的結構由動詞的類別所左右，不同類型的動詞就適用不同句子結構。英文的動詞還必須依照不同的時態或特殊的句型（如假設語氣）作不同的變化，相對地，由於中文並沒有這樣的動詞變化，臺灣學生在學習動詞時態的變化上往往遭遇困難，無法精準掌握變化規則而運用錯誤。本書除了在第一章介紹五種英文基本動詞類型之外，另外在第六章再介紹英文動詞的進階類型，請同學詳讀練習。

動詞的形成

　　英文動詞數量繁多，除了既有的動詞之外，也可以由動詞字尾與字首結合名詞或形容詞而構成動詞，如下列例子：

(1) 名詞加上動詞字尾

例如：class + ify → classify, symbol + ize → symbolize,

(2) 形容詞加上動詞字尾

例如：pure + ify → purify, short + en → shorten

(3) 動詞字首加上名詞

例如：en + danger → endanger, be + friend → befriend

(4) 動詞字首加上形容詞

例如：en + large → enlarge, be + little → belittle

常用動詞字尾與字首	
-ify	classify, intensify, simplify, beautify, purify,
-ize	specialize, symbolize, globalize, organize, memorize
-en	shorten, widen, broaden, tighten
-ate	activate, motivate, innovate, intimidate, authenticate
en-	encourage, enrich, ensure, endanger, enlarge
be-	befriend, belittle

2.2 名詞 (nouns)

名詞是作為表現動詞的主角（**主詞**）或接受動詞的對象（**受詞**），最基本且最簡單的句子結構只須具備一個不及物動詞，搭配一個擔任主詞的名詞，例如：*The baby smiles.*；或是由一個名詞當作主詞，加上一個及物動詞與一個當作受詞的名詞，而形成結構完整的句子，例如：*God created the world.*；另外，當動詞為不完全及物動詞時，名詞也用來作為**受詞補語**，屬於句子結構不可或缺的元素，例如：*They named the baby Timothy.* 這個句子中的受詞補語 Timothy 一旦移除，句子成為 *They named the baby. 結構就有缺陷，而無法表達完整的涵義。相對地，名詞作為非限定用法的同位語時，即非構成簡單句的必要元素，予以省略並不會影響句子的結構，例如：*Jerry's mother, a physician, serves at a local hospital.* 如果把句子中的同位語名詞 *a physician* 移除，留下來 *Jerry's mother serves at a local hospital.*，並不影響句子原有的結構，因此該名詞並非句子結構的必要元素。

　　單一的名詞即可構成名詞片語，或是名詞也可以與形容詞、現在分詞、過去分詞、介系詞片語、與不定詞片語等結合成為名詞片語，例如：

an apartment, a nice apartment with two bedrooms, an apartment located downtown, a fully furnished apartment, a person of interest, a person suspected of stealing, a suspicious person talking on the phone outside the house 等等。

名詞的形成
　　英文名詞的形成可以是：
(1) 形容詞加上名詞字尾
　　例如：different + ence → difference, happy + ness → happiness,
　　　　　special + ty → specialty, patient + ce → patience, warm + th → warmth
(2) 動詞加上名詞字尾
　　例如：create + ion → creation, develop + ment → development,

drive + er → driver, assist + ant → assistant, detect + ive → detective

（注意：-ive 可以作為形容詞的字尾，也可以作為名詞的字尾。）

(3) 名詞加上名詞字尾

例如：art + ist → artist, Taiwan + ese → Taiwanese, friend + ship → friendship

king + dom → kingdom, neighbor + hood → neighbor-hood

常用名詞字尾	
-al	approval, arrival, proposal, refusal,
-ance	appearance, endurance, ignorance, performance
-ence/-ency	difference, patience, reference, tendency
-cy	efficiency, emergency,
-dom	freedom, kingdom, wisdom
-ion/-ation/-sion	creation, generation, formation, examination, expression
-hood	likelihood, childhood, neighborhood
-ment	adjustment, achievement, indictment, movement, payment
-ty/-ity	specialty, safety, honesty, sensitivity, activity, purity, reality
-ness	kindness, happiness, friendliness, illness, eagerness
-th	strength, length, width, warmth

常用名詞字尾	
-ar/-er/-or（人）	liar, scholar, beggar, employer, driver, singer, visitor, survivor
-er/-or（物）	trigger, fertilizer, cooker, elevator, refrigerator, indicator
-ship	friendship, scholarship, penmanship, relationship
-ant	assistant, servant, inhabitant,
-ian	Christian, politician, physician
-ist	activist, artist, dentist, scientist, novelist
-ee	employee, attendee, nominee, trainee
-al	approval, professional
-ese/-n/ian/ish	Taiwanese, Japanese, Asian, American, Canadian, Irish, British
-tive	detective, relative, representative
-ism	idealism, tourism, capitalism

2.3 代名詞 (pronouns)

　　英文的代名詞種類不少，包括：人身代名詞（主格與受格）、所有代名詞、不定代名詞、指示代名詞、反身代名詞、疑問代名詞、相互代名詞、關係代名詞。以下分別說明其用法：

(1) 人身代名詞（主格與受格）

　　人身代名詞分成主格與受格，依不同人稱與單複數使用不同的代名詞，如下表所列。

人身代名詞				
	主格		受格	
	單數	複數	單數	複數
第一人稱	I	we	me	us
第二人稱	you	you	you	you
第三人稱	he/she	they	him/her	them
第三人稱（事物）	it	they	it	them

(2) 所有代名詞

所有代名詞分成所有格形容詞與所有格代名詞，依不同人稱與單複數使用不同的代名詞，如下表所列。

所有代名詞				
	所有格形容詞 （出現在名詞之前）		所有格代名詞 （單獨使用）	
	單數	複數	單數	複數
第一人稱	my	our	mine	ours
第二人稱	your	your	yours	yours
第三人稱	his/her	their	his/hers	theirs
第三人稱（事物）	its	their	its	theirs
			代表事物的所有格 代名詞極少使用	

(3) 不定代名詞

不定代名詞有些屬於單數，有些屬於複數，有些則是單複數皆可，如下表所列。不定代名詞都可以當主詞或受詞，若要變成所有格，則需在字尾加上 's。

不定代名詞	
單數	another, any, anybody, anyone, anything, each, everybody, everyone, everything, neither, nobody, none, nothing, oneself, other, somebody, someone, something
複數	both, few, many, several
單數或複數	all, any, most, none, some

(4) 指示代名詞

指示代名詞只有單數的 this 和 that，以及複數的 these 和 those，如下表所列。

指示代名詞	
單數	this, that
複數	these, those

(5) 反身代名詞

反身代名詞可以當作**受詞**，表示動作是由某人或某物加諸在自己身上如：*She sent herself an email.*，或是 *The child washed himself.*，或是 *The kitten groomed itself.*；反身代名詞也可以用來**強調語氣**，如：*He himself painted the house.*，或是 *The dog itself open the refrigerator.*

反身代名詞		
	單數	複數
第一人稱	myself	ourselves

反身代名詞		
	單數	複數
第二人稱	yourself	yourselves
第三人稱	himself herself	themselves

(6) 疑問代名詞

疑問代名詞有五個：who, whom, whose, which, what，用來**引導 WH 疑問句，是構成 WH 疑問句的獨立子句必要的元素。**疑問代名詞有的可以當作**主詞**，如 who, which, what，有的可以當作**主詞補語**，如 who, whose, what，有的可以當作**受詞**，如 whom, which, what，如下表所示。

疑問代名詞	功能	例句
who （人的主格）	主詞	Who sent you the gift?
	主詞補語	Who is your best friend?
whom （人的受格）	受詞	Whom (Who) did you have dinner with last night?（口語上往往以 who 代替 whom）
whose （人的所有格）	主詞補語	Whose is that fancy car?
which （人或物）	主詞	Which belongs to you?
	受詞	Which does she like best?
what（物）	主詞	What caused the accident?
	受詞	What are you thinking about?

疑問代名詞	功能	例句
	主詞補語	What is he? He is a fashion designer. What are these? These are smart glasses.

另外，whose, which, what 也可以用作**形容詞**，修飾後面所接的名詞，例如：Whose house is that? 或 Which sofa did the couple buy?，或是 What color did she paint her room?，不可與代名詞的作用混淆。

(7) 相互代名詞

英文的相互代名詞只有兩個片語：each other 和 one another，相互代名詞的使用條件有二：(1)涉及兩者或三者以上，以及(2)彼此之間做同樣的動作或有同樣的感受，例如：

James and his wife are talking to **each other**.

All of the group members help **one another** with their project.

The two sisters gave **each other** gifts.

Jack and Mary love **each other**.

Both teams fought hard against **each other**.

The players are competing with **one another** for the championship.

The students congratulated **each other** at the commencement.

由以上的例句，我們瞭解到 each other 與 one another 只能作**為動詞或介系詞的受詞**，而不能當作主詞。涉及到兩者彼此之間的情況限用 each other，而涉及到三者或更多時則 each other 或 one another 皆可使用。實際的運用上，each other 較常使用，one another 較少使用。

相互代名詞		
兩者彼此之間	限用 **each other**	The two sisters gave **each other** gifts.
三者或以上彼此之間	可用 **each other** 或 **one another**	Students congratulated **each other** at the commencement. The players are competing with **one another** for the championship.

(8) 關係代名詞

關係代名詞有 who, which, that, whom, whose 等五個，關係代名詞雖然是代名詞的一種，但是與代名詞的作用卻不盡相同，關係代名詞除了用來指稱先行詞，更重要的是關係代名詞具有相當於連接詞的作用，用來構成形容詞子句。在寫作上，運用形容詞子句來與獨立子句結合成為複句是很重要的技巧，因此如何將簡單句化身為形容詞子句便是其中的關鍵步驟，而什麼情況選用哪一個關係代名詞，來取代句子中與先行詞重覆的名詞，牽涉到幾個因素：(1) 是限定用法還是非限定用法，(2) 其先行詞是人或非人或整個句子，以及 (3) 其所取代的名詞是主格、所有格、還是受格，例如：

非限定用法／非人／主格

Taipei Zoo keeps many kinds of animals.

Taipei Zoo is the largest one in the country.

→ Taipei Zoo, **which** is the largest one in the country, keeps many kinds of animals.（以 which 取代第二句的 Taipei Zoo）

限定用法／人／主格

Tourists visit Taipei Zoo.

Tourists enjoy seeing all kinds of animals.

→ Tourists **who** visit Taipei Zoo enjoy seeing all kinds of animals.（以 **who** 取代第一句的 tourists）

（有關關係代名詞的使用與形容詞子句的運用將在從屬子句的形容詞子句一章中詳細說明。）

關係代名詞的選用如下表所示。

限定用法關係代名詞			
先行詞	主格	所有格	受格
人	who 與 that 通用	whose	who（不能用在介系詞後面） whom（目前較少使用，但一定用在介系詞後面）
非人	that（美式英文） which（英式英文）	whose	which 與 that 通用 （which 一定用在介系詞後面；that 不能用在介系詞後面，在代名詞或是由最高級所修飾的名詞後面一定用 that）

非限定關係代名詞			
先行詞	主格	所有格	受格
人	who	whose	whom（目前較少使用，但在介系詞後面一定要用 whom） who（不能用在介系詞後面）
非人	which	whose	which
前面整個句子	which	N/A	N/A

2.4 形容詞 (adjectives)

▶▶ ### 2.4.1 形容詞的形成

英文的形容詞的結構可以是由：

(1) 名詞加上形容詞的字尾

例如：courage + ous → courageous, expense + ive → expensive,

beauty + ful → beautiful, friend + ly → friendly

其中特別要注意的是 -ly 形容詞字尾，很容易跟 -ly 副詞字尾混淆：

名詞 + ly → 形容詞（如：lovely, timely, daily, monthly, yearly）

形容詞 + ly → 副詞（如：instantly, absolutely, frankly）

(2) 動詞加上形容詞的字尾

例如：act + ive → active, create + ive → creative, ignore + ant → ignorant, differ + ent → different, consider + ate → considerate

常用形容詞字尾	
-full	wonderful, useful, helpful, successful, doubtful
-ous	famous, gracious, marvelous
-able/ible	valuable, expandable, likable, enjoyable, responsible, re-sistible
-ish	foolish, childish, selfish
-ive	active, explosive, expensive, intensive, instrusive
-ly	friendly, lovely, daily, timely
-some	lonesome, troublesome
-al/-ial	formal, fictional, national, global, official, industrial, en-vironmental
-ic/-ical	heroic, economic, classic, classical, practical, economical
-ant	significant, pleasant, ignorant
-ary	elementary, customary, exemplary
-ate	fortunate, passionate, considerate
-ent	different, consistent, sufficient
-ory	compulsory, contradictory, obiligatory, mandatory
-y	cloudy, sunny, shaky, breezy, windy
-less	fealess, flawless, careless, useless, endless
-ing	interesting, fascinating, promising, charming, touching
-ed	learned, limited, short-sighted

▶▶ 2.4.2 形容詞的作用

形容詞是用來修飾名詞，或是作為主詞補語與受詞補語。形容詞修飾名詞時，並非句子結構不可或缺的元素，例如：*The big ship sails.* 句子中 big 用來修飾名詞 ship，如果將它移除，*The ship sails.* 句子結構依舊完整，只會影響 ship 這個名詞指稱的範圍，而不影響句子的結構。

　　然而，**形容詞若是作為主詞補語或受詞補語，則屬於句子結構中必要的元素**，一旦少了它，句子結構就瓦解，句子就不成句子，無法表達完整的涵義，例如：*The food tastes good.* 句中動詞 tastes 屬於不完全不及物動詞，其適用的句型必須在動詞後面接主詞補語，而形容詞 good 即是作為主詞 food 的補語。如果缺少了主詞補語 good，句子只剩下 *The food tastes.* 就不成句子，而無法表達完整的涵義。又例如：*The story makes her sad.* 這個句子的動詞屬於不完全及物動詞，結構上必須在受詞之後接受詞補語，如果把句子中的受詞補語 sad 拿走，句子只剩下 *The story makes her.* 就不是完整的結構，無法表達完整的涵義。

2.5 副詞 (adverbs)

　　副詞在英文中運用極為廣泛，可分為 (1) **單純副詞**、(2) **疑問副詞**、(3) **連接副詞**、與 (4) **關係副詞**。其中單純副詞與疑問副詞運用在單一的獨立子句，連接副詞用來連接前後兩個獨立子句，關係副詞則運用在形容詞子句。

(1) **單純副詞在英文中用來修飾動詞、形容詞（片語）、副詞（片語）、或整個句子。單純副詞依其作用可以用來表達時間、地點、狀態、程度、頻率。單純副詞在句子中出現的位置也很有彈性，可以出現在句首、句中、句尾**，是讓句子生動表達的重要成份。但有趣的是，副詞並非構成簡單句的必要元素，例如：***Fortunately***, *she passed the test.* 如果將副詞 fortunately 從句子中移除，句子成為 *She passed the test.* 結構完全不受影響；或例如：*She passed the test **quite easily**.* 如果把句子中的兩個副詞 quite 及 easily 同時刪除，句子成為 *She passed the test.* 其結構依舊完整無缺，仍然可以表達完整的涵義。

貼心提醒

> 英文的副詞形成通常是在形容詞之後加上字尾 -ly，例如：fortunate 變成 fortunately，clever 變成 cleverly，courageous 變成 courageously，或是 instant 變成 instantly；然而某些英文的**形容詞與副詞**卻是**同形**，例如：**hard, early, fast, high, low, near, late, long, first**
>
> 其中某些形容詞與副詞同形的單字字尾如果加了 -ly，雖然還是副詞，但意義卻大不相同，例如：
>
> **high**（高）+ **ly → highly**（非常地、高度地）
> **near**（靠近）+ **ly → nearly**（幾乎、差不多）
> **hard**（堅硬、刻苦、困難）+ **ly → hardly**（幾乎不、簡直不）
> **late**（遲、晚）+ **ly → lately**（近來）
> **most**（最多、最高程度）+ **ly → mostly**（大部分地、一般地）

(2) **疑問副詞**包括有 **when, where, how, why**，出現的位置在句首，功能在引導出一個 WH 疑問句，而疑問副詞是構成 **WH 疑問句的必要元素**，一旦缺少了疑問副詞，WH 疑問句就轉為 Yes/No 疑問句了。例如：*Where did you go last night?* 如果將疑問副詞 where 從句子中剔除，句子變成 *Did you go last*

night?，這是 Yes/No 疑問句，而非 WH 疑問句了！

(3) **連接副詞**則是用來連接前後兩個獨立子句，以轉承前後句子的語氣，例如：*She likes the new sofa very much.* ***However****, she doesn't have enough budget to buy it.* 或是 *She has found a new job in a different city;* ***therefore****, she is ready to move there.*

(4) **關係副詞 (when, where, how, why)** 與疑問副詞外觀一模一樣，但是功能完全不同。疑問副詞的功能是引導出 WH 疑問句，而**關係副詞的功能則與關係代名詞相同，是用來引導出形容詞子句**，例如：*This is the restaurant* ***where*** *I met my wife.* 或是 *A new era began in 2007,* ***when*** *the iPhone was first introduced.*

2.6 介系詞 (prepositions)

　　介系詞的功能是要引導出介系詞片語，也就是介系詞之後一定會接名詞或動名詞作爲其受詞，兩者共同構成一個介系詞片語，例如：***in*** *the park,* ***of*** *living,* ***from*** *heaven,* ***into*** *the ocean,* ***at*** *home,* ***for*** *celebrating,* ***under*** *the tree* 等等，而**介系詞片語的功能則是用來修飾名詞、形容詞、動詞**，例如：*children in the park, cost of living, music from heaven, safe at home, good for celebrating, run into the sea, sit under the tree*。介系詞若是與某一個動詞結合成爲**片語動詞**，例如：put off（延期）是由動詞 put 與介系詞 off 所構成的片語動詞，則介系詞 off 爲該片語動詞不可或缺的元素，除此之外，介系詞和介系詞片語都不是構成句子的必要元素。

2.7　連接詞 (conjunctions)

　　連接詞有三種：對等連接詞 (coordinating conjunctions)、從屬連接詞 (subordinating conjunctions)、與相關連接詞 (correlative conjunctions)，**對等連接詞及相關連接詞**可以用來**連接兩個相同詞類的字詞**，例如：*He **and** Nita are working in the same office.* 或是 ***Neither** he **nor** Nita is married.*；也可以用來**連接兩個獨立子句**，例如：*He eats a lot, **yet** he is in good shape.* 或是 ***As** you sow, **so** shall you reap.*。相對地，**從屬連接詞**則是用來連接主要子句與從屬子句，例如：*He is in good shape **because** he plays sports a lot.* 這三種連接詞都是英文句型靈活變化的很重要的元素，但都不是構成簡單句的必要元素。

2.8　感嘆詞 (interjections)

　　常用的感嘆詞有 Ah, Aha, Alas, Darn, Gee, Gosh, Hey, My goodness, Oops, Ugh, Uh-huh, Um, Well, Wow, Yuck 等等，感嘆詞用來表達各種不同情緒，如開心、驚訝、哀傷、憤怒、錯愕、或其他等等情緒，通常出現在句首，並以驚嘆號或逗點與句子隔開。值得注意的是，感嘆詞與句子的結構無關，它不修飾句子中任何單字或片語，句子中也沒有任何單字或片語修飾它，感嘆詞僅僅純粹表達情緒而已。從這個角度來看，許多文法學家因此認為感嘆詞是最不重要的詞類，而在正式書信與寫作上也都避免使用感嘆詞。

2.9 助動詞 (auxiliaries)

　　英文的助動詞分為兩大類：(1) **基本助動詞**，與 (2) **情態助動詞**，兩者各有其不同的功能。基本助動詞有三個：be, have, 以及 do，其本身無詞意，是用來幫助動詞形成不同的句型，本身依句子時態與主詞單複數而變化；情態助動詞則用來幫助動詞表達不同的語氣或態度，包括有：can, could, may, might, will, would, should, ought to, had better, must。

▶▶ 2.9.1 基本助動詞

　　英文基本的助動詞有三個：**be, have,** 以及 **do**，有趣的是這三個字也都可以作為動詞使用，同學要注意其不同的用法。例如：

作為助動詞的功能

He **is** practic**ing** English conversations.（助動詞 **is** 用來幫助動詞表達現在進行式）

He **has done** a great job.（助動詞 **has** 用來幫助動詞表達現在完成式）

He **did** not give up.（助動詞 **did** 用來幫助動詞形成否定句）

作為動詞的功能

She **is** my English tutor.（**is** 為句子動詞，意思為**是**。）

She **has** more than 10 students.（**has** 為句子動詞，意思為**有**。）

She **is doing** a good job.（**is doing** 為句子動詞，意思為**做**。）

這三個基本助動詞分別扮演不同的角色與功能,並且依動詞時式與主詞的人稱與單複數而變化。

(1) 助動詞 be

助動詞 be 的變化形依依動詞時式與主詞的人稱與單複數而有不同,而其功能為表達動詞時態或被動語態,詳如下列表格所示:

助動詞 be 的變化形		
現在式	am	主詞 I
	is	主詞第三人稱單數代名詞或名詞,不可數名詞
	are	主詞第一人稱複數 we,第二人稱 you,第三人稱複數代名詞或名詞
過去式	was	主詞 I,第三人稱單數代名詞或名詞,不可數名詞
	were	主詞第一人稱複數 we,第二人稱 you,第三人稱複數代名詞或名詞
進行式	being	全部
完成式	been	全部

助動詞 be 的功能		
助動詞	功能	例句
am/is/are	現在進行式	She **is** cooking in the kitchen.
was/were	過去進行式	The children **were** playing baseball in the park.
am/is/are	現在式被動語態	They **are** selected by the committee.
was/were	過去式被動語態	The house **was** sold to a new couple.
being	進行式被動語態	The restaurant is **being** renovated.
been	完成式被動語態	My application has **been** reviewed.

(2) 助動詞 have

助動詞 have 只有一種功能，就是幫助動詞表達現在完成式，而其變化形僅有兩種：have（適用於主詞爲非第三人稱單數者），以及 has（適用於主詞爲第三人稱單數者）。

助動詞 have 的功能		
助動詞	功能	例句
have	現在完成式	We **have** accomplished our goal.
has	現在完成式	The cat **has** eaten all the food in the bowl.

(3) 助動詞 do

助動詞 do 的變化形依動詞時式與主詞人稱及單複數而有所不同，包括 do, does, did 三種。而其功能有四：可以用來幫助動詞構成疑問句與否定句，或是用來加強語氣，或是用來代替前面的動詞。

助動詞 do 的變化形		
現在式	do	其他主詞
	does	主詞第三人稱單數代名詞或名詞，不可數名詞
過去式	did	全部

助動詞 do 的功能		
助動詞	功能	例句
do/does/did	疑問句	Does he play basketball?
do/does/did	否定句	The plane did not fly due to bad weather.

助動詞 do 的功能		
助動詞	功能	例句
do/does/did	加強語氣	You do work hard.
do/does/did	代替前面的動詞	She types faster than her teacher does.

▶▶ 2.9.2 情態助動詞

英文的情態助動詞有 **can, could, may, might, will, would, should, ought to, had better, must**，其與基本助動詞都是出現在原型動詞之前；不同的是，情境助動詞是帶有涵義的助動詞，用**來幫助動詞表達各種不同的語氣或態度**，如能力、意願、請求、許可、命令、客氣、告誡、或提議，但是**相同的情境助動詞在不同用法中會表達不同的意思**。

(1) 表達能力：can, could

She can run marathon.

He could do 100 push-ups without stopping.（could 表達過去具備的能力）

(2) 表達請求許可：may, can, could

May I talk to the manager?（正式且有禮貌）

Could I talk to the manager?（較有禮貌）

Can I talk to the manager?

(3) 表達允許：may, can（不能用 **could**）

Employees may wear casual clothes on Fridays.

You cannot keep pets in the apartment.

(4) 表達建議或提議：should, could

You should take the shuttle bus to the airport.

We could go to the mall to enjoy the cool air.

(5) 表達可能性：may, might, could

She may have dinner with us.（may 表達可能性較大）

She might quit her job.（might 表達可能性較小，或是 may 的過去式）

(6) 表達必須或告誡：must

It's very late. You must go home now.

You must not steal.

(7) 表達忠告或建議：should, ought to, had better

You don't look well. You should go see a doctor.

You have made a mistake. You ought to apologize to your colleagues.

The storm is coming. We had better stay indoors.

(8) 表達請求或希望：will, would, can, could

Will you buy me a sandwich?

Would you buy me a sandwich?（would 較有禮貌）

Can we eat ice cream?

Could I pick up the parcel later?（could 較有禮貌）

(9) 表達命令：will

You will report to the office tomorrow morning at eight.

2.10 動狀詞 (verbals)

　　英文八大詞類中的**動詞**，可以再**加以變化**。英文的動詞可以變身為不同形式的動狀詞，包括**不定詞、動名詞、現在分詞、與過去分詞**，分別扮演不同的功能，並且運用極廣。動詞一旦化身為動狀詞，雖然已經失去作為句子動詞的功能，但動狀詞仍舊保留動詞的其他特性，例如動狀詞可以加受詞，且其內部也可以有修飾副詞，而構成片語。換句話說，動狀詞不能當作句子的動詞，只能扮演其他的角色，例如動名詞可以當主詞或受詞，不定詞可以當名詞或用來修飾名詞或動詞，分詞可以用來修飾名詞等等，分別舉例說明如下：

(1) 不定詞 (infinitives)

　　不定詞的形式為 to + 原形動詞，如 to succeed, to enjoy, to read，或是 to + be + 形容詞，如 to be happy, to be respectful 等等，不定詞可以扮演好幾種不同的功能，例如：

To triumph requires persistence.

（不定詞 to triumph 作為名詞，當句子**主詞**）

Everyone wants **to enjoy**.

（不定詞 to enjoy 作為名詞，當**受詞**）

His parents want him **to be happy**.

（不定詞 to be happy 作為名詞，當**受詞補語**）

Our goal is **to succeed**.

（不定詞 to succeed 作為名詞，當**主詞補語**）

She is happy **to read**.

（不定詞 to read 作爲名詞，當**副詞**，修飾 happy）

He has a novel **to read**.

（不定詞 to read 作爲名詞，當**形容詞**，修飾 a novel）

(2) 動名詞 (gerunds)

動名詞由動詞原型字尾加上 -ing (V-ing) 所形成，其**功能與名詞相同**，可以當作句子的<u>主詞</u>，<u>動詞的受詞</u>，<u>補語</u>，或是<u>介系詞的受詞</u>。

例如：

Fishing is fun.（fishing 爲動名詞，作爲句子的**主詞**。）

He loves **fishing**.

（fishing 爲動名詞，作爲動詞 loves 的**受詞**。）

His favorite outdoor activity is **fishing**.

（fishing 爲動名詞，作爲**主詞補語**。）

On weekends, he looks forward to **fishing**.

（fishing 爲動名詞，作爲介系詞 to **的受詞**。）

(3) 現在分詞 (present participles)

現在分詞的形式與動名詞相同，都是動詞原型後面加 -ing (V-ing)，但是作用與動名詞不同。現在分詞的功能與形容詞相同，用來修飾名詞或及名詞同類語。**不及物動詞與及物動詞均可變化爲現在分詞**，如以下例子：

The young singer is a **rising** star.

（不及物動詞 rise 化身爲現在分詞 rising）

India is an **emerging** power.

（不及物動詞 emerge 化身爲現在分詞 emerging）

The room is filled with **soothing** music.

（及物動詞 sooth 化身爲現在分詞 soothing）

She is an **intimidating** boss.

（及物動詞 intimidate 化身爲現在分詞 intimidating）

(4) 過去分詞 (past participles)

　　過去分詞就是及物動詞三態的第三態，它跟動詞的完成式外觀形式相同，但是功能不同。只有**及物動詞才能化身爲過去分詞，當作形容詞來使用**，其功能是要修飾名詞或當作補語，如以下例子：

They found **fossilized** dinosaurs.

（過去分詞修飾名詞 dinosaurs）

This is a **restricted** area.（過去分詞修飾名詞 area）

I left my car **unlocked**.（過去分詞作爲受詞補語）

She had her hair **dyed**.（過去分詞作爲受詞補語）

　　在動狀詞一章中，我們會更詳細舉例說明不定詞、動名詞、現在分詞、與過去分詞的功能及用法，請同學們仔細研讀。

2.11 英文單字的種類與功能打通關

　　說明畫底線的單字屬於哪一種類型以及其功能。

　　示範：**She** plays **the piano well**.

→ She 代名詞作爲主詞，the piano 名詞作爲 plays 的受詞，well 副詞修飾 plays

1. She (1) **is** (2) **proud** to be a (3) **working** mother.

　　(1) ＿＿＿＿＿＿ (2) ＿＿＿＿＿＿ (3) ＿＿＿＿＿＿

2. The problems (1) **never** (2) **seemed** (3) **easy**.

   (1) ＿＿＿＿＿＿＿ (2) ＿＿＿＿＿＿＿ (3) ＿＿＿＿＿＿＿

3. Technologies (1) **have** advanced (2) **tremendously** in the (3) **past** decade.

   (1) ＿＿＿＿＿＿＿ (2) ＿＿＿＿＿＿＿ (3) ＿＿＿＿＿＿＿

4. Insufficient (1) **preparation** may result in (2) **poor** performances.

   (1) ＿＿＿＿＿＿＿＿＿＿＿ (2) ＿＿＿＿＿＿＿＿＿＿＿

5. (1) **How** (2) **far** can the electric motorcycle (3) **go** without replacing the battery?

   (1) ＿＿＿＿＿＿＿ (2) ＿＿＿＿＿＿＿ (3) ＿＿＿＿＿＿＿

6. (1) **Did** (2) **you** buy a book (3) **or** a video?

   (1) ＿＿＿＿＿＿＿ (2) ＿＿＿＿＿＿＿ (3) ＿＿＿＿＿＿＿

7. People (1) **like** (2) **to eat** ice cream in the summer.

   (1) ＿＿＿＿＿＿＿＿＿＿＿ (2) ＿＿＿＿＿＿＿＿＿＿＿

8. We (1) **should** (2) **stay** (3) **here**.

   (1) ＿＿＿＿＿＿＿ (2) ＿＿＿＿＿＿＿ (3) ＿＿＿＿＿＿＿

9. (1) **When** will the bus (2) **arrive**?

   (1) ＿＿＿＿＿＿＿＿＿＿＿ (2) ＿＿＿＿＿＿＿＿＿＿＿

10. (1) **Singing** with friends in a karaoke is (2) **definitely** (3) **relaxing**.

   (1) ＿＿＿＿＿＿＿ (2) ＿＿＿＿＿＿＿ (3) ＿＿＿＿＿＿＿

11. The (1) **slender** girl (2) **runs** really (3) **fast**.

   (1) ＿＿＿＿＿＿＿ (2) ＿＿＿＿＿＿＿ (3) ＿＿＿＿＿＿＿

12. The city government (1) **announced** new (2) **regulations** for street (3) **parking**.

   (1) ＿＿＿＿＿＿＿ (2) ＿＿＿＿＿＿＿ (3) ＿＿＿＿＿＿＿

13. (1) **Who** (2) **bought** the new handbag for (3) **her**?

(1) _____ (2) _____ (3) _____

14. He (1) **pays** US$750 for the (2) **monthly** (3) **rent**.

(1) _____ (2) _____ (3) _____

15. (1) **Has** the baby been (2) **sleeping** for (3) **over** two hours?

(1) _____ (2) _____ (3) _____

16. (1) **What** (2) **did** they say about our (3) **company's** new branch?

(1) _____ (2) _____ (3) _____

17. (1) **Can** you come (2) **to** my place (3) **soon**?

(1) _____ (2) _____ (3) _____

18. The insect (1) **appears** (2) **harmless**.

(1) _____ (2) _____

19. (1) **Where** can I find the post office (2) **and** a Japanese restaurant?

(1) _____ (2) _____

20. Repairing the (1) **damaged** car (2) **cost** her (3) **nearly** US$2,000.

(1) _____ (2) _____ (3) _____

21. The (1) **player** (2) **surprisingly** (3) **won** the championship.

(1) _____ (2) _____ (3) _____

22. (1) **Why** are (2) **so** many students (3) **absent** today?

(1) _____ (2) _____ (3) _____

23. The suspect (1) **may** hire a lawyer (2) **to defend** him.

(1) _____ (2) _____

24. Eating (1) **too** (2) **much** sugar (3) **increases** risk of cancer.

(1) ＿＿＿＿＿＿ (2) ＿＿＿＿＿＿ (3) ＿＿＿＿＿＿

25. The cost of (1) **living** has (2) **become** (3) **increasingly** expensive.

(1) ＿＿＿＿＿＿ (2) ＿＿＿＿＿＿ (3) ＿＿＿＿＿＿

26. She (1) **offered** him a job (2) **working** at a store (3) **run** by a Taiwanese.

(1) ＿＿＿＿＿＿ (2) ＿＿＿＿＿＿ (3) ＿＿＿＿＿＿

27. The store (1) **established** in 2002 (2) **has** a reputation for (3) **its** friendly services.

(1) ＿＿＿＿＿＿ (2) ＿＿＿＿＿＿ (3) ＿＿＿＿＿＿

28. (1) **Those** interested in (2) **traveling** (3) **may** find this Website very useful.

(1) ＿＿＿＿＿＿ (2) ＿＿＿＿＿＿ (3) ＿＿＿＿＿＿

29. The man (1) **carrying** a suitcase could (2) **be** a salesman.

(1) ＿＿＿＿＿＿＿＿＿ (2) ＿＿＿＿＿＿＿＿＿

30. (1) **Certain** patients need special (2) **care** (3) **to recover**.

(1) ＿＿＿＿＿＿ (2) ＿＿＿＿＿＿ (3) ＿＿＿＿＿＿

第三章 動狀詞 (Verbals)

為了說明動狀詞的來源與功能，我們先來看底下這個句子：

The **exciting sighting** of an **unidentified flying** object marked a special moment **to remember** for the witnesses.

令人亢奮目睹不明飛行物一事為目擊者留下了一個難以忘懷的特別時刻。

這個短短的簡單句在主部中出現了**動名詞 sighting**，作為句子的主詞；**現在分詞 exciting 修飾 sighting**，**過去分詞 unidentified 與現在分詞 flying 修飾名詞 object**；而在述部中則使用了**不定詞 to remember** 修飾名詞 moment。

由這個簡單的例句，我們可以窺見英文的動狀詞有不同種類，各自肩負不同的功能，並且在句子的自我內部擴充過程中運用極為頻繁，屬於非常重要的詞類。同學如能嫻熟使用動狀詞，寫出來的英文句子就會更加豐富。

動狀詞是由動詞衍生而來，雖然仍舊保留了動詞的部分特性，例如**可以加受詞**，如 practicing shooting 或是 to avoid misunderstanding，或是**內部可以有修飾副詞**，如 to work hard，但動狀詞**已失去作為句子中動詞的功用**，而是當作名詞或形容詞或副詞的功能來使用。動狀詞一共有四類：動名詞 (gerunds/V-ing)，不定詞 (infinitives/to V)，現在分詞 (present participles/V-ing)，和過去

分詞 (past participles/V-ed)。

3.1 動名詞 (gerunds/V-ing)

　　動名詞由動詞原型字尾加上 -ing (V-ing) 所形成，其功能與名詞相同，可以當作句子的**主詞**、**動詞的受詞**、**補語**，或是**介系詞的受詞**。

(1) 動名詞作爲句子的主詞

　　Working part-time is now very common among college students.（working 作爲句子的**主詞**。）

(2) 動名詞作爲動詞的受詞

　　We enjoyed **watching** the game in the stadium.

　　（watching 作爲動詞 enjoyed 的**受詞**。）

(3) 動名詞作爲主詞補語

　　One of her hobbies is **collecting** dolls.

　　（collecting 作爲**主詞補語**。）

(4) 動名詞作爲介系詞的受詞

　　The young couple is fond **of camping**.

　　（camping 作爲介系詞 of 的受詞）

　　She is good **at creating** emoji.

　　（creating 作爲介系詞 at 的受詞）

3.2 不定詞 (infinitives/to + VR)

不定詞是由 to 加上原形動詞 (verb root/VR) 所構成，其功能可作為**名詞**、**形容詞**、**副詞**。

(1) 不定詞作為名詞

To win is the goal of every player in the game.

（to win 作為**名詞**，當作句子的**主詞**。）

He wants **to enter** the famous university.

（to enter 作為**名詞**，當作動詞 want 的**受詞**。）

Her goal is **to succeed**.

（to succeed 作為**名詞**，當作主詞 her goal 的**補語**）

His parents want him **to be happy**.

（to be happy 作為**名詞**，當作受詞 him 的**補語**）

(2) 不定詞作為形容詞

As a college student, Tom has a lot of homework **to do** every week.（to do 作為**形容詞**，修飾名詞 homework。）

(3) 不定詞作為副詞

As it was getting late, they were anxious **to leave**.

（to leave 作為**副詞**，修飾形容詞 anxious。）

The government responded quickly **to rescue** people trapped in the flood.（to rescue 作為**副詞**，修飾動詞 responded。）

3.3 現在分詞 (present participles/V-ing)

　　英文的分詞有兩種：現在分詞 (present participles) 和過去分詞 (past participles)。形式不同，但是功能相同。其作用與形容詞相同，都是用來修飾名詞及名詞同類語。

　　現在分詞的形式與動名詞相同，都是動詞原型後面加 -ing (V-ing)，但是**作用與動名詞不同**。現在分詞的功能與形容詞相同，用來修飾名詞或及名詞同類語。不及物動詞與及物動詞均可變化為現在分詞，如以下例子：

(1) 不及物動詞變化為現在分詞（表達的是自身的動作）

　　a **singing** bird 吟唱的小鳥

　　（sing 為不及物動詞）

　　increasing opportunities 不斷增加，越來越多的機會

　　（increase 為不及物動詞）

(2) 及物動詞變化為現在分詞（表達的是該動作對其他人或事物的影響）

　　a **fascinating** story 引人入勝的故事

　　（fascinate 為及物動詞）

　　disturbing messages 令人不安的訊息

　　（disturb 為及物動詞）

　　an **inspiring** speech 振奮人心的演講

　　（inspire 為及物動詞）

　　an **exhausting** task 令人筋疲力竭的任務

　　（exhaust 為及物動詞）

貼心提醒

V-ing 的形式 (form) 與功能 (function)

英文的 動詞 +ing (V-ing)，一樣的形式，卻有三種不同的性質與功能：(1) 動詞進行式，(2) 動名詞，以及 (3) 現在分詞。三者形式相同，都是 V-ing，極容易混淆，但是三者的功能完全不同。動詞的進行式是句子中與主詞搭配的動詞，動名詞則是作為名詞的功能，而現在分詞則是作為形容詞的功能。

V-ing 的三種性質與功能

性質	功能	例句
動詞進行式	動詞	The population of the city is **growing** fast.
動名詞	名詞	**Growing** plants is fun.
現在分詞	形容詞	The new policies are for dealing with the **grow-ing** population.

3.4 小試身手

分辨下列劃底線部分為動詞進行式、動名詞或現在分詞

1. The Website features <u>uplifting</u> news stories. _____

2. They are <u>practicing</u> for tomorrow's game. _____

3. The team is aimed at <u>exploring</u> the deep ocean. _____

4. The <u>recovering</u> economy is likely to boost sales of new cars.

_____

5. Bears try to eat as much as they can before <u>hibernating</u>.

_____

6. Group discussions are <u>stimulating</u>. _____

7. <u>Smoking</u> is a traditional way to preserve meat. _____

8. A <u>touching</u> story makes people cry._____

9. She is looking forward to <u>meeting</u> with her roommate.

_____

10. She bought an antique <u>sewing</u> machine in a flea market.

_____

11. Most passengers were able to escape from the <u>sinking</u> ship.

_____

12. The new English teacher is (1) <u>applying</u> a new (2) <u>teaching</u> method in the writing class.

(1) _____ (2) _____

13. The company is (1) <u>considering</u> a new (2) <u>marketing</u> strategy to boost its sales.

(1) _____ (2) _____

14. The archaeology team has accomplished an (1) <u>astonishing</u> task in (2) <u>uncovering</u> the ancient burial site.

(1) _____ (2) _____

15. (1) <u>Exporting</u> machinery to Europe is (2) <u>helping</u> the company to recover from recession.

(1) _____ (2) _____

3.5 過去分詞 (past participles/V-ed)

　　過去分詞就是及物動詞三態的第三態，它跟動詞的完成式外觀形式相同，但是功能不同。**只有及物動詞才能化身為過去分詞，當作形容詞來使用，其功能是要修飾名詞或當作補語，而所表達的是人或事物受到外來動作的影響。**

　　下列例子說明過去分詞的功能：

(1) 過去分詞作為形容詞來修飾名詞

an **arranged** marriage 由他人安排（媒妁）的婚姻

an **abandoned** factory（遭人）廢棄的工廠

a **broken** heart 破碎的心

a **satisfied** customer 感到滿意的顧客

a **cloned** sheep 被複製的羊

a **distorted** image 受到扭曲的形象

money well **spent** 使用恰當的金錢

A penny **saved** is a penny **earned**. 一分一毫都要省，省下來的才是真正賺到手的，也就是聚沙成塔的意思。

(2) 過去分詞作為形容詞來當作受詞補語

They had the new air conditioner **installed**.
（他們**請人安裝**了新的冷氣機。）

I had my car **fixed**.（我**請人修好**了我的車子。）

The school got him **punished**.（學校使他**接受處罰**。）

When you leave, please keep the door **unlocked**.
（離開時門請**不要鎖上**。）

The police found the little boy severely **abused**.

（警察發現這個小男孩嚴重**受虐**。）

3.6 如何正確使用現在分詞與過去分詞

什麼時候該用現在分詞，什麼時候該用過去分詞，臺灣學生往往分不清楚，容易出錯。我們以下列例子來說明現在分詞與過去分詞如何區分其涵義，以及如何正確使用。

(1) 現在分詞由不及物動詞變化而來（表達的是自身的動作）

現在分詞的可以是由**不及物動詞**衍生而來，例如 sparkling light（閃亮的燈光），所表達的是自身的動作，**不涉及其他人或事物**。

以下為更多由不及物動詞變化而來的現在分詞例子：

They watched the **rising** sun（昇起的太陽）.

（The sun rises. 太陽**昇起**）

They have maintained **lasting** relationship（持續的關係）.

（The relationship lasts. 關係**持續**）

Be careful with the **boiling** water（滾熱的水）.

（The water boils. 水**滾**了）

(2) 現在分詞由及物動詞變化而來（表達的是該動作對其他人或事物的影響）

現在分詞也可以是由**及物動詞**衍生而來，例如 startling news

（令人驚嚇的新聞），所表達的是**該動作對其他人或事物的影響**（The news startles people. 新聞令人驚嚇）。

以下為更多由及物動詞變化而來的現在分詞例子：

She is an **amazing** teacher.（令人驚嘆的老師）
（She amazes people. 她令人感到驚嘆）

He is an **inspiring** speaker.（令人受到激勵）
（He inspires people. 他令人受到激勵）

Hiking is an **interesting** outdoor activity.
（令人感到興趣的戶外活動）
（Hiking interests people. 登山健行令人感到興趣）

The police have gathered **convincing** evidence of the crime.
（令人信服的證據）
（The evidence convinces people. 證據令人信服）

(3) 過去分詞由及物動詞變化而來（表達的是人或事物受到外來動作的影響）

過去分詞的來源與現在分詞不同，過去分詞只能是**由及物動詞衍生而來**，所表達的是**人或事物受到外來動作的影響**，例如 smoked salmon（被煙燻過的鮭魚），鮭魚不能自己煙燻自己，而是有人以煙燻的方式處理鮭魚；或是 a spoiled child（被寵壞的小孩），小孩不能自己寵壞自己，而是有人把他寵壞了。

He is an **underestimated** student.（被人低估的學生）

（He is underestimated by people. 他被人低估）

Visitors are not allowed to enter the **restricted** area.（受限制的區域）

（The area is restricted. 這個區域受到限制）

We found a cabin on an **isolated** island.（被隔絕的小島）

（The island is isolated. 這個小島被隔絕）

The company sells **imported** cars.（從國外被輸入的汽車）

（The cars are imported. 車子是從國外被輸入的）

The team discovered **fossilized** dinosaurs.（被變成化石的恐龍）

（The dinosaurs are fossilized. 恐龍被變成化石了）

Japanese like **pickled** vegetables very much.（醃過的蔬菜）

（The vegetables are pickled. 蔬菜被醃過）

She had her hair **dyed**.（頭髮被染色）

（Her hair was dyed. 她的頭髮被染色）

小小測試：現在分詞或過去分詞

1. 造成汙染的廢棄物 polluting or polluted waste?
2. 隱藏的照相機 a hiding or hidden camera?
3. 竄起的歌手 a rising or risen star?
4. 噁心的行為 a disgusting or disgusted act?

5. 縮短的假期 a shortening or shortened vacation?
6. 慈愛的母親 a caring or cared mother?
7. 遲到的祝賀 belating or belated congratulations?
8. 令人心碎的歌 a heartbreaking or heartbroken song?
9. 自動提款機 (ATM) an Automating or Automated Teller Machine?
10. 蒸餾水 distilling or distilled water?

3.7 小試身手

依中文涵義填入現在分詞或過去分詞，必要時需加上相反詞的字首。

示範：

an **unidentified** (identify) **flying** (fly) object 不明飛行物（UFO 幽浮飛碟）

---

1. a _____ (redefine) program 重新定義的計畫
2. the _____ (surround) area 周遭區域
3. _____ (recall) vehicles 召回的車輛
4. _____ (blind) light 刺眼的光線
5. the _____ (promise) land 應許之地
6. _____ (uplift) news 振奮人心的新聞
7. _____ (encourage) words 鼓勵人的言詞
8. a _____ (destroy) city 遭毀滅的城市
9. _____ (convince) evidence 令人信服的證據

10. ＿＿＿＿＿＿＿＿ (upload) files 已上傳的檔案

11. an ＿＿＿＿＿＿＿＿ (solve) case 未破的案子

12. a ＿＿＿＿＿＿＿＿ (suspend) driver's license 吊銷的駕照

13. ＿＿＿＿＿＿＿＿ (refresh) activities 恢復精神的活動

14. ＿＿＿＿＿＿＿＿ (explore) issues 尚未探討的議題

15. a ＿＿＿＿＿＿＿＿ (hide) treasure 隱藏的寶物

16. ＿＿＿＿＿＿＿＿ (overwhelm) pressure 招架不住的壓力

17. a ＿＿＿＿＿＿＿＿ (certify) accountant 有執照的會計師

18. ＿＿＿＿＿＿＿＿ (organize) crimes 黑道集團犯罪

19. ＿＿＿＿＿＿＿＿ (amaze) grace 奇異恩典

20. a ＿＿＿＿＿＿＿＿ (delay) flight 延遲的班機

21. ＿＿＿＿＿＿＿＿ (sharpen) skills 熟練的技術

22. a ＿＿＿＿＿＿＿＿ (calculate) plan 精心策劃的計畫

23. ＿＿＿＿＿＿＿＿ (classify) files 機密文件

24. ＿＿＿＿＿＿＿＿ (fall) leaves 落葉

25. an ＿＿＿＿＿＿＿＿ (amuse) story 有趣的故事

26. an ＿＿＿＿＿＿＿＿ (activate) software 已啟動的軟體

27. an ＿＿＿＿＿＿＿＿ (notice) event 未受注意的事件

28. a ＿＿＿＿＿＿＿＿ (please) personality 討人喜歡的個性

29. ＿＿＿＿＿＿＿＿ (civilize) people 文明人

30. a ＿＿＿＿＿＿＿＿ (deteriorate) condition 惡化中的狀態

31. ＿＿＿＿＿＿＿＿ (upgrade) equipment 升級的配備

32. a ＿＿＿＿＿＿＿＿ (mislead) argument 誤導的論證

33. ＿＿＿＿＿＿＿＿ (qualify) applicants 符合資格的應徵者

34. ＿＿＿＿＿＿＿＿ (expect) guests 不請自來的客人

35. an ＿＿＿＿＿＿＿＿ (overhaul) engine 大修過的引擎

36. an ＿＿＿＿＿＿＿＿ (defeat) team 零敗的球隊

37. the _____ (unfold) truth 揭露的真相

38. _____ (accumulate) rainfall 累積雨量

39. an _____ (invite) dessert 誘人的甜點

40. _____ (deafen) music 震耳欲聾的音樂

41. _____ (steal) items 失竊物品

42. an _____ (appeal) résumé 引人注目的履歷

43. a _____ (prove) theory 經過證實的理論

44. _____ (integrate) marketing 整合的行銷

45. a _____ (tempt) offer 誘人的出價

46. an _____ (enlarge) picture 放大的圖片

47. a _____ (worry) mother 憂心的母親

48. _____ (enhance) security 加強的保全

49. _____ (deceive) looks 會令人受騙的外觀

50. _____ (endanger) species 瀕臨危險的物種

3.8 動狀詞打通關

　　空格中填入恰當的動狀詞（不定詞、現在分詞、動名詞、或過去分詞）

1. The store is selling bicycles to students at a _____ (reduce) price.

2. At the age of 62, Grace is now attending a ballroom _____ (dance) class every Wednesday.

3. The kids are looking forward to the _____ (come) of the Christmas.

4. Many companies are testing self-_____ (drive) vehicles.

5. The _____ (travel) time from Taipei to Los Angeles by plane is about 12 hours.

6. _____ (empower) words are always helpful in _____ (boost) employees' morale.

7. As a _____ (satisfy) customer, she sent a card to the company to show her appreciation.

8. The new rules _____ (regulate) the use of cellphones on campus will take effect next month.

9. The businessman was betrayed by his most _____ (trust) friend.

10. As a _____ (forgive) mother, Sarah never hesitates _____ (help) her rebellious son.

11. The prosecutor submitted the _____ (convince) evidence to the jury and the judge.

12. She is lucky to be hired by a _____ (promise) company.

13. The _____ (devastate) parents mourned over the tragic loss of their baby.

14. His mission is to set the _____ (suppress) people free.

15. _____ (homeschool) can be _____ (demand) for parents.

16. The _____ (inspire) speech sparked _____ (surprise) reforms of the country.

17. Her colleagues consider Mary a hardworking but sometimes _____ (intimidate) supervisor.

18. When she comes home from work, she likes to listen to _____ _____ (comfort) music.

19. She had her _____ (bore) room _____ (repaint).

20. The fast _____ (grow) population in the urban area is a _____ (threaten) problem in _____ (house).

21. _____ (shoot) the basketball 300 times a day is _____ (exhaust).

22. The church can be a _____ (stabilize) force in a _____ (trouble) society.

23. The little girl doesn't mind _____ (do) all the house-work for her _____ (disable) mother.

24. The _____ (miss) antique car was found _____ (abandon) in a _____ (park) lot.

25. We want _____ (obtain) the _____ (desire) outcomes of the _____ (excite) experiment.

26. When her husband went down with illness, she got plenty of help from the _____ (support) group.

27. The more time people spent _____ (browse) the Web site, the more envious they felt.

28. After the boy went _____ (miss), the police searched the _____ (surround) areas thoroughly, but he was nowhere to be found.

29. Dr. Newby, a well-_____ (train) physician from the United States, is committed to _____ (offer) medical services to indigenous people in Taiwan.

30. It can be _____ (challenge) to cheer up an _____ (irritate) baby, but one mom has found the secret for _____ (brighten) her daughter's mood: Katy Perry!

第四章 片語 (Phrases)

　　英文的簡單句由主部與述部所構成，其中**主部可以是名詞片語、不定詞片語、或是動名詞片語；述部則是動詞片語，必須依照動詞不同類別搭配不同的必要元素而構成**。句子的主部與述部皆可進一步作自我內部擴充，以表達更豐富、更明確的含義。在介紹各類型的片語之前，我們先來檢視剖析以下的英文句子：

例一：這艘建造於 1985 年的船隻 正在航行橫越太平洋。

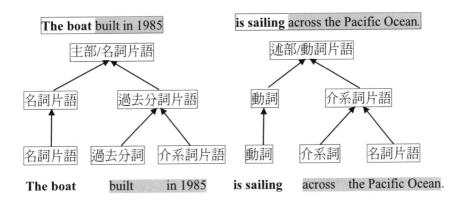

句子結構剖析：

1. 句子的主部為名詞片語，包含三個片語：(1) 名詞片語 **the boat** 為主部的必要元素，(2) 介系詞片語 **in 1985** 與過去分詞 built 組成 (3) 過去分詞片語 **built in 1985**，(1) 跟 (3) 共同構成主部的名詞片語 **the boat built in 1985**。

2. 句子述部的動詞片語包含三個部分：(1) 現在進行式的完全不及物動詞 **is sailing** 為述部的必要元素，(2) 名詞片語 **the Pacific Ocean** 與介系詞 **across** 組成 (3) 介系詞片語 **across the Pacific**

Ocean，(1) 跟 (3) 共同構成述部的動詞片語 **is sailing across the Pacific Ocean**。

例二：熟諳一種外國語言 可以是用來賺錢的技能。

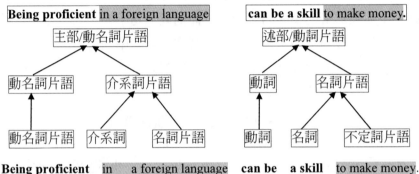

句子結構剖析：

1. 句子的主部為動名詞片語，包含兩個部分：(1) 動名詞片語 **being proficient**，為主部的必要元素，以及 (2) 介系詞片語 **in a foreign language**；(1) 跟 (2) 共同構成主部的動名詞片語 **being proficient in a foreign language**。

2. 句子述部的動詞片語包含三個部分：(1) 不完全不及物動詞 **can be**，(2) 名詞 **a skill** 作為主詞補語，(1) 跟 (2) 為句子不可或缺的部分；另外 (3) 不定詞片語 **to make money**，用來修飾 a skill，兩者構成擴充的名詞片語 **a skill to make money**；三者共同構成述部的動詞片語 **can be a skill to make money**。

例三：人工智慧的應用 將會深深地改變我們的生活。

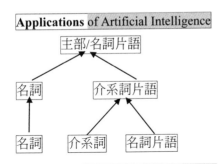

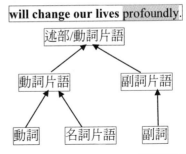

句子結構剖析：

1. 句子的主部爲名詞片語，包含兩個部分：(1) 名詞 **applications** 爲主部的必要元素，以及 (2) 介系詞片語 **of Artificial Intelligence**，用來修飾 applications，兩者構成擴充的名詞片語 **applications of Artificial Intelligence**，作爲主部。

2. 句子述部的動詞片語包含三個部分：(1) 未來式完全及物動詞 **will change**，(2) 名詞片語 **our lives**，作爲受詞，(1) 和 (2) 爲述部的必要元素；另外 (3) 副詞 **profoundly**，用來修飾 will change，形成擴充的動詞片語 **will change our lives profoundly**，作爲句子的述部。

例四：| 堪薩斯來的宣教士**布萊恩** | 前來臺灣教英文 |。

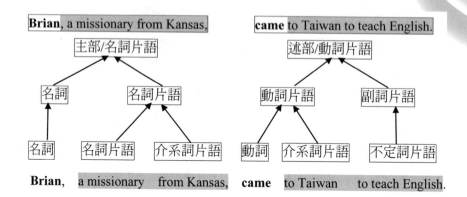

句子結構剖析：

1. 句子的主部為名詞片語，包含兩個部分：(1) 專有名詞 **Brian**，
   為主部不可或缺的元素，以及 (2) 名詞片語 **a missionary from
   Kansas**，是由名詞 a missionary 和介系詞片語 from Kansas 組
   成，作為 Brian 的同位語，並非主部必要的元素，兩者共同構成
   主部 **Brian, a missionary from Kansas,**

2. 句子述部的動詞片語包含三個部分：(1) 完全不及物動詞
   came，為述部不可或缺的元素，(2) 介系詞片語 **to Taiwan**，
   以及 (3) 不定詞片語 **to teach English**；(2) 與 (3) 都是修飾
   came，但都不是述部的必要元素，與 (1) 共同構成句子的述部
   came to Taiwan to teach English。

例五：在花蓮經營一家民宿 使得這對夫婦忙碌不停。

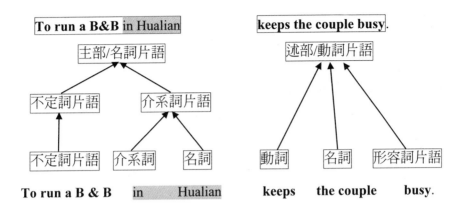

句子結構剖析：

1. 句子的主部為不定詞片語，包含兩個部分：(1) 不定詞片語 **to run a B&B**，為主部不可或缺的元素，(2) 介系詞片語 **in Hualian**，用來修飾 to run，但非必要元素，兩者共同構成主部 **to run a B&B in Hualian**。

2. 句子述部的動詞片語包含三個元素：(1) 不完全及物動詞 **keeps**，(2) 名詞 **the couple**，作為 keeps 的受詞，以及 (3) 形容詞片語 **busy**，作為受詞 the couple 的補語；這三個部分都是述部的必要元素，三者共同構成述部 **keeps the couple busy**。

　　從以上的例句分析，我們瞭解到英文句子是由各種不同的片語所構成，包括：名詞片語、動名詞片語、不定詞片語、分詞片語、副詞片語、介系詞片語、同位語片語、以及句子中的核心元素動詞片語。

　　不同的片語各有其功能，例如名詞片語、動名詞片語、不定詞片語可以作為句子的主詞，分詞片語用來修飾名詞，副詞片語用來修飾動詞或形容詞或副詞，而介系詞片語則可修飾名詞或動詞等等，接下來我們就要一一介紹各種不同的片語及其功能。

4.1 片語依其本質分類

片語的定義與分類

　　英文片語指的是不具備主詞與動詞結構的一個或多個單字，換句話說，片語可以是由一個單字或多個單字所組成，但還不足以構成句子的結構。

　　片語的分類有兩種方式：一種是依照**片語的本質**分類，包括：

(1) 名詞片語

(2) 動詞片語

(3) 形容詞片語

(4) 副詞片語

(5) 介系詞片語

(6) 不定詞片語

(7) 動名詞片語

(8) 分詞片語

　　另外一種則是依照**片語的功能**加以分類，而有：

(1) 副詞片語

(2) 形容詞片語

(3) 同位語片語

▶ 4.1.1 名詞片語 (noun phrases)

名詞片語的主體當然就是名詞。名詞片語可以只是單一的一個名詞所構成，如 Taiwan；也可以是一個名詞加上它的修飾詞所構成，如 a beautiful island。名詞片語的功能跟名詞一樣，有多種用途，它可以當作主詞、受詞、補語、同位語。

例如：

Taiwan is **a beautiful island**.

上句中 Taiwan 是句子的<u>主詞</u>，而 a beautiful island 則是當作<u>主詞補語</u>。

A famous singer will visit **Taiwan**.

上句中 a famous singer 是句子的<u>主詞</u>，而 Taiwan 則是當作 visit 的<u>受詞</u>。

Taiwan, **a beautiful island**, attracts **many foreign tourists**.

上句中 Taiwan 是句子的<u>主詞</u>，a beautiful island 則是 Taiwan 的<u>同位語</u>，而 many foreign tourists 則是 attracts 的<u>受詞</u>。

▶ 4.1.2 動詞片語 (verb phrases)

動詞片語的主體就是帶頭的動詞。動詞片語的結構非常多樣，分別舉例說明如下：

(1) 最單純的動詞片語是由單一一個完全不及物動詞所構成 (S. + Vi.)，沒有受詞，也沒有修飾詞，如：

The girls **are singing**.

(2) 由完全不及物動詞加修飾詞所構成 (S. + Vi. + Adv.)，如：

The girls **are singing beautifully**.（名詞片語作爲主詞 + 動詞

片語）

(3) 由一個完全及物動詞加上受詞所構成 (S. + Vt. + O.)，如：

The girls **are singing old songs**.（名詞片語作爲主詞 + 動詞片語）

(4) 由不及物動詞加上介系詞片語所構成(S. + Vi. + Prep. P.)，如：

The girls **come from different countries**.（名詞片語作爲主詞 + 動詞片語）

(5) 由不完全及物動詞加上受詞及受詞補語所構成 (S. + Vt. + O. + O.C.)，如

The girls **name their group Flash**.（名詞片語作爲主詞 + 動詞片語）

(6) 由及物動詞加上受詞及介系詞片語所構成 (S. + Vt. + O. + Prep. P.)，如

The girls **provide the young generation with popular songs**.（名詞片語作爲主詞 + 動詞片語）

(7) 由及物動詞加上受詞及受詞的修飾詞 (S. + Vt. + O. + Prep. P.)，如

The girls **draw fans of different ages**.（名詞片語作爲主詞 + 動詞片語）

(8) 由不完全不及物動詞加上主詞補語所構成 (S. + Vi. + S.C.)，如

The girls **are becoming famous**.（名詞片語作爲主詞 + 動詞片語）

以上的例句都說明了英文簡單句的結構是由主詞加上動詞片語所構成，也就是：

名詞片語／主部 + 動詞片語／述部 → 構成一個完整的簡單句

（這裡以名詞片語作爲主詞，除此之外，**動名詞片語或不定詞片語或名詞子句也可以作爲主詞，詳述於後**）

說明

名詞片語作為廣義的主詞（或稱為**主部，subject**），而名詞片語中的名詞即是狹義的主詞，這個名詞的單複數就決定了動詞片語中動詞的單複數。

動詞片語在文法上也稱為**述部 (predicate)**，其主體為其中的動詞，句子的時態表現在動詞的時態變化上，例如現在式、過去式、未來式、進行式、完成式等等。

因此，英文的簡單句結構也可以分解為：

Subject（主部）+ **Predicate**（述部）= **Simple Sentence**（簡單句）

▶▶ 4.1.3 形容詞片語 (adjective phrases)

　　單一的形容詞即可構成一個形容詞片語，用來**修飾名詞片語或動名詞片語**、或是作爲**主詞補語**，例如：a **kind** lady，a **beautiful** painting，或是**形容詞之前加上副詞**也可構成形容詞片語，例如 a **very kind** lady，an **incredibly beautiful** painting。

(1) 形容詞片語**修飾名詞片語**

> A **young** girl shares her food with the homeless.（**young** 修飾 girl）
>
> The **rich** man bought a **very expensive** car.（**rich** 修飾 man，**very expensive** 修飾 car，副詞要放在形容詞之前）

(2) 形容詞片語修飾動名詞片語

> **Regular** exercising is good for health.（**regular** 修飾 exercising）
>
> **Insufficient** practicing resulted in **poor** batting in the baseball game.（**insufficient** 修飾 practicing，**poor** 修飾 batting）
>
> He was put in jail for **extremely reckless** driving.（**extremely reckless** 修飾 driving）
>
> Her **rather creative** teaching makes her the most popular professor in the department.（**rather creative** 修飾 teaching）

(3) 形容詞片語作為主詞補語

> This winter is **warm**.
>
> This winter is **unseasonably warm**.
>
> Most people cannot stay **calm** during a crisis.
>
> She feels **somewhat uncomfortable** in front of new classmates.

(4) 形容詞片語作為受詞補語

> The tragic story made the little boy **terribly sad**.
>
> The blanket kept me **unexpectedly warm** at night.

▶▶ 4.1.4 副詞片語 (adverbial phrases)

單一的副詞即可構成副詞片語，用來修飾動詞片語、形容詞片語、現在分詞片語、過去分詞片語，例如：

The police **quickly** solved the case.（副詞 quickly 修飾動詞 solved）

She made a reservation of a hotel room **yesterday**.

副詞前面加上副詞也可以構成副詞片語，例如：

The boy swims **really fast**.

(1) 副詞片語修飾動詞片語

> The mother spoke **softly** to her baby.
>
> He has been trying **very hard** to improve his writing.
>
> **Cautiously**, the security guard opened the suspicious parcel.
>
> The hunter disappeared in the woods **mysteriously**.
>
> **Simultaneously**, the film is shown in theaters in major cities of the country.
>
> The Japanese princess **unprecedentedly** married to a commoner and **inevitably** lost her royal status.

(2) 副詞片語修飾形容詞片語

> All tasks of each group member are **equally** important.
>
> He easily carried out a **seemingly** difficult mission.
>
> The carpenter delivered **totally** impressive woodwork in renovating the house.

Abraham, a **highly** honorable man, has been named the new chief of the department.

The university aggressively recruits **exceptionally** outstanding students to their graduate programs.

(3) 副詞片語修飾現在分詞片語

The author has finally finished writing a story **undoubtedly** fascinating to children

The congressman made a speech **undeniably** intriguing patriotism.

The government offers incentives **hopefully** luring foreign investments.

Students **anxiously** waiting for the results of the test may not sleep well at night.

The chef **unselfishly** sharing his recipes on the social media is getting famous quickly.

The young lady performed a talent show stunning the judges **unexpectedly**.

(4) 副詞片語修飾過去分詞片語

She is dissatisfied with the steak apparently **over** cooked.

The girl found treasures **unintentionally** left in the basement.

The company recently released a van **specifically** designed for the disabled.

They got the little gifts **randomly** distributed to the audience.

Messages **wrongly** sent to the recipient may cause serious troubles.

Their job is to get shipments **always timely** delivered to the buyer.

▶▶ 4.1.5 介系詞片語 (prepositional phrases)

介系詞片語的結構很容易辨別，它的開頭一定是介系詞，後面加上名詞片語或動名詞片語而構成。

介系詞片語可以用來**修飾名詞**，**與形容詞片語功能相同**；也可以用來**修飾動詞、動名詞片語、不定詞片語**，**與副詞片語功能相同**。

例如：

(1) 介系詞片語的功能為形容詞片語

The toy **in his hand** is mine.
（介系詞片語由 in 及 his hand 所構成，其作用是用來**修飾名詞片語** the toy，相當於**形容詞片語**的功能。）

The singing **of the housewife** astonished the judges.
（介系詞片語由 of 及 the housewife 所構成，其作用是用來**修飾動名詞片語** the singing，相當於**形容詞片語**的功能。）

(2) 介系詞片語的功能爲副詞片語

The mother is preparing dinner **in the kitchen**.

（介系詞片語由 in 及 the kitchen 所構成，其作用是用來<u>**修飾動詞**</u> is preparing，相當於<u>副詞片語</u>的功能。）

She expressed her gratitude **by sending a card**.

（介系詞片語由 by 及 sending a card 所構成，其作用是用來<u>**修飾動詞**</u> expressed，相當於<u>副詞片語</u>的功能。）

Out of curiosity, they attend the Youth Bible Study every Friday evening.

（介系詞片語由 out of 及 curiosity 所構成，其作用是用來<u>**修飾動詞**</u> attend，相當於<u>副詞片語</u>的功能。）

Running a marathon **in such a hot weather** can be harmful.

（介系詞片語由 in 及 such a hot weather 所構成，其作用是用來<u>**修飾動名詞片語**</u> running a marathon，相當於<u>副詞片語</u>的功能。）

To survive **in the wild without prepared food** is very challenging.

（兩個介系詞片語由 in 及 the wild 與 without 及 prepared food 所構成，其作用都是用來<u>**修飾不定詞片語**</u> to survive，相當於<u>副詞片語</u>的功能。）

▶▶ 4.1.6 不定詞片語 (infinitive phrases)

不定詞片語是由不定詞所開頭的片語，也就是 **to + 原型動詞**的結構。不定詞由動詞變化而來，雖然不能作爲句子的動詞，但還保留了動詞的一些特性，例如不定詞之後可以接受詞或受詞與受詞補語 (to earn money, to have the air conditioner repaired, to text her a message)，或是不定詞可以加上副詞片語來修飾它 (to air the game live, to cooperate with the authorities)。

(1) 由完全不及物動詞轉換而來的單一不定詞即可構成不定詞片語，例如 to excel；
(2) 由不完全不及物動詞轉換而來的不定詞加上補語，例如 to become a programmer；
(3) 由完全及物動詞轉換而來的不定詞加了受詞，例如 to invent the device；
(4) 由完全不及物動詞轉換而來的不定詞加了受詞與補語，例如 to make customers happy；
(5) 由完全不及物動詞轉換而來的不定詞加上副詞，例如 to think creatively；
(6) 由完全不及物動詞轉換而來的不定詞加上介系詞片語，例如 to decide without consulting someone，都可以構成不定詞片語。

不定詞片語的功能

不定詞片語的功能有三方面：<u>名詞片語的功能</u>，<u>形容詞片語的功能</u>，以及<u>副詞片語的功能</u>。

(1) 不定詞片語的功能為<u>名詞片語</u>

> **To die for the country** is a soldier's honor.
> （不定詞片語當作<u>主詞</u>，是<u>名詞片語</u>的功能。）
> They are planning **to spend the winter in Florida**.
> （不定詞片語當作<u>受詞</u>，是<u>名詞片語</u>的功能。）
> The company's strategy is **to stay competitive in the market**.
> （不定詞片語當作<u>主詞補語</u>，是<u>名詞片語</u>的功能。）

(2) 不定詞片語的功能為<u>形容詞片語</u>

> The house has a big garage **to park three cars**.
> （不定詞片語作為形容詞片語，修飾名詞 garage）
> The students seemed **to be very excited**.
> （不定詞片語作為<u>主詞補語</u>，是<u>形容詞片語</u>的功能。）

(3) 不定詞片語的功能為<u>副詞片語</u>

> We arrived early **to get good seats**.
> （不定詞片語作為<u>副詞片語</u>，修飾動詞 arrived。）
> As a college student, she intends to work part-time at night **to support herself**.
> （不定詞片語作為<u>副詞片語</u>，修飾不定詞 to work part-time）

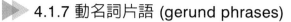

4.1.7 動名詞片語 (gerund phrases)

　　動名詞片語是以動名詞為主體的片語，動名詞由動詞變化而來，雖然不再能夠當作句子的動詞，卻還保有動詞的特性，例如動名詞之後可以接受詞 (reading novels)，也可以接受詞和受詞補語 (making everyone happy)，以及動名詞前後可以接副詞片語加以修飾 (proactively preparing for the game, nervously reporting news at the crime scene)；除此之外，動名詞也具備了名詞的特性，例如可以在動名詞前後加上形容詞片語來修飾它 (consistent weightlifting, the singing of the birds) 等等。

(1) 由完全不及物動詞轉換而來的單一動名詞可以構成動名詞片語，例如 swimming, skiing；
(2) 由不完全不及物動詞轉換而來的動名詞加上補語，例如 feeling embarrassed；
(3) 由完全及物動詞轉換而來的動名詞之後加上受詞，例如 writing an essay；
(4) 由不完全及物動詞轉換而來的動名詞之後加上受詞與補語，例如 naming one's dog Watermelon；
(5) 動名詞前後加上副詞片語或形容詞片語，例如 doing the chores reluctantly, graceful dancing，都可以構成動名詞片語。

　　動名詞片語的作用跟名詞片語相同，可以當作**主詞**，**受詞**，**補語**，以及**同位語**。

(1) 動名詞片語的功能為主詞

> **Singing** makes children happy.
> （動名詞本身即構成動名詞片語，當作句子的主詞。）
> **Achieving the goal** requires hard work.
> （動名詞加上受詞構成動名詞片語，當作句子的主詞。）
> **Naming one's dog Watermelon** is really funny.
> （動名詞加上受詞及受詞補語構成動名詞片語，當作句子的主詞。）

(2) 動名詞片語的功能為動詞的受詞

> She enjoys **reading novels**.
> （動名詞加上受詞構成動名詞片語，當作動詞的受詞。）
> They love **fishing during the summer**.
> （動名詞加上介系詞片語構成動名詞片語，當作動詞的受詞。）

(3) 動名詞片語的功能為主詞補語

> His favorite pastime is **playing video games**.
> （動名詞加上受詞構成動名詞片語，當作主詞補語。）
> The best part of the video was **the graceful dancing of the little girl**.
> （動名詞之前加上形容詞以及之後加上介系詞片語構成動名詞片語，當作主詞補語。）

(4) 動名詞片語的功能爲介系詞的受詞

> They won the prize for **designing the new device for recycling plastic containers**.
> （動名詞加上受詞構成動名詞片語，當作<u>介系詞的受詞</u>。）
> The new reporter is nervous about **reporting news at the crime scene**.
> （動名詞加上受詞及介系詞片語構成動名詞片語，當作<u>介系詞的受詞</u>。）

(5) 動名詞片語的功能爲同位語

> Her ambition, **becoming a certified accountant**, will be fulfilled soon.
> （動名詞加上補語構成動名詞片語，當作<u>主詞的同位語</u>。）
> Hundreds of thousands of tourists come to the Alps to experience the most popular sport in winter, **skiing**.
> （單一動名詞構成動名詞片語，當作<u>不定詞受詞的同位語</u>。）

▶▶ 4.1.8 分詞片語 (participial phrases)

　　分詞片語的主體即是帶頭的**現在分詞** (present participles) 或**過去分詞** (past participles)，分詞由動詞變化而來，雖然不再能夠當作句子的動詞，卻還保有動詞的特性，例如：由不完全不及物動詞變化而來的現在分詞 becoming 加上主詞補語 a translator，構成現在分詞片語 becoming a translator；或是由完全及物動詞變化而來的過去分詞加上後面的受詞或修飾詞所構成，**其作用與形容詞相同**。

　　現在分詞片語及過去分詞片語均有兩種用法：一種是放在名詞

或名詞片語後面，但是**不加逗點的限定用法**，另外一種是分詞與其所修飾的名詞或名詞片語之間必須**用逗點隔開的非限定用法**。

(1) 限定用法分詞片語（分為限定用法現在分詞片語以及限定用法過去分詞片語）

   (a) 限定用法現在分詞片語

   例一：[People **living in Seattle**] appreciate its mild climate.

> **說明**
>
> living in Seattle 是現在分詞片語，用來**修飾名詞** people，**名詞與分詞之間不加逗點**，兩者構成一個名詞片語 people living in Seattle，其含義是指居住在西雅圖的居民，而非指稱所有的人，因此是限定的用法。這樣的用法其實也是由**主動語態的限定用法形容詞子句所簡化而來**的。

   例二：The tourists are looking for [stores **selling local delicacies**].（現在分詞片語**修飾名詞** stores）

   (b) 限定用法過去分詞片語

   例一：[Soldiers **sent to the front**] are proud to fight for their country.

> **說明**
>
> sent to the front 是過去分詞片語，用來修飾 soldiers，名詞與分詞之間不加逗點，兩者構成一個名詞片語 soldiers sent to the front，其含義是指被派往前線的軍人，而非指稱所有的軍人，因此是限定的用法。這樣的用法其實也是**由被動語態的限定用法形容詞子句所簡化而來**的。

例二：Customers are willing to pay more money for [home appliances **manufactured in Japan**].

（過去分詞片語**修飾**名詞片語 home appliances）

（**關於形容詞子句及其如何簡化爲現在分詞片語與過去分詞片語，將在形容詞子句的篇章中詳細解說。**）

(2) 非限定用法的分詞片語

非限定用法的分詞片語是由非限定用法的形容詞子句簡化而來，若該形容詞子句爲**主動語態**，則簡化爲**現在分詞片語**；若該形容詞爲**被動語態**，則簡化爲**過去分詞片語**。非限定用法的分詞片語與另一個**主詞相同的句子結合**，即可構成英文寫作上經常運用的**分詞構句**的句型。（有關形容詞子句的用法將在子句一章中詳細解說）

我們先用以下的例句來說明非限定用法的分詞片語是如何變化而來：

(a) 非限定用法現在分詞片語（由主動語態句子轉化而來）

Cindy saw the beautiful house.（主動語態）

Cindy made a quick decision to buy it.

（前提：**兩個句子的主詞必須相同：Cindy**）

步驟一：先把**主動語態**的句子轉換爲**非限定用法形容詞子句**

Cindy saw the beautiful house. → **who saw the beautiful house**

步驟二：將子句跟**另一個主詞相同的句子結合**

→ Cindy, **who saw the beautiful house,** made a quick decision to buy it.

步驟三：再把子句簡化為現在分詞片語，即可完成分詞構
句的句型。

→ Cindy, **seeing the beautiful house,** made a quick decision to buy it.

或是將分詞片語移到句首：

→ **Seeing the beautiful house,** Cindy made a quick decision to buy it.

(b) 非限定用法過去分詞片語 （由被動語態句子轉化而來）

Joshua was inspired by the news story. （被動語態）

Joshua wrote the fascinating novel.

（前提：兩個句子的主詞必須相同：**Joshua**）

步驟一：先把被動語態的句子轉換為非限定用法形容詞子句

Joshua was inspired by the news story. → **who was inspired by the news story**

步驟二：將子句跟另一個主詞相同的句子結合

Joshua, **who was inspired by the news story,** wrote the fascinating novel.

步驟三：再將子句簡化為過去分詞片語

→ *Joshua,* ***inspired by the news story,*** *wrote the fascinating novel.*

或是將分詞片語移到句首：

→ ***Inspired by the news story,*** *Joshua wrote the fascinating novel.*

4.2 片語依其功能分類

片語依其功能分類，有 (1) 副詞片語，(2) 形容詞片語，以及 (3) 同位語片語。

▶▶ 4.2.1 副詞片語 (adverbial phrases)

副詞片語的功能與副詞相同，用來修飾動詞、形容詞、現在分詞、過去分詞、不定詞。廣義的副詞片語包括**單一的副詞**以及**加了修飾詞的副詞**，例如 very seriously；另外，前面所介紹的不同本質的片語中，**介系詞片語**及**不定詞片語**也具備副詞片語的功能。

(1) 副詞片語本身即是副詞片語的功能

> The little boy runs **really fast**.
> （really fast 為<u>副詞片語</u>，用來修飾動詞 runs。）
> She types **incredibly speedily and accurately**.
> （incredibly speedily and accurately 為<u>副詞片語</u>，用來修飾動詞 types。）

(2) 介系詞片語的功能為副詞片語

> The children are playing **in the yard**.
> （介系詞片語 in the yard，用來**修飾動詞** are playing，因此它的功能屬於**副詞片語**。）
> The man jumped **off the cliff into the ocean**.

（off the cliff 與 into the ocean 都是介系詞片語，都是用來**修飾動詞** jumped，因此它的功能屬於<u>副詞片語</u>。）

(3) 不定詞片語的功能爲副詞片語

The foreign students are happy **to study here**.
（不定詞片語 to study here，用來**修飾形容詞** happy，因此它的功能屬於**副詞片語**。）
I am proud **to stand with my son**.
（不定詞片語 to stand with my son，用來**修飾形容詞** proud，因此它的功能屬於副詞片語；另外有一個介系詞片語 with my son，用來**修飾不定詞** to stand，因此它的功能也屬於**副詞片語**。）

▶▶ 4.2.2 形容詞片語 (adjective phrases)

　　形容詞片語的功能與形容詞相同，用來作爲補語或修飾名詞片語或動名詞片語。廣義的形容詞片語包括**單一的形容詞**以及**加了修飾詞的形容詞**，例如 very beautiful；除此之外，前面所介紹的不同本質的片語中，**介系詞片語，不定詞片語，及分詞片語**都具備形容詞片語的功能

(1) 形容詞片語

He has become **more independent**.
（more independent 是<u>形容詞片語</u>，當作<u>主詞</u>he 的<u>補語</u>。）
The bride is a **very beautiful** lady.
（very beautiful 是**形容詞片語**，**修飾名詞** lady。）

(2) 介系詞片語作爲形容詞片語

> The manufacturing **of bicycles** has become modernized.
> （介系詞片語 **of bicycle** 用來**修飾動名詞** the manufacturing，其功能屬於<u>形容詞片語</u>。）
> It will be the first mall **in our city**.
> （介系詞片語 **in our city** 用來修飾名詞 mall，其功能屬於<u>形容詞片語</u>。）

(3) 不定詞片語作爲形容詞片語

> They are carrying out a dangerous mission **to rescue the hostages**.
> （不定詞片語 **to rescue the hostages** 用來修飾名詞 mission，其功能屬於<u>形容詞片語</u>。）
> The lawyer gave her a consent form **to be signed**.
> （不定詞片語 **to be signed** 用來修飾名詞 form，其功能屬於<u>形容詞片語</u>。）

(4) 現在分詞片語作爲形容詞片語

> Applicants **waiting for the interview** seemed nervous.
> （現在分詞片語 **waiting for the interview** 用來修飾名詞 applicants，其功能屬於<u>形容詞片語</u>。）
> Some people like to eat in restaurants **serving exotic food**.
> （現在分詞片語 serving exotic food 用來**修飾名詞** restaurants，其功能屬於<u>形容詞片語</u>。）

(5) 過去分詞作為形容詞片語

> The furniture **donated to the orphanage** will be shipped tomorrow.
> （**過去分詞片語 donated to the orphanage** 用來**修飾名詞** furniture，其功能屬於<u>形容詞片語</u>。）
> They like to buy produce **grown by local farmers**.
> （**過去分詞片語 grown by local farmers** 用來**修飾名詞** produce，其功能屬於<u>形容詞片語</u>。）

▶▶ **4.2.3 同位語片語** (appositive phrases)

　　同位語片語出現在名詞或名詞相等語（亦即先行詞）的後面或前面，它的形式可以是名詞片語，動名詞片語，不定詞片語，或是介系詞片語；而其功能則是用來解釋，分辨，或重新命名其先行詞。

　　我們用以下的例句來說明同位語如何變化而來：

(1) 名詞片語作為同位語

> Steve Jobs was **the creator of the iPhone**.
> → 先把句子簡化為名詞片語 **the creator of the iPhone**
> Steve Jobs started the era of smartphones.
> → 再將名詞片語放在先行詞 Steve Jobs **後面**，成為它的同位語（記得要在先行詞後面及同位語後面加逗點）
> → Steve Jobs, **the creator of the iPhone,** started the era of smartphones.

Dr. Hoffman is **a renowned scholar**.

→ 先把句子簡化爲名詞片語 **a renowned scholar**

Dr. Hoffman will conduct the research.

→ 再將名詞片語放在先行詞 Dr. Hoffman **前面**，成爲它的同位語（記得要在同位語後面加逗點）

→ **A renowned scholar,** Dr. Hoffman, will conduct the research.

His wife is **a famous pianist**.

→ 先把句子簡化爲名詞片語 **a famous pianist**

His wife will perform in the concert tomorrow night.

→ 再將名詞片語放在先行詞 his wife **後面**，成爲它的同位語（記得要在先行詞後面及同位語後面加逗點）

His wife, **a famous pianist**, will perform in the concert tomorrow night.

(2) 不定詞片語作爲同位語

Her father's dream is **to build a house in the farm**.

→ 先把句子簡化爲不定詞片語 **to build a house in the farm**

Her father's dream may come true one day.

→ 再將不定詞片語放在先行詞 her father's dream **後面**，成爲它的同位語（記得要在先行詞後面及同位語後面加逗點）

Her father's dream, **to build a house in the farm**, may come true one day.

(3) 動名詞片語作爲同位語

> The only solution to the financial crisis is **cutting down spending**.
>
> → 先把句子簡化爲動名詞片語 **cutting down spending**
>
> The manager knows the only solution to the financial crisis.
>
> → 再將動名詞片語放在先行詞 the only solution to the financial crisis **後面**，成爲它的同位語（記得要在先行詞後面加逗點）
>
> → The manager knows the only solution to the financial crisis, **cutting down spending**.

(4) 介系詞片語作爲同位語

> The ancient burial place of royalty is **in the suburbs of the city**.
>
> → 先把句子簡化爲介系詞片語 **in the suburbs of the city**
>
> The ancient burial place of royalty was discovered by an archaeological team last year.
>
> → 再將介系詞片語放在先行詞 the ancient burial place of royalty **後面**，成爲它的同位語（記得要在先行詞後面及同位語後面加逗點）
>
> → The ancient burial place of the royalty, **in the suburbs of the city**, was discovered by an archaeological team last year.

同位語片語又可依其是否必要而分為兩種：(1) **必要**的稱為**限定用法**，及 (2) **非必要**的稱為**補充用法**。
例如：

(1) 限定用法同位語片語

<u>**We African Americans**</u> are fighting against racial discrimination.

此句中的 we 是句子的主詞，也是同位語片語 African Americans 的先行詞，兩者之間不加逗點，表示這個同位語片語是必要的；如果省略了 African Americans 這個同位語片語，我們就無從知道主詞 we 所指的是什麼人了。

(2) 補充用法同位語片語

<u>**The French Open**</u>, <u>**a major tennis tournament**</u>, is often referred to as Roland Garros.

此句中的主詞是 the French Open，而在兩個逗點之間的 a major tennis tournament 則是用來補充說明主詞的同位語片語，並非必要的，如果將其省略，也不會影響主詞的指稱對象。

從以上的例子，我們知道逗點對同位語片語的使用很關鍵，若是**限定用法**的同位語片語，**不可以加逗點**；若是**補充用法**，則需**加逗點**。

寫出下列句子中劃底線的片語

(a) 是何種本質的片語（名詞片語：名片；動詞片語：動片；介系詞片語：介片；不定詞片語：不片；動名詞片語：動名片；現在分詞片語：現分片；過去分詞片語：過分片；形容詞片語：形片；副詞片語：副片）

(b) 並說明其功能。

示範：(1)Kevin, (2)an international student (3)from Australia (4)studying at Feng Chia University, (5)loves (6) beef noodles (7)very much.

Ans. (1) (a) 名片 (b) 主詞，(2)(a) 名片 (b) 同位語，(3)(a) 介片 (b) 修飾 student，(4)(a) 現分片 (b) 修飾 student，(5)(a) 動片 (b) 句子述部，(6)(a) 名片 (b) 作為 loves 的受詞，(7)(a) 副片 (b) 修飾動詞 loves

---

1. Scientists (1) at the Penn Museum in Philadelphia (2) accidentally discovered a 6,500-year-old skeleton in the basement.

   (1)(a) _____ (b) _____

   (2)(a) _____ (b) _____

2. (1) Exhausted, the truck driver decided (2) to take a break.

   (1)(a) _____ (b) _____

   (2)(a) _____ (b) _____

3. (1) Paying attention in the class is the key to (2) effective learning.

   (1)(a) _____ (b) _____

   (2)(a) _____ (b) _____

4. (1) To enter a national university is (2) her goal.

   (1)(a) _____ (b) _____

   (2)(a) _____ (b) _____

5. Most politicians often fail (1) to keep their promises (2) made during the elections.

   (1)(a) _____ (b) _____

   (2)(a) _____ (b) _____

6. (1) Enacted on July 1, 2015, the new law requires employers to give employees two days off (2) in a week.

   (1)(a) _____ (b) _____

   (2)(a) _____ (b) _____

7. (1) Performing skillfully, the young musician (2) astounded the audience.

   (1)(a) _____ (b) _____

   (2)(a) _____ (b) _____

8. Players (1) competing in the tournament are trying (2) their best to win the championship.

   (1)(a) _____ (b) _____

   (2)(a) _____ (b) _____

9. The committee (1) will interview the candidates (2) applying for the scholarship.

   (1)(a) _____ (b) _____

   (2)(a) _____ (b) _____

10. (1) Manufactured in 1960, the car is still (2) in good shape.

(1)(a) —————————— (b) ——————————

(2)(a) —————————— (b) ——————————

11. The theory (1) proposed by Dr. Collins (2) has been very popular in the past 20 years.

(1)(a) —————————— (b) ——————————

(2)(a) —————————— (b) ——————————

12. (1) People wishing to qualify for the job must first pass (2) the English language test.

(1)(a) —————————— (b) ——————————

(2)(a) —————————— (b) ——————————

13. The amusement park, (1) established in the 1970s, are still attracting (2) hundreds of thousands of tourists every year.

(1)(a) —————————— (b) ——————————

(2)(a) —————————— (b) ——————————

14. Winning the first prize, the contestant was (1) extremely excited (2) to give thanks to God.

(1)(a) —————————— (b) ——————————

(2)(a) —————————— (b) ——————————

15. The apartment renovated (1) two years ago offers the residents (2) satisfying facilities.

(1)(a) —————————— (b) ——————————

(2)(a) —————————— (b) ——————————

16. The next step for him (1) after finishing the vocational training is to find a job (2) matching his expertise.

(1)(a) —————————— (b) ——————————

(2)(a) —————————— (b) ——————————

17. The canned food (1) tainted during the manufacturing process has been sold (2) to many retail stores.

(1)(a) _____ (b) _____

(2)(a) _____ (b) _____

18. (1) Before the meeting, he gathered his staff (2) to go over the agenda (3) prepared the day before.

(1)(a) _____ (b) _____

(2)(a) _____ (b) _____

(3)(a) _____ (b) _____

19. Experts are urging people to avoid (1) using cellphones (2) in the dark (3) to protect their eyes.

(1)(a) _____ (b) _____

(2)(a) _____ (b) _____

(3)(a) _____ (b) _____

20. Before (1) going on a cruise trip to Hong Kong, she asked her friend (2) to feed her cat (3) twice a day.

(1)(a) _____ (b) _____

(2)(a) _____ (b) _____

(3)(a) _____ (b) _____

4.4 片語組合練習

將各題中的片語與句子基本結構結組合成一個簡單句，以完成中文英譯。

示範：*規律地練習的目的在於增強肌肉記憶。*

The purpose is...

to reinforce, of practicing, muscle memory, regularly

→ ***The purpose of practicing regularly is to reinforce muscle memory.***

1. 這個由市政府所開發的手機應用程式透過手機提供乘客所有市公車到每一個站預估抵達時間。

   The mobile app provides passengers…

   of all city buses, developed by the city government, with an estimated arrival time, via cellphones, to every stop

   _____

   _____

2. 在南臺灣種植芒果的果農今年由於恰當的天氣獲利頗豐。

   …the farmers made profits.

   in southern Taiwan, this year, considerable, due to suitable weather, growing mangos

   _____

   _____

3. 這位修車工人非常有效率，僅僅花了半個小時就找到故障的零件並換上新的了。

   The mechanic is…

   the defected part, spending half an hour, with a new one, and replacing it, just, very efficient, identifying

   _____

   _____

4. 壽司，一種目前在外國人中間很受歡迎的普通日本食物，其實有了正確的材料和工具在你自家的廚房製作並不難。

Sushi is…

not difficult, among foreigners nowadays, actually, with the right ingredients and tools, popular, to make, in your own kitchen, a common Japanese food

_____

_____

5. 要獲得一份優厚薪水的工作，除了在其領域的專業，也需要創意和溝通技巧。

In addition to…, …requires…

the expertise, and communication skills, in the field, to get a high-paying job, creativity

_____

_____

6. 身爲職業母親，她很高興在母親節收到一張來自她八歲女兒、有著甜蜜話語的卡片。

As a working mother, she is…

a card, on Mother's Day, very happy, from her eight-year-old daughter, to receive, with sweet words

_____

_____

_____

7. 來自世界各地的遊客受到吸引，從 Eagle Point 的天空步道，一座往外延伸超過峽谷邊緣 70 英呎的玻璃橋，觀看大峽谷

Tourists are attracted.

over the rim, from the Skywalk at Eagle Point, to view the

Grand Canyon, from all over the world, extending 70 feet out, of the Canyon, a glass bridge

_____

_____

_____

8. 這家爲年輕人製造衣著的服裝公司在他們流行服裝的設計上已經做了大膽的改變，以保持市場上的競爭力。

The apparel company has made changes.

in their fashion design, to stay competitive, producing garments, for the youth, in the market, bold

_____

_____

_____

9. 經歷了一段難過的期間之後，她終於克服了悲傷，並且重新獲得對生命的熱忱。

After…, she has overcome…

and regained passion, finally, the grief, for life, going through a difficult time

_____

_____

_____

10. 由血汗工廠的工人製造的產品爲公司在全球市場賺可觀的高利潤。

Products make profits.

at sweatshops, high, by workers, in the global market, tremendously, for the company, manufactured

_____

_____

_____

第五章 簡單句的內部擴充

5.1 簡單句如何進行內部擴充

簡單句由所需的必要元素構成之後，已經成型的簡單句可以運用**名詞、形容詞、副詞、分詞、或各種片語**加在**原有結構內的適當位置**，進行**簡單句的內部擴充**，使簡單句所表達的內容更加豐富，但結構仍然維持簡單句。

例一：
機器人會**說話**。（「說話」為完全不及**物動詞**）
The robot | can talk | . (**S.** + **Vi.**)

（神奇的）機器人會（像人類一樣）說話。
需要加入一個現在分詞與一個介系詞片語：
神奇的：Amazing，像人類一樣：like humans
→ *The **amazing** robot can talk **like humans**.*

例二：
他們**發現**了寶藏。（「發現」為完全及**物動詞**）
They | found the treasure | . (**S.** + **Vt. + O.**)

（太令人驚訝了），他們（運用先進科技）發現了（失蹤的）寶藏。

需要加入一個副詞、一個介系詞片語、與一個現在分詞：

太令人驚訝了：Surprisingly，運用先進科技：with advanced technologies，失蹤的：missing

→ *Surprisingly, they found the **missing** treasure **with advanced technologies**.*

例三：

食物**嚐起來**好吃。（「嚐起來」為**不完全不及物動詞**）

| The food | tastes good | . (S. + | Vi. + SC. |)

（這個餐廳所供應的）（墨西哥）食物嚐起來（**真的**）好吃。

需要加入一個過去分詞片語、一個形容詞、與一個副詞：

這個餐廳所供應的：served in the restaurant，

墨西哥：Mexican，真的：really

→ *The **Mexican** food **served in the restaurant** tastes **really** good.*

例四：

這趟旅行**使得**每一位都開心。（「使得」為**不完全及物動詞**）

| The trip | made everyone happy | . (S. + | Vt. + O. + OC. |)

這趟（**兩週**）（去歐洲的）旅行使得（旅行團的）每一位都（**極度**）開心。

需要加入一個形容詞、兩個介系詞片語、與一個副詞：

兩週的：two-week，去歐洲的：to Europe，旅行團的：in the tour group，極度：extremely

→ *The **two-week** trip **to Europe** made everyone **in the tour group extremely** happy.*

例五：

她朋友**寄**給她一份禮物。（「寄」為**授與動詞**）

Her friend | sent her a gift . (**S. +** | **Vt. + O2. + O1.**)

她（**在澳洲讀書的**）朋友（**上個禮拜**）寄給她一份（**特別的**）禮物。

需要加入一個現在分詞片語、一個副詞片語、一個形容詞：

在澳洲讀書的：studying in Australia，上個禮拜：last week，特別的：special

→ *Her friend **studying in Australia** sent her a **special** gift **last week**.*

 5.1.1 小試身手：簡單句的內部擴充

　　將括號中的單字與片語放置在簡單句中的恰當位置以完成句子英譯。

1. 這塊地的地主蓋了好幾間小木屋給人家租用作為度假住宿。

　　句子基本結構：The owner built cabins.

　　(to stay, several, for vacations, to rent, of the land, for people)

　　＿＿＿＿＿＿＿＿＿＿＿＿＿＿＿＿＿＿＿＿＿＿＿＿＿＿＿＿

　　＿＿＿＿＿＿＿＿＿＿＿＿＿＿＿＿＿＿＿＿＿＿＿＿＿＿＿＿

2. 修微積分這門很硬的課程的學生花好幾個小時準備該科期末考。

　　句子基本結構：Students spent hours.

　　(of Calculus, demanding, many, for its final exam, the course, preparing, taking)

　　＿＿＿＿＿＿＿＿＿＿＿＿＿＿＿＿＿＿＿＿＿＿＿＿＿＿＿＿

　　＿＿＿＿＿＿＿＿＿＿＿＿＿＿＿＿＿＿＿＿＿＿＿＿＿＿＿＿

3. 我最要好的朋友之一 Tina 昨天晚上傳訊息給我，邀請我下禮拜六晚上去參加她的慶生聚會。

句子基本結構：Tina texted me a message.

(inviting me, next Saturday night, one of my best friends, to her birthday party, last night)

_____

_____

4. 對花生過敏的人必須避免食用含有該成份的食物。

句子基本結構：People must avoid eating food.

(containing, allergic, such ingredient, to peanuts)

_____

_____

5. 實力龐大的多國企業一直在影響很多開發中國家政府的政策，以便在全球市場拓展他們的生意。

句子基本結構：The corporations have been influencing policies.

(in the global market, powerful, government's, to expand their businesses, multi-national, in many developing countries)

_____

_____

6. 這位老婆婆經營餐廳，以低價賣傳統的臺灣麵食給大學生，事實上每個月生意都虧錢。

句子基本結構：The old lady is losing money.

(over business, at low prices, to college students, running a restaurant, selling, every month, actually, traditional Taiwanese noodles)

_____

_____

7. 在人口稠密的現代化城市，於夜晚期間有各別種不同的燈光點亮，光害非常嚴重。

句子基本結構：Light pollution is serious.

(very, with, populated, during the night, turned on, in cities, of lights, modern, many different kinds)

8. 由日本人所建造連接東京和大阪的子彈列車是於 2007 年正式啓用的臺灣高鐵的原型。

句子基本結構：The bullet train is the prototype.

(officially, of Taiwan High Speed Rail, connecting Tokyo and Osaka, launched in 2007, built by Japanese)

9. David 的上司派給他一項富有挑戰性的工作，帶領一群由三十位電腦專家的團隊執行一項人工智慧的計畫。

句子基本結構：David's boss assigned him a job.

(a group, an AI project, 30 computer specialists, challenging, to lead, composed of, to implement)

10. 經過過去幾個月無數次會議冗長時間的討論，雙方終於同意要一起合作開發鄰近國家首都的土地。

句子基本結構：…, the two sides agreed.

(in the past few months, the land, after, finally, in numerous meetings, of the country, in developing, long-hour discussions, the capital, near, to collaborate)

_____

_____

▶▶ 5.1.2 小試身手：完成句子英譯

1. 這位住在對街的男士就業於一家日本餐廳擔任廚師以維持他一家的生計。

   句子基本結構：The man works in a restaurant.

   _____

   _____

2. 這對來自加拿大興奮的年輕夫婦在女嬰出生前把他們的女嬰取名為 Angel。

   句子基本結構：The couple named their baby girl Angel.

   _____

   _____

3. 我們英文老師胡老師給我們一份作業要在周末去跟母語人士說英文。

   句子基本結構：Ms. Hu gave us an assignment.

   _____

   _____

4. 現在很多不同產業的工廠正運用現代科技，包括大數據與物聯網，來有效改進其生產，以便在全球市場保持競爭力。

   句子基本結構：Factories are using technologies.

   _____

   _____

5. 昨天晚上我媽媽為我二十歲的姊姊準備的生日蛋糕看起來漂亮又好吃。

句子基本結構：The cake looked pretty and delicious.

5.2 中翻英解題祕技

　　本節以大學入學英文科測驗中的句子中翻英題目為例，來說明如何剖析英文句子的基本結構，並透過句子內部擴充完成句子英譯。首先看到中文句子，要先確認英文句子所要使用的動詞類型，以及句子的基本結構所需包含的必要元素，接著將基本結構翻譯成英文，然後運用各種單字與片語進行句子的內部擴充，最後完成全句的英譯。

中文句子的英譯過程包括：
(1) 確認句子的動詞類型與基本結構
(2) 將基本結構中文翻成英文
(3) 進行句子內部擴充，完成全句英譯。

　　接下來，我們以學測與指考中翻英的兩個題目為例子，示範演練如下：

題目一：
(1) 相較於他們父母的世代，現今年輕人享受較多的自由和繁榮。
(2) 這個快速改變的世界中，他們必須學習有效地因應新的挑戰。（105 年學測）

---

(1)「相較於他們父母的世代，現今<u>年輕人享受</u>較多的<u>自由和繁</u>
<u>榮</u>。」

第一步：確認句子的動詞類型與基本結構

本句的動詞「享受」為**完全及物動詞**，句子的基本結構包含三
個必要元素：

| 主詞 S. | + | 完全及物動詞 Vt. + 受詞 O. |

全句的基本結構為：

| 年輕人 | 享受 + 自由和繁榮 |

第二步：將基本結構翻成英文

Young people enjoy freedom and prosperity.

第三步：進行句子內部擴充

（相較於他們父母的世代），（現今）年輕人享受（較多的）
自由和繁榮

需要在原有的句子中加入一個過去分詞片語與兩個單字：

相較於他們父母的世代：compared to the generation of
their parents，

現今：nowadays，較多的：more

完成全句英譯

→ *Compared to the generation of their parents, nowadays*
  *young people enjoy **more** freedom and prosperity.*

(2)「這個快速改變的世界中，<u>他們必須學習有效地因應新的挑</u>
<u>戰</u>。」

第一步：確認句子的動詞類型與基本結構

本句的動詞「學習」為**完全及物動詞**，句子的基本結構包含三

個要素：

主詞 ＋ 完全及物動詞 ＋ 受詞

全句的基本結構為：

他們 必須學習 ＋ 因應新的挑戰

第二步：將基本結構翻成英文

They must learn to respond to new challenges.

第三步：進行句子內部擴充

（**這個快速改變的世界中**），他們必須學習（**有效地**）因應新的挑戰。

需要在原有的句子中加入一個介系詞片語與一個副詞：

這個快速改變的世界中：in this fast changing world，有效地：effectively

完成全句英譯

In this fast changing world, they must learn to respond to new challenges effectively.

經過上述的步驟，完成題目一的兩句中文英譯如下：

(1) 相較於他們父母的世代，現今年輕人享受較多的自由和繁榮。

Compared to the generation of their parents, young people nowadays enjoy more freedom and prosperity.

(2) 這個快速改變的世界中，他們必須學習有效地因應新的挑戰。

In this fast changing world, they must learn to respond effectively to new challenges.

題目二：
(1) 臺灣便利商店的密集度是全世界最高的，平均每兩千人就有一家。
(2) 除了購買生活必需品，顧客也可以在這些商店繳費，甚至領取網路訂購之物品。（104年指考）

(1)「臺灣便利商店的<u>密集度是</u>全世界<u>最高的</u>，平均每兩千人就有一家。」

第一步：確認句子的動詞類型與基本結構

本句的動詞為「是」，屬於不完全不及物動詞，句子的基本結構包含三個要素：

主詞 + 不完全不及物動詞 + 主詞補語

全句的基本結構為：

密集度 是 + 最高的

第二步：將基本結構翻成英文

The density is the highest.

第三步：進行句子內部擴充

（臺灣便利商店的）密集度是（全世界）最高的，（平均每兩千人就有一家）。

需要在原有的句子中加入兩個介系詞片語與一個現在分詞片語：

臺灣便利商店的：**of the convenience stores in Taiwan**

全世界：**in the world**

平均每兩千人就有一家：**averaging one for every two thou-**

sand people

完成全句英譯

*The density **of the convenience stores in Taiwan** is the highest **in the world**, averaging one for every two thousand people.*

(2)「除了購買生活必需品，顧客也可以在這些商店<u>繳費</u>，甚至<u>領取</u>網路訂購之<u>物品</u>。」

第一步：確認句子的動詞類型與基本結構

本句的動詞有兩個：「繳」跟「領取」，二者都屬於完全及物動詞，因此本句的基本結構包含了五個要素：

主詞 ＋ 完全及物動詞一 ＋ 受詞一 ＋ 完全及物動詞二 ＋ 受詞二

全句的基本結構為：

顧客 可以繳 ＋ 費 ＋ 領取 ＋ 物品

第二步：將基本結構依動詞類型句構翻成英文

Customers can pay bills and pick up goods/items.

第三步：進行句子內部擴充

（除了購買生活必需品），顧客（也）可以（在這些商店）繳費，（甚至）領取（網路訂購之）物品。

需要在原有的句子中加入兩個介系詞片語，兩個副詞與一個過去分詞片語：

除了購買生活必需品：in addition to purchasing/buying daily necessities,

也：also，在這些商店：in these stores，甚至：even，網路

訂購之：ordered online

完成全句英譯

*In addition to purchasing/buying daily necessities, customers can **also** pay bills **in these stores** and **even** pick up goods/items **ordered online.***

經過上述的步驟，完成題目二的兩句中文英譯：

(1) 臺灣便利商店的密集度是全世界最高的，平均每兩千人就有一家。

The density of the convenience stores in Taiwan is the highest in the world, averaging one for every two thousand people.

(2) 除了購買生活必需品，顧客也可以在這些商店繳費，甚至領取網路訂購之物品。

In addition to purchasing/buying daily necessities, customers can also pay bills in these stores and even pick up goods/items ordered online.

　　由以上出自學測跟指考的兩個中翻英題目的示範演練，我們學會了如何分析判斷句子的動詞類型，以及句子的基本結構所包含的必要元素，並依照步驟，先完成基本結構的英譯，再透過句子內部的擴充，最後完成全句英譯。這樣的中譯英技巧不僅可以運用在筆譯上，也可以在英文寫作上有所發揮，幫助同學寫出合乎英文文法的句子。

5.3 簡單句內部擴充挑戰題

　　運用各式動詞句型及各類片語，將下列中文句子<u>翻成一句簡單</u><u>句</u>英文。（劃底線的部分是句子的基本結構）

> 示範：
> *他<u>接到在辦公室加班的老板來電之後匆匆地離開晚宴</u>。*
> ***He left the dinner party in a hurry after getting a call from his boss working overtime in the office.***

1. 這位地震中受困於倒塌的大樓中的<u>受害者</u>，在黑暗中<u>保持</u>冷靜並設法藉由敲打牆壁<u>發出</u>信號求救。

　　_____

　　_____

2. Richardson 博士，一位著名的兒童教育專家，<u>設立了這所</u>透過各種不同學習活動來開發兒童潛能的<u>學校</u>。

　　_____

　　_____

3. 在溫哥華取得飯店管理碩士學位後，<u>她留在當地</u>，在一家飯店擔任業務經理的助手，開始她的職業生涯。

　　_____

　　_____

4. Seth 是一位在臺北一家法國餐廳工作有抱負的年輕廚師，打算有一天要在上海跟另一位廚師開一家高級餐廳。

_____

_____

5. 這家從前國營、二十年前私有化的釀酒廠，如今生產世界上最好的啤酒之一，年銷售七億美金。

_____

_____

6. 為了適應美國文化，這位來自日本為 NBA 球隊跳舞的啦啦隊員刻意像美國人一樣穿著，並且盡她最大努力改進她的英語能力。

_____

_____

_____

7. 這個新蓋的運動中心，位於本市最大的公園對面，以低價提供市民練習或比賽的三面室內籃球場和一座游泳池。

_____

_____

_____

動詞進階篇 |

流淚撒種的　必歡呼收割

（聖經 詩篇 126:5）

Those who sow with tears will reap with songs of joy.

(Psalm 126:5)

第六章 動詞進階句型

英文動詞句型變化繁多，除了前文所介紹的五種基本句型之外，本章再進一步介紹六種動詞句型：

(1) 不及物動詞 + 介系詞 + 受詞

(2) 及物動詞 + 受詞 + 介系詞 + 受詞

(3) 使役動詞

(4) 動詞 + 動名詞

(5) 引述動詞

(6) 片語動詞

6.1 不及物動詞 + 介系詞 + 受詞 (intransitive verbs followed by prepositional phrases)

這一類的動詞屬於不及物動詞，因此後面不能直接結合受詞，必須先搭配一個**特定的介系詞**，才能在其後接一個受詞，組成完整的動詞片語，再與主部結合成為完整的句子。要特別注意的是，它所搭配的特定介系詞並無規則可循，只能強記。

其句型為：

| 主部 S. | + | 述部 / 不及物動詞 Vi. + 介系詞 Prep. + 受詞 O. |

| The farm house | belongs to my father |.
這個農舍**屬於**我父親所有。

The basketball team **is relying on the star player** .
這個籃球隊**依靠**這位明星球員。

The laid-off workers **resorted to legal procedures** .
被裁員的工人**訴諸**法律途徑。

Many public servants **are complaining about their reduced benefits** .
很多公務員都在**抱怨**他們被縮減的福利。

有些動詞**涵義相同**，卻適用**不同的句型**，例如：

arrive **at/in** + 受詞 = reach + 受詞

（兩者都是抵達某目的地的意思，但 arrive 為完全不及物動詞，
而 reach 則為完全及物動詞，後面必須接受詞。）

consist **of** + 受詞 = comprise + 受詞（由…組成，包含）

cope **with** + 受詞 = tackle + 受詞（處理，應付）

常用 不及物動詞 + 介系詞 + 受詞 句型的動詞

abide by 遵守（法律）	improve on 改善
adhere to 堅持，黏著於…	insist on 堅持
aim at 對準…目標	insure against 防範…發生
amount to 總計，等同於…	interfere with 阻擾 干擾
appeal to 訴諸…手段	invest in 投資
apologize to 向…道歉	lead to 導致…後果

apply for 申請，應徵	leave for 前往
arrive at/in 抵達	long for 期盼
associate with 與…相關聯	look after 照顧
attend to 照顧	look for 尋找
believe in 信仰	object to 反對
belong to 屬於	pay for 為…付出代價
bump into 無意中碰見	prepare for 為…作準備
care about 關心	profit from 從…獲利
care for 喜歡	qualify for 具有…的資格
cater to 迎合	react against 對…作出反應
collide with 相撞	refer to 指稱，提及，查詢
complain about 抱怨	relate to 與…相關
concentrate on 專注於	rely on 依賴
conform to 遵守，符合	resort to 訴諸…手段
consist of 包括，含有	respond to 回應
contribute to 有所貢獻於	result from 由…所導致
cope with 處理，應付	result in 導致…結果
depend on 依賴，取決於	search for 搜尋
dispose of 丟棄	specialize in 專精於，擅長
dream about 夢見	stem from 源自
dream of (=imagine) 夢想	succeed in 在…成功
emerge from 浮現，出現	suffer from 受…病痛之苦
engage in 致力於	sympathize with 同情
hint at 暗示	think of 想到…，考慮
hunger for 渴望	

選擇恰當的介系詞

( ) 1. Students with programming skills will qualify _____ the part-time job.

     A.of   B.at   C.for   D.in

( ) 2. Hikers should not dispose _____ any garbage along the trail or in the woods.

     A.of   B.to   C.for   D.in

( ) 3. The builder conforms _____ the regulations and laws in building the house.

     A.to   B.at   C.on   D.with

( ) 4. The puppy hungers _____ its owner's companionship.

     A.of   B.about   C.for   D.in

( ) 5. The photographer has been engaging _____ capturing the beauty of old towns.

     A.for   B.with   C.in   D.to

( ) 6. The missionary adhered _____ her religious belief when persecuted.

     A.to   B.at   C.on   D.into

( ) 7. The rescue team is searching _____ survivors in the derailed train.

     A.for   B.with   C.about   D.to

( ) 8. The restaurant introduced new dishes to cater _____ young customers.

     A.of   B.to   C.for   D.in

( ) 9. The babysitter attends _____ the little boy during the weekend.

A.for　　　　B.about　　　C.with　　　　D.to

(　) 10. The ambulance collided ＿＿＿ a truck when going through an intersection.

A.for　　　　B.at　　　　C.in　　　　D.with

▶▶ 6.1.2 小試身手

　　使用 不及物動詞＋介系詞＋受詞 的句型將下列中文句子翻成英文。

1. 每一位國民都應該**遵守**法律。(abide)

_____

2. 警察快速地**回應**這個緊急狀況。(respond)

_____

3. 這場車禍意外**肇因於**天候不佳。(result)

_____

4. 這份探討學習英語最佳策略的問卷**包含**了二十個題目。(consist)

_____

_____

5. 嫌犯的母親**阻擾**了警察的調查。(interfere)

_____

6. 多數澎湖的居民**反對**設立賭場。(object)

_____

7. 耶穌**同情**窮人和病人所受的苦。(sympathize)

_____

8. 公寓的房客經常**抱怨**不斷漲價的月租。(complain)

_____

9. 大部分大學生在接近學期結束時都**專心在準備**期末考。(concentrate, prepare)

_____

_____

10. 公司或個人不應該**丟棄**有毒廢棄物。(dispose)

_____

11. 我們規律地運動且正確地攝食可以**防範**健康問題。(insure)

_____

12. 每一位研究團隊的成員都對計畫的傑出成果**有所貢獻**。(contribute)

_____

13. 經常閱讀英文小說自然會對一個人的英文程度**帶來**明顯的進步。(lead)

_____

14. 父母和其兒女的衝突往往**來自於**溝通不足與不同的價值觀。(result)

_____

_____

15. 這位經驗老到的眼科醫師**專精於**眼睛雷射手術。(specialize)

6.2 及物動詞 + 受詞 + 介系詞 + 受詞 (Vt. + O. + Prep. + O.)

　　某一些及物動詞的句型比較特殊，必須先在其後面接一個受詞，然後再接一個特定的介系詞，最後再接一個受詞，才能構成完整的動詞片語，進而與主部結合構成完整的句子。此類動詞所接的介系詞是特定的，並無規則可循，必須熟記。此類動詞的句型為：

主部 S. + 及物動詞 Vt. + 受詞 O. + 介系詞 prep. + 受詞 O.

The judge based his decision on constitutional rights .
（法官依據憲法的權利作出裁決。）

The coach blamed the tight schedule for the basketball team's loss .
（教練將球隊輸球怪罪在密集的賽程。）

The law entitled women to the right to vote .
（法律賦予婦女投標的權利。）

常用 及物動詞 + 受詞 + 介系詞 + 受詞 句型的動詞

associate + O. + with 把…和…聯想或聯繫在一起	entrust + O. + to 將…託付某人
attribute + O. + to 把…歸功於…	entrust + O. + with 託付某人….
base + O. + on (upon) 把…作為…的依據	forgive + sb. + for + sth. 原諒某人某事
compare A to B 比較 A 跟 B	incorporate + O. + into 將…併入或整合

confine + O. + to 把…侷限（限制）在…	prevent + O. + from 預防或防止…免於…
confront + O. + with 使…與…面對或對質	provide + O.（人）+ with（物／人）提供某人…
dedicate + O. + to 1. 把…全然用於… e.g. She dedicated her life to the family. 2. 把…獻給… e.g. He dedicated his success to his parents.	provide + O.（物／人）+ for（人）提供…給某人
	regard + O. + as 視…為…
	remind + O. + of 提醒某人….
	return + O. + to 把…歸還給…
deprive + O. + of 剝奪某人某樣權利	rob + O. + of 強取某人的…
direct + O. + to 將注意力或談話指向…	supply + O.（物）+ to（人）提供…給某人
divide + O. + into 將…分成….	supply + O.（人）+ with（物）提供某人…
	suspect sb. of sth. 懷疑某人做了某事
	trust + O. + with 託付某人…
entitle + O. + to 給於某人某樣權利	view + O. + as 看待…為…
	warn + O. + of 警告某人某事

6.2.1 小試身手

在下列空格中填入恰當的介系詞

1. The new mayor **regards** creating new jobs ＿＿＿＿＿ his top priority.

2. The court ruling **deprived** the mother ＿＿＿＿＿ her custody over her children.

3. The Internet **provides** the younger generation ＿＿＿＿＿ different kinds of online resources never seen before.

4. The government investigator **suspected** the officer ＿＿＿＿＿ embezzlement.

5. Government officials **warn** the residents ＿＿＿＿＿ possible landslides as another typhoon is approaching with likely heavy rainfall.

6.2.2 小試身手

使用 及物動詞 + 受詞 + 介系詞 + 受詞 的句型將下列中文句子翻成英文

1. 她母親身爲營造公司的執行長總是把挑戰視爲轉機。

＿＿＿＿＿＿＿＿＿＿＿＿＿＿＿＿＿＿＿＿＿＿

＿＿＿＿＿＿＿＿＿＿＿＿＿＿＿＿＿＿＿＿＿＿

2. 這個卓越教師的故事讓我想起我國中時的英文老師。

＿＿＿＿＿＿＿＿＿＿＿＿＿＿＿＿＿＿＿＿＿＿

＿＿＿＿＿＿＿＿＿＿＿＿＿＿＿＿＿＿＿＿＿＿

3. 去年新訂的一項規則防範球員免於受傷。

＿＿＿＿＿＿＿＿＿＿＿＿＿＿＿＿＿＿＿＿＿＿

4. 我們應該把球隊的勝利歸功於教練。

5. 化學老師把班上學生分爲五人一組作實驗。

6. 導遊將遊客引導至以其現代藝術作品的收藏聞名的美術館。

7. 來自加拿大的護士宣教士把她的一生奉獻給臺灣民衆。

8. 新的規範會不會剝奪藍領工人自願加班的權利呢？

6.3 使役動詞 (causative verbs)

一、典型使役動詞

一般認爲使役動詞有五個：**make, have, let, get, help**，這五個動詞各有其**不同的涵義**與所適用的**句型**。

涵義 ：

1. **make** 意指**強迫某人做某事**或**使某人接受外力而產生某種狀況或結果**

   例如：Our teacher **makes us memorize** 100 new words every week.

   我們老師**強迫我們**每個禮拜**背** 100 生字。

   Our teacher **makes us disciplined** for breaking rules.

我們老師**使我們**在違反規定時**接受處罰**。

2. **have** 意指要求某人做某事或使某人／某物接受外力而產生某種狀況或結果

例如：Our teacher **has us clean** the classroom before going home.

我們老師**要求我們**回家前**打掃**教室。

Our teacher **had one of the classmates suspended** for one day.

我們老師**讓**班上一個同學**遭到停止來校**一天。

Our teacher **had his desk mopped** (by someone).

我們老師**讓**他的桌子（由別人）**擦乾淨了**。

3. **let** 意指允許某人做某事或使某人／某物接受外力而產生某種狀況或結果

例如：Our teacher **does not let us eat** in the class.

我們老師**不允許我們**在課堂上**吃**東西。

Our teacher **lets his notebook be used** by us.

我們老師**讓**他的筆電**被我們使用**。

4. **get** 意指說服或鼓勵某人做某事或使某人／某物接受外力而產生某種狀況或結果

例如：Our teacher **got us to volunteer** for community services.

我們老師**讓我們志願去做**社區服務。

Our teacher **got some of our classmates selected** to join the school band.

我們老師**讓**我們班上幾個同學**被挑選**加入學校樂隊。

Our teacher **got her hair permed**.
我們老師**把她的頭髮給燙了**。

5. **help** 意指**協助某人做某事**
例如：Our teacher **helps us prepare** for the exam.
我們老師**幫助我們準備**考試。

適用句型：

1. **make, have, let, help** 共用的句型為
make/have/let/help + 人 + 原型動詞，
2. **make, have, get** 共用的句型為
make/have/get + 人／物 + 過去分詞，
3. **get** 單獨使用的句型為 **get + 人 + 不定詞**，
4. **let** 單獨使用的句型為 **let + 人／物 + be + 過去分詞**。

Make (1)	
涵義	強迫某人做某事，相當於 force or require someone to take an action
句型	**make + 人 + 原型動詞**
例句	My mother **made me eat** pig liver soup to enhance my energy. 我母親**強迫我吃**豬肝湯增強體力。 The coach **makes the basketball players practice** shooting 500 times a day. 教練**要求籃球選手**一天**練習**投籃 500 次 The English teacher **makes her students read** at least two chapter books every month. 英文老師**要求她的學生**每個月至少**閱讀**兩本章節書。

Make (2)	
涵義	使某人接受外力而產生某種狀況或結果
句型	**make + 人 + 過去分詞**
例句	The foreign tourist tried to **make himself understood** when asking for directions. 問路的時候外國遊客努力要**讓別人瞭解她說的話**。 The agency **makes him consulted** by a therapist every week. 機構**要他**每個禮拜**接受**心理治療師的**諮商**。

Have (1)	
涵義	要求某人做某事 / 要某人負責做某事，相當於 ask someone to do something/give someone the responsibility to do something
句型	**have + 人 + 原型動詞**
例句	The architect **had her assistant present** the model of the newly designed concert hall. 建築師**要她的助理展示**新設計的音樂廳的模型。 The founder of the pineapple cake shop **had his eldest son take** over the business. 這家鳳梨酥店的創始人**要他的長子接管**生意。

Have (2)	
涵義	使某人接受外力而產生某種狀況或結果
句型	**have + 人 + 過去分詞**
例句	The detective **had the suspect detained**. 刑警**讓**嫌疑犯加以**拘留**。 The FBI **will have the witness** well **protected** in a safe place. 聯邦調查局**將會讓證人**在安全的地方**受到妥善的保護**。

Have (3)	
涵義	使某物接受外力而產生某種狀況或結果
句型	**have + 物 + 過去分詞**
例句	The new owner **had the house remodeled** (by someone). 新屋主讓房子（由別人）**重新整修**。 She had **her ears pierced** (by someone) to wear earrings. 她讓**她的耳朵**（由別人）**穿洞**以便戴耳環。

Let (1)	
涵義	允許某人做某事，相當於 permit or allow someone to do something
句型	**let + 人 + 原型動詞**
例句	The mayor **let the protestors submit** their requests. 市長**讓抗議者提交**他們的請求。 The professor **let the students bring** their notes with them to take the final exam. 教授**容許學生帶**筆記來考期末考。

Let (2)	
涵義	使某人接受外力而產生某種狀況或結果
句型	**let + 人 + be + 過去分詞**
例句	The social worker promised **not to let the children be separated** from her parents. 社工人員承諾**不會讓小孩跟他們父母分開**。 The doctor **let the patient be released** from the hospital five days after the surgery. 手術後五天，醫生**讓病人得以出院**。

Let (3)	
涵義	使某物接受外力而產生某種狀況或結果
句型	**let + 物 + be + 過去分詞**
例句	He **let his swimming pool be used** by the neighbors for free. 他**讓**他的游泳池免費**被**鄰居**使用**。 The library **will let the new books be shelved** once they are categorized. 一旦完成分類，圖書館就**會將讓新書上架**。

Get (1)	
涵義	說服或鼓勵某人做某事，相當於 convince or encourage someone to do something
句型	**get + 人 + 不定詞**
例句	After a long discussion, the lawyer **got his client to take** the deal **and plead** guilty. 經過長時間討論，律師**使得其當事人接受協議並認罪**。 The business consultant **got the CEO to agree** to restructure the 26-year-old company. 商業顧問**使執行長同意重整** 26 年的公司組織。

Get (2)	
涵義	使某人接受外力而產生某種狀況或結果
句型	**get + 人 + 過去分詞**
例句	The young father finally **got the twin babies bathed and clothed**. 年輕的爸爸終於**把攣生寶寶洗好澡穿好衣服**了。 The parents **got their baby baptized**. 父母**讓**他們的嬰兒**受洗**了。

Get (3)	
涵義	使某物接受外力而產生某種狀況或結果
句型	**get + 物 + 過去分詞**
例句	He **got his car serviced** before driving it to go around Taiwan. 他**把他的車子給人保養好**才開車去環島臺灣。 His boss told him to **get the contract signed** as soon as possible. 他的老闆告訴他盡快**把合約簽好**。

Help	
涵義	協助某人做某事，相當於 assist someone in doing something
句型	**help + 人 + 原型動詞 / 不定詞**（目前多數偏向使用**原型動詞**。）
例句	The flight attendant **helped the two passengers switch** seats. 空服員**協助兩位乘客交換**位子。 The guests **helped the hostess clean** up the table **and do** the dishes after dinner. 客人吃完晚餐後**幫助女主人清理餐桌並清洗碗盤**。

make, have, let, get 的區別

這三個動詞所表達的涵義有程度上的差異，我們以下列例句加以說明：

(1) His parents **made** him work part-time during college.

他的父母**強迫**他在讀大學時打工。

（最強烈的使役動詞，違背受迫者的意願，受迫者無法抗拒。）

(2) His parents **had** him work part-time during college.

他的父母**要**他在讀大學時打工。

（稍微強烈的使役動詞，雖然違背被要求者的意願，但後者也照做了。）

(3) His parents **let** him work part-time during college.

他的父母**允許／讓**他在讀大學時打工。

(4) His parents **got** him **to work** part-time during college.

他的父母**說服**他在讀大學時打工。（後者經過溝通後，接受前者的意見而行動。）

二、類使役動詞

除了以上所介紹的典型使役動詞，英文也有許多動詞具備類似的涵義，卻是套用不同的句型，例如：

(1) 套用的句型為 V. + 人 + 不定詞

The private school requires students to wear uniforms to school.

這家私立學校**要求學生穿著**制服上學。

The professor asked his assistant to apply for government's subsidy.

教授**請她的助理申請**政府的補助。

The salesman successfully persuaded the couple to buy the new car.

銷售員成功地**說服這對夫妻購買**這部新車。

The company allows the employees to work with flexible hours.

這家公司**容許員工**以彈性工時**上班**。

The loss of the election caused the ruling party to reexamine its policies.

選舉失利**促使執政黨重新檢討**其政策。

(2) 套用的句型為：V. + 人 + to + be + 過去分詞

The captain ordered the soldiers to be trained to prepare for fighting under severely cold weather. 隊長**命令士兵們接受訓練**以預備在嚴寒天氣下戰鬥。

The customs requires passengers to be checked thoroughly before boarding the plane. 海關**要求乘客**在登機前**接受澈底檢查**。

(3) 套用的句型為：V. + 人 / 物 + 現在分詞（只有 **keep** 適用本句型）

The secretary kept the visitor waiting in the lobby.
祕書**讓訪客**在大廳**等候**。

With limited human resources, the manager is trying his best to keep the factory running .
以有限的人力資源，經理盡他最大努力**讓工廠繼續作業**。

類使役動詞
allow 容許 , **ask** 請求 , **cause** 促使 , **convince** 說服 , **enable** 使…能夠… , **force** 強迫 , **lead** 帶領 , **persuade** 說服 , **permit** 許可 , **motivate** 激勵 , **need** 需要 , **order** 命令 , **require** 要求 , **want** 要…做…
句型一：V. + 人 + 不定詞
The new equipment **enables the scientists to conduct** new studies. 新設備**使科學家能夠進行**新的研究。

句型二：V. + 人 + to + be + 過去分詞
His wife **convinced him to be treated** by a chiropractor.   他妻子**說服他接受**整脊師的**治療**。
句型三：V. + 人／物 + 現在分詞
The school **keeps the underachieving students going** to school during summer break. 學校**使低成就學生**在暑假期間**繼續**上學。

 6.3.1 小試身手

使用 使役動詞 句型將下列中文句子翻成英文

1. 他在面試之前剪了頭髮。(get)

_____

2. 睡覺之前我們讓冷氣繼續運轉。(keep)

_____

3. 公司要求其員工穿著正式服裝上班。(have)

_____

4. 冰箱的發明使我們能夠隨時享受新鮮冰涼的食物。(allow)

_____

_____

5. 目前在有些國家，貧困仍舊會迫使兒童去工作賺錢。(force)

_____

_____

6. 她的律師讓她與出版社簽下這份合約書來銷售她新的小說。(get)

_____

_____

7. 我的上司說服我休假一整個禮拜。(convince)

8. 她昨天把她新車送洗以便迎接農曆年的到來。(have)

9. 他的成功的故事激勵很多弱勢學生更加努力。(motivate)

10. 足球教練迫使球員在雨中受訓以預備下個球季的賽事。(make)

11. 這個房地產經紀人 (realtor) 說服了這位退休的工程師買了一間附有游泳池的房子。(persuade)

12. 這位教授讓他的計畫書 (proposal) 被教育部通過了。(get)

13. 他的創新點子讓他獲得升遷。(get)

14. 實驗失敗促使研究人員嘗試新的方法。(cause)

15. DNA 的證據使法官能夠將被告定罪。(enable)

16. 便宜的票價使得更多年輕人可以參加演唱會。(let)

17. 警察使犯罪現場澈底加以搜索。(have)

18. 動物園管理員讓獅子們每天早上從籠子裡放出來。(let)

19. 醫生讓病人接受 X 光檢查。(have)

20. 他的健身教練要求他每天做五十下伏地挺身和五十下仰臥起坐。(make)

6.4 動詞 + 動名詞 (Verb + V-ing)

　　一般而言，動詞之後如果接了另外一個動詞，後面的動詞會形成不定詞 (infinitive)，也就是 "to + 原型動詞"。但有一些動詞比較特殊，後面所接的動詞會形成動名詞，包括 **(1) V-ing**、**(2) be-ing + 形容詞**、**(3) being + 名詞**、**(4) being + 介系詞片語**、以及 **(5) being + 過去分詞**，引導出動名詞片語，兩者組合成完整的動詞片語，進而與主部構成完整的句子，表達完整的涵義。

　　此類動詞的句型有五種。

(1) 主部 S. + 動詞 + V-ing

She **enjoyed watching** the magic show.
她看魔術表演看得很開心。

The company **will avoid making** the same mistake.
公司將會**避免犯**同樣的錯誤。

The research **involves conducting** experiments in the lab.
這項研究**包含**了在實驗室**進行實驗**。

(2) 主部 S. + 動詞 + being + 形容詞

The patient **has endured being ill** for over a month.

病人已經**忍受生病**超過一個月了。

(3) 主部 S. + 動詞 + being + 名詞

The young girl **imagines being a princess** living in a beautiful castle.

年輕女生**想像是**住在美麗城堡的公主。

(4) 主部 S. + 動詞 + being + 介系詞片語

The hiker **recalled being in dangerous situations** under the bad weather.

登山客**記得**在惡劣天氣下**身處危險的情況**。

The taxi driver **denies being out of control** after the accident.

計程車司機在事故發生後**否認失控**。

(5) 主部 S. + 動詞 + being + 過去分詞

Transfer students didn't **anticipate being treated** nicely by new classmates.

轉學生不**預期會受到**新同學良好的**對待**。

The reporter **described being attacked** by protestors during the demonstration.

記者**描述**在示威過程**遭到**抗議者**攻擊**。

後面接動名詞的動詞

admit 承認	continue 繼續	finish 完成	quit 退出、放棄
appreciate 感激	defend 防禦	fancy 猜想	recall 回憶起
anticipate 預期	deny 否認	imagine 想像	regret 懊悔
avoid 避免	delay 延遲	involve 涉及	report 報導、描述
bear 忍受	describe 描述	keep 持續…	resent 怨恨
cease 停止不做	discontinue 中斷	mention 提及	resist 抗拒
celebrate 慶祝	dislike 厭惡	mind 介意	risk 冒…風險
commence 開始	endure 容忍、忍受	miss 錯過 思念	stand 忍受
complete 完成	enjoy 喜歡、享受	postpone 延期	stop 停止不做
consider 考量	explain 解釋	practice 練習	suggest 建議

 6.4.1 小試身手

使用 動詞接動名詞 的句型將下列中文句子翻成英文

1. 抽菸三十年之後他終於戒菸了。

_____

2. 她否認接受工作邀約去上海就業。

_____

3. 她後悔沒有出國念碩士。

_____

4. 大部分的員工不介意加班。

_____

5. 忠實的顧客持續爲了其好吃的派而回來這個糕餅店 (pastry shop)。

_____

_____

6. 非法的外國勞工再也不能忍受被其雇主剝削 (exploit) 了。

_____

_____

7. 他們冒著賠錢的風險研發新產品。

_____

8. 她無法停止思念她正在日本工作的女兒。

_____

9. 貪腐的市長承認從營建公司收賄。

_____

10. 寵物店 (pet shop) 的店主正在考慮開一家新店面來迎合需求。

_____

_____

11. 地震生還者感激從倒塌的建築物中被救出來。

_____

_____

12. 這位成功的企業家提到儘管有嚴峻的挑戰他還是無所畏懼。

_____

_____

13. 滿懷抱負的學生幻想是跨國企業的執行長。

_____

_____

14. 職業自由車選手一天練習騎單車 100 公里。

_____

15. 這位名人不喜歡處在有敵意的環境。

___

6.5 引述動詞 (reporting verbs)

　　英文的引述動詞後面可以接名詞子句或不定詞，在這裡先介紹接不定詞的句型，引述動詞之後接名詞子句的句型則留待名詞子句時再加以說明。引述動詞接不定詞的句型有兩種：(1) **引述動詞加不定詞**，(2) **引述動詞加受詞加不定詞**。

▶▶ 6.5.1 引述動詞 + 不定詞

例如：

He agreed that he would join the research team

→ He agreed to join the research team.

She claimed that she owned the property.

→ She claimed to own the property.

適用此類句型的動詞有：

引述動詞 + 不定詞
agree 同意 ask 詢問 claim 宣稱 demand 強烈要求 offer 提供 promise 承諾 propose 提議 refuse 拒絕 threaten 威脅

The professor advised her that she take four courses in the first semester.

→ The professor **advised** **her** **to take** four courses in the first semester.

The manager reminded her that she would give a presentation the next day.

→ The manager **reminded** **her** **to give** a presentation the next day.

適用此類句型的動詞有：

引述動詞 + 受詞 + 不定詞
advise 建議採取 ask 詢問 beg 哀求 convince 說服 encourage 鼓勵 forbid 禁止 instruct 指示 吩咐 invite 邀請 order 命令 persuade 說服 remind 提醒 tell 告訴 urge 敦促 warn (not to) 警告（不要做…）

貼心提醒

"suggest" 不是引述動詞，因此不可以寫成 *My teacher suggests me to read more story books.

使用引述動詞將下列中文句子翻成英文。

1. 警衛敦促住戶立刻離開大樓因為有火災警報。

---

2. 學校教師威脅要罷課。

---

3. 他父母說服他接手他們的家庭事業。

---

4. 教授警告她的學生考試不要作弊。

---

5. 這個強悍的男生拒絕在拔河比賽中放棄。

---

6. 他提議聘請西班牙文老師來訓練我們的職員。

---

7. 他在越南經營家具工廠的大學同學邀請他去那裡觀光旅遊。

---

8. 他們禁止他們小孩去網咖。

---

9. 醫生透過電話指示計程車司機協助孕婦在車子裡接生 (deliver) 嬰兒。

---

10. 妳先生已經答應帶妳去加勒比慶祝結婚二十週年嗎？

6.6 片語動詞 (phrasal verbs)

要瞭解片語動詞，我們先來看以下的一段敘述：

Emily **got up**（起床）at 6:20. After breakfast, she **put on**（穿上）a nice dress and **set off**（出發）for work. She **ran across**（偶遇）an old friend, Gloria, on her way to the train station. Gloria asked Emily to **eat out**（到餐廳用餐）with her that night to **catch up.**（交談以瞭解近況）Emily said she had to **look after**（照顧）her children after work, so they **put off**（延後）the dinner until the weekend. Later, when Emily **got into**（進入）her office, she **turned on**（打開）the computer and **went over**（查看）her schedule of the day. She had **come up with**（想出）a new idea the other day, so she **set up**（安排）a meeting to **talk** it **over**（討論）with her associates. The meeting **turned out**（發展結果）very well, and everyone was **looking forward to**（期待）**carrying out**（執行）the new idea.

以上短短的敘述，使用了十七個英文的**片語動詞**，這些都是很常見的片語動詞，卻分別屬於不同類型，接下來我們就要深入瞭解英文的片語動詞。

▶▶ 6.6.1 何謂片語動詞

片語動詞跟動詞片語不同，片語動詞是動詞，而動詞片語則是片語，兩者不可混爲一談。片語動詞是英文中很另類的一種動詞，片語動詞可以是由：

(1) 一個動詞結合一個介副詞（particle，表面上為介系詞，但其作用是副詞的功能，因此稱為介副詞）而成，例如 He *wakes up* at five every morning.；或

(2) 一個動詞結合一個介系詞所構成，例如 He *stood by* his best friend.；或是

(3) 由一個動詞結合兩者所構成，例如 People *look up to* brave soldiers.。

　　可見片語動詞的核心是動詞，然而片語動詞的涵義往往無法從個別的單字涵義加以推敲出來，例如 *give up* 為放棄的意思，但是 give 的字義與放棄完全無關。正因如此，片語動詞必須以整體看待，我們也無法預測其組合之後的涵義，而需要個別學習不同的片語動詞，例如 *take after* someone 所表達的涵義是*長得像*某人，而 *look after* someone 意思是*照顧*某人。片語動詞雖然是較口語化的用法，但也廣泛使用於寫作，而不同的片語動詞也適用不同的句型結構，例如有的片語動詞為不及物，例如 *pass out*；有的為及物，例如 *go over*；有的及物片語動詞可以拆開，例如 *fill* the form *out*，有的不可以拆開，例如 *look into* something；不一而足，變化繁多。因此，我們在寫作上使用片語動詞時，必須注意其結構上的變化，才能運用得當。

▶▶ 6.6.2 片語動詞的分類

　　片語動詞依其後是否必須接受詞而分為兩大類：(1) 不及物片語動詞，其結構為：動詞 + 介副詞，及 (2) 及物片語動詞；而及物片語動詞又可以分為 (a) 片語動詞的結構為：動詞 + 介系詞 + 受詞，其動詞與介系詞的組合**不可以分開**，(b) 動詞片語的結構為：動詞 + 介副詞 + 介系詞 + 受詞，其動詞與介系詞的組合**不可以分**

開，以及 (c) 片語動詞的結構爲：動詞 + 介副詞 + 受詞或是動詞 + 受詞 + 介副詞，其動詞與介副詞的組合**可以分開**，如下表所示。

（**不可以分開的**屬於**介系詞**，如 call **on** a friend；而**可以分開的**則是屬於**介副詞**，如 turn the light **on**）。

另外，有些片語動詞可以兼具及物與不及物的用法，例如：hang up 或 hang up the phone 都是掛斷電話的意思，

片語動詞（依其後有無受詞而分類）	
(1) 不及物片語動詞 （動詞 + 介副詞）	My car ***broke down*** yesterday.（車子壞了）
(2) 及物片語動詞 （動詞 + 介系詞 + 受詞 / 不可分開）	The police will ***look into*** the case.（調查） The police will ***look into*** it .
(3) 及物片語動詞 （動詞 + 介副詞 + 介系詞 + 受詞 / 不可分開）	He is trying to ***keep up with*** other students in the class.（跟上） He is trying to ***keep up with*** them .
(4) 及物片語動詞 （動詞 + 介副詞 + 受詞 / 可分開）	She ***put on*** a nice dress for the dinner.（穿上） She ***put*** a nice dress ***on*** for the dinner. She ***put*** it ***on*** for the dinner.（受詞爲**代名詞**，必須放置在**可分開的**動詞和介副詞之間）

(1) 不及物片語動詞： 動詞 + 介副詞

The thief ***got away***（逃走）.（**away** 是介副詞，get away 爲不及物片語動詞，後面不接受詞。）

She reluctantly ***gave up***（放棄）.（**up** 是介副詞，give up 爲不

及物片語動詞，後面不接受詞。）

(2) 及物片語動詞：動詞 + 介系詞 + 受詞 / 動詞與介系詞不可以分開

My sister will *look after* my children .（照顧）（**after** 是介系詞，引導出一個介系詞片語 after my children，look 與 after 不可分開。）

My sister will *look after* them .（受詞 them 爲代名詞，其位置仍然在介系詞之後）

She *ran into* her high school classmate at a fast food restaurant.（不期而遇，碰見）（**into** 是介系詞，引導出一個介系詞片語 into her high school classmate，ran 與 into 不可分開。）

She *ran into* him at a fast food restaurant.（受詞 him 爲代名詞，其位置仍然在介系詞之後）

(3) 及物片語動詞：動詞 + 介副詞 + 介系詞 + 受詞 / 動詞與介系詞不可以分開

The young boy *came up with* a brilliant idea for saving water.（想出一個做法）（**up** 爲介副詞，而 **with** 則爲介系詞，come up with 爲及物片語動詞，介系詞 with 後面接受詞。）

The young boy *came up with* that .（受詞 **that** 爲代名詞，其位置仍然在介系詞之後）

She wants to *get rid of* all the old furniture （丟棄）before moving to the new apartment.（**rid** 爲介副詞，而 **of** 則爲介系詞，get rid of 爲及物片語動詞，介系詞 of 後面接受詞。）

She wants to *get rid of* it .（受詞 **it** 爲代名詞，其位置仍然在介系詞之後）

(4) 及物片語動詞： 動詞 + 介副詞 + 受詞 ╱ 動詞 + 受詞 + 介副詞
    動詞與介副詞可以分開

He turned on the air conditioner . （打開電器開關）（**on** 是
介副詞，turn on 為及物片語動詞，**後面接受詞**。）

He turned the air conditioner on .

He turned it on . （受詞 **it** 為代名詞，必須置於動詞與介副詞
之間）

 6.6.3 常用片語動詞與例句

不及物片語動詞：動詞 + 介副詞	
break down 故障 損壞	The old washing machine broke down yesterday.
carry on 繼續	Despite the severe weather, the mountain climbers carried on.
catch on 變得流行	The new style of sneakers is catching on among professional players.
catch up 交談以瞭解彼此近況	Grace had dinner with her brother to catch up.
come to 恢復知覺	He was hit on the head by a baseball and became unconscious for a few minutes before finally coming to again.
drop by 臨時造訪	My best friend has moved to a new house. He told me to drop by anytime.
eat out 到餐廳吃飯	The couple decided to eat out to celebrate their anniversary.

不及物片語動詞：動詞 + 介副詞	
end up 結果、最後到達	She worked very hard and ended up being admitted to a prestigious university. They traveled across the United States and ended up in Seattle.
get by 生存	He barely gets by with the minimum wage.
give in 讓步、屈服	After several negotiations with the union, the corporation gave in at last.
go on 繼續	The game could not go on if the light went out.
keep away 遠離、保持距離	The child's mother told him to keep away from the swing.
look out 注意	School children are asked to look out when crossing the street.
make up 和好	The couple finally made up after not talking to each other for three days.
pass away 過世	Their grandfather passed away last year.
pass out 昏倒 失去知覺	The old man passed out after walking under the sun for hours.
run out 用盡	The detergent has just run out.
set off 出發	They set off early in the morning.
show off 炫耀	My brother likes to show off when skateboarding.
show up 現身	He didn't show up in the gathering.
take off 起飛	The plane took off just 10 minutes ago.
take over 接手、接管、接任	Once the owner retires, his son will take over.
turn out 發展結果	The negotiation turned out well.

不可分開及物片語動詞：動詞＋介系詞＋受詞	
call on 拜訪	She called on one of her colleagues last weekend.
go out 燈火熄滅	The candles went out one by one.
get over 從病痛康復、走過心情低潮	He finally got over the flu after taking three days off. It won't be easy for her to get over the grief of the loss of her mother.
go over 複習、檢視、查看	Good students go over the materials before the exam.
go through 經歷困境	Her best friend helped her go through the most difficult time of her life.
go through 仔細檢查、搜查	He will go through the old photos and digitize them.
look after 照顧	My mother helped our neighbors look after their three-year-old daughter.
look into 調查	The school will look into the accident.
run across 偶遇	She ran across her old schoolmate at a bar.
run into 遇見	He ran into a famous basketball player in the gym.
stand by 支持	He stood by his best friend because of trust.
take after 與…相像	The daughter takes after her mother.
wait on（在餐廳）服務客人	The manager wants experienced waitresses to wait on celebrities at dinner.

不可分開及物片語動詞（三個字）：動詞 + 介副詞 + 介系詞 + 受詞	
catch up with 迎頭趕上	The developing countries in Southeast Asia are catching up with industrialized countries.
check up on 檢視、調查	The light went out. The electrician was checking up on the fuse box.
come up with 提出構想、做法	During the discussion, they came up with a satisfying solution.
come up with 拿出具體的東西	We need to come up with enough cash before the deadline.
cut down on 縮減開銷	The company cuts down on the expense of electricity by limiting the use of air conditioners in the office.
drop out of 中途退學	He dropped out of college due to financial difficulties.
get along with 與…相處得來	The star player did not get along with the teammates.
get away with 逃避責罰	Due to lack of hard evidence, the murderer got away with the punishment for his crime.
get rid of 去除、擺脫、丟棄	He wants to get rid of most of his books before retiring.
get through with 完成	We will get through with the geography project this weekend.
keep up with 跟上步伐	Some of the elderly just cannot keep up with the fast development of the digital era.
look forward to 期待	We are looking forward to the cruise tour to Alaska

不可分開及物片語動詞（三個字）：動詞＋介副詞＋介系詞＋受詞	
look down on 瞧不起	The rich tend to look down on the poor.
look out for 注意	When camping in the woods, people should look out for wild animals.
look up to 尊敬	Tribal people look up to great hunters.
put up with 忍受（某人或某事）	The professor cannot put up with the students for their tardiness and laziness. Athletes must put up with harsh training to excel.
run out of 耗盡	After working for over 12 hours, she ran out of energy.

可分開及物動詞片語：動詞＋介副詞＋受詞／動詞＋受詞＋介副詞	
blow up 引爆	They blew up the old building in a matter of seconds.
bring up 提起、提到	She brought up how she barely escaped a car accident.
bring up 養育	The single mother brought up five children.
call off 取消	They called off the game due to the bad weather.
carry out 執行	They will carry out the new project.
check out 檢查	We must check out the surroundings when camping.
do something over 重做（動詞和介副詞必須分開）	He didn't do the assignment properly, so he had to do it over.
figure out 弄明白	The old man finally figured out it was a scam.

可分開及物動詞片語：動詞 + 介副詞 + 受詞 / 動詞 + 受詞 + 介副詞	
fill out 填表	Students are asked to fill out the application form online.
fill up 填滿、裝滿、加滿	He filled up the gas tank of the car at the gas station.
give away 免費送出	The newly open supermarket is giving away small gifts to every customer.
hand in 繳交	He handed in the report yesterday.
hang up 掛斷電話	She hung up the phone because she didn't want to talk to her boyfriend anymore.
hang up 懸掛	They will hang up an oil painting on the wall in the living room.
hold up 使延遲	The heavy snow held up the road construction.
hold up 搶劫	He held up a tourist and got away.
leave out 遺漏、省略	Did you leave out anything in preparing the documents?
let down 使…失望	He promised to his parents that he would not let them down.
look over 檢視、查看	The roof is leaking. He needs to look it over.
look up 查閱	He usually looks new words up in online dictionaries.
make up 捏造、虛構	He made up a funny story to entertain the kids.
make out 聽清楚、弄明白	It was very noisy. I couldn't make out what he was saying.

可分開及物動詞片語：動詞 + 介副詞 + 受詞 / 動詞 + 受詞 + 介副詞	
pick out 挑選出	The interviewers will pick out three candidates from the applicants.
pick up 拿起來	She picked up the parcel at the convenience store.
pick up 習得	He picked up French during his childhood in Paris.
point out 指出來	The witness pointed the suspect out.
put away 收起來存放	We put away heavy jackets and sweaters during the summer.
put off 延期、延後舉行	They put off the concert due to low ticket sales.
put out 撲滅	The chef quickly put out the fire in the kitchen.
roll out 推出	The car dealer has just rolled out a special deal for pick-up trucks.
set apart 區分	The quality of their work sets them apart from their rivals.
set up 安排、建置、佈置	They set up a meeting for the student representatives to meet with the president of the university.
take down 寫下來、做筆記	She is a serious student. She takes down what the professor teaches in every class.
take off 脫掉	It is inappropriate if one doesn't take off his hat in a restaurant.
take out (someone) 殺害	The sniper took out the kidnapper at the scene.
take over 接手、接管、接任	The new general manager will take over the operation of the company.

可分開及物動詞片語：動詞 + 介副詞 + 受詞 / 動詞 + 受詞 + 介副詞	
talk someone into something 說服某人做某事（動詞與介副詞必須分開）	The children talked their parents into buying a new minivan.
talk over 討論	He is not sure about what courses to take next semester. He wants to talk it over with the department chair.
think over 認真地考慮	Several universities have offered her fellowships, and she will think it over before making a decision.
try on 試穿	It is alright for the customers to try on the new clothes before making purchases.
try out 試用	Some stores allow people to try out their products before buying them.
turn down 拒絕、回絕	The company has offered him a job, but he turned it down.
turn down 調低音量	She turned the TV down, so she could talk on the phone.
turn up 調高音量	To lighten up the atmosphere, he turned the music up.
turn off 關掉（電燈、電腦、冷氣、電扇…）	He turned the computer off before going out.
turn on 打開（電燈、電腦、冷氣、電扇…）	She turned the air conditioner on as soon as she entered the apartment.

可分開及物動詞片語：動詞 + 介副詞 + 受詞／動詞 + 受詞 + 介副詞	
use up 用盡	She has used up the detergent.

 6.6.4 小試身手

使用片語動詞完成以下句子

1. James has not seen his best friend in high school for over 35 years. Yesterday they finally got together. They must have a lot to _____ _____ .

2. The authorities have to _____ _____ the football game due to security concern. They will reschedule the game to next week.

3. She drove her car to the gas station just in time before it _____ _____ _____ gas.

4. The president of the car company vowed to _____ _____ a completely new model next year to attract younger buyers.

5. Interestingly, the son looks just like the mother while the daughter _____ _____ the father.

6. Before Lunar New Year, people in Taiwan _____ _____ _____ old clothes and buy new ones for good luck.

7. After viewing the footage of the surveillance camera, the detective immediately _____ _____ the identity of the intruder

8. The professor asked her students not to ＿＿＿＿＿＿ her ＿＿＿＿＿＿ in the final exam. After all, she has taught them everything they needed to know.

9. The university offered Cindy a scholarship, but she ＿＿＿＿＿ it ＿＿＿＿＿ because she didn't like the cold weather there.

10. The air pollution was so bad that they could not ＿＿＿＿＿ ＿＿＿＿＿ ＿＿＿＿＿ it any more. They decided to move to another city for health sake.

11. They ＿＿＿＿＿ ＿＿＿＿＿ the wedding procedure in the church yesterday before the wedding day to make sure it would be perfect.

12. The school will have to ＿＿＿＿＿ ＿＿＿＿＿ ＿＿＿＿＿ their annual budget as the number of students is decreasing.

13. The coach asked his assistant to ＿＿＿＿＿ ＿＿＿＿＿ his job training the players for a few days because he was sick.

14. The police officer eventually ＿＿＿＿＿ the suspect's mother ＿＿＿＿＿ giving her son's whereabouts by promising not to harm him.

15. The boss didn't like my monthly report. I had to ＿＿＿＿＿ it ＿＿＿＿＿ .

16. People need to ＿＿＿＿＿ ＿＿＿＿＿ the forms online to apply for a job nowadays.

17. They had to ＿＿＿＿＿ ＿＿＿＿＿ the meeting until next week because of the approaching typhoon.

18. Our neighbor downstairs was playing music too loud. I went to knock on his door and asked him to ＿＿＿＿＿ ＿＿＿＿＿

the volume.

19. The cyclist is going so fast that no one could _____ _____ _____ him. He certainly will be the winner of the game.

20. This is a good program, and we need to hire some experts to _____ it _____ .

6.7 動詞句型打通關

使用恰當的動詞句型將下列句子翻成英文。

1. 新總統沒有**任命**她出任德國的大使。

_____

2. 她把這份英文文件**翻成**日文。

_____

3. 公司是否**認為**這個促銷活動非常成功？

_____

4. 這個非官方組織正在**招募**志工去照顧老人。

_____

5. 這位教授**專長於**分析消費者的行為。

_____

6. 為了找到比較好的工作，他正在**考慮**學習西班牙語。

_____

7. 她把那部同款的車子**誤認**為是她先生的。

_____

8. 安全帶**保護**駕駛和乘客**免於**嚴重的受傷。

_____

9.反對黨**指控**總統濫用其職權。

10.這個老舊的吸塵器**壞掉**了。（片語動詞）

11.他**比較喜歡**早上喝黑咖啡。

12.老師**要求**學生避免犯相同的錯誤。

13.好幾家衛星工廠**供應**這家汽車製造廠不同的零件。

14.這個委員會**由**十一位委員**組成**。

15.從臺北來的轉學生跟班上同學**相處融洽**。（片語動詞）

16.念了一個小時的英文之後，我就**累**了。

17.科學家把這個現象跟氣候變遷**聯想在一起**。

18.他一向**支持**他的隊友。（片語動詞）

19.他的缺乏耐心**導致**他的計畫失敗。

20.這份工作**提供**給他很好的機會應用他的專長。

21.砍伐森林**剝奪**了野生動物的棲息地。

---

22. 網路搜索引擎**使**我們很快獲得各種不同的資訊。

_____

23. 這個錯誤的決定**使**公司**付出**鉅額的虧損（的代價）。

_____

24. 圖書館正在把舊雜誌**免費送人**。（片語動詞）

_____

25. 他們把這次的成功**歸諸於**他的富有創意的策略。

_____

26. 學校新的措施能夠**防止**學生上課缺席嗎？

_____

27. 在戰爭期間，這個母親把她生病的嬰兒**託付給**隔壁的護士。

_____

28. 地震過後，政府為受害者**提供**臨時住所、食物、和醫療。

_____

29. 我們產品的標示都**符合**政府的規定。

_____

30. 他們**期待著**觀看兩支籃球隊間緊張的比賽。（片語動詞）

_____

31. 開車前往花蓮之前她**加滿**油箱。（片語動詞）

_____

32. 我的老闆**指示**我中午以前要把花送去給客人。

_____

33. 他的不當行為**使**他被公司開除了。

_____

34. 這所大學**決定**把這兩個系合併成一個新的系。

_____

35. 工作內容**涉及**在辦公室接電話以及拜訪潛在的客戶。

第七章 被動語態 (Passive Voice)

　　爲了說明英文的被動語態與中文的差異，我們先來看看底下的中英對照的例句：

球員受傷，整個球季報銷，大喊：我<u>完了</u>！
英文說：I'<u>m done</u>!

跑馬拉松的跑者抵達終點時都**筋疲力竭**了。
英文說：The marathon runners <u>were exhausted</u> when they reached the finish line.

汽車故障送修，修車廠打電話來說：車子<u>修好了</u>。
英文說：Your car <u>has been fixed</u> .

新聞報導：這家公司<u>涉及</u>一宗洗錢犯罪。
英文說：The company <u>is involved in</u> a money laundering crime.

公務人員<u>有權利享有</u>政府提供的福利。
英文說：The public servants <u>are entitled to</u> benefits offered by the government.

找工作時看徵才廣告，心想：我**夠資格**。
英文說：I <u>am qualified</u> for the job.

你通知買家說：樣品**已經遞送了**。

英文說：The sample **has been shipped**.

旅行社說：機票昨天**訂好了**。

英文說：Your plane ticket **was booked** yesterday.

房東對房客說：你的房租必須在這個月底**繳清**。

英文說：Your rent must **be paid** by the end of this month.

　　以上的例子說明了中文在表達被動語態時不像英文那麼明顯嚴謹，句子中不見得會出現「被」；反觀英文的被動語態則必須遵守一定的規則，句子的動詞依時態與主詞的單複數作不同的變化，其中最明顯的特徵就是 **be + 過去分詞**，句子中只要出現這樣的動詞片語，就可以確認是被動語態的句型。

　　被動語態有其通常適用情況，本篇將會一一舉例說明，並讓同學透過練習確實掌握其句型結構的變化，而能在寫作與翻譯時嫻熟使用被動語態。

7.1　使用被動語態的時機

　　為了 (1) **強調句子中接受動作的受詞**，(2) **主事者比較沒那麼重要**，或是 (3) **主事者身分不明**的時候，主動語態的句子往往會改寫成被動語態，而**將受詞轉換成句子的主詞**，同時要**把動詞改寫成 "be" 動詞加 "過去分詞"**。而原來主動語態中的主詞，則移到被動**語態句子動詞之後，並加上 by**（但狀態動詞則會使用其他的介系詞）。

例如：

規定要求學生要穿制服上學。

The code requires **students** to wear uniforms to school.

（"students" 是 "requires" 的<u>受詞</u>。）

學生依規定必須穿制服上學。

Students are required **by the code** to wear uniforms to school.

（"students" 是句子的<u>主詞</u>，動詞 "requires" 改寫成 "**are re-quired**"。）

警方找到失竊的車子。

The police found **the lost vehicle**.（"the lost vehicle" 是 "found" 的<u>受詞</u>。）

失竊的車子由警方找到了。

The lost vehicle was found **by the police**.

（"the lost vehicle" 轉換成句子的<u>主詞</u>，動詞 "found" 改寫成 "**was found**"。）

Sam Johnson 於 1985 年成立這家公司。

Sam Johnson established **the company** in 1985.

（"the company" 是 "established" 的受詞）

這家公司由 Sam Johnson 於 1985 年成立。

The company was established **in 1985** **by Sam Johnson**.

（"the company" 轉換成句子的<u>主詞</u>，動詞 "established" 改寫成 "**was established**"。）

他們可能會把小孩送去寄養家庭。

They may send **the child** to a foster home.

（主動語態句子中 "the child" 是 "send" 的**受詞**）

小孩可能會由他們送去寄養家庭

The child may be sent **to a foster home** **by them.**

（"the child" 轉換成句子的**主詞**，動詞 "may send" 改寫成 "**may be sent**"）

7.2 被動語態的句型與結構

▶▶ 7.2.1 被動語態的句型（Be + P.P. 過去分詞）

　　被動語態的句型其中必要的兩個元素是 "**be**" 動詞與 "**過去分詞**"，而 be 動詞則由原來主動語態的**動詞時態**與**主詞的人稱及單複數**所決定。換句話說，我們將主動語態的句子改寫成被動語態時，不可以改變句子的時式。任何一個子句，包括獨立子句和從屬子句，如果結構中具備了 be 動詞 + 過去分詞的元素，這個子句就一定是被動語態了！（如下列表格的例句與句型分析）

被動語態句型

動詞時態	句型
簡單現在式 I **am flattered**. The new teacher **is liked** by the students. Four movie stars **are nominated** for the award.	S + (am, is, are) + P.P. （主詞及其單複數決定現在式 be 動詞的選用）
簡單過去式 A new bill **was passed** by the Congress to further protect the endangered species. More than 100 small trees **were planted** in the park.	S + (was, were) + P.P. （主詞單複數決定過去式 be 動詞的選用）

動詞時態	句型
簡單未來式 More workers **will be hired**. The old computers **will be replaced**.	S + **will** + **be** + **P.P.** （will 表達這個句子是未來式，而 be 動詞一律為原型）
現在進行式 The car **is being repaired** by the mechanic. The new orders **are** now **being processed** online.	S + **(am, is, are)** + **being** + **P.P.** （括號內現在式的 be 動詞由主詞及其單複數決定，表達這個被動語態的句子是現在式；而 **being** 則表達這個句子是進行式。）
過去進行式 The dinner **was being prepared** by the wives. The suspects **were being investigated** by the police.	S + **(was, were)** + **being** + **P.P.** （括號內的過去式 be 動詞由主詞單複數決定，表達這個被動語態的句子是過去式；而 **being** 則表達這個句子是進行式。）
現在完成式 The house **has been remodeled**. Millions of smartphones **have been sold**.	S + **(has, have)** + **been** + **P.P.** （括號內的 **has 或 have** 由主詞單複數決定，表達現在；而 **been** 則表達這個句子是完成式。）

動詞時態	句型
未來完成式 The corporation **will have been established** for 40 years by 2017. The great paintings **will have been stolen** for 10 years by next month.	**S + will + have + been + P.P.** （未來完成式的被動語態，不論主詞的人稱及其單複數，一律使用 **will + have + been + P.P.**，**will** 表達未來；**have + been** 表達這個句子是**完成式**。）
過去完成式 The flight **had been canceled** before the storm hit the area. The villagers **had been evacuated** before the volcano erupted.	**S + had + been + P.P.** （過去完成式的被動語態，不論主詞的人稱及其單複數，一律使用 **had + been + P.P.**；**had** 表達是**過去**，**been** 表達這個句子是**完成式**。）
助動詞 + 原型動詞 Your dinner **can be ordered** over the phone. The term project **must be submitted** online. He **may be fined** for parking here.	**S + 助動詞 + be + P.P.** （不論主詞的人稱及其單複數，一律使用原來主動語態句子中的助動詞以及 be 動詞原型動詞。）

 貼心提醒

被動語態句型中以 get 取代 be 動詞

英文被動語態的句型結構的必備要素為 be 動詞 + 過去分詞，其中的 be 動詞也可以以 get 取代，例如有人去應徵工作，後來收到通知說錄取了，便可以對別人開心地說：*I got hired.* 後來工作表現優異，獲得升遷，便可以說：*I have gotten promoted.* 好景不常，公司遭到併購，人力裁減，遭到資遣，便可以說：*I got laid off.* 之後一家海外企業透過獵人頭公司找上他，要聘請他到越南任職，他便可以說：*I got offered a job working for a multina-tional corporation in Vietnam.*

▶▶ 7.2.2 小試身手

　　空格中填入適當的助動詞（如果需要的話），be 動詞及過去分詞。

1. 嫌犯已經被目擊證人指認出來了。

   The suspect ＿＿＿＿＿ ＿＿＿＿＿ ＿＿＿＿＿ by the eyewit-ness.

2. 安樂死在臺灣合法化了嗎？

   ＿＿＿＿＿ mercy killing ＿＿＿＿＿ ＿＿＿＿＿ in Taiwan?

3. 這份合約必須在月底前簽署完成。

   The contract ＿＿＿＿＿ ＿＿＿＿＿ ＿＿＿＿＿ by the end of the month.

4. 這個節目由本公司所贊助。

   The program ＿＿＿＿＿ ＿＿＿＿＿ by our company.

5. 棒球比賽因雨延期了嗎？

   ＿＿＿＿＿ the baseball game ＿＿＿＿＿ ＿＿＿＿＿ due to the rain?

6. 會計系統是否正在電腦化中？

   ＿＿＿＿＿ the accounting system ＿＿＿＿＿ ＿＿＿＿＿?

7. 昨天晚上，有八位舞者被挑選出來在典禮中表演。

   Last night, eight dancers ＿＿＿＿＿ ＿＿＿＿＿ to perform in
   the ceremony.

8. 病人上個禮拜被診斷出患了老年癡呆症。

   The patient ＿＿＿＿＿ ＿＿＿＿＿ with dementia last week.

9. 在她打電話詢問之前，她的申請已經得到許可了。

   Her application ＿＿＿＿＿ ＿＿＿＿＿ ＿＿＿＿＿ before she
   made the call to inquire.

10. 專案小組昨天提出了多少個方案？

    How many projects ＿＿＿＿＿ ＿＿＿＿＿ by the Task
    Force?

11. 數以百萬的難民已經被歐洲許多國家收容了。

    Millions of refugees ＿＿＿＿＿ ＿＿＿＿＿ ＿＿＿＿＿ by
    several countries in Europe.

12. 聖誕禮物在聖誕夜之前正在由大家準備中。

    Christmas presents ＿＿＿＿＿ ＿＿＿＿＿ ＿＿＿＿＿ by ev-
    eryone before the Christmas Eve.

13. 這個有機農場種植了很多不同的蔬菜。

    Many different vegetables ＿＿＿＿＿ ＿＿＿＿＿ in this or-
    ganic farm.

14. 更多的醫生和護士已經被派遣到強烈地震受災最嚴重的小鎮。

    More doctors and nurses ＿＿＿＿＿ ＿＿＿＿＿
    to the towns hardest hit by the strong earthquake.

▶▶ 7.2.3 By 連同原來主動語態主詞的省略

　　被動語態的句子在下列三種情況**不會提及動詞的動作是由誰做
的**，而會把 by 連同原來主動語態主詞同時省略：

(1) 句子所要表達的著重在動作本身，而動作是誰做的不重要或不明的。

(2) 為了禮貌上不歸罪特定的人。

(3) 為了規避責任而刻意不提及動作是由誰所做的。

(1) 句子所要表達的著重在動作本身，而動作是誰做的不重要或不明的。

例如：

*規則已經修改了。*The regulations have been revised.

這項計畫的用意是要讓民眾欣賞他們自我的文化。
The project is intended for people to appreciate their own culture.

*逃犯已經遭到逮捕。*The fugitive has been arrested.

新的規定是訂來阻止吸菸的。
The new rules were set up to discourage smoking.

*合約正在討論中。*The contract is being discussed.

會議重新排程到下周二。
The meeting is rescheduled to next Tuesday.

*車子昨天失竊的。*The car was stolen yesterday.

*建議觀眾酌情自行定奪。*Viewer discretion is advised.

(2) 爲了禮貌上不歸罪特定的人

例如：

造成了一項意外。 An accident was caused. （Instead of "An accident was caused by him."）

這個災難是可以避免的。 The disaster could have been prevented.

(3) 爲了規避責任而刻意不提及動作是由誰所做的

例如：

他受命要把證據掩蓋掉。

He was ordered to cover up the evidence.

這項活動是設計來吸引年輕選民。

The campaign was designed to appeal to young voters.

英文中有許多用詞習慣以被動語態表達，例如：

您過獎了！英文則是說：*I'm flattered!*

或是員工年終收到老闆犒賞一臺 BMW 轎車，一時之間，感激興奮到不知所措，無法言語，難以招架之際，英文遇到這樣的情緒，會說：*I'm overwhelmed!*

或是某人得意忘形之際而說錯話、做錯事，事後後悔了，便可以託詞說：*I was carried away.*

或是籃球員在比賽中老是進不了球，露出沮喪的表情，播報的記者就會說：*He must be frustrated.*

或是舊屋重新整修後煥然一新，屋主見到負責設計與施工的建築師佩服不已，英文就說：*I'm very impressed!*

以下爲常用的被動語態習慣用語：

被動語態習慣用語	
be carried away 得意忘形而失言或失態	The winner of the boxing game got carried away and said something rather inappropriate.
be blown away 震驚、震撼	When his friends saw him a year later, they were blown away by how much weight he had lost.
be embarrassed 丟臉、尷尬	He was embarrassed at the counter when he found out he didn't have his wallet with him.
be excited 感到興奮	The fans were excited to see the movie star at the airport.
be exhausted 累壞了	Having finished the graduation project, the team members were totally exhausted.
be flattered 過獎了	Thank you for your compliment, but I'm flattered.
be frightened 害怕	The boy was frightened in the haunted house.
be frustrated 沮喪、挫敗	She was frustrated after failing to be hired as a flight attendant.
be impressed 佩服、開了眼界	The board of the tech company was impressed by the new CEO's performance in his first year.
be interested 感興趣	Infants are interested in learning their mother tongues.
be lost 迷路、迷網	The foreign tourists were lost in the big city.
be overwhelmed 因情緒的喜或悲而招架不住	The unemployed single father was overwhelmed when winning a twenty million lottery. The president was overwhelmed when he learned

被動語態習慣用語	
	the devastating accident causing hundreds of casualties.
be qualified 有資格	People over 65 are qualified for the subsidy for national health insurance from the city government.
be relieved 鬆了一口氣	The mayor was relieved when the kidnapped celebrity was rescued without being harmed.
be ripped off 被敲竹槓	Sam paid $20 for a used screw in a junk yard. His friend said he was ripped off.
be satisfied 滿意	The customer was not satisfied as she was not served nicely.
be scared 害怕	Jessica is tough enough not to be scared to go bungee jumping on her twentieth birthday.
be supposed to 照理應該	Parents are not supposed to leave their young children alone at home.
be surprised 驚訝	The passenger flying from Taipei to Sydney was surprised to be upgraded to the business class for free.
be tired 累了	She was tired after jogging for nearly an hour.
be tired of 厭倦	Rebecca was tired of having to put up with her boyfriend's tardiness.
be worried (about) 擔心	The foreign student was worried when the civil war broke out in her home country.

▶▶ 7.2.4 小試身手

主動語態與被動語態的互換

1. Google offers many kinds of free services.

   Many kinds of free services ＿＿＿＿＿ ＿＿＿＿＿ by Google.

2. The lady ＿＿＿＿＿ an instant message to her boss.

   An instant message was sent to her boss by the lady.

3. The company has announced the new marketing strategies.

   The new marketing strategies ＿＿＿＿ ＿＿＿＿ ＿＿＿＿

   by the company.

4. They will postpone the game if it rains tomorrow night.

   The game ＿＿＿＿＿ ＿＿＿＿＿ ＿＿＿＿＿ if it rains tomor-

   row night.

5. Doctors and nurses are treating the injured passengers on the

   crashed bus in the Emergency Room.

   The injured passengers on the crashed bus ＿＿＿＿＿ now

   ＿＿＿＿＿ ＿＿＿＿＿ in the Emergency Room by doctors

   and nurses.

6. The professor corrected many grammatical errors in her pa-

   per.

   Many grammatical errors in her paper ＿＿＿＿＿ ＿＿＿＿＿

   by the professor.

7. People in this city will always remember what he has done for

   them.

   What he has done for the people in this city ＿＿＿＿ always

   ＿＿＿＿＿ ＿＿＿＿＿ by them.

8. Europeans ＿＿＿＿＿ ＿＿＿＿＿ ＿＿＿＿＿ America until

   Christopher Columbus first reached the New World in 1492.

America had not been discovered by Europeans until the New World was first reached by Christopher Columbus in 1492.

9. The government ＿＿＿＿＿ ＿＿＿＿＿ five scientists to carry out the research.

Five scientists have been assigned by the government to carry out the research.

10. The committee members ＿＿＿＿＿ now hotly ＿＿＿＿＿ the proposed budget before voting.

The proposed budget is now being hotly debated by the committee members before voting.

7.3 狀態動詞的被動語態 (passive stative verbs)

狀態動詞的被動語態有兩個特徵：1. 這類動詞通常使用被動語態句型，2. 這類的被動語態所使用的介系詞通常不是 by，而是各自使用不同的介系詞；如下表所列：

被動語態狀態動詞	連用介系詞	中文涵義
be accustomed	to	習慣於
be annoyed	with	被…惹惱
be committed	to	致力於
be composed	of	由…組成
be concerned	about	關切
be connected	with/to	與…有關聯、與…相連接
be covered	with	被…覆蓋
be crowded	with	擠滿了…

被動語態狀態動詞	連用介系詞	中文涵義
be devoted	to	奉獻於
be disappointed	at	對…失望
be done	with	完成
be dressed	in	穿著
be equipped	with	配備有
be excited	about	對…感到興奮
be exposed	to	暴露於
be filled	with	充滿
be finished	with	完成
be frightened	of	對…感到害怕
be involved	in	參與…之中、涉及於
be known	for	以…聞名
be limited	to	侷限於
be located	in	位於
be made	of	由…所製造（物理變化）
	from	由…所製造（化學變化）
be married	to	與某人為夫妻關係
be opposed	to	反對
be pleased	with	對…感到滿意開心
be qualified	for	符合…的資格
be related	to	與…相關
be satisfied	with	對…感到滿意
be worried	about	對…感到憂慮，擔憂

在每一句的三個空格中填入適當的 **be 動詞、過去分詞、及所**
連用的介系詞。

1. People should not ＿＿＿＿ ＿＿＿＿ ＿＿＿＿ the sunlight too much in the summer.（暴露於）

2. Parents ＿＿＿＿ ＿＿＿＿ ＿＿＿＿ the government's
   new tuition policy.（被…惹惱）

3. College graduates majoring in English ＿＿＿＿ ＿＿＿＿
   ＿＿＿＿ this position.（符合…的資格）

4. Professor Chen ＿＿＿＿ ＿＿＿＿ ＿＿＿＿ developing
   new computer technologies.（奉獻於）

5. The father ＿＿＿＿ ＿＿＿＿ ＿＿＿＿ his son's aca-
   demic progress as he has been working part-time since entering the college.（關切）

6. The largest shopping mall in the nation ＿＿＿＿ ＿＿＿＿
   ＿＿＿＿ our city.（位於）

7. Mr. and Mrs. Johnson ＿＿＿＿ now ＿＿＿＿ ＿＿＿＿
   the loud noise produced by the airplanes.（習慣於）

8. The auditorium ＿＿＿＿ ＿＿＿＿ ＿＿＿＿ students as
   a concert was going on in there.（擠滿）

9. The committee ＿＿＿＿ ＿＿＿＿ ＿＿＿＿ seven
   members.（由…組成）

10. The children ＿＿＿＿ ＿＿＿＿ ＿＿＿＿ the lost dog.
    （擔心）

11. ＿＿＿＿ you d＿＿＿＿ ＿＿＿＿ your home assign-
    ment?（完成）

12. Tina _____ _____ _____ her finest clothes when she attended the party last night.（穿著）

13. Research has revealed that learners' reading ability _____ _____ _____ their vocabulary size.（與…相關）

14. Timothy _____ _____ _____ the field trip. （對…感到興奮）

15. The table _____ _____ _____ all kinds of delicious foods.（被…覆蓋）

16. On her birthday, Julia received a box that _____ _____ _____ presents.（裝滿）

17. After many days' work, the team finally f_____ _____ _____ the experiment.（完成）

18. Weeks after the disastrous earthquake, people _____ still _____ _____ the aftershocks.（對…感到害怕）

19. Jessica _____ _____ _____ several student clubs when she was in college.（參與）

20. The main dishes served in this restaurant _____ _____ beef and chicken.（偏限於）

21. In Taiwan, most computers _____ _____ _____ the Internet.（與…相連接）

22. Everyone except the manager _____ _____ _____ the new business model.（反對）

23. She _____ _____ _____ a movie star.（與某人為夫妻關係）

24. The car _____ _____ _____ a sunroof and the cruise control.（配備有…）

25. The teacher _____ very _____ _____ the out-

come of the test.（對…感到開心）

26. Investors _____ _____ _____ the company's profit gained last year.（對…感到滿意）

27. The group _____ _____ _____ environmental protection.（致力於）

28. She likes to wear pants that _____ _____ _____ natural fabrics such as cotton or wool.（由…所製作）

29. Kending _____ _____ _____ its beautiful sand beaches.（以…聞名）

30. The fans _____ _____ _____ the game results because their favorite team had been defeated.（對…感到失望）

7.4 動狀詞被動語態

英文的動狀詞一共有四種：動名詞、現在分詞、過去分詞、不定詞，其中除了過去分詞，其他三種均有主動語態與被動語態兩種句型結構，隨著時態而做的變化。不同類別的動狀詞其被動語態的功能也有所不同，以下分別以例句說明：(1) **動名詞被動語態**、(2) **現在分詞被動語態**、與 (3) **不定詞被動語態**。

(1) 動名詞被動語態

動名詞的被動語態分爲 (A) **現在式被動語態**與 (B) **現在完成式**被動語態兩種，分別表列說明如下。

A. 動名詞現在式被動語態

動名詞被動語態 A	
現在式：Be + 過去分詞	
例句	功能
Being appreciated makes people happy.（被人表示感激）	句子主詞
Children do not like **being lectured**.（被說教）	動詞受詞
She is dedicated to protecting pets from **being abused**.（受虐）	介系詞受詞
The biggest joy of an orphan is **being adopted**.（被領養）	主詞補語

B. 動名詞現在完成式被動語態

動名詞被動語態 B	
現在完成式：Having been + 過去分詞	
例句	功能
Having been diagnosed with diabetes will make her change her diets drastically.（被診斷出）	句子主詞
The grandchildren enjoyed **having been pampered** by their generous grandparents.（得到寵愛）	動詞受詞
The young oncologist reacted strongly against **having been excluded** from the medical research project.（被排除在外）	介系詞受詞
The most exciting moment for Jasmine last year was **having been commended** in the conference for her incredible contributions.（接受表揚）	主詞補語

句型結構說明：

動名詞現在完成式被動語態可能由現在完成式動詞或由過去完成動詞變化而來。

(a) 動名詞現在完成式被動語態由現在完成式動詞變化而來

She has been diagnosed with diabetes. It will make her change her diets drastically.

→ **Having been diagnosed** with diabetes will make her change her diets drastically.

(b) 動名詞現在完成式被動語態由過去完成式動詞變化而來

She had been diagnosed with diabetes. It made her change her diets drastically.

→ **Having been diagnosed** with diabetes made her change her diets drastically.

(2) 現在分詞被動語態

現在分詞的被動語態其功能與形容詞相同，都是用來修飾名詞及名詞同類語。現在分詞的被動語態分為 (A) **現在式**被動語態與 (B) **現在完成式**被動語態兩種，分別表列說明如下。

A. **現在分詞現在式被動語態**

現在分詞被動語態 A	
現在式：**Being** + 過去分詞	
例句	功能
Being listed as one of the best outlet stores to shop, it is now rolling out a series of luring sales.（名列）	修飾句子主詞

現在分詞被動語態 A	
現在式：Being + 過去分詞	
例句	功能
The indigenous people, **being deprived** of their rights to hunt in National Parks, are protesting before the Legislative Yuan in Taipei.（被剝奪）	修飾句子主詞
He finally cut a deal to sell his art collections, **being coveted** by many potential buyers.（被覬覦）	（修飾名詞片語 art collections）

句型結構說明 ：

　　現在分詞現在式被動語態可能**由現在式動詞或由過去式動詞變化而來**。

　　The store is/was listed as one of the best outlet stores to shop. It is now rolling out a series of luring sales.

　　→ **Being listed** as one of the best outlet stores to shop, it is now rolling out a series of luring sales.

　　The indigenous people is/was deprived of their rights to hunt in National Parks, so they are protesting before the Legislative Yuan in Taipei.

　　→ The indigenous people, **being deprived** of their rights to hunt in National Parks, are protesting before the Legislative Yuan in Taipei.

　　He finally cut a deal to sell his art collections. They are/were coveted by many potential buyers.

→ He finally cut a deal to sell his art collections, **being coveted** by many potential buyers.

B. 現在分詞現在完成式被動語態

現在分詞被動語態 **B**	
現在完成式：**Having Been** + 過去分詞	
例句	功能
The price of the medication, **having been prescribed** by the physician, is going to increase by 6% starting this month.（由…所的開處方）	修飾名詞
Having been denied entry to the country due to invalid passports, the foreign tourists will be forced to take the next flight to return to their home country.（遭到拒絕）	修飾主詞

句型結構說明：
　　現在分詞現在完成式被動語態可能由**現在完成式動詞或由過去完成式動詞變化而來**。

(a) 現在分詞現在完成式被動語態由現在完成式動詞變化而來
　　The foreign tourists **have been denied** entry to the country due to invalid passports, so they will be forced to take the next flight to return to their home country.
　　→ **Having been denied** entry to the country due to invalid passports, the foreign tourists will be forced to take the next flight to return to their home country.

(b) 現在分詞現在完成式被動語態由過去完成式動詞變化而來

The foreign tourists **had been denied** entry to the country due to invalid passports, so they were forced to take the next flight to return to their home country.

→ **Having been denied** entry to the country due to invalid passports, the foreign tourists were forced to take the next flight to return to their home country.

（有關現在分詞被動語態的句型結構與運用請詳閱第九章分詞構句）

(3) 不定詞的被動語態

不定詞的被動語態分為 (A) 現在式被動語態與 (B) 現在完成式的被動語態兩種，分別表列說明如下。

A. 不定詞現在式被動語態

不定詞被動語態 A	
現在式：To Be + 過去分詞	
例句	功能
To be assigned the job is a great honor.（受指派）	句子主詞
Students like **to be encouraged** in the class.（被鼓勵）	動詞受詞
Higher tariffs will be imposed on more items of goods **to be imported** from the country as retaliation.（進口）	修飾名詞
The police officers are thrilled **to be equipped** with newly released high-power weapons and top-of-the-line gadgets to crack down on crimes.（得到裝備）	修飾過去分詞 thrilled

不定詞被動語態 A	
現在式：To Be + 過去分詞	
例句	功能
The best way to recover from serious injuries is **to be assisted** by physical therapists to go through the long process of rehabilitation.（接受協助）	主詞補語

B. 不定詞現在完成式被動語態

不定詞被動語態 B	
現在完成式：To Have Been + 過去分詞	
例句	功能
To have been forgiven humbled the drunk driver killing two motorcyclists.（蒙原諒）	句子主詞
The student was devastated **to have been withdrawn** from the debate team.（被拉掉）	修飾過去分詞 devastated
The executive order requiring every scooter to be equipped with Anti-lock Breaking System（ABS）**to have been revoked** made everyone relieved.（被撤回）	修飾名詞 order
He was thankful to God **to have been set** free from the prison after having been proved innocent.（被釋放）	thankful 的補語

▶▶ 7.4.1 小試身手

將劃底線的中文翻譯成英文的被動語態的動名詞、現在分詞、不定詞（一個空格填寫一個英文單字）。

1. 被提名為年度歌唱獎的最佳女歌手讓她覺得光榮。

_____ _____ the best female singer of the annual singing award makes her proud.

2. 沒有人喜歡被同儕霸凌。

No one likes _____ _____ _____ by the peers.

3. 要接受檢驗的產品放置在這裡。

Products _____ _____ _____ are placed here.

4. 勤奮工作的員工喜歡因他們的貢獻得到獎勵。

Hard-working employees enjoy _____ _____ for their contributions.

5. 工作六個月後得到升遷是對他的才華和表現的肯定。

_____ _____ _____ after working for just six months is a recognition of his talent and performance.

6. 電視節目製作人對於被觀眾批評感到失望。

The producer of TV program is disappointed at _____ _____ by the audience.

7. 被說軟弱惹惱了這位職業美式足球選手。

_____ _____ _____ annoys the professional football player.

8. 學生們接到通知因為快速逼近的颱風要提早離開學校而興奮地瘋狂。

Students went excitedly crazy to _____ _____ _____ to leave school earlier due to the fast approaching typhoon.

9. 被錄取進入哈佛大學，Patrick 立刻打電話給父母親及高中老師報這個大好消息。

_____ _____ _____ to Harvard University, Patrick immediately called his parents and high school teacher about the wonderful news.

10. 要修改的提案會在今天下午的會議討論。

The proposal ＿＿＿＿＿ ＿＿＿＿＿ ＿＿＿＿＿ will be discussed in the meeting this afternoon.

7.5 被動語態打通關

中譯英填充

1. 今晚餐桌上會上什麼菜？

＿＿＿＿＿ ＿＿＿＿＿ ＿＿＿＿＿ ＿＿＿＿＿ on the table tonight?

2. 沒有人喜歡被他們信賴的朋友所出賣。

No one likes ＿＿＿＿＿ ＿＿＿＿＿ ＿＿＿＿＿ by their ＿＿＿＿＿ friends.

3. 比賽被打敗令人失望。

＿＿＿＿＿ ＿＿＿＿＿ in a game is ＿＿＿＿＿.

4. 遊客受到警告不要餵食野生動物。

Tourists ＿＿＿＿＿ ＿＿＿＿＿ ＿＿＿＿＿ ＿＿＿＿＿ ＿＿＿＿＿ the wild animals.

5. 這群孩子真的很享受接受招待去遊樂園玩。

The kids really enjoyed ＿＿＿＿＿ ＿＿＿＿＿ to the amusement park.

6. 得到老師的讚美會鼓勵學生學習。

＿＿＿＿＿ ＿＿＿＿＿ by the teacher encourages students ＿＿＿＿＿ ＿＿＿＿＿.

7. 臺灣製造的鞋子在很多國家都有賣。

Shoes _____ in Taiwan _____ _____ in many countries.

8. 當代藝術家所創作的藝術品將於下週展示。

The artworks _____ _____ _____ _____ will _____ _____ next week.

9. 五位來自不同領域科學家的團隊已經被政府指派來執行這項保育計畫。(assign)

A team of five scientists _____ different _____

_____ _____ _____ to _____ _____ the preservation project.

10. 美國各地很多百貨公司由於獲利快速下滑正在被關閉中。

Many department stores across the United States _____

_____ _____ _____ due to fast _____ profits.

7.6 被動語態挑戰題

使用被動語態完成下列句子的英譯

1. 新的行銷策略已於上周五的會議上由執行長宣佈，並將在下一季實施。(announce, implement)

   _____

2. 意外事故中受傷的乘客們正在急診室由醫師治療中。(treat)

   _____

3. 蔬菜必須加以清洗才能拿來煮。(wash)

   _____

4. 今年到年底銷售業績最好的業務員將會升任經理。(promote)

_____

5. 昨晚比賽前的歌曲由一位由地主球隊老闆所邀請的著名歌手演唱。(sing)

_____

_____

6. 張小姐，應徵者當中最優秀的，將受到公司聘用。(hire)

_____

_____

7. 為這個城市服務了八年的市長將永遠由市民所銘記。(remember)

_____

8. 獵殺受當局保護的動物可能會遭到嚴懲。(punish)

_____

9. 這一棟由著名建築師設計的圖書館已經獲得認證為綠建築了。(certify)

_____

_____

10. 所有在工廠加工的食品都必須經過政府的檢驗後才能在市面上販售。(inspect)

_____

_____

句型變化篇 |

他們必如鷹展翅上騰　奔跑卻不困倦　行走卻不疲乏

（聖經 以賽亞書 40:31）

They will soar on wings like eagles; they will run and
not grow weary, they will walk and not be faint.

(Isaiah 40:31)

第八章 子句 (Clauses)

　　爲了說明英文子句的類型與功能，我們先來看以下介紹臺灣的句子：

After the foreign tourists read the introduction from the pamphlet, they will learn that Taiwan, which is an island with many scenic high mountains, is an amazing country that is known for its people who are warm and hospitable as well as for its flourishing high-tech industry.

這句英文包含了：
一個副詞子句
after the foreign tourists read the introduction from the pamphlet

一個獨立子句
they will learn (that Taiwan is an amazing country).

一個名詞子句
that Taiwan is an amazing country（嵌入在獨立子句之中，作爲動詞 learn 的受詞）

兩個非限定用法形容詞子句
1. which is an island with many scenic high mountains（對於其所修飾的先行詞 Taiwan 提供額外的資訊）
2. who are warm and hospitable（修飾先行詞 people）

一個限定用法形容詞子句

that is known for its people who are warm and hospitable as well as for its flourishing high-tech industry.（修飾先行詞 coun-try）

以開車來比喻英文寫作，這樣的句子已經不是轎車，而是大型聯結車了！要開這種聯結車，技術要高超，經驗要豐富，稍有差池，輕則擦撞，重則車毀人亡，不可不慎！要寫出這樣複雜的長句子，當然要先把基本功培養好，先練好簡單句，再來練合句及複句，最後才是複合句。

想要正確地寫出如此複雜的英文句子，我們必須透徹瞭解英文不同類型的子句及其功能，這也正是本篇的重點，包括：子句的結構，獨立子句的形成及如何透過對等連接詞結合為合句，從屬子句的類型（名詞子句、副詞子句、形容詞子句）與功能，從屬子句與獨立子句如何透過從屬連接詞結合成為複句，副詞子句與形容詞子句簡化為片語，以及數個獨立子句如何轉變而結合成一個複句或複合句。

8.1 英文子句的類別與結構

英文的子句概分為兩種：獨立子句與從屬子句，**獨立子句**本身具備了完整的〔主部 + 述部〕的結構，足以表達完整的涵義，從而可以構成一個簡單句；**從屬子句**雖然也具備了〔主部 + 述部〕的結構，卻不足以表達完整的涵義，而必須嵌入或依附於獨立子句（主要子句），二者共同組成複句，從屬子句才有意義。底下我們

要介紹 (1) 獨立子句的結構，(2) 從屬子句的結構，以及 (3) 由獨立子句與從屬子句搭配組合的四種類型的句子：簡單句、合句、複句及複合句。

8.1.1 獨立子句的結構

　　英文的子句，都必須具備〔主詞／主部 + 動詞／述部〕的結構，主部由名詞片語、動名詞片語、不定詞片語所構成，片語中的名詞、動名詞、不定詞即是子句的主詞；而述部則由動詞片語所構成，片語中的動詞即是子句的動詞，且動詞片語是否需要其他必要元素由動詞的類型所決定，動詞與這些其他必要的元素共同構成動詞片語，也就是述部；述部與主部結合便構成了獨立子句，進而形成簡單句。

　　例如：

The cellphone is ringing .

分析說明：

單一名詞 "**the cellphone**" 為主詞，同時構成主部；"**is ringing**" 為現在進行式動詞，屬於**完全不及物動詞**，不需要其他元素即可構成動詞片語，作為述部；主部與述部共同構成獨立子句，也就是簡單句 "**The cellphone is ringing.**"。

The cellphone on the coffee table looks fancy .

分析說明：

名詞 "**the cellphone**" 為主詞，與結構上非必要的元素介系詞片語 "on the coffee table" 共同構成名詞片語，作為主部；動詞為 "looks"，屬於不完全不及物動詞，必須搭配結構上必要的元素主詞補語 "fancy" 才能構成完整的動詞片語 "**looks fancy**"，作為述部；主部與述部共同構成獨立子句，也就是簡單句 "**The cell-phone** on the coffee table **looks fancy**."。

The girl *sitting next to me* **bought the cellphone** *from an online store last month*.

分析說明：

名詞 **"the girl"** 爲主詞，與結構上非必要的元素現在分詞片語 "sitting next to me" 共同構成名詞片語，作爲主部；動詞爲 "bought"，屬於完全及物動詞，必須搭配結構上必要的元素受詞 "the cellphone" 才能構成完整的動詞片語 **"bought the cellphone"**，這個動詞片語又加上結構上非必要的元素介系詞片語 "from an online store" 與副詞片語 "last month" 予以擴充爲 "bought the cellphone from an online store last month"，作爲述部；主部與述部共同構成獨立子句，也就是簡單句 "**The girl** sitting next to me **bought the cellphone** from an online store last month."。

Buying the cellphone **cost her 500 dollars**.

分析說明：

動名詞 "buying" 爲主詞，必須搭配結構上必要的元素受詞 "the cellphone"，才能構成完整的動名詞片語 **"buying the cellphone"**，作爲主部；動詞爲 "cost"，屬於不完全及物動詞，必須搭配結構上必要的元素受詞 **"her"** 以及受詞補語 **"500 dollars"**，才能構成完整的動詞片語 **"cost her 500 dollars"**，作爲述部；主部與述部共同構成獨立子句，也就是簡單句 **"Buying the cellphone cost her 500 dollars"**.。

所謂的簡單句指的是其**結構簡單**，僅由一組主部 + 述部的元素即可構成，並非其內容簡單，正如前面章節所述，簡單句可以透過內部的擴充形成**內容豐富**的句子，仍然維持簡單句的結構。例如：

The A350-900s equipped with Rolls-Royce Trent XWB84 engines are to be delivered beginning in 2021, with deliveries of the A350-1000s powered by Rolls-Royce Trent XWB97 engines to start in the third quarter of 2022. (Taipei Times)

本句的字數很多，但其基本結構為 *The A350-900s are to be delivered.* 仍然是**簡單句**。

相對地，有些句子**字數不多**，結構卻極為**複雜**，例如：

The man who lost his briefcase said that he would reward generously the finder who would return it to him.

本句的主要子句為 *The man said* + **名詞子句（受詞）**，另外搭配了兩個形容詞子句，句子結構為**複句**。

Since our space journey started, we have left so much trash there that scientists are now concerned that if we don't clean it up, we may all be in mortal danger.（102 學測）

本句的主要子句為 *we have left so much trash there*，另外搭配了三個副詞子句與一個名詞子句，句子結構為**複句**。

▶▶ 8.1.2 從屬子句的結構

　　從屬子句是由獨立子句變化而來，若是在獨立子句的開頭加上**從屬連接詞**或**關係代名詞**或**關係副詞**，則化身為**從屬子句 (dependent clauses)**，因此雖然其具備了主詞／主部＋動詞／述部的結構，但卻必須內嵌或依附於獨立子句中，而無法獨自構成完整的句子。例如：

that the cellphone is ringing

（that＋獨立子句＝從屬子句＝**名詞子句**）

whether the cellphone is ringing

（whether＋獨立子句＝從屬子句＝**名詞子句**）

when the cellphone is ringing

（when＋獨立子句＝從屬子句＝**副詞子句**）

which/that is ringing

（關係代名詞 which/that 取代了主詞＝從屬子句＝**形容詞子句**）

where the cellphone is ringing

（關係副詞 where＋獨立子句＝從屬子句＝**形容詞子句**）

　　從屬子句依其功能分為三類：(1) <u>名詞子句</u> (noun clauses)，(2) <u>副詞子句</u> (adverbial clauses)，(3) <u>形容詞子句</u> (adjective clauses or relative clauses)

▶▶ 8.1.3 由獨立子句與從屬子句所構成的四種句子類型

　　獨立子句本身即可構成一個簡單句 (simple sentences)，而獨立子句也可以和另一個獨立子句結合，構成合句 (compound sentences)；獨立子句也可以和從屬子句結合，構成**複句 (complex** sentences)；而合句也可以再崁入從屬子句，構成**複合句 (compound complex sentences)**。

英文的句子，不論其長短，不論如何變化，不外乎就是由獨立子句和從屬子句所構成的四種型態：(1) 簡單句 (2) 合句 (3) 複句及 (4) 複合句，沒有其他的類型！換句話說，我們所寫出來的英文句子，一定是這四種句子類型的其中一種，如果不是的話，我們所寫的句子就是不合文法的 (ungrammatical)。因此，要寫出結構正確又富有變化的英文句子，必須澈底瞭解英文子句的結構和功能，以及獨立子句和從屬子句彼此如何搭配變化。

在子句這一章，我們會詳細介紹：
(1) 獨立子句及三種從屬子句（名詞子句、副詞子句、形容詞子句）的結構與功能
(2) 獨立子句與獨立子句如何結合成為合句
(3) 名詞子句如何嵌入獨立子句構成複句
(4) 副詞子句與形容詞子句如何依附於獨立子句形成複句
(5) 副詞子句如何簡化為省略子句
(6) 如何正確使用限定用法及非限定用法形容詞子句
(7) 形容詞子句如何簡化為片語
(8) 複句的結構
(9) 複合句的結構
(10) 如何將數個簡單句結合成為複句或複合句

8.2 獨立子句 (independent clauses)

　　獨立子句由主部與述部所構成，主部爲名詞片語或與名詞片語相同功能的片語所構成，而述部則由動詞片語所構成。動詞片語的必要元素依動詞類型而有所不同，例如完全不及物動詞只需動詞本身即可構成完整的動詞片語，與主部共同構成一個完整的獨立子句，如：The baby is sleeping；若是完全及物動詞則除了動詞本身之外，還需要接受詞才能構成完整的動詞片語，再與主部共同形成完整的獨立子句，如：Everyone adores the baby。

　　獨立子句本身可以單獨存在，並構成一個**簡單句**；也可以跟另外一個獨立子句，以對等連接詞結合，成爲一個**合句**；也可以跟從屬子句結合，構成**複句**。

▶▶ 8.2.1 獨立子句本身構成的簡單句：五種基本動詞句型

　　這一節我們以五種基本動詞的句型來說明獨立子句的結構以及其所必須具備的元素。

---

(1) 完全不及物動詞 (S. + Vi.)

The baby *is talking*.

主部／名詞片語 + 述部／現在進行式動詞片語 ＝ 獨立子句
＝ 簡單句

---

(2) 完全及物動詞 (S. + Vt. + O.)

The baby | *loves + music* .

主部 / 名詞片語 + 現在式動詞 + 受詞

= 主部 / 名詞片語 + 述部 / 現在式動詞片語 = 獨立子句

= 簡單句

---

(3) 不完全不及物動詞 (S. + Vi. + S.C.)

The baby | *is + cute* .

= 主部 / 名詞片語 + 現在式動詞 + 主詞補語

= 主部 / 名詞片語 + 述部 / 現在式動詞片語 = 獨立子句

= 簡單句

---

(4) 不完全及物動詞 (S. + Vt. + O.C.)

The baby | *calls + the cat + Mimi* .

= 主部 / 名詞片語 + 現在式動詞 + 受詞 + 受詞補語

= 主部 / 名詞片語 + 述部 / 現在式動詞片語

= 獨立子句 = 簡單句

---

(5) 授與動詞 (S. + Vt. + O2 + O1)

The baby | *gives + mother + a smile* .

= 主部 / 名詞片語 + 現在式動詞 + 間接受詞 + 直接受詞

= 主部 / 名詞片語 + 述部 / 現在式動詞片語

= 獨立子句 = 簡單句

以上 (1)-(5) 的句子都是由一個獨立子句所構成的簡單句，其中都包含了主部 / 名詞片語 + 述部 / 動詞片語的基本結構，以及

依動詞類型所需的必要配件。以汽車來比喻，這四個獨立子句所構成的簡單句都屬於基本配備的陽春車，結構單純，傳達簡單易懂的涵義。

8.2.2 分辨獨立子句與片語的差異

前面 (1)-(5) 的五個例句，其結構具備了所必要的最基本元素，因此句子雖然簡短，仍然足以構成獨立子句，進而形成簡單句。這種僅含有基本必要元素的簡單句，可以透過內部的擴充而形成字數多的長句子，而其架構依然維持簡單句的結構。反觀一長串的英文字湊在一起，如果不具備〔主部 + 述部〕的結構，字數再多，充其量也僅僅是片語而已。現在我們來檢視分析下列 (6)-(11) 的句子：

---

(6)

The research team with members from different countries
is conducting a study on the effects of genetically modified
foods on human health .

= 主部 S. / 名詞片語 + 現在進行式動詞 Vt. + 名詞片語 / 受詞 O.

= 主部 / 名詞片語 + 述部 / 現在進行式動詞片語

= 獨立子句 = 簡單句

句子的基本結構為：The research team is conducting a study.
經過內部擴充後，成為涵義更豐富的簡單句。

---

(7)

To boost the economy , *the government* *has been imple-*

menting many major construction projects throughout the country since two years ago .

= 不定詞片語 + 名詞片語 S. + 現在完成進行式動詞 Vt. + 名詞片語 O.

= 不定詞片語 + 主部／名詞片語 + 述部／現在完成進行式動詞片語

= 獨立子句 = 簡單句

句子基本結構為：The government has been implementing construction projects.

經過內部擴充後，成為涵義更豐富的簡單句。

---

(8)

Helping my parents with some home projects always *requires trips* to Sutherlands *and enjoyable rides* through town with my dad in his red Chevy pick-up .

= 主部／動名詞片語 S. + 副詞 + 現在式動詞 Vt. + 名詞片語／受詞 O.

= 主部／動名詞片語 + 述部／現在式動詞片語

= 獨立子句 = 簡單句

句子基本結構為：Helping my parents requires trips and rides.
經過內部擴充後，成為涵義更豐富的簡單句。

(9)

Professor Huang, a specialist in food science , ***has been
invited*** to deliver a speech at an international conference
organized by a food company selling many kinds of local
delicacies .

= 主部／名詞片語 S. ＋ 同位語 ＋ 現在完成式被動語態動詞
V. ＋不定詞片語／副詞片語＋介系詞片語／副詞片語

= 主部／名詞片語 ＋ 同位語 ＋ 述部／現在完成式被動語態
動詞片語

= 獨立子句 = 簡單句

句子基本結構爲：Professor Huang has been invited.
經過內部擴充後，成爲涵義更豐富的簡單句。

(6) 到 (9) 的句子由許多單字與片語所組成，結構看起來似乎
很複雜，但仔細分析其組成元素，這些句子其實仍然是由**主部 +
述部所構成的單一獨立子句，從而構成簡單句**。其中都包含了**名詞
片語 + 動詞片語的基本結構**，以及**其他依動詞類型的句型結構所
需要的元素**。除此之外，(6) 到 (9) 的句子也分別使用了不同類型
的片語，經過句子內部擴充之後，豐富了句子的內容，成爲涵義更
豐富的簡單句。也就是說這部由獨立子句組成的汽車，結構單純，
除了具備必要的基本配備之外，還加裝了各類的修飾語及連接詞的
選配，算是豪華配備的汽車，而得以表達更豐富的涵義。

反觀以下 (10) 和 (11)，乍看之下像是句子，仔細分析後，卻
發現並**不具備主詞 + 動詞的基本結構**，自然也就**缺乏了主部與述**

部的完整結構，而無法形成一個獨立子句的。由此可見，我們如果把一堆單字和片語拼湊起來，但卻**缺少主詞 + 動詞的結構，所拼湊的文字至多僅能構成片語而已**，並無法構成一個簡單句。換句話說，一旦缺少了**動詞（有如汽車的引擎）**或**主詞（有如車身）**，再多的單字或片語（汽車配件）也無法構成一個完整的句子（汽車）。不過，一旦我們補上關鍵的配備（引擎或車身），這些單字和片語就具備了主詞加動詞的結構，而搖身一變，成爲獨立子句所構成的簡單句，也就是一部可以開動的汽車了！

---

(10)

Hosted a seminar at the Taiwan Council of Agriculture on *Small Farm Food Processing Management*

這一些單字與片語所組成的文字並非句子，其結構只是以動詞 **hosted** + 名詞／受詞 **a seminar** 爲核心的**動詞片語**，只有引擎，缺少了主詞的車身。

我們可以用底下的補救方法完成簡單句的結構：

在原來的動詞片語前面補上名詞片語 **the renowned scholar** 作爲主詞，便具備了 主詞＋過去式動詞＋受詞 以及 主部／名詞片語＋述部／過去式動詞片語 的基本結構，成爲**獨立子句**，而構成一個簡單句了：

The renowned scholar *hosted a seminar* at the Taiwan Council of Agriculture on Small Farm Food Processing Management .

= S. + Vt. + O. （完全及物動詞）

= 獨立子句 = 簡單句

(11)

*A relaxing and joyous **evening** with good friends over Korean BBQ and traditional Taiwanese desserts*

這一些單字與片語所組成的文字並非句子，其結構只是以 evening 為核心的**名詞片語**，可以作為主詞或主詞補語，我們可以用底下 (a)、(b) 兩種補救方法完成簡單句的結構：

(a) 以名詞片語作為主詞補語

補上主詞 it（車身）和動詞 was（引擎），便具備了 主詞 + 過去式動詞 + 名詞片語 / 主詞補語 以及 主部 / 名詞片語 + 述部 / 過去式動詞片語 的基本結構，成為**獨立子句**，而構成一個簡單句了：

It ***was a*** relaxing and joyous ***evening*** with good friends over Korean BBQ and traditional Taiwanese desserts .

= S. + Vi. + S.C. （不完全不及物動詞）

= 獨立子句 = 簡單句

(b) 以名詞片語作為主詞

補上動詞與 created 以及名詞片語 a great memory 作為動詞的受詞，便具備了 主詞 + 過去式動詞 + 受詞 以及 主部 + 述部 / 過去式動詞片語 的基本結構，成為**獨立子句**，而構成一個簡單句了：

A relaxing and joyous ***evening*** with good friends over Korean BBQ and traditional Taiwanese desserts ***created a great memory***.

= S. + Vt. + O. （完全及物動詞）

= 獨立子句 = 簡單句

從以上的例子，我們瞭解到：要把單字跟片語組合成為一個獨立子句，最關鍵的就是必須具備**主詞／主部＋動詞的基本結構**，再依不同類型動詞的句型結構要求，加入所需要的其他元素，與動詞共同構成動詞片語，也就是句子的述部，如此，**主部／名詞片語＋述部／動詞片語**即可構成完整的獨立子句，從而形成簡單句。

　　例如**不完全不及物動詞**所構成的獨立子句，除了要具備主詞加不及物動詞的基本結構之外，還必須加入**主詞補語**，其句型結構才能完整表達涵義；或是**不完全及物動詞**所構成的獨立子句，除了要具備主詞加不及物動詞的基本結構之外，還必須加入**受詞補語**，其句型結構才能完整表達涵義。而其他的片語或修飾語則屬於選配，並非不可或缺，其有無並不影響獨立子句的結構。

　　接下來，我們要介紹獨立子句如何與另外一個獨立子句結合，而構成另一種句子的型態，也就是<u>合句 **(compound sentences)**</u>。

▶▶ 8.2.3 合句：以對等連結詞結合兩個獨立子句

　　一個獨立子句即可構成一個簡單句，並傳遞一個完整的訊息給讀者。在英文寫作時，我們也可以將兩個獨立子句，運用**對等連接詞 (coordinating conjunctions)** 加以結合，構成一個**合句**，同時傳遞兩個完整的訊息給讀者。必須注意的是，要將兩個獨立子句結合，不能只在其間加上逗點，一定要以對等連接詞加以結合，否則就是不合文法的連寫句了。我們用以下的例句來說明：

(1) Julia wanted to learn Japanese culture.
(2) She decided to spend one year in Osaka as an exchange student.

句子 (1) 和 (2) 都是由獨立子句所構成的簡單句，分別傳遞兩個完整的訊息。而這兩個簡單句依照其邏輯關係，可以選用恰當的對等連接詞加以結合，構成一個新的合句 (3)。**英文的對等連接詞一共有七個：and, but, or, so, nor, for, yet**，在這裡句子 (1) 是句子 (2) 的原因，因此我們選用對等連接詞 so，將兩個獨立子句結合，形成一個合句 (3)。

→ (3) **Julia wanted to learn Japanese culture, <u>so</u> she decided to spend one year in Osaka as an exchange student.** (合句)

這個合句 **(3) 所表達的涵義**跟底下的句子是一致的，但是後者屬於**複句**，是由獨立子句與副詞子句所構成，因此兩者的**句子型態**不同：

Because Julia wanted to learn Japanese culture, (副詞子句／從屬子句) she decided to spend one year in Osaka as an exchange student (獨立子句／主要子句). (複句)

貼心提醒

在結合成合句時，兩個獨立子句之間除了必須有**對等連接詞**之外，在第一個獨立子句最後的地方還要加上一個**逗點**，才算完整，否則仍是不合英文文法，如下例所示：

* Julia wanted to learn Japanese culture <u>so</u> she decided to spend one year in Osaka as an exchange student. (culture 後面**少了逗點**，因此本句不合英文文法)

但若僅僅在兩個獨立子句之間加上逗點，而**缺少對等連接詞**的話，也是不合文法的，如下例所示：

* Julia wanted to learn Japanese culture, she decided to spend one year in Osaka as an exchange student.（連寫句）

接下來，我們用更多的例句來說明，如何以對等連接詞結合兩個獨立子句，構成一個新的合句。

Mr. Kent is an English teacher. He earns a lot of money by writing novels.

→ Mr. Kent is an English teacher, **and** he earns a lot of money by writing novels.（而且）（注意：在第一個獨立子句最後的地方要加上一個逗點。）

The lady is 75 years old. She bikes 30 miles on every sunny day.

→ The lady is 75 years old, **yet** she bikes 30 miles on every sunny day.（仍然）

The students can submit an electronic file of the assignment via the Internet.
They can hand in a hard copy to the professor's office.

→ The students can submit an electronic file of the assignment via the Internet, **or** they can hand in a hard copy to the professor's office.（或者）

By the time she got to the airport, the flight had been canceled.

She had to take the train instead.

→ By the time she got to the airport, the flight had been canceled, **so** she had to take the train instead.（所以，因此，於是）

Cathy was hoping to get a promotion last year.

Her performance was not good enough.

→ Cathy was hoping to get a promotion last year, **but** her performance was not good enough.（但是，然而，不過，可是）

He did not attend the meeting. He did not answer the phone.

→ He did not attend the meeting, **nor did** he answer the phone.
（也沒有）
（注意：使用 **nor** 連接前後兩個獨立子句時，**後面的獨立子句必須倒裝**。）

He cannot be late for work anymore. He will be fired.

→ He cannot be late for work anymore, **or** he will be fired.（否則）

The rain finally stopped. She went out to jog.

→ The rain finally stopped, **so** she went out to jog.（所以，因此，於是）

They have decided to move to a cheaper apartment.

The rent has gone up too high.

→ They have decided to move to a cheaper apartment, **for** the rent has gone up too high.（因為，由於）

依照兩個獨立子句的邏輯關係，填入恰當的對等連接詞，以完成合句。

1. Her bike was stolen, ＿＿＿＿＿＿ she had to walk home from the park.

2. The budget was not approved, ＿＿＿＿＿＿ they would not drop the proposed project.

3. He did not invest in the stock market, ＿＿＿＿＿＿ did he invest in the real estate.

4. She is on a diet, ＿＿＿＿＿＿ she really wants to eat ice cream.

5. They recycle almost everything, ＿＿＿＿＿＿ doing so can help protect the environment.

6. She loves sports, ＿＿＿＿＿＿ she plays badminton every week.

7. The earthquake destroyed their house, ＿＿＿＿＿＿ they did not give up on themselves.

8. The employees can choose to work from 9:00 to 18:00, ＿＿＿＿ ＿＿＿＿ they can choose to work from 8:00 to 17:00.

9. The workers were hoping for a pay raise, ＿＿＿＿＿＿ the results of the negotiation between the factory owner and the union were disappointing.

10. We are moving to Taipei, ＿＿＿＿＿＿ my father has found a new job there.

11. The research team has not found any evidence to support the theory, ＿＿＿＿＿＿ the researchers insist on their theory.

12. The citizens are fleeing their country, _____ a civil war has broken out between the government and the rebels.

13. The new smartphones have been sold out, _____ they have to order more.

14. She likes drinking coffee every morning, _____ she prefers it black.

15. Children have never been very good at listening to their elders, _____ they have never failed to imitate them. (*James A. Baldwin*)

▶▶ 8.2.5 合句中翻英（必須以對等連接詞連接兩個獨立子句）

1. 科技讓我們的生活更舒適，然而它也被利用來犯罪。（93 年指考）

_____

_____

2. 人類對外太空所知非常有限，但長久以來我們對它卻很感興趣。（94 年學測）

_____

_____

3. 閱讀對孩子有益，所以老師應該多鼓勵學生到圖書館借書。（95 年學測）

_____

_____

4. 近二十年來我國的出生率快速下滑，這可能導致我們未來人力資源的嚴重不足。（99 年指考）

_____

_____

5. 專家警告我們不應該再將食物價格低廉視爲理所當然，因爲全球
   糧食危機已經在世界許多地區造成嚴重的社會問題。（97 年指
   考）

   _____

   _____

8.3 連寫句 (run-on sentences)

　　從前面的說明，我們知道一個獨立子句即可構成一個簡單句，
若是要把兩個獨立子句結合，除了必須使用恰當的對等連接詞來連
接前後兩個獨立子句，也必須在第一個獨立子句之後加上逗點，這
樣才能完成正確的合句的結構。我們在連接兩個或更多個獨立子句
時，有可能犯兩個錯誤：(1) **逗點拼接句 (comma splices)**，以及
(2) **融合句 (fused sentences)**，兩者都必須加以更正，以成爲合文
法的句子。

▶▶ 8.3.1 逗點拼接句 (comma splices)

　　獨立子句之間**沒有使用對等連接詞**，而**僅僅使用逗點** (comma) 來連接，這樣的構句就形成了**逗點拼接句** (comma splices) 或
稱爲**逗點謬誤** (comma faults)，屬於句子結構的瑕疵，在英文寫作
上是不能接受而必須加以更正的錯誤。例如：

　　* _She bought a new backpack, she will give it to her friend_
　　　 as a gift.（**逗點拼接句**）

　　更正方法如下：

1. 將兩個獨立子句分別寫成兩個簡單句

She bought a new backpack. She would give it to her friend as a gift.

2. 使用恰當的對等連接結合兩個獨立子句

She bought a new backpack, **and** she would give it to her friend as a gift.

3. 使用分號分開兩個獨立子句

She bought a new backpack; she would give it to her friend as a gift.

4. 將其中一個獨立子句改成從屬子句

She bought a new backpack, **which** she would give to her friend as a gift.

（將第二個獨立子句改成<u>非限定用法的形容詞子句</u>）

8.3.2 融合句 (fused sentences)

　　獨立子句之間既<u>無對等連接詞</u>，也<u>無任何標點符號</u>時，這樣的構句就形成了融合句 (fused sentences)，也是錯誤的句子結構，必須加以更正。例如：

　　It was a lovely day they decided to have a picnic in the park.（**融合句**）

　　更正方法如下：

1. 將兩個獨立子句分別寫成兩個簡單句

It was a lovely day. They decided to have a picnic in the park.

2. 使用恰當的對等連接結合兩個獨立子句

It was a lovely day, so they decided to have a picnic in the park.

3. 使用分號分開兩個獨立子句

It was a lovely day; they decided to have picnic in the park.

4. 將其中一個獨立子句改成從屬子句

The decided to have a picnic in the park because it was a lovely day.

（將第一個獨立子句改成副詞子句）

（有關獨立子句如何轉換成為從屬子句的技巧細節將在從屬子句單元詳細介紹。）

▶▶▶ 8.3.3 小試身手

使用恰當的對等連接詞改正下列結構錯誤的連寫句。

1. She has found a better job, she will quit her current job.

_____

2. The new immigrants are taking English language classes English is not their native language.

_____

3. Several companies had made offers to buy the patent, the

young inventor turned them down.

_____

_____

4. The basketball player had a severe cold he played an incredible game by scoring 40 points.

_____

_____

5. They did not buy new furniture they did not buy a new refrigerator.

_____

6. The tourists have packed their luggage, they are ready to check out.

_____

7. She likes to work out she spends two hours a day in the fitness center.

_____

8. He is now driving an electric car it is good for the environment.

_____

9. The old man wanted to withdraw money from his bank account at an ATM he forgot the password.

_____

_____

10. The university wanted to recruit elite students to its graduate programs, it offers them full scholarships.

_____

_____

8.4 從屬子句 (dependent / subordinate clauses)

從屬子句皆從從獨立子句變化而來，因此都具備有 主詞／主部＋動詞／述部 的結構，但卻不能單獨構成一個簡單句，而是必須與獨立子句**結合成為複句**。

從屬子句與獨立子句的區別在於**從屬子句都由從屬連接詞開頭**，從屬子句的開頭有可能是名詞子句的標記連接詞，引導出一個**名詞子句**；也可能是從屬副詞連接詞，引導出一個**副詞子句**；或是由關係代名詞，引導出一個**形容詞子句**。

名詞子句無論是作為句子的主詞、受詞、受詞補語、形容詞補語，都是句子**結構上不可或缺的元素**。

副詞子句與句子結構無關，而是用來**提供更多的資訊**，如事件發生的**時間、原因、順序、後果、條件**等等。

形容詞子句用來修飾名詞，與句子的結構無關，但其中的**限定用法形容詞子句，屬於表達涵義上必要的元素**；非限定用法形容詞子句則是補充用法，提供額外的資訊，屬於**表達涵義上非必要的元素**。

我們用下列例句加以說明：

(1) 名詞子句

律師確信<u>被告是無辜的</u>。

The lawyer believes $\boxed{\text{that}}$ **the defendant is innocent**.

（**that** 是標記名詞子句的連接詞，引導出名詞子句。**名詞子句不能單獨構成句子，必須內嵌於前面的獨立子句**，作爲動詞 believes 的**受詞**；因爲是**內嵌**，所以名詞子句作爲受詞是屬於**句子結構必要的元素**，兩者結合成爲一個**複句**。）

(2) 副詞子句

這位律師<u>自從十年前加入這家律師事務所之後</u>已經打贏很多大型官司。

The lawyer has won many big cases $\boxed{\text{since}}$ **she joined the law firm ten years ago**.

（**since** 爲從屬連接詞，引導出副詞子句。**副詞子句不能單獨構成句子，必須依附於前面的獨立子句**，因爲是**依附**，所以副詞子句**並非句子結構不可或缺的元素**，兩者也結合成爲一個**複句**。）

(3) 形容詞子句

這位律師已經幫助了很多<u>弱勢的</u>人。

The lawyer has helped many people $\boxed{\text{who}}$ **are underprivileged**.

（**who** 是關係代名詞，引導出一個形容詞子句。**形容詞子句不能單獨構成句子，必須依附於前面的獨立子句**，因爲是**依附**，所以形容詞子句**並非句子結構不可或缺的元素**，兩者也結合成爲一個複句。）

接下來，我們就要詳細介紹這三種不同類型的從屬子句（名詞子句、副詞子句、形容詞子句），包括它們的結構及功能，以便我們在英文寫作時能夠正確且靈活地運用從屬子句，將其內嵌或依附於獨立子句中，構成複句；或是在合句中再加入從屬子句而構成複合句，如此可以寫出結構較為複雜，富有變化，又合乎文法的英文句子，而能夠透過複句及複合句表達更豐富的涵義。

另外在副詞子句及形容詞子句部分，我們要進一步探討如何將副詞子句簡化為省略子句，以及如何將形容詞子句簡化為不同類型的片語，進而將原來的複句簡化成為簡單句。這些變化都是我們在英文寫作時必須熟練運用的技巧。

8.5 名詞子句 (noun clauses)

名詞子句為從屬子句，由敘述句、WH 疑問句、Yes/No 疑問句變化而來，並且扮演不同功能，例如：

1. 在浴室裏，父子兩人假裝**他們是躲藏在山洞裏**。
   *In the bathroom, the father and the son pretended **that they were hiding in a cave**.*
   （名詞子句由**連接詞 that** + 敘述句 **they were hiding in a cave** 變化而來，作為現在**動詞 pretended 的受詞**。）

2. 我們正努力絞盡腦汁想知道**這個事情能夠如何解決**。
   *We are trying to figure out **how the issue can be resolved**.*
   （名詞子句由 **WH 疑問句 How can the issue be resolved?** 變

化而來 → **how the issue can be resolved**，作為**介系詞的受詞**。）

3. **飛機航班是否準時**要視天氣狀況而定。
Whether the flight will be on schedule *depends on the weather condition.*
（名詞子句由 **Yes/No 疑問句 Will the flight be on schedule?變化而來 → Whether the flight will be on schedule**，作為句子的主詞。）

　　接下來我們要介紹名詞子句的功能，不同類別的名詞子句如何從敘述句與疑問句變化而來，以及在寫作上如何運用不同類別的名詞子句，充分發揮其功能。

▶▶ 8.5.1 名詞子句的功能

　　名詞子句的功能**與名詞相同**，可以作為**主詞**、**受詞**以及**主詞補語**；另外名詞子句也可以當作**形容詞補語**，但是名詞不能當作形容詞補語。當名詞子句作為主詞、受詞、主詞補語時，是嵌入在片語或獨立子句之中，屬於句子結構中不可或缺的元素，唯有當名詞子句作為形容詞補語時，是依附於獨立子句中，而非句子結構中不可或缺的元素。例如：

(1) 名詞子句作為 主詞

　　正確的飲食於健康有益是無庸置疑的。
That proper diet is good for health is beyond doubt.

　　Brian 在魔術表演中所表現的完全讓觀眾嚇到了。

What Brian performed in the magic show totally shocked the audience.

暴風雨是否會來襲還不確定。
Whether the storm will come is uncertain.

(2) 名詞子句作為 動詞的受詞

Brian 的父母不知道**他會變魔術**。
Brian's parents don't know **that he can do magic tricks**.

你有嘗試過**這部車可以跑多快**嗎？
Have you tried **how fast the car can run**?

她在考慮**是否要買一臺新電腦**。
She is considering **whether / if she will buy a new computer**.

(3) 名詞子句作為 主詞補語

Brian 所變的魔術之一是**他讓自己消失不見了**。
One of Brian's magic tricks is **that he makes himself disappear**.

這個國家的政治發展已經變成**分析家之前所預測的**。
The political development of the country has become **what the analyst predicted**.

主要的擔心是**新的領導人是否能夠將組織翻轉**。

The main concern is **whether / if the new leader can turn the organization around**.

(4) 名詞子句作爲 介系詞的受詞

教授要我們專注在這個理論如何解釋這樣的現象。

The professor wants us to concentrate on **how the theory explains the phenomenon**.

這個年輕的媽媽正在考慮是否應該辭去工作成爲全職母親。

The young mother is thinking about **whether she should quit her job to be a fulltime mother**.

(5) 名詞子句作爲 現在分詞的受詞

考量生活費過去幾年來已經有所上漲，政府已經決定把基本工資漲到每小時 15 塊美金。

Considering **that the living cost has been up in the past few years**, the government has decided to raise the minimum wage to US$15 per hour.

後悔在大學新鮮人頭一年不夠認眞念書，她誓言從現在開始要在課業的努力上保持專注。

Regretting **that she did not work hard enough during the freshman year in college**, she vows to stay focused on academic efforts from now on.

(6) 名詞子句作爲 動名詞的受詞

陪審團被誤導而相信被告在這個謀殺案中是無辜的。

The jury were fooled into believing **that the accused was** innocent in the murder case.

承認他一直以來對同事太過嚴苛，對經理而言一點也不容易。
Admitting **that he has been too harsh on the colleagues** is certainly not easy for the manager.

(7) 名詞子句作爲 形容詞的補語 （非句子結構中不可或缺的元素）
Brian 很開心他的朋友們享受他的魔術表演。
Brian is happy **that his friends enjoyed the magic show**.

他們不確定他們什麼時候會到達。
They are not sure **when they will arrive**.

新任的執行長感到樂觀，公司明年的銷售會有可觀的成長。
The new CEO is optimistic **that the company will have a substantial growth in sales next year**.

▶▶ 8.5.2 名詞子句的形成

　　名詞子句的形成可以是 (1) **在敘述句的開頭加上連接詞 that 所構成**，或是 (2) **由疑問句變化而成**。由疑問句變化而來的名詞子句又分爲兩種情況：一種是由 **WH 疑問句**變化而成，另一種則是由 **Yes/No 疑問句**變化而成。詳細說明如下：

名詞子句的形成	
敘述句加上連接詞 **that**	Jesus said **that** He was the way, the truth, and the life. **That** the sun rises in the east is predictable. She is grateful **that** she is blessed in her life.
WH 疑問句變化而成	They are investigating **why** it happened. **What** the teacher announced yesterday surprised everyone. 疑問詞：**who, what, why, where, when, how**（＋形容詞／副詞）, **which**（＋名詞）, **whose**（＋名詞）, **whom**
Yes/No 疑問句變化而成	We don't know **whether/if** she wants to join us **or not**. **Whether** he can keep the dog is up to his parents.

1. 敘述句變成名詞子句

　　這一類的變化最簡單，在運用的時候也不容易出錯，只要在敘述句的開頭加上連接詞 that 即可，例如：

　　That the Earth is round is beyond doubt.（敘述句開頭加 **that** 成為名詞子句，作為句子的主詞。）

　　（名詞子句作為主詞時，連接詞 **that** 是不可以省略的！）

He confirmed |that| the medical team had found the cure.
（敘述句開頭加 that 成爲名詞子句，作爲 confirmed 的受詞。）

The investigation **revealed** |that| **the failure of the break
system caused the accident**.（敘述句開頭加 **that** 成爲名詞子句，
作爲 confirmed 的受詞。）

（名詞子句作爲受詞時，連接詞 **that** 是可以省略的！）

2. WH 疑問句轉換成名詞子句

WH 疑問句變成名詞子句的過程如以下說明：

例如：

|How| **did** the magician **do** the trick?（**WH 疑問句**）

→ |how| the magician **did** the trick（名詞子句）

（how 之後的疑問句改成肯定句）

|Where| **does** your brother **work**?（**WH 疑問句**）

→ |where| your brother **works**（名詞子句）

（where 之後的疑問句改成肯定句）

|How many| bicycles **has** the company **sold** since 2010?
（**WH 疑問句**）

→ |how many| bicycles the company **has sold** since 2010
（名詞子句）

（how many 之後的疑問句改成肯定句）

|What| **will** she **invent** next time?（**WH 疑問句**）

→ |what| she **will invent** next time（名詞子句）

→（what 之後的**疑問句改成肯定句**）

WH 疑問句與名詞子句的差別：
(1) 疑問句是完整的句子，因此句尾有問號；名詞子句是從屬子句，本身不能單獨構成句子，必須內嵌在獨立子句中，因此子句句尾沒有句點或問號。
(2) 名詞子句的結構與直述句相同，並非疑問句的結構。

以下是更多 **WH 疑問句變成名詞子句**的例子：

When are they coming? 他們什麼時候來？（**WH 疑問句**）
→ **when they are** coming 他們什麼時候來（**名詞子句**）
Do you know **when they are coming?** 你知道**他們什麼時候來嗎**？（**名詞子句**）

Why did it happen? 這事爲什麼發生呢？（**WH 疑問句**）
→ **why it** happened 這事爲什麼發生（**名詞子句**）
Are they going to investigate **why it happened**? 他們會去調查**這事爲什麼發生嗎**？（**名詞子句**）

How cute is the puppy? 小狗有多可愛呢？（**WH 疑問句**）
→ **how cute** the puppy **is** 小狗有多可愛（**名詞子句**）
We are wondering **how cute the puppy is**. 我們心裡在想小狗有多可愛。（**名詞子句**）

How wonderful was the present? 禮物有多棒呢？（**WH 疑問句**）

→ **how wonderful** the present **was** 禮物有多棒（**名詞子句**）

The little girl realized **how wonderful the present was**. 小女孩明白了**禮物有多棒**。（**名詞子句**）

How often does she go shopping for groceries?
她多久去購買一次生鮮呢？（**WH 疑問句**）

→ **how often** she **goes** shopping for groceries 她多久去購買一次生鮮（**名詞子句**）

Her husband doesn't know **how often she goes shopping for groceries**.
她先生不知道**她多久去購買一次生鮮**。（**名詞子句**）

WH 子句之前不可以再加上 "that"，因此不可以寫成

*They don't know **that why** it happened.

正確寫法為：They don't know **why** it happened.

3. Yes/No 疑問句轉換成名詞子句

Yes/No 疑問句變成名詞子句一共有兩種不同的變化，其轉換過程說明如下：

Is he a good doctor?（Yes/No 疑問句）

→ I wonder if he is a good doctor.（名詞子句）
（Yes/No 疑問句改寫成肯定句，再於肯定句之前加上 **if**）

→ I wonder whether he is a good doctor.（名詞子句）

（Yes/No 疑問句改寫成肯定句，再於肯定句之前加上 **whether**）

補充說明：

if/whether 名詞子句也會與 "or not" 一起使用，如以下例句：

*I wonder if he is a good doctor **or not**.*

*I wonder whether he is a good doctor **or not**.*

*I wonder whether **or not** he is a good doctor.*

但是學術寫作講求精簡，因此盡量避免使用 **or not**.

貼心提醒

if/whether 名詞子句之前不可以再加上 "that"，因此**不可以**寫成

*He doubted **that whether** he would ever find the answer.

正確寫法為：He doubted **whether** he would ever find the answer.

8.5.3 WH 名詞子句的功能

WH 疑問句一旦變成名詞子句，就可以擔任不同的角色，包括：

(1) WH 名詞子句作為 受詞

(2) WH 名詞子句作為 主詞

兩者都可以嵌入於獨立子句中，與其結合成為複句。

1. WH 名詞子句作爲受詞

(a) 名詞子句嵌入在 肯定句 中作爲 受詞

Everyone wants to know **how the magician did the trick** .
They are trying to figure out **how many bicycles the company has sold since 2010** .

（句子最後的標點符號爲**句點**，而非問號，因爲整個句子的結構是肯定句，而非疑問句。）

(b) 名詞子句嵌入在 疑問句 中作爲 受詞

Do you know **where your brother works** ?
Can anyone predict **what she will invent next time** ?

（句子最後的標點符號爲**問號**，而非句點，因爲整個句子的結構是疑問句，而非肯定句。）

2. WH 名詞子句作爲主詞

魔術師是如何變這個戲法仍然是個謎團。
How the magician did the trick is a mystery.

你哥哥在何處工作依舊是祕密。
Where your brother works remains a secret.

自從去年以來公司賣了多少電動機車將於今天記者會公開。

How many electric scooters the company has sold since last year will be disclosed in the press conference today.

她下次會發明什麼令大家好奇。

What she will invent next time makes everyone curious.

新房子多久會蓋好端視天氣如何。

How soon the new house will be built is up to the weather.

學費多貴視學生是否來自本州或其他地方。

How expensive the tuition is depends on whether the students are from the state or other places.

（名詞子句作為主詞視為單數）

 8.5.4 whether / if 名詞子句的功能

　　Yes/No 疑問句轉換成名詞子句時，所用的連接詞是 **if 或 whether** 就是 " **是否** " 的意思。這類的 whether / if 名詞子句的作用包括：

(1) **whether** / **if** 引導的名詞子句內嵌於敘述句或疑問句中作為**動詞的受詞**

(2) **whether** / **if** 引導的名詞子句依附於敘述句或疑問句中作為**形容詞的補語**

(3) **whether** 引導的名詞子句內嵌於敘述句或疑問句中作為**介系詞的受詞**

(4) whether 引導的名詞子句內嵌於敘述句或疑問句中作爲**主詞補語**

(5) whether 引導的名詞子句內嵌於敘述句中作爲**句子的主詞**

　　上述的五種作用中，(1) 跟 (2) 的名詞子句都可以由 **whether 或 if** 引導，但是 (3)、(4)、(5) 的名詞子句則**只有 whether** 可以引導。

貼心提醒

Whether 名詞子句與 if 名詞子句兩者皆可作為動詞的受詞與形容詞的補語，但只有 **whether** 名詞子句才能作爲介系詞的受詞，主詞補語，以及句子的主詞。

1. whether / if 名詞子句作爲動詞的受詞

(a) whether / if 名詞子句內嵌於敘述句中作爲動詞的受詞：

我們想知道是否應該穿著正式服裝去參加宴會。

We are wondering whether / if we should wear formal clothing to the party.

這位專家無法判定這幅畫作是否爲眞跡。

The expert can't determine whether / if the painting is authentic.

公司想要知道**這個業務員是否誠實**。

The company wants to know | **whether / if** | **the salesman is honest**.

他們不知道**他們是否能捱過這種嚴苛的訓練**。

They didn't know | **whether / if** | **they could survive the harsh training**.

說明：因為整句的結構是**敘述句**，所以句尾標點符號是**句點**。連接詞 **if/whether** 不能省略！

(b) whether / if 名詞子句內嵌於 疑問句 中作為 受詞 ：

你知不知道**這臺機器是否可以運作**嗎？

Do you know | **whether / if** | **the machine works**?

你知不知道**這場表演是否會準時開始**呢？

Do you know | **whether / if** | **the show will start on time**?

你知不知道**電費帳單是否已經繳**了呢？

Did you know | **whether / if** | **electricity bill had been paid**?

說明：因為整句的結構是**疑問句**，所以句尾標點符號是**問號**。連接詞 **whether / if** 不能省略！

2. whether / if 名詞子句作爲形容詞補語

(a) whether / if 名詞子句，內嵌於 敘述句 中作爲 形容詞補語

> 他們不確定**她是不是受害者其中一位**。
>
> They were not **sure** whether / if she was one of the victims.
>
> 他不確定**這個疾病是否會傳染**。
>
> He was not **certain** whether / if the disease was infectious.

(b) whether / if 名詞子句，內嵌於 疑問句 中作爲 形容詞補語

> 她還不確定**她是否要買一臺新的洗衣機**嗎？
>
> Is she not **sure** whether / if she wants to buy a new washing machine?
>
> 他們不確定**他們是否要搭乘遊輪去度假**嗎？
>
> Were they not certain whether / if they would go on a vacation on a cruise?

3. whether 名詞子句作爲介系詞的受詞

由 **whether** 引導的名詞子句可以作爲**介系詞的受詞**，但是由 **if** 引導的名詞子句則不可以。

(a) whether 名詞子句，內嵌於 敘述句 中作爲 介系詞的受詞

> 他們在討論**新的措施是否會有效**。
>
> They are talking about whether the new measures will be

effective.

研究人員正試圖弄明白**曝露在陽光下是否有助於治療癌症**。

The researchers are trying to figure out whether exposing to sunlight will help treat the cancer.

(b) whether 名詞子句，內嵌於 疑問句 中作爲 介系詞的受詞

調查人員有沒有已經調查了**是否人爲疏失造成這起意外**呢？

Has the investigator looked into whether human errors caused the accident?

這個會議會不會把焦點放在**服裝的規定是否應該要修改**呢？

Will the meeting focus on whether the dress code should be modified?

4. whether 名詞子句作爲主詞補語

　　由 **whether** 引導的名詞子句可以作爲**主詞補語**，但是由 **if** 引導的名詞子句則**不可以**。

(a) whether 名詞子句內嵌於敘述句，作爲 主詞補語 。

爭議點在於**我們是否應該繼續使用核能發電**。

The issue is whether we should continue to use nuclear power.

(b) 由 **whether** 引導的名詞子句內嵌於疑問句，作為 主詞補語 。

是否要辯論的題目是不是**大麻是否應該合法化**？

Is the topic of the debate whether recreational cannabis should be legalized?

5. whether 名詞子句作為主詞

　　由 **whether** 引導的名詞子句可以作為句子的**主詞**，但是由 **if** 引導的名詞子句則**不可以**。

(a) whether 名詞子句內嵌於敘述句，作為句子的 主詞 。

是否要送他們小孩上私立學校令他們困擾。

Whether they should send their kids to a private school puzzles them.

（名詞子句作為主詞視為單數）

(b) whether 名詞子句內嵌於疑問句，作為句子的 主詞 。

能否讓小孩養寵物是不是由媽媽決定呢？

Is whether the kids can keep a pet up to their mother?

（名詞子句作為主詞視為單數）

⟩⟩ 8.5.5 小試身手

填入適當的的連接詞以完成句子中的名詞子句

(一) 名詞子句作為主詞

1. _____ the magician did the trick is a mystery.

2. _____ she said was convincing.

3. _____ the experiment failed to prove the theory is yet to be determined.

4. _____ far the new invention will take us is still unknown.

5. _____ she has done for the community deserves everyone's respect.

6. _____ learning how to play tennis requires a lot of practice discourages many potential learners.

7. _____ much the project will cost is hard to estimate now.

8. _____ the team will win the championship depends very much on the players' competitiveness and team work.

(二) 名詞子句作為受詞或補語

1. A: Do you know _____ he will leave the country?

   B: I think it's next week.

2. The researcher will conduct an experiment to find out _____ the use of smartphones affects one's social skills.

3. Are they not sure _____ they can hunt geese in this area?

4. A: There are so many children in the park. Can you tell me
   _____ one your child is?

   B: Oh, she is the one playing on the swing.

5. The investigation team will try to determine _____
   human errors caused the plane crash.

6. It is essential _____ modern citizens understand the
   importance of sustainable use of our natural resources.

7. That Jesus sacrificed himself on the cross revealed _____
   precious God's grace is.

8. A: Did the police discover _____ the thief hid the stolen items?

   B: Yes, they found them in an abandoned house.

9. The new president vows _____ he will revive the
   economy of the country.

10. She has proven herself through _____ she coped with
    the adversity.

11. They don't know _____ they will succeed in the end;
    however, they will keep doing _____ they are doing
    now.

12. She was disappointed _____ her students did not do
    well in the exam.

13. Are they not certain _____ students can take more
    than 25 credit hours in a semester?

14. A recent poll indicated _____ companies plan to in-
    crease their hiring of new college graduates by 8.6% this year.

15. Have they figured out _____ they should build a deck
    in the back of their house?

➤➤ 8.5.6 名詞子句打通關

使用名詞子句將劃底線部分翻成英文

1. 此項研究結果顯示睡眠不足可能導致嚴重的疾病。

   The results of the study reveal _____

   _____.

2. Julia 很傷心，她把新買的智慧手機搞丟了。

   Julia was sad _____.

3. 市政府將要決定這個方案以有限的預算是否可行。

   The city government will decide _____

   _____.

4. 我們可能無法完全體會父母們願意為他們的孩子付出什麼代價。

   We may not fully realize _____

   _____.

5. 全球化可能造成工業化國家與開發中國家之間更大的差距是目前的熱門話題。

   _____ is

   now a hot topic.

6. 你在質疑她是否會成為軍中好的領導者嗎？

   Are you questioning _____

   _____?

7. 是否應該要蓋一座新的國際機場是新政府的主要議題。

   _____ is a major is-

   sue for the new government.

8. 這項研究計畫是否能夠達成其目標取決於研究團隊的努力與合作。

   _____ depends

on the efforts and collaboration of the research team.

9. 她最大的成就是經過多年的努力獲得了電腦博士學位。

Her greatest achievement is _____

_____

10. 這項手術是否必要仍在討論中。 _____

_____ is still in discussion.

11. 新的商業區的開發會如何影響環境將會是聽證會的焦點。

_____ will

be the focus of the hearing.

12. 他們聽到臺北舊公寓的房租有多貴是不是很驚訝？

Were they surprised to hear _____

_____?

13. 他們正在探討改變飲食是否能夠幫助治癒癌症。

They are looking into _____

_____.

14. 上星期參訪過孤兒院之後，他們意識到他們多麼幸運有他們自己的家庭以及他們可以為孤兒們做什麼。

After visiting the orphanage last week, they realized _____

_____ and

_____.

15. 在高階寫作課，學生將學習什麼是研究報告以及他們應該如何進行研究。

In the advanced writing class, _____

_____.

8.5.7 名詞子句挑戰題

將全句翻成英文，劃底線的部分要使用名詞子句。

1. 天氣狀況是不是將會決定這座新的體育館的建造什麼時候可以完成呢？

_____

_____

2. 政府正在考量基因改造食品的強制標示是否應該由法律加以規範。

_____

_____

_____

3. 我們從課本所學到的只是人類知識的一小部分，而我們從人生經驗所學到的比較珍貴。

_____

_____

_____

4. 這架飛機怎麼墜毀的還在調查當中。

_____

5. 我們是否要容許員工彈性上班將會在下週的會議上討論並以投票決定。

_____

_____

_____

6. 即將畢業的大學生表示說他們非常感激系上教授這四年來在課堂上所教導他們的。

_____

_____

_____

7. 讀研究所期間她是否需要兼差打工是不是她最主要的關切呢？

_____ ?

8. 機器人實在不可思議，他們組裝汽車比工人有效率多了，所以將來機器人是否在其他製造業會取代人工是不難預測的。

_____

_____

9. 要成為為國際航空公司工作的職業機師非常困難不會阻擋他追尋他開飛機的夢想。

_____

_____

10. 價格跟品質將會決定一項新產品能否在競爭激烈的市場生存下來。

_____

_____

11. 研究人員正專注在新的方法是否會導致所期望的結果。

_____

_____

12. 僅僅藉由曝露在其中即可習得人類語言的能力是內建在我們腦袋裏一事，著實令人驚嘆。

_____

_____

13. 知道智慧家電用品會是市場上的熱門商品，這家公司已經投資了一大筆可觀的經費來研發該類產品。

_____

_____

14. 要證明這個理論是正確的需要進行設計恰當的實驗。

_____

_____

15. 預測豪大雨會再持續幾天，氣象局警告河邊的居民應該注意洪水爆發。

_____

_____

 8.5.8 名詞子句與引述動詞

　　名詞子句作爲受詞往往是接在**引述動詞** (reporting verbs) 之後，如以下例句：

The new manager **proposes** **that** **the company adopt a new organizational structure to improve its efficiency**.

The mayor **concluded** **that** **the city government would build a new school in the fast developing area**.

　　引述動詞也可以先接受詞，再接名詞子句，例如：

They **informed** **us** **that** **the proposal had been approved**.

Her boss **promised** **her** **that** **she would get a raise**.

因此，我們歸納出來**引述動詞 + 名詞子句**句型有兩種，列表如下：

引述動詞 + 名詞子句	
引述動詞 + **that** 名詞子句	He admitted that he had lied.
引述動詞 + 受詞 + **that** 名詞子句	Her boss promised her that she would get a raise.

1. 引述動詞 + that 名詞子句

引述動詞使用於引述句 (reported speech)，最常見的就是 "say" 和 "tell"。

例如：

He **said that he would sign the contract**.（動詞 say + that + 名詞子句）

He **told me that he would sign the contract**.（動詞 tell + 受詞 + that + 名詞子句）

除了這兩個動詞之外，英文還有其他許多常用的引述動詞，這些引述動詞的用法有的跟 "say" 句型一樣，有的跟 "tell" 句型一樣。以下分別加以介紹。

與 "say" 一樣句型的引述動詞：動詞 + that 名詞子句			
add 進一步表示	believe 相信	**demand*** 要求	hope 希望
admit 承認	boast 吹噓	deny 否認	imagine 想像
advise* 忠告	claim 宣稱	determine 決定	imply 暗示
agree 同意	comment 評論	doubt 懷疑	indicate 指出 / 表明
allege 宣稱	complain 抱怨	estimate 估計	**insist*** 堅持
announce 宣佈	confess 認錯 / 認罪	explain 解釋	mean 意謂
answer 回答	confirm 確認	fear 害怕	mention 提及
argue 論理 / 辯解 / 主張	consider 考量 / 認為	feel 感覺	note 注意到 / 指明
assert 斷言	declare 宣告	guarantee 保證	observe 觀察

與 "say" 一樣句型的引述動詞：動詞 + that 名詞子句			
persuade 說服	recommend* 推薦	reveal 揭露 / 顯示	understand 了解
pledge 誓言 / 許諾	request 請求	say 說	verify 驗證 / 證實
pray 祈禱	remark 發表談話	state 敘述	vow 發誓
predict 預測	remember 記得	suggest* 建議	warn 警告
prefer* 偏好	repeat 重覆	suppose 假定	wonder 心中想著
promise 承諾	reply 回答	think 認為 / 考慮	worry 擔憂
propose* 提議	report 報告	threaten 威脅	
reason 推理	regret 後悔		

例句：

The government announced that there would be a tax reduction next year.

They estimated that repairing the house might cost over ten thousand dollars.

貼心提醒

advise, demand, insist, prefer, propose, recommend 以及 suggest 這幾個動詞後面所接的名詞子句中的主要動詞必須用**原型動詞**。

如以下例句：

The doctor **suggests** (that) he **exercise** (not exercises) at least thirty minutes a day.

The landlord **insisted** (that) we **pay** (not paid) the rent once in three months.

2. 引述動詞 + 受詞 + that + 名詞子句

這一類的句型是在引述動詞後面先接受詞，再接 that 所引導的名詞子句。

例如：

The spokesman **told the reporters that** the hostage had been rescued.

The teacher **reminded the students that** the assignment would be due next week.

與 "tell" 一樣句型的引述動詞：動詞 + 受詞 + that 名詞子句	
advise* 忠告 / 勸告	promise 答應 / 保證
assure 使確信 / 使放心	reassure 使放心 / 使消除疑慮
convince 使信服 / 說服	remind 提醒
inform 告知 / 提供訊息	tell 告訴
notify 通知 / 告知	warn 警告
persuade 說服 / 勸服	

例句：

The committee **informed Steven** that he should submit the necessary files before Friday.

The realtor **convinced the lady** that it was the best time to purchase a new house.

> **advise** 這個動詞後面所接的名詞子句中的動詞必須用**原型動詞**。
> 例如：The lawyer advised his client that he **file**（原型動詞）a
> lawsuit against the government.

1. 引述動詞的時態為簡單現在式或現在式進行式，名詞子句的時
   式可能是簡單現在式、現在進行式、簡單未來式、或現在完成
   式。

   例如：

   She **says / is saying** that she **wants** to buy us hamburgers.

   She **says / is saying** that she **is buying** us hamburgers.

   She **says / is saying** that she **will (may, can)** buy us hamburgers.

   She **says / is saying** that she **has bought** us hamburgers.

2. 引述動詞的時式為簡單過去式或過去進行式，名詞子句的時態
   可能是簡單過去式、過去進行式，助動詞 will, may, can 要改
   成 would, might, could，或是過去完成式。

   例如：

   She **said / was saying** that she **wanted** to buy us hamburgers.

   She **said / was saying** that she **was buying** us hamburgers.

She **said / was saying** that she **would (might, could)** buy us hamburgers.

She **said / was saying** that she **had bought** us hamburgers.

▶▶ 8.5.9 小試身手

使用引述動詞及名詞子句將下列中文句子翻成英文（一個空格填一個英文單字）

1. 這位市長候選人估計選舉至少會讓她花掉至少三千萬臺幣。

The _____ running for Mayor _____ that the _____ will _____ her at least NT$30,000,000.

2. 新的高中校長向家長承諾說他在他領導下學校會成爲卓越。

The new _____ of the high school _____ the parents that under his _____ the school would _____ .

3. 營養專家建議她少吃油炸的食物。

The _____ _____ that she _____ less _____ _____ food.

4. 研究人員宣稱他們找到老人痴呆症的原因了。

The researchers _____ that they have _____ the _____ of _____ .

5. 一位食品科學專家透露某些食物會增強我們的免疫系統。

An _____ in food science _____ that certain foods will _____ our _____ .

6. 籃球隊教練要求球員準時到球場練球。

The coach of the basketball team d_____ed the players

_____ to the basketball _____ _____

_____ to _____ .

7. 氣象學者警告說溫室效應將使海平面上升並淹沒海岸邊的城市。

_____ _____ that _____ _____

would _____ the sea level to _____ and inun-

date cities in _____ areas.

8. 精神科醫師建議病患要他每天服用處方的藥物。

The psychiatrist a_____ed the _____ that he

_____ the _____ medications on a daily _____ .

9. 研究結果指出曝露於電子產品可能會對兒童有負面的影響。

The _____ of the study _____ that

to _____ devices may have a _____ impact

_____ children.

10. 在昨天的辯論過程中，對手主張全球化對跨國企業比對開發中
    國家的個人更有利。

During the debate yesterday, the _____

that _____ _____ multinational _____

more than the _____ in the _____ countries.

8.5.10 引述名詞子句挑戰題

翻譯全句為英文，劃底線部分要使用名詞子句。

1. 專家們斷言特斯拉的電動汽車很快將嚴重威脅到傳統汽車產業。

_____

_____

2. 汽車駕駛被抓到超速，然而他辯解說他是急著送他太太去醫院。

3. 經過三天的搜尋，搜救隊透過無線電證實他們已經找到失蹤的登山客生還但是虛弱。

4. 建築師堅持所有用來蓋這間飯店的材料要符合政府的規定。

5. 工廠的工人抱怨說太差的工作環境導致工作效率不佳。

6. 諮商期間，教授建議 (advise) 他繼續在生物化學領域攻讀 (pursue) 博士學位。

7. 抗議群眾要求 (demand) 政府立刻釋放上個月被逮捕的反對黨的政治領袖。

8. 從 DNA 化驗所得到的新證據顯示嫌犯並未犯下這個罪行。

9. 在令人佩服的簡報之後，這家廣告公司說服了這家軟性飲料製造商它可以為其新產品製作最有創意的電視和網路廣告。

10.昨天的會議上，財務分析師提議公司與其市場上的主要競爭對手合併，但是她也提醒大家合併時會有風險。

_____

_____

_____

8.6 副詞子句 (adverbial clauses)

　　副詞子句，是以不同的從屬連接詞來表達不同的涵義，例如**地點、時間、方式、原因、結果、條件**等等。副詞子句為從屬子句，必須與獨立子句結合形成結構完整的複句。

　　副詞子句依附於獨立子句所構成的複句句型有兩類：
1. **副詞子句在前，獨立子句在後**。（中英文結構相同）
  Because it was raining, they decided to stay home.
  因為下雨，他們決定待在室內。

  Even though it's very hot in the summer, the old man never turns on the air conditioner.
  儘管夏天非常炎熱，這位老人家從來不開冷氣。

2. **獨立子句在前，副詞子句在後**。（中英文結構可能不同，因為中文的副詞子句往往是出現在句子前面。）
  The children get excited **whenever they are watching cartoons**.
  每當小孩在看卡通的時候，（他們）就會感到興奮。

You may hurt your eyes **if you use the cellphone in the dark**.
如果在暗處使用手機，你可能會傷害到你的眼睛。

　　兩種句型的差別在於**副詞子句在前的情況，必須在副詞子句尾端加上逗點**，而獨立子句在前的情況則不必加逗點。

while 及 whereas 所引導的副詞子句屬於例外，即使放**在獨立子句之後，獨立子句尾端仍須加上逗點**。

People in modern cities enjoy convenient medical care, **whereas** those in rural areas have much less access to hospitals or clinics.

住在現代化都市的人享有便利的醫療，**反之在農村的人則僅有很少的醫院或診所可以去看病**。

8.6.1 副詞子句的功能與引導副詞子句的從屬連接詞

　　副詞子句的功能包括下列所要表達的涵義，而**不同的涵義**則用**不同的從屬連接詞**來表達：

副詞子句的功能	
目的	從屬連接詞
表達時間	after 在…之後, as 當…的時候, as soon as 一…就…, before 在…之前, once 一旦, (not)…until 直到…才…, when 在…的時候, since 自從…以來, while 當…的時候, by the time 到了…的時候, whenever 無論何時, every time 每次, the first time 第一次, the next time 下一次, the last time 上一次, (no sooner)…than 一…就…
表達地點	where 哪裡, wherever 無論哪裡, anywhere 任何地方, everywhere 每個地方
表達方式	as 像…一樣, as if 彷彿, as though 彷彿, like 像…一樣, the way 照…的方式
表達程度或比較	than 比…, as...as 如同…一樣…, (not) so...as（不）如同…一樣
表達原因	as 基於／隨著, because 因為, since 因為, now that 既然, in that 因為
表達結果	so + 形容詞…that 如此…以至於…, such + 名詞…that 如此…的一位…以至於…,
表達條件	if 如果／假使, unless 除非, only if 唯有在…的條件下, in case 萬一, as long as 只要, suppose 假設, whether…or not 無論是否
表達目的	in order that 為了…的目的, so that 為了…, lest 唯恐／免得
表達直接對比	while 與…同時, whereas 反之／鑒於…

副詞子句的功能	
目的	從屬連接詞
表達讓步	though 儘管…（可是），although 儘管…（可是），even though 儘管…（可是），while 然而，whereas 而，even if 即使，whichever (no matter which) 無論哪一個，whoever (no matter who) 無論什麼人，whenever (no matter when) 無論什麼時間

1. 表達時間 (after, as, as soon as, before, since, until, when, while, by the time, whenever, every time, the first time, the next time, the last time, no sooner… than)

When they arrived at the airport, a tour bus was waiting to pick them up.（當…的時候）

The gold medal winner has been practicing swimming since she was six.（自從）

The firefighters did not leave until the fire was completely put out.（直到）

As soon as the meeting was over, they rushed to the party.（一…，就…）

As railroads expanded west, hopeful settlers pushed into a territory that had been occupied for thousands of years by native Americans.（隨著）

The phone rang while she was cooking.（正當…時候）

The meeting had finished by the time he got there.（…的時候）

$\boxed{\text{Whenever}}$ there is a snow storm, the schools will be closed.
（無論什麼時候）

$\boxed{\text{Once}}$ the dog saw Lisa, it ran out of the house to her.（一⋯，就⋯）

No sooner had the little boy seen his mother $\boxed{\text{than}}$ he burst into tears.（一⋯就⋯）

（"no sooner⋯than" 所表達的涵義是主要子句跟副詞子句的狀況幾乎同時發生，而且 "no sooner" 引導的主要子句的時態為過去完成式，"than" 引導的副詞子句的時態則為簡單過去式，同時主要子句必須倒裝。）

這種句型可以改寫成以 "as soon as" 所引導的副詞子句與主要子句構成的複句如下：

= As soon as the little boy saw his mother, he burst into tears.
= The little boy burst into tears as soon as he saw his mother.
（注意：主要子句與副詞子句的時態均為簡單過去式。）

2. 表達地點 (where, wherever, anywhere, everywhere)

$\boxed{\text{Where}}$ there is a will, there is a way.（哪裡）

$\boxed{\text{Wherever}}$ the celebrity goes, many paparazzi will follow.（無論哪裡）

The police will find him anywhere he hides.（任何地點）

3. 表達方式 (as, as if, as though, like, the way)

He works really hard $\boxed{\text{as (/as if/as though/like)}}$ everyday were the last day of his life.（仿如，正如）

The coach trains the players the way he was trained.（以…
的方式）

4. 表達程度或比較 (than, as...as, so...as, the...the)

The object is closer than it appears in the mirror.（比… ）

He is not so smart as he thinks he is.（如同… ）

5. 表達原因 (as, because, given, since, now that, in that)

Now that she is an adult, she is legally responsible for what
she does.（既然）

They will get a discount since they are members.（既然，因
爲）

The team did not offer the player a new contract in that he
did not pass the physical examination.（因爲）

6. 表達結果 (so…that, such…that)

She is so intelligent that the math teacher likes to challenge her with difficult math problems.（so 後面要接
形容詞）

She is such an intelligent student that the math teacher
likes to challenge her with difficult math problems.（such
後面要接名詞或名詞片語）

7. 表達條件 (if, unless, only if, in case, whether…or not)

In case there is a fire, we should avoid taking the elevator.
（萬一）

We will stick to our original plan unless someone has a better solution.（除非）

The sales representative will receive an extra bonus only if he reaches the goal set by the company.（只有在….的條件下）

Whether you are convinced or not, you have to do it.（無論是否）

8. 表達目的 (in order that, so that, lest)

In order that the new restaurant will attract customers, it offers special discounts on the opening week.（爲了要….）

The owner of the house will have to renovate the house so that he can sell it at a better price.（才能夠達到…. 的目的）

The players spend time warming up lest they (should) get hurt in the game.

球員花時間熱身**以免**比賽時受傷。

= The players spend time warming up **for fear that** they **(should) get** hurt in the game.

= The players spend time warming up **for fear of getting** hurt in the game.

> ### 說明
>
> "lest" 所接的副詞子句中的動詞爲原形動詞，前面會出現 "should"，所表達的意思不是應該，而是**可能性**，並且**發生的可能性不高**。**"should" 可以省略**，而動詞仍舊維持原形動詞。"lest" 爲**正式用法**，僅用於非常正式的書面文件，目前較常使用表達相同涵義的句型是 "for fear that" 或是 "for fear of"。

9. 表達直接對比 (while, whereas)

While she loves classical music, her husband is a big fan of rock and roll.

The supermarkets in industrial countries dump tons of unsold food on a daily basis, whereas people in poor countries are starving.

（注意：**while** 及 **whereas** 所引導的副詞子句如果**放在獨立子句之後**，該獨立子句仍然須加逗點。）

10. 表達讓步 (though, although, even though, while, whereas, even if, whichever/no matter which, whoever/no matter who, whenever/no matter when)

Even though Danny is smaller than his opponent, he managed to beat him in the match.（儘管）

Whenever/No matter when you need help, we will always be there.（無論什麼時候）

You must keep working hard whichever/no matter which career path you choose.（無論哪一個）

▶▶ 8.6.2 小試身手

圈選恰當的從屬連接詞以完成句子中的副詞子句。

1. _____ the government announced the new college tuition policy, most of the college students and their parents angrily protested.

   A. Though　　B. When　　C. If　　　D. Unless

2. Many investors are selling their stocks _____ the economy is not looking good.

A. as   B. even though

C. until   D. in case

3. He went to the store and bought a gift for his girlfriend
   _____ he got his first pay check.

   A. once   B. as though   C. even if   D. as if

4. The professor promised the students he would take them to
   the KFC _____ they did well in the exam.

   A. until   B. unless   C. if   D. although

5. _____ the general public may put a lot of emphasis on
   a graduate's alma mater, hiring managers do not.

   A. While   B. Because   C. Since   D. As

6. The new product has created millions of revenue _____
   it was introduced six months ago.

   A. when   B. the way   C. though   D. since

7. _____ his friends do not believe in him, his wife remains his strongest supporter.

   A. As if   B. In that   C. Even if   D. Since

8. _____ the manager was in a meeting with an important
   client, he was interrupted by his secretary.

   A. Because   B. Now that   C. While   D. Whenever

9. _____ Mr. Huang's qualifications are better than other
   candidates, we should hire him as our new sales and marketing manager.

   A. Since   B. Although   C. Unless   D. As

10. The international flights will be delayed _____ the heavy
    snow on the runways is plowed and cleared in time.

    A. until   B. even though   C. unless   D. because

11. The rich woman lives a simple life _____ she didn't have not much money to spend.

   A. so that   B. although   C. now that   D. like

12. They will not stop protesting _____ the government abolishes the law prohibiting indigenous people to hunt in their own land.

   A. when   B. until   C. as soon as   D. once

13. _____ the guests have left the house, the couple need to start cleaning.

   A. If   B. Now that   C. Until   D. The way

14. The mechanic would not stop working _____ the engine was fixed and started running.

   A. as   B. whenever   C. until   D. while

15. _____ people in the past wrote letters to correspond, nowadays most people use smartphones to send instant messages to one another.

   A. Since   B. Whereas   C. The way   D. In case

16. The young girl determined to travel around the island by cycling _____ both of her hands had been amputated.

   A. although   B. as soon as   C. unless   D. after

17. _____(1)_____ we go hiking in the woods, we always bring umbrellas with us _____(2)_____ it rains.

   (1) A. Once   B. After   C. Even if   D. When

   (2) A. in case   B. even though   C. since   D. as

18. They hired the lawyer _____ he has won many civil lawsuits.

   A. while   B. as soon as   C. because   D. as if

19. The pastor gave me his cellphone number _____(1)_____ I could reach him _____(2)_____ I needed to.

(1) A. in that B. even though C. even if   D. so that

(2) A. until   B. whenever   C. while   D. as

20. He said he would return to Taiwan _____ he obtained his doctoral degree.

A. until   B. as soon as   C. as if   D. as

21. _____ college students from wealthy families travel abroad to enjoy the summer vacation, those who are on tuition loans may need to work during the summer to make ends meet.

A. As   B. Unless   C. If   D. While

22. Wisdom is the reward you get for a lifetime of listening _____ you'd preferred to talk. (*Doug Larson*)

A. in case   B. because   C. when   D. since

23. Be nice to people on your way up _____ you'll meet them on your way down. (*Wilson Mizner*)

A. because   B. only if   C. once   D. so that

24. _____ you cry because the sun has gone out of your life, your tears will prevent you from seeing the stars. (*Anonymous*)

A. As   B. As soon as   C. Unless   D. If

25. _____ she took over the company, its business has expanded to India and Russia.

A. When   B. The first time   C. Since   D. As

▶▶ 8.6.3 副詞子句簡化為省略子句 (elliptical clauses)

在寫作的運用上，如果副詞子句的主詞與獨立子句的主詞一致時，可以將副詞子句簡化成為省略子句，而仍然維持其所要表達的涵義。

副詞子句的簡化有三種情況：

(1) 副詞子句為主動語態

(2) 副詞子句為被動語態

(3) 副詞子句的動詞為 be 動詞

底下分別以例句說明其簡化過程：

1. 主動語態副詞子句簡化為省略子句

When **she** looked at the Statute of Liberty, **she** got very emotional.

（先決條件：副詞子句的主詞與獨立子句的主詞同為 **she**）

→ When **looking** at the Statue of Liberty, she got very emotional.

（主詞和 be 動詞同時省略，動詞改為現在分詞。）

→ **Looking** at the Statue of Liberty, she got very emotional.

（連接詞 when 也省略了）

After he had saved enough money, he left the company to start his own business.

→ **After having saved enough money**, he left the company to start his own business.

（主詞省略，動詞改為現在分詞片語）

→ **Having saved enough money**, he left the company to start his own business.

（主詞和連接詞 after 同時省略，動詞改為現在分詞片語）

2. 被動語態副詞子句簡化為省略子句

Though the young man is underpaid, he works as hard as other employees.

→ **Though underpaid**, the young man works as hard as other employees.

（主詞和 be 動詞同時省略，though 不能省略）

Before he was promoted, he had been teaching at the university for 15 years.

→ **Before being promoted**, he had been teaching at the university for 15 years.

（主詞省略，而 **before 由連接詞變身為介系詞，因此 be 動詞改為動名詞**，作為**介系詞的受詞**，before 不能省略。）

before 已經由連接詞變身為**介系詞**，因此若改寫成 **Before promoted**, he had been teaching at the university for 15 years. 這個句子是**不合文法**，是**錯誤的**。

After she is appointed the new manager of the branch office in Germany, she will have to leave her country next week.

→ **After being appointed the new manager of the branch office in Germany**, she will have to leave her country.

（主詞省略，而 **after** 由連接詞變身為介系詞，因此 **be** 動詞改為動名詞，作為介系詞的受詞，after 不能省略。）

after 已經由連接詞變身為**介系詞**，因此若改寫成 **After appointed** the new manager of the branch office in Germany, she will have to leave her country. 這個句子是**不合文法**，是**錯誤的**。

3. 副詞子句的動詞為 be 動詞時簡化為省略子句

(1) be 動詞後面接介系詞片語

Whenever you are in trouble, you can always call me.

→**Whenever in trouble**, you can always call me.

（主詞和 **be** 動詞同時省略，whenever 不能省略）

(2) be 動詞後面接形容詞片語

Unless he is insane, he will be sentenced to life in prison for what he has committed.

→**Unless insane**, he will be sentenced to life in prison for what he has committed.

（主詞和 **be** 動詞同時省略，unless 不能省略）

(3) be 動詞後面接名詞片語

Although he was an experienced detective, he could not solve the mysterious case.

→**Although an experienced detective**, he could not solve the mysterious case.

（主詞和 **be** 動詞同時省略，although 不能省略）

重點提醒：

副詞子句簡化為省略子句時，其前提是**副詞子句與主要子句的主詞兩者必須一致**，否則會造成**脫節修飾語**的錯誤，如下列例子：

While working out in the basement, her cellphone rang.
這個句子似乎可以翻成中文為：**在地下室健身時，她的手機響了。**

乍看之下好像正確，其實是不合英文文法的。因為原來的**副詞子句的主詞為 she**，而**主要子句的主詞卻是 her cellphone**，**兩者並不一致**，從而造成**脫節修飾語**。
正確的寫法如下：
While working out in the basement, she heard her cellphone ring.

（有關脫節修飾語請詳讀第十二章**誤置與脫節修飾語**）

▶▶ 8.6.4 小試身手

將下列句子中的副詞子句簡化為省略子句

1. Even though the song is simple in its lyrics and melody, it has become very popular.

---

2. When it was first introduced, the new model did not attract

many buyers.

3. Although she was the only eyewitness, she refused to testify in the court.

4. After he had obtained the certificate, he asked for a raise.

5. Unless one is proven guilty, a person is assumed innocent.

6. The car will be parked in the evidence garage after it is impounded.

7. Before he became a Christian, he had been leading a miserable life.

8. Don't hesitate to express your opinions if you are in a meeting with your colleagues.

9. She runs marathons several times a year though she is no longer young.

10. Before she wrote the bestselling novel, she had been a school teacher.

11. Tourists won't miss visiting the National Palace Museum when they are in Taipei.

12. Tom will be promoted after he has been successfully trained in the program.

_____

13. She would not easily give up when she was determined to do something.

_____

14. Since she quit her job, she has managed to open an online store selling frozen dumplings.

_____

15. While they were hiking, they found a wounded rabbit.

_____

▶▶ 8.6.5 副詞子句挑戰題

中翻英（劃底線的部分為副詞子句）

1. 蚊子<u>一旦叮咬過某些傳染病的患者</u>，就可能將病毒傳給其他人。（105 年指考）

_____

_____

2. 大部分學生不習慣自己解決問題，<u>他們總是期待老師提供標準答案</u>。（98 年學測）

_____

_____

3. <u>如果我們只為自己而活</u>，就不會真正地感到快樂。（96 年學測）

_____

_____

4. <u>只要我們持續認真努力</u>，我們會學會流利地說外國話。

5. 雖然不允許室內抽菸的規定遭到許多癮君子的反對，對不抽菸的人它的確是一大福音。（95 年指考）

6. 除非牠們在這個禮拜被領養，否則這些小狗會被安樂死。

7. 正當北極熊在寒冷的冬天獵取食物，棕熊則是在冬眠等候春天。

8. 工廠工人不會停止罷工直到雇主同意提高他們的工資並改善他們的工作環境。

9. 無論你是否信服，你都必須接受調查的結果。

10. 每天數以千計的墨西哥人非法穿越邊界進入美國為了要能夠在那裡過較好的生活。

8.7 形容詞子句 / 關係子句 (adjective / relative clauses)

形容詞子句 (adjective clause)，又稱為**關係子句** (relative clause)，依其作用不同而分成兩類：1. **限定用法的 (restrictive)** 形容詞子句，與 2. **非限定用法的 (non-restrictive)** 形容詞子句。

限定用法的形容詞子句又稱為**必要的 (essential)** 形容詞子句，而非限定用法的形容詞子句則又稱為**非必要的 (non-essential)** 形容詞子句。

1. 限定用法形容詞子句

中文的形容詞子句出現在所修飾的名詞或名詞片語之前，如：**喜愛運動的** 人 ；而英文的形容詞子句通常是緊跟在所修飾的名詞或名詞片語（也就是先行詞／前置詞）之後，如： people **who like sports**；或是盡可能地靠近先行詞，如： a house in Seattle **that costs less than one million dollars**。此為**限定用法**，先行詞與限定形容詞子句兩者之間**不需加逗點**，例如：

喜愛運動的 人 喜歡與好友一起觀賞電視實況轉播的比賽。
people **who like sports** enjoy watching live games on TV with good friends.

從以上的例子，我們知道**普通名詞**，像是 people，students，restaurants，teacher，movie，device，其指**稱的對象範圍很大**，當我們在這樣的普通名詞之後加上一個**限定用法**的形容詞子句，便可以**限定縮小其指稱的範圍**，而變成

<u>people</u> **who like sports** 喜歡運動的 人

<u>students</u> **whose parents are immigrants** 父母爲移民的 學生

<u>restaurants</u> **that sell seafood** 賣海鮮的 餐廳

<u>the teacher</u> **who influenced me the most** 影響我最深的 那位老師

<u>the movie</u> **which we watched last night** 我們昨晚看的 那部 電影

<u>a device</u> **that combines a cellphone with a handheld computer** 一種結合手機與手持電腦的 裝置 。

　　但若是把限定用法的形容詞子句從句子中移除，雖然不會影響句子的結構，但是該名詞所指稱的對象就無法界定了，也因此，**<u>限定用法的形容詞子句</u>又稱爲必要的形容詞子句。**

　　我們以下用集合的觀念與圖形，來說明限定用法形容詞子句對其先行詞指稱的對象所產生的變化：

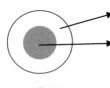

→ people（普通名詞指稱的對象爲大的集合）

→ **people who like sports**（名詞後面加了限定用法形容詞子句，<u>指稱的對象縮小爲小的集合</u>）

→ students（普通名詞指稱的對象爲大的集合）

→ **students whose parents are immigrants**（名詞後面加了限定用法形容詞子句，<u>指稱的對象縮小爲小的集</u> <u>合</u>）

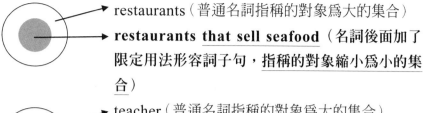

restaurants（普通名詞指稱的對象為大的集合）

restaurants that sell seafood（名詞後面加了限定用法形容詞子句，指稱的對象縮小為小的集合）

teacher（普通名詞指稱的對象為大的集合）

the teacher who influenced me the most（名詞後面加了限定用法形容詞子句，指稱的對象為特定的一位老師）

movie（普通名詞指稱的對象為大的集合）

the movie which we watched last night（名詞後面加了限定用法形容詞子句，指稱的對象為特定的一部電影）

a device（普通名詞指稱的對象為大的集合）

a device that combines a cellphone with a handheld computer（名詞後面加了限定用法形容詞子句，指稱的對象縮小為小的集合）

2. 非限定用法形容詞子句

若是**非限定用法**，則形容詞子句與所修飾的名詞或名詞片語（也就是先行詞）兩者之間**必須加上逗點**隔開，例如：

展示中國古代皇室手工藝品的國立故宮博物院 每年吸引數以百萬的觀光客。

National Palace Museum , **which exhibits ancient Chinese imperial artifacts,** draws millions of tourists annually.

於1876年獲得電話專利的亞歷山大貝爾 創立了貝爾電話公司。

Alexander Graham Bell , **who received the telephone pat-ent in March 1876,** founded the Bell Telephone Company.

而就**專有名詞**而言，其**指稱的對象已經明確**，不需要再加以界定，所以會用非限定用法的形容詞子句接在其後，並以逗點隔開，其目的在**提供額外的訊息**，因此，若是把非限定用法的形容詞子句從句子中移除，例如：

National Palace Museum , ~~**which exhibits ancient Chinese imperial artifacts,**~~ draws millions of tourists annually.

Alexander Graham Bell , ~~**who received the telephone pat-ent in March 1876,**~~ founded the Bell Telephone Company.

如此修改並不會影響其所修飾的名詞的涵義與指稱的對象，也不會影響句子的結構，因此，非限定用法的形容詞子句又稱爲**補充用法的形容詞子句**或**非必要的形容詞子句**。

另外，如果從**上下文已經知道該普通名詞所指稱的對象**時，普通名詞也會使用**非限定**的形容詞子句提供額外的訊息，例如：

He took **photos** of the house for sale. When his wife saw **the photos,** which he sent to her over the cellphone, she was very pleased.

出現在第二句的普通名詞 the photos 其指稱的對象（待售房子的照片）已經清楚明確，因此後面所接的形容詞子句爲**非限定用**

法，即使該形容詞子句從句子中挪去，也不影響句子的結構，而讀者也清楚知道該普通名詞所指稱是什麼。

3. 限定用法形容詞子句與非限定用法形容詞子句所隱含的意思

我們以下列兩個例句來說明限定用法跟非限定用法的形容詞子句所表達的不同涵義及及其適用情況：

(1) My sister who works at a bank is getting married next month.

(2) My sister, who works at a bank, is getting married next month.

在例句 (1) 中，my sister 這個名詞片語後面接了一個**限定用法的形容詞子句 who works at a bank**，兩者之間沒有以逗點隔開，所傳達的訊息是寫這句話的人有**不只一位姊妹**，因此才需要以限定用法的形容詞子句來限定 my sister 這個名詞片語所指稱的對象是在銀行上班的那一位姊妹。換句話說，寫這句話的人除了有一位姊妹是在銀行上班，另外還有別的（至少一位）姊妹是在其他場所上班。

而在例句 (2) 中，my sister 這個名詞片語後面接了一個**非限定用法的形容詞子句 who works at a bank，子句前後分別以逗點隔開**，其指稱的對象已經明確了，因此所傳達的訊息表明寫這句話的人**只有一位姊妹**，所以非限定用法的形容詞子句又稱為非必要的形容詞子句。

從以上的說明，我們瞭解到**限定用法的形容詞子句和非限定用法的形容詞子句對所修飾的名詞（也就是先行詞），產生什麼影響與涵義的變化**，並且瞭解到什麼時候適用限定用法的形容詞子句，又什麼時候適用非限定用法的形容詞子句，而不至於傳遞了錯誤的訊息。

8.7.1 限定用法形容詞子句

　　限定用法（必要）的形容詞子句的作用是要確定所修飾的名詞（也就是先行詞）指稱的對象，或限定所必須具備的條件或適用的範圍，或是給予定義說明其功能與特質。我們用以下的例子加以說明：

　　修好我車子的 汽車師傅原來是我朋友的叔叔。

The mechanic who fixed my car turned out to be my friend's uncle.

（形容詞子句的作用在 **確定先行詞 mechanic 所指稱的對象**。）

　　這家跨國企業新聘用的 執行長採用新的國際行銷策略。

The CEO who the multinational corporation newly hires adopts new international marketing strategies.

（形容詞子句的作用在 **確定先行詞 CEO 所指稱的對象**。）

　　這個運動員已經創下了一項 很難打破的 紀錄

The athlete has set **a record** that will be very difficult to break .

（形容詞子句的作用在 **說明先行詞 a record 的特徵**。）

　　他們想要租一間 靠近傳統菜市場的 公寓

They want to rent **an apartment** that is close to a traditional market .

（形容詞子句的作用在 **限定先行詞 an apartment 所必須具備的條件**。）

去年的表現達到公司所設定的目標的業務代表會獲得百分之十五的加薪。

Sales representatives **whose** performance reached the target set by the company will get a 15% raise.

（形容詞子句的作用在**限定先行詞 sales representatives 所指稱的範圍。**）

電腦就是**為多重目的處理數位資訊的**一種電子裝置。

A computer is **an electronic device** that processes digital information for multiple purposes .

（形容詞子句的作用在**定義說明先行詞 an electronic device 的功能。**）

8.7.2 限定用法形容詞子句所使用的關係代名詞

從以上的幾個例句，我們也發現到，每一個形容詞子句都由一個關係代名詞開頭，並且不同性質的先行詞要適用不同的關係代名詞 (relative pronouns)；因此，要正確地使用限定用法的形容詞子句，必須知道什麼時候選用什麼關係代名詞。先行詞依其性質分為兩大類：人及非人，而關係代名詞的又依其作用分為主格，所有格，及受格。我們先看完以下的中英對照的例句之後再來列表說明。

想要報名參加海外暑期課程的同學必須在四月底之前繳交申請表。

Students who want to sign up for the overseas summer program must submit the application form by the end of

April.

（先行詞 students，屬人；關係代名詞的作用為主格，用 **who**。）

這個非政府組織正在招募 專長是土木工程的 志工。

The NGO is recruiting **volunteers whose** expertise is civil engineering .

（先行詞 volunteers，屬人；關係代名詞的作用為所有格，用 **whose**。）

接受總統指派為談判代表的 政府官員將於下周二啓程。

Government officials who the president has appointed representatives for the negotiation will depart next Tuesday.

（先行詞 government officials，屬人；關係代名詞的作用為受格，用 **who**。）

包裹所應該送達的 客戶一直都沒有收到該包裹。

The customer to whom the parcel was supposed to be shipped never received it.

（先行詞 the customer，屬人；關係代名詞的作用為受格，且出現在介系詞後面，必須用 **whom**。）

市政府計畫給予 使用綠能的 家庭補助。

The city government is planning to give subsidies to **households** that / which use green energy .

（先行詞 households，屬非人；關係代名詞的作用為主格，用 that 或 which。）

爲了要蓋新廠房，這家企業正在尋找一塊 面積大約 15 英畝的 地。

To build a new factory, the corporation is looking for a piece of **land** whose area is around 15 acres .

（先行詞 land，屬非人；關係代名詞的作用爲**所有格**，用 **whose**。）

他們買給母親的 **禮物** 要到她生日那天才會揭曉。

The gift that / which they bought for their mother will not be disclosed until her birthday.

（先行詞 the gift，屬非人；關係代名詞的作用爲**受格**，用 **that** 或 **which**。）

意外發現歷史文物所在的 **教堂** 建於五百多年前。

The church in which the historical relics were accidentally found was built over 500 years ago.

（先行詞 church，屬非人；關係代名詞的作用爲**受格**，且出現在介系詞 in 後面，必須用 **which**。）

這家畫廊會購買任何 這位知名藝術家遺留下來的 作品。

The gallery will buy **anything** that the famous artist left behind .

（先行詞 anything，屬非人；關係代名詞的作用爲**受格**，且出現在代名詞 anything 後面，必須用 **that**。）

這是這對喜劇演員 所表演過的 **最搞笑的秀**。

It was **the funniest show** that the tandem comedians had ever performed.

（先行詞 **the funniest show**，屬非人；關係代名詞的作用為**受格**，且出現在由最高級 the funniest 所修飾的名詞 show 後面，必須用 **that**。）

由以上的例句我們可以歸納出在不同情況下應如何選用特定的限定用法關係代名詞，如下表所列：

限定用法關係代名詞			
先行詞	關係代名詞的作用		
	主格	所有格	受格
人	who 與 that 通用	whose	**who**（不能用在介系詞後面） **whom**（目前較少使用，但一定用在介系詞後面）
非人	**that** （美式英文） **which** （英式英文）	whose	**which** 與 **that** 通用 （**which** 一定用在介系詞後面；**that** 不能用在介系詞後面，但是在代名詞後面或是由最高級所修飾的名詞後面則必須用 **that**）

目前在實際的英文寫作上，選用限定用法關係代名詞的規則變化如下：

1. 限定用法<u>人的主格</u>關係代名詞常見<u>口說的 **that** 與正式的 **who** 通用</u>。

2. <u>**人的受格**</u>關係代名詞，<u>**除非是出現在介系詞後面，whom 已經**</u>

較少使用，在美式英語寫作中**多已使用 who**：

3. 限定用法**非人的主格**關係代名詞也常見 **which 與 that 通用**，

4. **非人的受格**關係代名詞，**除非是出現在介系詞後面必須使用 which**，**that 與 which 也已經通用**。

　　由此可見，過去嚴格的限定用法關係代名詞的使用已經逐漸由口說的習慣用法轉移到寫作，因而產生規則的鬆動，而有了通用的彈性，不過其中**唯一不變的是所有格的關係代名詞 whose**。

　　1. **人的限定用法的受格**關係代名詞如果出現在**介系詞後面**，一定要用 **whom**，不可以用 who。例如：

　　The lady **with whom** they had dinner last night was a famous artist.

　　2. **非人的限定用法受格**關係代名詞如果出現在**介系詞後面**，一定要用 **which**，不可以用 that。例如：

　　The boat **on which** we are now boarding is bound for Alaska.

　　3. **非人的限定用法受格**關係代名詞如果出現在**代名詞或是由最高級所修飾的名詞後面**，一定要用 **that**。例如：

　　He promised that he would do **anything that** his wife requested.

　　Landing a high-paying job in San Francisco is **the best** thing **that** ever happened to her.

▶▶ 8.7.3 限定用法形容詞子句由關係副詞 (relative adverbs) 所引導

形容詞子句通常以關係代名詞來指稱先行詞，並引導該形容詞子句，但先行詞若是表達**地點**或**時間**或**理由**時，則可以使用**關係副詞**來引導形容詞子句。英文的關係副詞有三個：**where, when, why**。以關係副詞開頭的形容詞子句乍看之下好像是名詞子句，但其實不是，差別在於形容詞子句之前會出現先行詞，而名詞子句則沒有。

先行詞	關係副詞
地點	**where (in which, at which, on which)**
時間	**when (in which, at which, on which)**
動機 / 原因 / 理由	**why**

我們以下列例句說明其用法：

(1) where

Every class in Taiwan's schools has its own fixed classroom **where** (= **in which**) its students take all the courses, except for computer courses and laboratory work.（限定用法，**先行詞為何地**。）

It's really convenient to have a convenience store around the corner **where** (= **at which**) people can pay bills, withdraw cash from an ATM, or even purchase tickets.

(2) when

The 1990s were a time **when** (= **in which**) the information technologies started to boom.（限定用法，**先行詞為何時**。）

I remember it was a lovely day **when** (= **on which**) we had a barbecue in the backyard with our friends.

從以上的例子，我們知道關係副詞中的 **where** 和 **when** 是由 介系詞 +which 轉換而來的。

(3) why（關係副詞 **why** 只會用在限定形容詞子句）

The actual motive **why** he committed the crime remained unknown.（限定用法，先行詞為**動機**。）

The nice neighborhood was the reason **why** I moved here. （限定用法，先行詞為**原因或理由**。）

▶▶ 8.7.4 限定用法形容詞子句的形成

接下來，我們就要來說明如何**將一個簡單句轉換成為限定用法的形容詞子句**，包括兩種情況，總共十一種類型的變化：（一）使用關係代名詞指稱先行詞的八種類型，包括人的主格、所有格、受格，以及人的受格出現在介系詞之後的四種情況，加上非人的主格，所有格、受格，以及非人的受格出現在介系詞之後的四種情況，一共八種類型。（二）使用關係副詞 where, when, why 引導形容詞子句的三種類型。

(一)使用關係代名詞指稱先行詞（一共八種類型）

(1) She teaches history.

→ **who / that** teaches history（以 who 或 that 取代 she，完成限定形容詞子句）

主詞 she 作為先行詞，其性質是**人**，又是**主格**，因此選用的**關**

係代名詞為 **who** 或是 **that**。

(2) **Andy's** car is stolen.（簡單句）

    →**whose** car is stolen（以 whose 取代 Andy's，完成限定形容詞子句）

所有詞 her 作為先行詞，其性質是**人**，又是**所有格**，因此選用的**關係代名詞為 whose**。

(3) The college students admire **the entrepreneur** for his innovative business model.

    →the colleges students admire **who / whom** for his innovative business model（以 who 或 whom 取代 the entrepreneur）

    →**who / whom** the college students admire for his innovative business model（將 who 或 whom 移到子句前端，完成限定用法形容詞子句）

受詞 the entrepreneur 作為先行詞，其性質是人，又是受格，因此選用的關係代名詞為 **who 或 whom**。（**whom 已經很少使用在現代美式英文寫作上，除非是出現在介系詞後面。**）

(4) They sent the gift to **their beloved uncle**.

    →They sent the gift to **whom**（以 whom 取代 their beloved uncle）

    →**to whom** they sent the gift（將 to whom 移到子句前端，完成限定形容詞子句）

受詞 their beloved uncle 作為先行詞，其性質是**人**，又是**受格**，因為是出現**在介系詞後面的受詞**，因此必須選用**關係代名詞 whom**，而不能使用 who。再把介系詞 to 跟關係代名詞 whom 一起移到子句的開頭位置，就形成了限定用法的形容詞子句了。

(5) **The flight** was delayed.

→ **that**（美式）/ **which**（英式）was delayed（以 that 或 which 取代 the flight，完成限定形容詞子句）

主詞 the flight 作爲先行詞，其性質是**非人**，又是**主格**，因此選用的**關係代名詞爲 that**（美式）/ **which**（英式）。

(6) **The horse's** leg is injured.

→ **whose** leg is injured（以 whose 取代 the horse's，完成限定形容詞子句）

所有詞 the horse's 作爲先行詞，其性質是**非人**，又是**所有格**，因此選用的**關係代名詞爲 whose**。

(7) The department is offering **new courses**.

the department is offering **which / that**（以 which 或 that 取代 new courses）

which / that the department is offering（將 which 或 that 移到子句前端，完成限定形容詞子句）

受詞 new courses 作爲先行詞，其性質是**非人**，又是**受格**，選用的關係代名詞爲 **which 或 that**，再把 which 或 that 移到子句開頭的位置，就形成了限定用法的形容詞子句了。

(8) We lived in **the house** when we first moved to Sydney.

→ we live in **which** when we first moved to Sydney.（以 which 取代 the house）

→ **in which** we live when we first moved to Sydney.（將 in which 移到子句前端，完成限定形容詞子句）

先行詞 the house 爲簡單句中**介系詞 in 的受詞**，其性質是**非人**，又是**受格**，但因爲是出現**在介系詞後面，因此必須選用關係代名詞 which**，而不能使用 that。再把介系詞 in 跟關係代名詞 which 一起移到子句的開頭位置，就形成了限定用法的形容詞子句了。

(二) 使用關係副詞 where, when, why 引導限定形容詞子句

(9) We can pay bills at **a convenience store**.

→ we can pay bills at **which**（以 which 取代 a convenience store）

→ **at which** we can pay bills（將 at which 移到子句前端，完成限定形容詞子句）

→ **where** we can pay bills.（將 at which 轉換成關係副詞 where 來引導限定形容詞子句）

(10) She graduated from college in **2011**.

→ she graduated from college in **which**（以 which 取代 2011）

→ **in which** she graduated from college（將 in which 移到子句前端，完成限定形容詞子句）

→ **when** she graduated from college（將 in which 轉換成關係副詞 when 來引導限定形容詞子句）

(11) His friend is angry with him for **the reason**.

→ his friend is angry with him for **which**（以 which 取代 the reason）

→ **for which** his friend is angry with him（將 for which 移到子句前端，完成限定用法形容詞子句）

→ **why** his friend is angry with him（將 for which 轉換成關係副詞 why 來引導限定用法形容詞子句）

▶▶ 8.7.5 小試身手

　　將以下簡單句劃底線的名詞片語，依其性質與作用改為適當的關係代名詞（主格，所有格，或受格）或關係副詞，再將整句改寫成形容詞子句。

　　Example: **Most people** enjoy watching movies. → **who** / **that** enjoy watching movies

1. **They** have participated in the community services.

_____

2. They have participated |in| **the community services**.

_____

3. **The two sides** have agreed to the deal.

_____

4. The two sides have agreed |to| **the deal**.

_____

5. The conference is taking place **in the hotel**.

_____

6. **The dog** is chasing a scooter.

_____

7. The dog is chasing **a scooter**.

_____

8. The family decided to move to Australia **for a better environment**.

_____

9. **The manager's** assistant is taking online courses to develop more business skills.

10. The manager's assistant is taking **online courses** to develop more business skills.

_____

11. The manager's assistant is taking online courses to develop **more business skills**.

_____

12. The doctor saved **the little child** by transplanting a man's kidney.

_____

13. The government will give **grants** to innovative inventors.

_____

14. Barry proposed to his girlfriend **in this restaurant**.

_____

15. The government will give grants to **innovative inventors**.

_____

16. **Applicants** speak English and Spanish.

_____

17. The new nurse in the emergency room coped with **the urgent situation** professionally.

_____

18. People in Taiwan have barbecues everywhere **on the Moon Festival**.

_____

19. Applicants speak **English and Spanish**.

_____

20. **The cat's** hair is orange.

_____

▶▶ 8.7.6 限定用法形容詞子句與獨立子句結合

　　經過以上的練習，我們已經學會如何將簡單句改寫成限定形容詞子句，接下來，我們可以運用這個技巧，將兩個簡單句融合成為一個包含限定形容詞子句的複句了。

　　當兩個簡單句**含有相同的普通名詞或名詞片語**時，我們可以將其中一個簡單句裡面共同的普通名詞或名詞片語，依其類別（人或非人；主格或所有格或受格）改成適當的關係代名詞，而另一個維持不變的簡單句中共同的普通名詞或名詞片語即是關係代名詞的先行詞，如此就可以先將一個簡單句轉換成**限定用法的形容詞子句**，然後再與另外一個維持不變的簡單句結合，成為一個新的複句。

　　我們用以下十一個例子來說明：

（一）**八種由不同的關係代名詞來指稱不同類別先行詞的情況**，包括人的主格、所有格、受格，以及人的受格出現在介系詞之後的四種情況，加上非人的主格、所有格、受格，以及非人的受格出現在介系詞之後的四種情況，一共八種類型；以及

（二）**三種由關係副詞 where, when, why 來引導形容詞子句的情況**，如何選用恰當的關係代名詞來取代共同的名詞或名詞片語，將其中一個簡單句轉換為限定用法的形容詞子句，放置於獨立子句中先行詞的後面，用來修飾該先行詞，從而依附於維持不變的另一個獨立子句，兩者結合成為複句。

(一) 由關係代名詞來指稱不同類別的先行詞（一共八種類型的變化）

例一 先行詞屬人的主格：

(1) **These elderly people** like biking very much.（這些老人家熱

愛騎單車。）

(2) **These elderly people** are planning to travel around Taiwan by bike.

（這些老人家正計畫騎車環繞臺灣。）

步驟一：以人的主格關係代名詞 **who / that** 取代句子 (1) 的共同名詞片語 these elderly people，完成限定形容詞子句。

→ **who / that** like biking very much

步驟二：再將限定形容詞子句與維持不變的句子 (2) 結合成為一個複句

→ These elderly people **who / that like biking very much** are planning to travel around Taiwan by bike.

（**熱愛騎單車的**這些老人家正計畫要騎車環繞臺灣。）

例二 先行詞屬人的所有格：

(1) **The lady's** son was missing.（**那位女士的**兒子走失了。）

(2) The police notified **the lady** that they had found him.

（警察通知**那位女士**說他們已經找到他了。）

步驟一：以人的所有格關係代名詞 whose 取代句子 (1) 的共同名詞 the lady，完成限定形容詞子句。

→ **whose** son was missing

步驟二：再將限定形容詞子句與維持不變的句子 (2) 結合成為一個複句

→ The police notified the lady **whose son was missing** that they had found him.

（警察通知那位**兒子走失的**女士說他們已經找到他了。）

：

(1) The baseball team signed **the young player**.（這支棒球隊簽下這位年輕球員。）

(2) **The young player** will play as a starting pitcher.

（這位年輕球員將會以先發投手出賽。）

步驟一：以人的受格關係代名詞取代句子 (1) 的共同名詞片語 the young player

→ the baseball team signed **who / whom**

步驟二：再將 **who / whom** 移到子句前端，完成限定形容詞子句。

→ **who / whom** the baseball team signed

步驟三：再將限定形容詞子句與維持不變的句子 **(2)** 結合成為一個複句。

→ The young player **who / whom the baseball team signed** will play as a starting pitcher.

（**這支棒球隊簽下的**這位年輕球員將會以先發投手出賽。）

例四 先行詞屬人的受格，並且出現在介系詞後面：

(1) The land with several hot springs belongs to **the old farmer**.

（這塊有數個溫泉的土地屬於**這位老農**所有。）

(2) The hotel chain is negotiating a land purchase deal with **the old farmer**.

（這家連鎖旅館正在與**這位老農**洽商土地購買交易。）

步驟一：以人的主格關係代名詞 whom 取代句子 (1) 的共同名詞片語 the old farmer（出現在介系詞後面，不能用 who。）

→ the land with several hot springs belongs to **whom**

步驟二：將 to whom 移到子句前端，完成限定形容詞子句。

→ to whom the land with several hot springs belongs

步驟三：最後再將限定形容詞子句與維持不變的句子 (2) 結合成為一個複句

The hotel chain is negotiating a land purchase deal with the old farmer to whom the land with hot springs belong.

（這家連鎖旅館正在與土地所屬的老農洽商土地購買交易。）

例五 先行詞屬非人的主格：

(1) **The team** won the first prize in the competition.（這個團隊贏得競賽首獎。）

(2) **The team** consisted of five college students.（這個團隊是由五位大學生組成。）

改法一：句子 (1) 轉換成限定形容詞子句，句子 (2) 維持不變。

步驟一：以非人的主格關係代名詞 **that**（美式）/ **which**（英式）取代句子 (1) 的共同名詞 the team

→ **that**（美式）/ **which**（英式）won the first prize in the competition

步驟二：再將限定形容詞子句與維持不變的句子 (2) 結合成為一個複句

→ The team **that**（美式）/ **which**（英式）**won the first prize in the competition** consisted of five college students.

（贏得競賽首獎的團隊是由五位大學生組成。）

改法二：將句子 (2) 轉換成限定形容詞子句，句子 (1) 維持不變。

步驟一：以非人的主格關係代名詞 **that**（美式）/ **which**（英式）取代句子 (2) 的共同名詞 the tem，完成限定形容詞子句。

→ **that**（美式）/ **which**（英式）consisted of five college students

步驟二：再將限定形容詞子句與維持不變的句子 **(1)** 結合成爲一個複句

→ The team **that**（美式）/ **which**（英式）**consisted of five college students** won the first prize in the competition.
（由五位大學生組成的團隊贏得競賽的首獎。）

例六 先行詞屬非人的所有格：

(1) **The horse's** leg is injured.（這匹馬的腿受傷了。）

(2) **The horse** will not race for a while.（這匹馬將有一段時間不會出賽了。）

步驟一：以非人的所有格關係代名詞 **whose** 取代句子 (1) 的共同名詞 the horse，完成限定形容詞子句

→ **whose** leg is injured

步驟二：再將限定形容詞子句與維持不變的句子 **(2)** 結合成爲一個複句

→ The horse **whose leg is injured** will not race for a while.
（這隻腿受傷的馬將有一段時間不會出賽了。）

例七 先行詞屬非人的受格：

(1) He designed **the robot**.（他設計這臺機器人。）

(2) **The robot** will be first introduced next month.
（這臺機器人將於下個月首度亮相。）

步驟一：以非人的受格關係代名詞 **which / that** 取代句子 (1) 的共同名詞 the robot

→ he designed **which / that**

步驟二：再將 which / that 移到子句前端，完成限定形容詞子句。

→ **which / that** he designed

步驟三：最後再將限定形容詞子句與維持不變的句子 (2) 結合成為一個複句

→ The robot **which / that he designed** will be first introduced next month.

（這臺<u>他所設計的</u>機器人將於下個月首度亮相。）

例八 先行詞屬非人的受格，並且出現在介系詞後面：

(1) The patrons complained about **the poor service**.

（顧客對不佳的服務品質有所抱怨。）

(2) **The poor service** affects the business of the newly open restaurant.

（不佳的服務品質影響這家新開張餐廳的生意。）

步驟一：以非人的受格關係代名詞 **which** 取代句子 (1) 的共同名詞片語 the poor service（出現在介系詞後面，不可以用 that）

→ the patrons complained about **which**

步驟二：再將 **about which** 移到子句前端，完成限定形容詞子句。

→ about **which** the patrons complained

步驟三：最後再將限定形容詞子句與維持不變的句子 (2) 結合成為一個複句

→ The poor service about **which the patrons complained** affects the business of the newly open restaurant.

（**顧客所抱怨的**不佳的服務品質影響這家新開張餐廳的生意。）

(二)由關係副詞 where, when, why 引導限定形容詞子句
（一共有三種類型）

例九 由關係副詞 where 引導形容詞子句

(1) They deliver parcels to **a convenience store**.
（他們寄送包裹到一家便利商店。）

(2) Customers can pick them up at **a convenience store**.
（顧客能夠在一家便利商店取貨。）

步驟一：以受格關係代名詞 **which** 取代句子 (2) 的共同名詞 a convenience store（出現在介系詞 at 後面，不可以用 that）

→ customers can pick them up at **which**

步驟二：將 **at which** 移到子句前端，完成限定形容詞子句

→ at **which** customers can pick them up（這時已經可以將此限定形容詞子句與維持不變的句子 (1) 結合成為一個複句了）

→ They deliver parcels to a convenience store at which customers can pick them up.

步驟三：再將 **at which** 轉換成關係副詞 **where**

→ They deliver parcels to a convenience store where customers can pick them up.
（他們把包裹寄送到一家**顧客能夠在那裡取貨的**便利商店。）

例十 由關係副詞 when 引導形容詞子句

(1) The boy is looking forward to **a sunny Saturday afternoon**.
（這男孩期待著一個晴朗的禮拜六下午。）

(2) He can play baseball with his friends on **a sunny Saturday**

afternoon.

（他可以在一個晴朗的禮拜六下午跟他的朋友們打棒球。）

步驟一：以受格關係代名詞 **which** 取代句子 (2) 的共同名詞片語 a sunny Saturday afternoon（出現在介系詞 on 後面，不可以用 that）

→ he can play baseball with his friends on **which**

步驟二：再將 **on which** 移到子句前端，完成限定形容詞子句。

→ on **which** he can play baseball with his friends（這時已經可以將此限定形容詞子句與維持不變的句子 (1) 結合成爲一個複句了）

→ The boy is looking forward to a sunny Saturday afternoon **on which** **he can play baseball with his friends**.

步驟三：再將 **on which** 轉換成關係副詞 **when**

→ The boy is looking forward to a sunny Saturday afternoon **when** **he can play baseball with his friends**.

（這男孩期待著一個他可以（在那時候）跟朋友們打棒球的晴朗的禮拜六下午。）

例十一 由關係副詞 **why** 引導形容詞子句

(1) The researchers explain **the reason**.（研究人員解釋原因。）

(2) Eating too much sugar is harmful to our health for **the reason**.

（吃太多糖對我們身體有害爲了這個原因。）

步驟一：以非人的受格關係代名詞 **which** 取代句子 (2) 的共同名詞 the reason（出現在介系詞 for 的後面，不能用 that）

→ eating too much sugar is harmful to our health $\boxed{\text{for}}$ **which**

$\boxed{步驟二}$：再將 for which 移到子句前端，完成限定形容詞子句

→ $\boxed{\text{for}}$ **which** eating too much sugar is harmful to our health（這時已經可以將此限定形容詞子句與維持不變的句子 (1) 結合成爲一個複句了）

→ The researchers explain the reason $\boxed{\text{for which}}$ **eating too much sugar is harmful to our health**.

$\boxed{步驟三}$：再將 **for which 轉換成關係副詞 why**

→ The researchers explained the reason $\boxed{\text{why}}$ **eating too much sugar is harmful to our health**.（研究人員解釋爲什麼吃太多糖對我們身體有害的原因。）

▶▶ **8.7.7 受格關係代名詞的省略**

限定用法的形容詞子句中的**受格關係代名詞可以省略**，並不影響子句的結構，如以下例句所示：

You met **the lady** last night at the party.

The lady was a model.

兩個簡單句結合成爲一個複句：

→ The lady $\boxed{\text{who / whom}}$ **you met last night at the party** was a model.

省略關係代名詞 who / whom：

→ The lady **you met last night at the party** was a model.

The student was granted a full scholarship.

Her teacher was very proud of **the student**.

兩個簡單句結合成爲一個複句：

The student $\boxed{\text{of whom}}$ **her teacher was very proud** was granted a full scholarship.

省略關係代名詞 whom，同時將介系詞 of 歸回原位：

The student **her teacher was very proud** $\boxed{\text{of}}$ was granted a full scholarship.

The diamond was very expensive.

He bought **the diamond** for his wife.

兩個簡單句結合成為一個複句：

→ The diamond **which / that** he bought for his wife was very expensive.

省略關係代名詞 which / that：

→ The diamond he bought for his wife was very expensive.

The doctor treated the patient with **a new drug**.

The new drug has just been approved by the authorities.

兩個簡單句結合成為一個複句：

→ The new drug $\boxed{\text{with which}}$ the doctor treated the patient has just been approved by the authorities.

省略關係代名詞 with which，同時將介系詞 with 歸回原位：

→ The new drug **the doctor treated the patient** $\boxed{\text{with}}$ has just been approved by the authorities.

▶▶ 8.7.8 小試身手

空格中填入恰當的限定用法關係代名詞或關係副詞

1. James is the only one in our office _____ mother tongue is not English.

2. Mary is the kindergarten teacher from _____ the children hear funny stories.

3. She is the professor _____ the Computer Science Department has just hired.

4. They can also send messages pointing out problems _____ need to be addressed, such as a streetlight _____ is not working.

5. She didn't tell her friends the reason _____ she broke up with her boyfriend.

6. His parents warns the babysitter not to feed their child any food _____ he is allergic to.

7. This is the laptop from _____ we retrieved the files _____ will serve as hard evidence.

8. It was a Sunday afternoon _____ we had a yard sale before we moved out of the old house.

9. A great leader is someone _____ can inspire people _____ follow him.

10. This is the restaurant _____ I met my wife for the first time.

11. He finally got to interview the author _____ novel had sold more than two million copies.

12. Not everything _____ can be counted counts, and not everything _____ counts can be counted. – *Albert Einstein*

13. This is the miracle _____ happens every time to those _____ really love; the more they give, the more they possess. – *Rainer Maria Rilke*

一、將下列各題中劃底線的簡單句改成限定用法形容詞子句，再與另一個簡單句結合成為複句。

1. The couple is looking to rent an apartment.
   The apartment's monthly rent is around NT$25,000.

   _____

2. Researchers are conducting a survey to find out the challenges.
   Foreign students may face the challenges when studying abroad.

   _____

   _____

3. The NGO is recruiting young people. Young people are willing to spend at least three years in poor countries helping children.

   _____

   _____

4. He is the programmer. The programmer developed the popular app for smart phones.

   _____

5. The number of vehicles has exceeded 10 million a year.
   The vehicles run across the suspension bridge.

   _____

6. As a daughter of a wealthy father, Sarah wants to marry to someone.

Someone has the same family background.

_____

_____

7. The airlines overbooked and offered cash as compensation for passengers.
Passengers were willing to take the next flight.

_____

_____

8. The Department of Architecture is hiring a young scholar.
The scholar's research focuses on green buildings.

_____

_____

9. The female applicant will report to the research and development department.
The manager interviewed the female applicant last week.

_____

_____

10. She remembers that it was a rainy day. She bought her first computer on that rainy day.

_____

_____

二、中翻英（劃底線部分為限定用法形容詞子句）

1. 科學家正尋求安全、乾淨又不昂貴的綠色能源，以滿足我們對電的需求。（100 年指考）

_____

_____

2. 有些**我們認爲安全的**包裝食品可能含有**對人體有害的**成分。（101 年指考）

_____

_____

3. **拍攝這些電影的**地點也成爲熱門的觀光景點。（101 年學測）

_____

_____

4. 這個計畫的目的是要把**已經表現突出的**研究生送往世界前一百大的大學去攻讀博士學位。

_____

_____

5. 新成立的航空公司正在招募**性向與英語能力適合接受訓練成爲機師的**年輕人。

_____

_____

▶▶ 8.7.10 英文限定用法形容詞子句與中文之間的轉換

英文的限定形容詞子句爲從屬子句，必須依附於獨立子句，才能出現在文句中，兩者結合構成一個複句。**英文的形容詞子句，無論其關係代名詞是主格、所有格、受格，都必須放在最可能靠近先行詞之後的位置**，例如：people **who are good at computer programming**，或是 companies **whose revenue exceeded one billion dollars**，或是 the mystery **that they have just solved**。若是先行詞後面接了介系詞片語，形容詞子句則置於介系詞片語之後，例如：people **in their twenties who are good at computer programming**。

相反地，中文句子的結構與英文不同，**關係代名詞為主格時，英文的限定形容詞子句會縮減為中文的形容詞片語，且會出現在所修飾的名詞之前**，例如：people **who are good at computer programming** 翻成中文為「**擅長電腦程式的人**」；**關係代名詞為所有格時，英文的限定形容詞子句也會縮減為中文的形容詞片語，並且可能出現在名詞之前或之後**，例如：professors **whose expertise is online marketing** 可以翻成中文「**專長為網路行銷的教授**」或是「**教授專長為網路行銷**」；而**關係代名詞為受格時，英文的限定形容詞子句在中文仍舊維持形容詞子句的結構，並且出現在所修飾的名詞之前**，例如：The restaurant **which they just opened in Seattle** 翻成中文「**他們剛在西雅圖開的餐廳**」。

(1) 關係代名詞為主格

The English teacher $\boxed{\text{who likes to play tennis}}$ teaches English grammar well.

英文的限定形容詞子句在中文以形容詞片語出現在所修飾的名詞之前：

→ $\boxed{\text{喜歡打網球的}}$ 那位英文老師文法教的很好。

The English teacher from Taichung $\boxed{\text{who likes to play tennis}}$ teaches English grammar well.

→ $\boxed{\text{喜歡打網球}}$ 來自臺中的那位英文老師文法教的很好。

→ 來自臺中、$\boxed{\text{喜歡打網球的}}$ 那位英文老師文法教的很好。

Motor vehicles $\boxed{\text{which are powered by electricity}}$ produce less pollution and noise.

$\boxed{\text{由電力提供動力的}}$ 車輛產生較少的汙染與噪音。

(2) 關係代名詞為所有格

A stadium whose main purpose is for playing basketball games can also be used for live concerts.

英文的限定形容詞子句在中文以形容詞片語出現在所修飾的名詞之前：

主要用途是比賽籃球的 體育館也可以用來作現場音樂會。

Students whose grades are among the top three of the class will be awarded by the principal.

英文的限定形容詞子句在中文以形容詞片語出現在所修飾的名詞之前：

→ 成績在班上前三名的 學生會獲得校長的獎勵。

英文的限定形容詞子句在中文以形容詞片語出現在所修飾的名詞之後：

→ 學生 成績在班上前三名的 會獲得校長的獎勵。

(3) 關係代名詞為受格

The suspects who the police arrested were involved in telephone frauds.

英文的限定形容詞子句在中文以形容詞子句出現在所修飾的名詞之前：

警察逮捕的 嫌犯涉及電話詐欺。

The house that they just bought is in a nice neighborhood.

英文的限定形容詞子句在中文以形容詞子句出現在所修飾的名詞之前：

→ 他們剛買的 房子位於很好的街區。

▶▶ 8.7.11 限定用法形容詞子句挑戰題

將下列句子中文翻成兩句或三句英文，再將其結合成括號內含有限定形容詞子句的中文英譯的複句。（劃底線部分為限定形容詞子句）

> 示範：
> (1) 上個月在臺南旅遊時我們在一家餐廳跟一位好朋友共進晚餐，(2) 這位好朋友在臺南已經住了超過三十年了。（1＋2：上個月在臺南旅遊時我們在一家餐廳跟一位在臺南已經住了超過三十年了的朋友共進晚餐。）
>
> (1) Last month when we were traveling in Tainan, we had dinner at a restaurant with a good friend.
>
> (2) The good friend has been living in Tainan for over thirty years.
>
> (1)+(2) Last month when we were traveling in Tainan, we had dinner at a restaurant with a good friend **who has been living in Tainan for over thirty years**.

1. (1) 我們在考慮要買這棟房子因為在鄰近地區有一座公園，(2) 我們的小孩可以在那座公園跟他們的朋友們玩耍。（1+2：我們在考慮要買這棟房子，因為在鄰近地區有一座我們的小孩可以在那裡跟他們的朋友們玩耍的公園。）

   (1) ＿＿＿＿＿＿＿＿＿＿＿＿＿＿＿＿＿＿＿＿＿＿

   (2) ＿＿＿＿＿＿＿＿＿＿＿＿＿＿＿＿＿＿＿＿＿＿

(1)+(2)_____

_____

_____

2.(1) 爲了舉辦這個活動，我們正在尋找一家鄰近國際機場，有寬
敞會議廳的旅館，(2) 會議廳能夠容納 200 人並提供西式餐點。
　（1+2：爲了舉辦這個活動，我們正在尋找一家鄰近國際機場，
有能夠容納 200 人並提供西式餐點的寬敞會議廳的旅館）

(1)_____

(2)_____

(1)+(2)_____

_____

3.(1) 教會爲低成就的學生設置課後課程，(2) 這些低成就的學生
已經逐漸改善他們的課業表現。（1+2：教會的課後課程爲其所
設置的這些低成就學生已經逐漸改善他們的課業表現。）

(1)_____

(2)_____

(1)+(2)_____

_____

4.(1) 我們公司捐贈了兩輛救護車給這家醫院，(2) 這家醫院提供
弱勢病患免費醫療。（1+2：我們公司捐贈了兩輛救護車的這家
醫院提供弱勢病患免費醫療。）

(1)_____

(2)_____

(1)+(2)_____

_____

5. (1) 這個碩士班以其創新且實用的課程著名，(1) 很多大學畢業生都在申請這個碩士班。（1+2：很多大學畢業生都在申請的碩士班以其創新且實用的課程著名。）

(1)_____

(2)_____

(1)+(2)_____

_____

6. (1) 昨天我去一座一座體育館看球，(2) 我最喜歡的 NBA 球隊連續三年在那裡贏得冠軍。（1+2：昨天我去一座我最喜歡的 NBA 球隊連續三年在那裡贏得冠軍的體育館看球賽。）

(1)_____

(2)_____

(1)+(2)_____

_____

7. (1) 搜救隊所今天下午救起一位遊客，(2) 這位遊客已經在巨大石頭下受困了好幾個小時。（1+2：搜救隊所今天下午救起的遊客已經在巨大石頭下受困了好幾個小時。）

(1)_____

(2)_____

(1)+(2)_____

_____

8. (1) 這位女士其實是一位臥底天使，(2) 她的公司年賺五百萬美金，(3) 她要在非洲偏遠村落為兒童蓋數個學校。（1+2：其公司年賺五百萬美金的這位女士是一位要在偏遠村落爲兒童蓋數個學校的臥底天使。）

(1)_____

(2)_____

(1)+(2)_____

_____

9.(1) 這位著名烘焙大師以其專業知識幫助經營不善的糕餅店，(2) 這些糕餅店都成功地翻轉了它們的生意。（1+2：這位著名烘焙大師所幫助的經營不善的糕餅店都成功地翻轉了它們的生意。）

(1)_____

(2)_____

(1)+(2)_____

_____

10.(1) 使我們公司更有競爭力對於我們未來的生意至爲關鍵，(2) 這正是爲什麼我們公司正在進行組織重整的理由。（1+2：使我們公司更有競爭力對於我們未來的生意至爲關鍵是我們公司正在進行組織重整的理由。）

(1)_____

(2)_____

(1)+(2)_____

_____

8.7.12 非限定用法形容詞子句

相較於限定用法的形容詞子句，**非限定用法的形容詞子句在句子的結構及語意上並非必要的**，其作用在於提供讀者有關先行詞的額外資訊，而不是要限定先行詞指稱的對象與範圍。因此，若是（一）**先行詞為專有名詞，其指稱的對象已經清楚明確**，（二）**先行詞為普通名詞，以非限定用法形容詞子句來解釋該名詞的涵義**，（三）**由上下文可以知道普通名詞之先行詞指稱的對象**，或是（四）以 **which** 用來**指稱前面的整個句子**，而不是前面句子裡的某一個名詞，這四種情況就必須使用**非限定用法的形容詞子句**，提供讀者額外的訊息。

如何選用非限定的關係代名詞與限定的關係代名詞的選用一樣，都必須依照**先行詞的性質**，及**關係代名詞的作用屬於主格、所有格、受格**而決定，我們先看完以下的中英對照的例句之後再來列表說明。

例一：

身為經驗豐富外科醫師的 **劉醫師**將為總統執行心臟開刀手術。
或是：

劉醫師 （他）是經驗豐富的外科醫師，將為總統執行心臟開刀手術。

→ **Dr. Liu**, who is an experienced surgeon, will perform heart surgery on the President.
（專有名詞指稱**特定的人**，關係代名詞為**主格 who**。）

例二：

其所著奇幻小說系列《哈利波特》銷售超過四億本的 **J．K．Rowling** 已經成為世界上最富有的作家之一。

或是：

J.K. Rowling, 其所著奇幻小說系列《哈利波特》銷售超過四億本，已經成為世界上最富有的作家之一。

→ **J.K. Rowling,** whose fantasy series of *Harry Potter* have sold more than 400 million copies , has become one of the wealthiest authors in the world.

（專有名詞指稱**特定的人**，關係代名詞為**所有格 whose**。）

例三：

她參加了由**林博士**所主持的工作坊，希望從他那裡學習如何更有效率地學習英文。

→ She participated in the workshop hosted by **Dr. Lin**, **from whom** she hoped to learn how to learn English more effectively .

（專有名詞指稱**特定的人**，關係代名詞為**受格 whom**。）

例四：

1964夏季奧林匹克運動會於**東京**舉行，該城市即將主辦 2020 夏季奧林匹克運動會。

→ The 1964 Summer Olympics was held in **Tokyo,** which will host the 2020 Summer Olympics .

（專有名詞指稱**特定的地方**，關係代名詞為**主格 which**。）

例五：

來自美國的 Rhodes 一家人喜歡外出到**星期五餐廳**用餐，它的餐點和氣氛令他們有思鄉的感覺。

→ The Rhodes from the US like to dine out at **TGI Fridays,** whose food and atmosphere make them feel nostalgic .

（專有名詞指稱**特定的地方**，關係代名詞為**所有格 whose**。）

例六：

其中多數是建造作為法老王的安葬所在的埃及金字塔已經由
為數甚多的科學家和考古學家所研究。

或是：

埃及金字塔，其中多數是建造作為法老王的安葬所在，已經
由為數甚多的科學家和考古學家所研究。

→ **Egyptian pyramids**, most of **which** were built as tombs
for the pharaohs , have been studied by many scientists and
archaeologists.

（專有名詞指稱**特定的物件**，關係代名詞為**受格 which**）

例七：

人們為了耶穌的降生而慶祝的**聖誕節**在很多國家是國定假日。
聖誕節，人們為了耶穌的降生而慶祝**該節日**，在很多國家是
國定假日。

→ **Christmas**, **which** people celebrate for the birth of Jesus,
is a national holiday in many countries.

（專有名詞指稱特定的節慶，關係代名詞為**主格 which**。）

例八：

數以萬計的遊客於新年元旦湧向加州的 Pasadena 去觀賞特色
為花車、鼓號樂隊以及騎兵隊的**玫瑰花車遊行**。

或是：

數以萬計的遊客於新年元旦湧向加州的 Pasadena 去觀賞**玫瑰**

花車遊行，其特色為花車、鼓號樂隊以及騎兵隊。

→ Tens of thousands of tourists flock to Pasadena, California on New Year's Day to watch **the Rose Parade,** which features floral floats, marching bands, and equestrian units .

（專有名詞指稱特定的活動，關係代名詞為主格 **which**。）

例九：

指定打擊，（他）是在棒球賽中代替投手打擊的選手，是不需要上場守備的強力打者。

→ **A designated hitter,** who hits for the pitcher in a baseball game , is a powerful hitter without having to play defense on the field.

（先行詞為**普通名詞**，使用**非限定**用法形容詞子句來**解釋該名詞的涵義**，關係代名詞為**主格 who**。）

例十：

我們以投幣方式從其購買飲料或零食的販賣機在現代都市非常普遍。

或是：

販賣機，我們以投幣方式從其購買飲料或零食，在現代都市非常普遍。

→ **Vending machines,** from **which** we purchase drinks or snacks by inserting coins or bills , are very popular in modern cities.

（先行詞為**普通名詞**，使用**非限定**用法形容詞子句來**解釋該名詞的涵義**，關係代名詞為**受格 which**。）

例十一：

經過兩個月的乾旱終於下雨了，這讓農民和政府都鬆了一口氣 。

→ **It finally rained after two months of drought,** which made farmers and the government relieved .

（先行詞爲整個句子，關係代名詞爲主格 **which**。）

看完這些例句，我們可以歸納出：英文的**非限定用法形容詞子句中，不同性質的先行詞必須使用特定的關係代名詞加以取代，並引導該形容詞子句**。其用法整理如下一單元。

▶▶ 8.7.13 非限定用法形容詞子句所使用的關係代名詞

英文的非限定用法的形容詞子句，依其先行詞之性質（人或非人）及所要取代的名詞的作用（主詞，所有詞，受詞）而使用不同的關係代名詞，如下表所示：

非限定關係代名詞			
先行詞	關係代名詞的作用		
	主詞／主格	所有詞／所有格	受詞／受格
人	**who**	**whose**	**whom**（目前較少使用，但在介系詞後面一定要用 **whom**） **who**（不能用在介系詞後面）
非人	**which**	**whose**	**which**
前面整個句子	**which**	N/A	N/A

從以上表格所顯示的，我們歸納出來以下的規則：

1. 先行詞屬人，**且關係代名詞為主格時，非限定關係代名詞為只能使用 who**，不能用 that，這個情況**與限定用法不同**。

2. 先行詞屬非人，**且關係代名詞為主格時，非限定關係代名詞只能使用 which**，也不能用 that，這個情況也**與限定用法不同**。

3. 先行詞為**前面整個句子時，非限定關係代名詞為只能使用 which**，不能用 that。

4. **關係代名詞為所有格**時，不論時屬人還是非人，一律使用 **whose**。

5. 先行詞屬人，且**關係代名詞為受格時**，非限定關係代名詞可以使用 **who 或 whom**，不過除非是出現在介系詞之後，否則 **whom 已經較少使用**；而 **who 則不能使用在介系詞之後**，這個情況**與限定關係代名詞相同**。

6. 先行詞屬非人，且**關係代名詞為受格時**，非限定關係代名詞**只能使用 which**，不能用 that，這個情況**與限定用法不同**。

以上有關如何選用正確的非限定關係代名詞的規則細節，同學必須分辨清楚，牢記在心，方能在寫作上純熟運用非限定形容詞子句，從而寫出合乎英文文法的複句。

▶▶ **8.7.14 非限定用法形容詞子句的形成**

我們用以下例句來示範非限定用法形容詞子句的使用情況以及其形成過程，包括四種不同先行詞的情況：（一）**先行詞為專有名詞，其指稱的對象已經清楚明確**，（二）**先行詞為普通名詞，以非限定用法形容詞子句來解釋該名詞的涵義**，（三）**由上下文可以知道普通名詞之先行詞指稱的對象**，以及（四）**which 用來指稱前面的整個句子**。

(一) 先行詞為專有名詞

先行詞為專有名詞時，其指稱的對象已經清楚明確，可以是指稱特定的人、地方、事物、事件、何地、何時，當我們使用一個句子來敘述該專有名詞時，可以同時在該名詞之後以非限定形容詞子句來敘述該名詞的特徵或所涉及的其他情況，提供給讀者額外的訊息。先行詞為專有名詞中的人、地方、物、及事件時，必須依據不同情況使用不同的關係代名詞來加以指稱，並引導該形容詞子句，這樣的情況較為普遍；若先行詞表達何地、何時的情況，則可以使用關係副詞 (when, where) 來引導非限定形容詞子句。

1. 專有名詞指稱特定的人

例一：

(1) **Dr. Symonds** is giving a speech in our school next week.
（句子敘述 Dr. Symonds 將要做的事）

(2) **Dr. Symonds** is a famous sociologist.（句子說明 Dr. Symonds 本身的一個特徵）

步驟一：先將句子 (2) 的主詞 Dr. Symonds 以**主格關係代名詞 who** 取代，轉換成非限定形容詞子句 → **who** is a famous sociologist

步驟二：再將非限定形容詞子句置於句子 (1) 的專有名詞 **Dr. Symonds** 之後，並以逗點隔開，完成複句的結構。→ **Dr. Symonds, who is a famous sociologist** , is giving a speech in our school next week.

例二：

(1) After teaching for 40 years, **Mrs. Welch** will retire next year.

（句子敘述 Mrs. Welch 將要做的事）

(2) Many students admire **Mrs. Welch**.（句子敘述 Mrs. Welch 其他的情況）

步驟一：先將句子 (2) 的受詞 Mrs. Welch 以**受格關係代名詞 who** 取代，轉換成非限定形容詞子句 → **who** many students admire

步驟二：再將非限定形容詞子句置於句子 (1) 的專有名詞 **Mrs. Welch** 之後，並以逗點隔開，完成複句的結構。

→ After teaching for 40 years, **Mrs. Welch,** who many students admire , will retire next year.

2. 專有名詞指稱特定的地方

(1) **Hawaii** is famous for its beautiful beaches and sunny weather.

（句子敘述 **Hawaii** 的狀況）

(2) **Hawaii** draws millions of local and foreign tourists every year.

（句子敘述 **Hawaii** 其他的狀況）

步驟一：先將句子 (2) 的主詞 **Hawaii** 以**主格關係代名詞 which** 取代，轉換成非限定形容詞子句 → **which** draws millions of local and foreign tourists every year

步驟二：再將非限定形容詞子句置於句子 (1) 的專有名詞 **Hawaii** 之後，並以逗點隔開，完成複句的結構。

→ **Hawaii,** which draws millions of local and foreign tourists every year , is famous for its beautiful beaches and sunny weather.

3. 專有名詞指稱特定的事物

(1) **The Statue of Liberty** is a symbol of freedom and democracy.

（句子敘述 the Statue of Liberty）

(2) **The Statue of Liberty** was a gift from the people of France to the United States.

（句子說明 the Statue of Liberty 本身的一個特徵）

步驟一：先將句子 (2) 的主詞 the Statue of Liberty 以主格關係代名詞 **which** 取代，轉換成非限定形容詞子句

→ **which** was a gift from the people of France to the United States

步驟二：再將非限定形容詞子句置於句子 (1) 的專有名詞 **the Statue of Liberty** 之後，並以逗點隔開，完成複句的結構。

→ **The Statue of Liberty,** which was a gift from the people of France to the United States , is a symbol of freedom and democracy.

4. 專有名詞指稱特定的事件或節慶

(1) Hoping to get rich overnight, thousands of gold miners flocked to San Francisco during **the California Gold Rush**.

（句子敘述涉及 the California Gold Rush）

(2) **The California Gold Rush** began on January 24, 1848 and peaked in 1852.

（句子說明 the California Gold Rush 本身的一個特徵）

步驟一：先將句子 (2) 的主詞 the California Gold Rush 以主格關

係代名詞 **which** 取代，轉換成非限定形容詞子句

→ **which** began on January 24, 1848 and peaked in 1852

步驟二：再將非限定形容詞子句置於句子 (1) 的專有名詞 **the California Gold Rush** 之後，並以逗點隔開，完成複句的結構。

→ Hoping to get rich overnight, thousands of gold miners flocked to San Francisco during **the California Gold Rush, which began on January 24, 1848 and peaked in 1852** .

(二) 先行詞為普通名詞，以非限定用法形容詞子句來解釋該名詞的涵義

(1) **A smartphone** incorporates functions of computers and phones.

(2) **A smartphone** allows people to download and upload all kinds of information and videos anytime anywhere.

步驟一：先將句子 (1) 的主詞 a smartphone 以**主格關係代名詞 which** 取代，轉換成非限定形容詞子句 → **which** incorporates functions of computers and phones

步驟二：再將非限定形容詞子句置於句子 (2) 的普通名詞 **a smartphone** 之後，並以逗點隔開，完成複句的結構。

→ **A smartphone,** **which incorporates functions of computers and phones** , allows people to have easy access to all kinds of information and videos anytime anywhere.

(三) 先行詞為普通名詞，由上下文已知其所指稱對象

(1) She bought **a new dress** in the department store yesterday.

(2) **The new dress** cost her $350.

(3) **The new dress** got ruined by spilled coffee at work today.

步驟一：先將句子 (2) 的主詞 the new dress 以**主格關係代名詞 which** 取代，轉換成非限定形容詞子句 → **which** cost her $350

步驟二：再將非限定形容詞子句置於句子 (3) 的普通名詞 **the new dress** 之後，並以逗點隔開，完成複句的結構。

→ She bought **a new dress** in the department store yesterday. **The new dress**, which cost her $350 , got ruined by spilled coffee at work today.

(四)which 用來指稱前面的整個句子（補述用法）

(1) The city government decided to suspend all classes on Monday due to the typhoon.

(2) It made both the teachers and the students very happy.

步驟一：以**主格關係代名詞 which** 取代句子 (2) 的代名詞 it，轉換成非限定形容詞子句 → **which** made both the teachers and the students very happy

步驟二：再將非限定形容詞子句置於句子 (1) 之後，並以逗點隔開，完成複句的結構。→ The city government decided to suspend all classes on Monday due to the typhoon, which made both the teachers and the students very happy .

（**which** 用來指稱前面的句子「**因為颱風的關係，市政府決定禮拜一停課**」，**此舉**使得老師和學生都很開心。）

注意：非限定用法的形容詞子句在寫作時必須跟它所修飾的先行詞以逗點隔開，並且該類型的形容詞子句若是放在句中，該子句的結尾也必須加上逗點。

▶▶▶ 8.7.15 以關係副詞引導的非限定形容詞子句

非限定用法的形容詞子句，大多是以關係代名詞來指稱先行詞，並引導該非限定形容詞子句；但先行詞若是表達**地點**或**時間**，則可以使用**關係副詞**來指稱先行詞，並引導該非限定形容詞子句。在限定用法，可以使用的關係副詞有表達地點的 where，表達時間的 when，以及表達原因的 why；而在**非限定用法**，則只能使用**表達地點的 where** 以及**表達時間的 when**，而 **where** 及 **when** 都是由 介系詞 + which 轉換而來，如下列例句：

人們得以目睹壯觀日出的 阿里山每年吸引數十萬的遊客。
Ali Mountain, where (= in which) people get to watch the magnificent sunrise , attracts hundreds of thousands of tourists annually.（先行詞為已知的地點）

臺灣民眾在**農曆除夕**享用傳統美食，當天家庭成員回到父母老家團圓。
People in Taiwan eat traditional food on **Lunar New Year's Eve,** when (= on which) family members return to their parents' home for reunion .（先行詞為已知的時間）

先行詞	關係副詞
地點	**where (in which, at which, on which)**
時間	**when (in which, at which, on which)**

(一) 以關係副詞 where 引導非限定形容詞子句

(1) Many people prefer to live in **Taichung**.（句子敘述涉及 Taichung）

(2) The weather is mild in **Taichung**.（句子說明 Taichung 本身的一個特徵）

先將句子 (2) 轉換成非限定形容詞子句

→ the weather is mild in **which**（以關係代名詞 **which** 取代 **Taichung**）

→ **in which** the weather is mild（將 **in which** 移到子句前端，完成非限定形容詞子句）

→ **where** the weather is mild（以關係副詞 **where** 取代 **in which**，來引導非限定形容詞子句）

再將非限定形容詞子句置於句子 (1) 的專有名詞 Taichung 之後，並以逗點隔開，完成複句的結構。

→ Many people prefer to live in **Taichung**, where the weather is mild .

(二) 以關係副詞 where 引導非限定形容詞子句

(1) They were celebrating their 35th wedding anniversary on **May 21, 2018**.

（句子敘述涉及 May 21, 2018）

(2) They received a wonderful gift from their children on **May 21, 2018**.

（句子說明 May 21, 2018 當天發生的某一件事）

先將句子 (2) 轉換成非限定形容詞子句

→ they received a wonderful gift from their children on **which**（以關係代名詞 **which** 取代 **May 21, 2018**）

→ **on which** they received a wonderful gift from their children（將 **on which** 移到子句前端，完成非限定形容詞子句）

→ **when** they received a wonderful gift from their children（以關係副詞 **when** 取代 **on which**，來引導限定形容詞子句）

再將非限定形容詞子句置於句子 (1) 的專有名詞 May 21, 2018 之後，並以逗點隔開，完成複句的結構。

They were celebrating their 35th wedding anniversary on **May 21, 2018,** when they received a wonderful gift from their children .

▶▶ 8.7.16 小試身手

依先行詞的類別和作用，填入適當的關係代名詞或關係副詞以完成非限定用法形容詞子句。

1. Julian's father, _____ parents immigrated to California from Taiwan in the 1960s, is now a famous physician in Los Angeles.

2. The study is exploring the effects of early exposures to more than one language in childhood. The results of the study, _____ was conducted by a group of linguists, will be presented in the conference next month.

3. Dr. Martin Lo, _____ is an expert in food science, was invited to make a speech in Taipei regarding food safety.

4. The old bridge, _____ was built more than a hundred years ago, will be demolished next week as the new one has been built to replace it.

5. The information is transmitted back to the control center, _____ has used the data to cut electricity costs by 25% and garbage costs by 20%.

6. The McDonald's in Taiwan, _____ children enjoy the happy meals and playrooms, has been sold to a Taiwanese businessman.

7. Native Americans, _____ culture is completely different from the white people, have long known how to use natural resources in a sustainable way.

8. In 2016, the Chicago Cubs finally won the World Series again after a 108-year drought, _____ made their fans crazily celebrate the victory everywhere in the city.

9. He had a car accident on Lunar New Year's Eve last year, _____ everyone was supposed to celebrate the coming of New Year.

10. Master Zhu, from _____ many students have learned how to sculpt, has set up a sculpture museum in Taipei.

11. The Sun Moon Lake, _____ was originally built for generating hydraulic power, has become one of the hottest tourist spots in central Taiwan.

12. Eric, the production manager, _____ has just been promoted, will be sent to the branch in Paris.

8.7.17 非限定用法形容詞子句與獨立子句的結合

　　當兩個簡單句**含有相同的專有名詞或已知指稱對象的普通名詞**時，我們可以將其中一個簡單句共同的名詞改成**關係代名詞**，而將簡單句轉換成**非限定用法的形容詞子句**，然後再與另外一個維持不變的簡單句結合，成為一個新的複句。必須注意的是，跟限定形容詞子句一樣，有的情況我們會使用關係代名詞來指稱先行詞並引導子句，有的情況則會將 介系詞 +which 轉換成關係副詞，而以關係副詞來引導非限定形容詞子句。因此，我們用以下九個例子來說明，包括有**七種情況**會使用**關**係代名詞來指稱不同類別的先行詞，以及另外**兩種情況**會使用**關係副詞 where 跟 when 來引導非限定形容詞子句**（why 只會用在限定用法），在不同的情況，如何將簡單句轉換為**非限定的形容詞子句**，再與**獨立子句**結合成為**複句**的過程。

1. 使用關係代名詞指稱先行詞的七種情況

例一 先行詞屬人的主格 ：

(1) **Steve Jobs** was the founder of Apple Company.

(2) **Steve Jobs** created the iPhone.

改法一：將句子 (1) 改為非限定形容詞子句，句子 (2) 維持不變。

步驟一 ：以人的主格關係代名詞 who 取代句子 (1) 的共同專有名詞 Steve Jobs, 完成非限定形容詞子句。

→ **who** was the founder of Apple Company

步驟二 ：再將非限定形容詞子句與維持不變的句子 (2) 結合成為一個複句

→ Steve Jobs, **who was the founder of Apple Company**, created the iPhone.

改法二：將句子 (2) 改爲非限定形容詞子句，句子 (1) 維持不變。

步驟一：以人的主格關係代名詞 who 取代句子 (2) 的共同專有名詞 Steve Jobs, 完成非限定形容詞子句。

→ **who** created iPhone

步驟二：再將非限定形容詞子句與維持不變的句子 (1) 結合成爲一個複句

→ Steve Jobs, **who created the iPhone,** was the founder of Apple Company.

例二 先行詞屬人的所有格：

(1) Dora's major is Art History.

(2) Dora wants to become a curator of an art museum one day.

步驟一：以人的所有格關係代名詞取代句子 (1) 的共同名詞 Dora's，完成非限定形容詞子句。

→ **whose** major is Art History

步驟二：再將非限定形容詞子句與維持不變的句子 (2) 結合成爲一個複句

→ Dora, **whose major is Art History,** wants to become a curator of an art museum one day.

例三 先行詞屬人的受格：

(1) People all over the world adore **Kate Middleton.**

(2) **Kate Middleton** married to Prince William on April 29, 2011.

步驟一：以人的受格關係代名詞取代句子 (1) 的共同專有名詞 Kate Middleton

→ people all over the world adore **who / whom**

步驟二：再將 **who / whom** 移到子句前端，完成非限定形容詞子句。

→ **who / whom** people all over the world adore

步驟三：再將非限定形容詞子句與維持不變的句子 (2) 結合成為一個複句

→ Kate Middleton, **who / whom people all over the world adore,** married to Prince William on April 29, 2011.

例四 先行詞屬人的受格，且關係代名詞出現在介系詞後面

(1) The airport in New York was named after **John F. Kennedy**.

(2) **John F. Kennedy** was a great leader in American history.

步驟一：以人的受格關係代名詞 **whom** 取代句子 (1) 的共同專有名詞 John F. Kennedy（出現在介系詞 after 後面，不能用 who）

→ the airport in New York was named after **whom**

步驟二：再將 **after whom 移到子句前端**，完成非限定形容詞子句。

→ after **whom** the airport in New York was named

步驟三：最後再將非限定形容詞子句與維持不變的句子 (2) 結合成為一個複句

→ John F. Kennedy, after **whom the airport in New York was named,** was a great leader in American history.

例五 先行詞屬非人的主格：

(1) ***The Adventures of Tom Sawyer*** is an 1876 novel by Mark Twain.

(2) ***The Adventures of Tom Sawyer*** tells a story of Tom Sawyer and his friend Huckleberry Finn.

改法一：將句子 (1) 改成非限定形容詞子句，句子 (2) 維持不變。

步驟一：以非人的主格關係代名詞取代句子 (1) 的共同專有名詞 *the Adventure of Tom Sawyer*，完成非限定形容詞子句。

→ **which** is an 1876 novel by Mark Twain

步驟二：再將非限定形容詞子句與維持不變的句子 (2) 結合成為一個複句

→ *The Adventures of Tom Sawyer*, <u>**which is an 1876 novel by Mark Twain,**</u> tells a story of Tom Sawyer and his friend Huckleberry Finn.

改法二：將句子 (2) 改成非限定形容詞子句，句子 (1) 維持不變。

步驟一：以**非人的主格關係代名詞 which** 取代句子 (2) 的共同專有名詞 *the Adventure of Tom Sawyer*，完成非限定形容詞子句。

→ **which** tells a story of Tom Sawyer and his friend Huckleberry Finn

步驟二：再將再將非限定形容詞子句與維持不變的句子 (2) 結合成為一個複句

→ *The Adventure of Tom Sawyer*, <u>**which tells a story of Tom Sawyer and his friend Huckleberry Finn,**</u> is an 1876 novel by Mark Twain.

：

(1) **Taipei 101's** fireworks on New Year's Eve is one of the greatest events in Taiwan.

(2) **Taipei 101** is an icon of modern Taiwan.

步驟一：以非人的所有格關係代名詞 **whose** 取代句子 (1) 的共同專有名詞 Taipei 101's，完成非限定形容詞子句。

→ **whose** fireworks on New Year's Eve is one of the greatest events in Taiwan

步驟二：再將非限定形容詞子句與維持不變的句子 (2) 結合成爲一個複句

→ Taipei 101, **whose fireworks on New Year's Eve is one of the greatest events in Taiwan,** is an icon of modern Taiwan.

例七 先行詞屬非人的受格：

(1) Her family depends on **Winnie's income**.

(2) **Winnie's income** will greatly increase as she has found a much better job.

步驟一：以非人的受格關係代名詞 **which** 取代句子 (1) 已知指稱對象的共同名詞片語 Winnie's income

→ her family depends on **which**

步驟二：再將 on which 移到子句前端，完成非限定形容詞子句。

→ **on which** her family depends

步驟三：最後再將非限定形容詞子句與維持不變的句子 (2) 結合成爲一個複句

→ Winnie's income, **on which her family depends,** will greatly increase as she has found a much better job.

2. 使用關係副詞 where, when 引導非限定形容詞子句的兩種情況

例八 使用關係副詞 where 來引導非限定形容詞子句

(1) Tourists enjoy rice noodles and other traditional delicacies in **Hsinchu**（新竹）.

(2) **Hsinchu** is widely known for its high-tech companies in the industrial park.

步驟一：以非人的受格關係代名詞 which 取代句子 (1) 的專有名詞 Hsinchu

→ tourists enjoy rice noodles and other traditional delicacies in **which**

步驟二：再將 **in which** 移到子句前端，完成非限定形容詞子句。

→ **in which** tourists enjoy rice noodles and other traditional delicacies

步驟三：再將 **in which** 轉換成關係副詞 **where**

→ **where** tourists enjoy rice noodles and other traditional delicacies

步驟四：最後再將非限定形容詞子句與維持不變的句子 (2) 結合成為一個複句

→ Hsinchu, **where tourists enjoy rice noodles and other traditional delicacies,** is widely known for its high-tech companies in the industrial park.

例九 使用關係副詞 **when** 來引導非限定形容詞子句

(1) Children receive presents on **Christmas**.

(2) People celebrate **Christmas** for the birth of Jesus Christ.

步驟一：以非人的受格關係代名詞 **which** 取代句子 (1) 的共同專有名詞 Christmas

→ children receive presents on **which**

步驟二：再將 **on which** 移到子句前端，完成非限定形容詞子句。

→ **on which** children receive presents

步驟三：再將 **on which** 轉換成關係副詞 **when**

→ **when** children receive presents

步驟四：最後再將非限定形容詞子句與維持不變的句子 (2) 結合成為一個複句

→ People celebrate Christmas, **when children receive presents,** for the birth of Jesus Christ.

▶▶ 8.7.18 英文非限定用法形容詞子句的位置與中文的轉換

英文的**非限定形容詞子句**與限定用法一樣，都必須放在最靠近先行詞之後的位置；相對地，關係代名詞為**主格或所有格**時，英文的非限定形容詞子句翻成中文後可能以不同的中文句子形式呈現，或是縮減為中文的片語，而其出現的位置可能在**先行詞之前或之後**；而關係代名詞若是**受格**時，英文的非限定形容詞子句在**中文的結構不盡相同，而其放置的位置也有不同的變化。**舉例說明如下：

(一) 關係代名詞為主格

例一：

National Museum of Natural Science, **which is a five-ven-ue complex,** is a major science learning center.

英文的非限定形容詞子句**可能以不同的中文句子形式呈現**：

→國立自然科學博物館，**本身是一座五個展覽場地的綜合建築**，是一個主要的科學學習中心。（**英文的非限定形容詞子句翻成中文後同樣出現在先行詞之後**）

→**本身是一座五個展覽場地的綜合建築**，國立自然科學博物館是一個主要的科學學習中心。（**英文的非限定形容詞子句翻成中文後反而出現在先行詞之前**）

→**本身是一座五個展覽場地的綜合建築的**國立自然科學博物館是一個主要的科學學習中心。（**英文的非限定形容詞子句翻成中文後反而出現在先行詞之前**）

英文的非限定形容詞子句**縮減為中文的名詞片語**：

→國立自然科學博物館，**一座五個展覽場地的綜合建築**，是一個主要的科學學習中心。（**縮減為中文的名詞片語，出現在先行詞之後**）

→**一座五個展覽場地的綜合建築**，國立自然科學博物館是一個主要的科學學習中心。（**縮減為中文的名詞片語，出現在先行詞之前**）

上述的例句中非限定形容詞子句可以縮減為中文的名詞片語，

這樣的句子結構變化如同英文將形容詞子句簡化爲名詞片語，作爲主詞的同位語：

→ National Museum of Natural Science, **a five-venue complex**, is a major science learning center.

→ **A five-venue complex**, National Museum of Natural Science is a major science learning center.

例二：

Mark Zuckerberg , **who co-founded Facebook in 2004,** has become one of the richest men on Earth.

英文的非限定形容詞子句可能以不同的中文句子形式呈現：

→ Mark Zuckerberg ，他於 2004 共同創建了臉書，已經成爲地表上最富有的人之一。（英文的非限定形容詞子句翻成中文後同樣出現在先行詞之後）

→ 於 2004 共同創建了臉書， Mark Zuckerberg 已經成爲地表上最富有的人之一。（英文的非限定形容詞子句翻成中文後反而出現在先行詞之前）

→ 於 2004 共同創建了臉書的 Mark Zuckerberg 已經成爲地表上最富有的人之一。（英文的非限定形容詞子句翻成中文後反而出現在先行詞之前）

英文的非限定形容詞子句縮減爲中文的動詞片語：

→ Mark Zuckerberg ，於 2004 共同創建了臉書，已經成爲地表上最富有的人之一。（縮減爲中文的動詞片語，出現在先行

詞之後）

→於 **2004 共同創建了臉書**，Mark Zuckerberg 已經成爲地
表上最富有的人之一。（**縮減爲中文的動詞片語，出現在先行
詞之前**）

上述例句中英文的非限定形容詞子句可以縮減爲動詞片語，
但在**英文句子的結構**，中文的動詞片語必須轉換成現在分詞片語
co-founding Facebook in 2004，才能用來修飾主詞 Mark Zuck-
erberg，如下列例句：

→ Mark Zuckerberg, **co-founding Facebook in 2004**, has
become one of the richest men on Earth.
→ **Co-founding Facebook in 2004**, Mark Zuckerberg has
become one of the richest men on Earth.

貼心提醒

同學如果按照中文結構寫成下列的英文句子
*Mark Zuckerberg, **co-founded** Facebook in 2004, has become
one of the richest men on Earth.*
這樣的句子結構就錯了！事實上這樣的結構錯誤常常出現在臺灣
學生的英文寫作，不可不慎！

（有關形容詞子句簡化爲現在分詞片語及過去分詞片語的技巧
請詳讀本篇後面的解說。）

(二) 關係代名詞為所有格

　　例如：

　　 Jeremy Lin , **whose sudden surge in NBA created Lin-sanity in 2012,** is now a point guard of the Toronto Raptors.

　　英文的非限定形容詞子句**可能以不同的中文句子形式呈現**：

→ 林書豪 ，**其突然崛起於 2012 年創造了林來瘋**，現在是多倫多暴龍隊的控衛。（**英文的非限定形容詞子句翻成中文後同樣出現在先行詞之後**）

→ **其突然崛起於 2012 年創造了林來瘋**， 林書豪 現在是多倫多暴龍隊的控衛。（**英文的非限定形容詞子句翻成中文後反而出現在先行詞之前**）

→ **突然崛起於 2012 年創造了林來瘋的** 林書豪 ，現在是多倫多暴龍隊的控衛。（**英文的非限定形容詞子句翻成中文後反而出現在先行詞之前**）

(三) 關係代名詞為受格

　　例一：

　　 Mr. Chen ，**to whom the billionaire gave his fortune in his will,** will set up a foundation for public health with the inherited wealth.

　　英文的非限定形容詞子句以中文形容詞子句的形式，出現在先行詞之前：

→ **這位億萬富翁在其遺囑中把財產留給他的** 陳先生 ，將會以其所繼承的財富設立一個公共健康的基金會。（**以中文形容詞子句**

的形式出現在先行詞之前）

英文的非限定形容詞子句縮減為中文名詞片語，<u>出現在先行詞之後</u>：

→ 陳先生，**也就是這位億萬富翁在其遺囑中把財產留給他的人**，將會以其所繼承的財富設立一個公共健康的基金會。（以中文名詞片語的形式出現在先行詞之後）

例二：

They have sold their house in Taipei , **which they bought twenty years ago.**

英文的非限定形容詞子句縮減為中文名詞片語，出現在先行詞之後：

→ 他們已經賣掉了臺北的房子，**就是他們二十年前所買的房子**（以中文名詞片語的形式出現在先行詞之後）。

英文的非限定形容詞子句以中文形容詞子句的形式，<u>出現在先行詞之前</u>：

→ 他們已經賣掉了**他們二十年前買的**臺北的房子。（以中文形容詞子句的形式出現在先行詞之前）

英文的非限定形容詞子句縮減為中文形容詞片語，出現在先行詞之前：

→ **二十年前買的**臺北的房子，他們已經賣掉了。（以中文形容詞片語的形式出現在先行詞之前）

由以上的例句，我們瞭解到中英文的句子結構差異極大，因此在英文寫作時，必須注意避免受到中文結構的影響，否則一不小心就寫出不合英文文法、怪裡怪氣的英文句子了。

 8.7.19 小試身手
　　改正下列句子中有關形容詞子句的錯誤

1. The young couple is looking for an apartment which monthly rent is around NT$15,000.

2. Tina has read 20 books during the summer break, and one of which is "*Kira, Kira,*" that is a novel written by a Japanese American author.

3. Steven Curry shoots sharply from three-point range, has created many new records in the NBA.

4. The Taiwan High Speed Rail that connects the major cities in the west coast of Taiwan represents the new era of Taiwan's transportation system.

5. The hunters are trying to figure out the reason how the wild boar escaped from the trap.

6. Donald Trump, is the President of the United States, holds a strong stance against illegal immigrants.

7. Kending National Park is the first national park in Taiwan was established in 1982.

8. Brain is a successful businessman, who is specialized in creative marketing, has just published a new book.

▶▶ 8.7.20 小試身手

　　將下列各題中劃底限的簡單句，依其作用，轉換成限定或非限定形容詞子句，再將該形容詞子句與維持不變的簡單句結合成為複句。

1. Dr. Huang graduated from the University of Delaware.
Dr. Huang is now a renowned professor at a prestigious university in Taiwan.

_____

_____

2. She has read eight books during this semester.
One of the eight books is "*When You Reach Me,*" a novel about making sacrifices for friends.

_____

_____

3. A virtual reality headset allows people to experience a three dimensional, computer generated environment when playing games.
A virtual reality headset can cost as much as $800.

_____

_____

4. The City Council initiated the plan to build a new shopping mall.

   A new shopping mall will be located in the outskirts of the city.

   _____

   _____

5. The Moon Festival is celebrated on the fifteenth day of August on the lunar calendar.

   Family members in Taiwan gather together for reunion on the Moon Festival.

   _____

   _____

6. The two-year study lead by Dr. White is aimed at finding out the key factors contributing to the fast economic growth of the country in recent years.

   The results of the study will be released next year.

   _____

   _____

7. The teacher invited the students to a dinner party at her house. The students participated in community services during the winter break.

   （說明：有些學生並未參與社區服務，而老師只邀請有參與社區服務的學生。）

   _____

   _____

8. My car has been running over 5,000 kilometers since its last maintenance.

The engine oil of my car needs to be changed.

_____

_____

9. Nathan is the new CEO of this multinational corporation operating in Taipei.
The amazing success of this corporation is attributed to Nathan's unique vision.

_____

_____

10. People in Taiwan like to shop at Costco.
A large variety of imported American foods are available at Costco.

_____

_____

▶▶ 8.7.21 小試身手

　　將下列句子翻譯成英文，句子中劃底限的部分要依上下文情況，選擇以限定或非限定形容詞子句加以翻譯。

1. Jennifer 的父親目前是洛杉磯出名的醫師，他是隨著雙親於 1970 年代由臺灣移民到加州。
Jennifer's father _____

_____

2. 爲這家高科技公司工作是他夢寐以求的機會。

_____

3. Tony 擁有物理治療碩士學位，他想要找一份和他的專長密切相關的工作。
With a master's degree in physical therapy, _____

_____

4. 昨天經理面試的其中一位女士是跟公司完美的搭配。

_____

was a perfect match for the company.

5. 臺灣的小學每一個班級都有自己的教室，學生在那裏上幾乎所有的課程。

In Taiwan, every class _____

6. 曝露在兩種語言同時說的環境的小孩會自然的學會那兩種語言。

_____

will acquire the two languages naturally.

7. 網路商店提供不常外出或住在偏遠地區的消費者很方便的購物方式。

Online stores provide _____ for

_____

8. 今年的聖誕派對我們會交換價錢不少於一千元臺幣的禮物。

_____

in the Christmas party this year.

9. 為了吸引國外投資者，政府必須創造一個安全無貪汙且低稅制的友善環境。

_____, the government must create _____

_____.

10. 殺人鯨是世界上最大型的掠食動物，會一起合作獵取獵物。

Killer whales _____

_____

11. 會兩種外語的人找到待遇好的工作的機會比只會一種外語的要好的多。

_____ have much better

chances of _____ than _____

_____

12. 李大師<u>在流行音樂產業工作多年</u>，是好幾首電影主題曲的作曲
者。

Master Lee _____

_____

13. <u>花時間陪自己孩子並且經常全家一起去度假</u>的父母跟孩子培養
出比較好的關係。

_____

_____ better relationships with them.

14. <u>曾經在日本打過職業棒球</u>的陳偉殷現在是美國大聯盟的先發投
手。

Weiyin Chen _____

_____

15. Sandra Bullock，<u>曾經在 2010 年贏得奧斯卡金像獎最佳女主
角</u>的著名電影明星，將擔任這部新片的導演。

_____

_____ will be the director of the new film.

8.7.22 形容詞子句挑戰題

將下列句子先按第一句中文翻成兩句或三句或四句英文，再將
其結合成括號內含有限定或非限定形容詞子句的中文英譯的複句。
（劃底線部分為限定或非限定形容詞子句）

1. (1) 氣候變遷主要肇因於化石燃料的消耗，(2) 農人受害於氣候
變遷最深。（1+2：<u>農人受其害最深</u>的氣候變遷，主要肇因於化
石燃料的消耗。）

(1)_____

(2)_____

(1)+(2)_____

_____

2. (1) Paul 精通英語和西班牙語，(2) 他擔任部門主管，(3) 這個部門負責開發海外市場。（1+2+3：精通英語和西班牙語的 Paul 在負責開發海外市場的部門擔任主管。）

(1)_____

(2)_____

(3)_____

(1)+(2)+(3)_____

_____

3. (1) 有機食品依據有機耕種標準所生產，(2) 有機食品越來越受到消費者的歡迎。（1+2：依據有機耕種標準所生產的有機食品，越來越受到消費者的歡迎。）

(1)_____

(2)_____

(1)+(2)_____

_____

4. (1) 世界大學運動會（The Universiade）是一項國際體育與文化盛事。(2) 世界大學運動會每兩年一次由不同城市舉辦。（1+2：世界大學運動會（The Universiade）是一項國際體育與文化盛事，每兩年一次由不同城市舉辦。）（106 年指考）

(1)_____

(2)_____

(1)+(2)_____

_____

5. (1) 在快速變遷的全球經濟體系下，一家公司需要經常為其員工辦理工作坊及現場訓練課程以提升其專業知識與技能。(2) 公司依賴員工的專業知識與技能來增強其生產力與競爭力。（1+2：在快速變遷的全球經濟體系下，一家公司需要經常為其員工辦理工作坊及現場訓練課程以提升公司所賴以增強其生產力與競爭力的員工的專業知識與技能）

(1)_____

_____

(2)_____

_____

(1)+(2)_____

_____

6. (1) 這項數百萬美金的醫學研究計畫是由一家大型製藥公司所資助，(2) 這項研究計畫正在招聘學者和研究人員，(3) 這些人員在生物科技領域學有專精。（1+2+3：這項由一家大型製藥公司所資助的數百萬美金的醫學研究計畫正在招聘在生物科技領域學有專精的學者和研究人員。）

(1)_____
(2)_____
(3)_____
(1)+(2)+(3)_____

_____

_____

7. (1) 經過多年的施工，美國終於在 1914 年完成並開放巴拿馬運河，(2) 該運河連接了大西洋和太平洋並大大縮短了時間，(3) 船隻花時間航行於這兩大洋之間航行。（1+2+3：經過多年的施工，美國終於在 1914 年完成並開放連接大西洋和太平洋的巴拿馬運河，並大大縮短了船隻航行於這兩大洋之間所花的時間。）

(1) _____

_____

(2) _____

_____

(3) _____

(1)+(2)+(3) _____

_____

8. (1) 他們祖母昨天正在慶祝八十大壽，(2) 他們已經祕密錄製了一段影片要祝賀她。(3) 當她看到這段影片非常開心地笑了。

（1+2+3：昨天正在慶祝八十大壽的他們的祖母，看到他們已經祕密錄製了要祝賀她的影片時，非常開心地笑了。）

(1) _____

(2) _____

(3) _____

(1)+(2)+(3) _____

_____

_____

9. (1) 大坑每天吸引很多登山客，(2) 一群年輕廚師曾經在不同餐廳工作，(3) 他們已經在大坑開了一家新餐廳，(4) 在這家餐廳登山客可以享用海鮮，(5) 海鮮是由澎湖每天空運來的。（在每天吸引很多登山客的大坑，一群曾經在不同餐廳工作的年輕廚師已經，新開了一家客人可以享受由澎湖每天空運來的海鮮的新餐廳。）

(1) _____

(2) _____

(3) _____

(4) _____

(5) _____

(1)+(2)+(3)+(4)+(5) _____

_____

_____

_____

8.8 複句 (complex sentences)

　　一個獨立子句加上至少一個從屬子句即可構成複句，也就是複句的結構中可能包含一個獨立子句（或稱主要子句）以及一個或數個相同或不同的從屬子句，如以下所示：

*To find out **what makes human screams unique***, *neuroscientist Luc Arnal and his team examined a bank of sounds containing sentences spoken or screamed by 19 adults.*（105年指考）

　　句子結構：獨立子句／主要子句 + **名詞子句** = 複句
　　　　　　　（名詞子句包含在不定詞片語之內）
　　獨立子句：主部 neuroscientist Luc Arnal and his team／述
　　　　　　　部 examined…19 adults
　　名詞子句：what makes human screams unique

Young children can acquire two languages at the same time **as long as they have enough exposure to both of them***.*

句子結構：獨立子句 / 主要子句 + **副詞子句** ＝ 複句

獨立子句：主部 young children / 述部 can acquire…the same time

副詞子句：as long as they have enough exposure to both of them

*Not long after World War II, Cartier-Bresson traveled east, spending considerable time in India, **where he met and photographed Gandhi shortly before his assassination in 1948**.* （104 學測）

句子結構：獨立子句 / 主要子句 + **形容詞子句** ＝ 複句

獨立子句：主部 Cartier-Bresson / 述部 not long…, traveled…in India,

非限定形容詞子句：where he met and photographed Gandhi shortly… in 1948

*Many people found the story of the Kiddie Stool inspiring **because it showed that with imagination, anyone can be an inventor**.* （105 學測）

句子結構：獨立子句 / 主要子句 + **副詞子句** + **名詞子句** ＝ 複句

獨立子句：主部 many people / 述部 found the story of the Kiddie Stool inspiring

副詞子句：because it showed + 名詞子句

名詞子句：that with imagination, anyone can be an inventor

*The report states **that 40% of all children across the region are currently not receiving an education, which is a result of two consequences of violence: structural dam-***

age to schools and the displacement of populations, also called "forced migration." （105 年指考）

　　句子結構：獨立子句 / 主要子句 + **名詞子句** + **形容詞子句**
　　　　　　　 ＝複句

　　獨立子句：主部 the report / 述部 states + 名詞子句

　　名詞子句：that 40% of all children across… an education, +
　　　　　　　非限定形容詞子句

　　非限定形容詞子句：which is a result… of populations, also
　　　　　　　　　　　 called "forced migration."

*A big difference between the Japanese school system and the American School system is **that Americans respect individuality, while the Japanese control the individual by observing group rules**.*

　　句子結構：獨立子句 / 主要子句 + **名詞子句** + **副詞子句**
　　　　　　　 ＝複句

　　（副詞子句包含在名詞子句之內）

　　獨立子句：主部 a big difference between… school system /
　　　　　　　述部 is + 名詞子句

　　名詞子句：that Americans respect individuality, + 副詞子句

　　副詞子句：while the Japanese control… by observing group
　　　　　　　rules

*In 1982, this story sparked the interest of a British air-force officer and long-distance runner called John Foden, **who wondered if it really was possible to run from Athens to Sparta and arrive the next day***.（102 年指考）

句子結構：獨立子句／主要子句 + **形容詞子句** + **名詞子句**
= 複句

（名詞子句包含在形容詞子句之內）

獨立子句：主部 this story／述部 in 1982, sparked…Foden +
限定形容詞子句

非限定形容詞子句：who wondered + 名詞子句

名詞子句：if it really was possible to run…and arrive the
next day

*Terrence Power, for example, complained **that after his
wife learned she had Wegener's disease, an uncommon dis-
order of the immune system**, they found it difficult to refuse
testing recommended by her physician.*（104 學測）

句子結構：獨立子句／主要子句 + **名詞子句** + **副詞子句** +
名詞子句 = 複句

（副詞子句包含在第一個名詞子句之內，第二個名詞子句則包
含在副詞子句中）

獨立子句：主部 Terrence Power／述部 for example, complained + 名詞子句

名詞子句：that + 副詞子句，they found it difficult…by her
physician

副詞子句：after his wife learned + 名詞子句

名詞子句：she had Wegener's disease, an uncommon disor-
der of the immune system

*The study shows **that** the need to bond with a social group
is **so** fundamental to humans **that** it remains the key determinant*

*of **whether we stay healthy or get ill**, even **whether we live or die**.*（103 年指考）

句子結構：獨立子句／主要子句＋**名詞子句＋副詞子句＋名詞子句＋名詞子句＝複句**

（後面的兩個名詞子句包含在副詞子句之內）

獨立子句：主部 the study／述部 shows ＋名詞子句

名詞子句：that the need to bond with a social group…to humans ＋副詞子句

副詞子句：so… that it remains… determinant of ＋名詞子句，even ＋名詞子句

名詞子句：whether we stay healthy or get ill

名詞子句：whether we live or die

***Although it becomes less experimental as usage grows**, you should keep in mind **that Bitcoin is a new invention that is exploring ideas that have never been attempted before**.*（103 年指考）

句子結構：獨立子句／主要子句＋**副詞子句＋名詞子句＋形容詞子句＋形容詞子句＝複句**

（兩個形容詞子句包含在名詞子句之內）

獨立子句：主部 you／述部 keep in mind ＋名詞子句

副詞子句：although it becomes less experimental as usage grows

名詞子句：that Bitcoin is a new invention ＋限定形容詞子句 ＋限定形容詞子句

限定形容詞子句：that is exploring ideas（前置詞為 invention）

限定形容詞子句：that have never been attempted before（前
置詞為 ideas）

 8.8.1 複句小試身手

分析下列句子結構以找出其中所包含的獨立子句與從屬子句。

示範：

*Consumers wonder if technology benefits society or only
those who control it.*

句子結構：獨立子句（內含名詞子句／名詞子句內含形容詞子句）

獨立子句：consumers wonder ＋ 名詞子句 ＋ 形容詞子句

名詞子句：if technology benefits society or only those ＋ 形容
詞子句

形容詞子句：who control it

---

1. Germs, which scientists call microbes, are actually very small
   organisms that can be seen only under a microscope.
   句子結構：＿＿＿＿＿＿＿＿＿＿＿＿＿＿＿＿＿＿＿＿＿
   子句：＿＿＿＿＿＿＿＿＿＿＿＿＿＿＿＿＿＿＿＿＿＿＿＿
   ＿＿＿＿＿＿＿＿＿＿＿＿＿＿＿＿＿＿＿＿＿＿＿＿＿＿＿
   ＿＿＿＿＿＿＿＿＿＿＿＿＿＿＿＿＿＿＿＿＿＿＿＿＿＿＿
   ＿＿＿＿＿＿＿＿＿＿＿＿＿＿＿＿＿＿＿＿＿＿＿＿＿＿＿

2. Even in areas where winds blow from the sea onto land, deserts can form if there is a mountain range between these lands
   and the sea.
   句子結構：＿＿＿＿＿＿＿＿＿＿＿＿＿＿＿＿＿＿＿＿＿

子句：_____

_____

_____

_____

3. A very important feature of DNA, which determines the complexity of the organism, is that the instructions it contains can be duplicated and passed to offspring.

句子結構：_____

子句：_____

_____

_____

_____

4. The key to understanding why reputable studies are so starkly divided on the question of what Facebook does to our emotional state may be in simply looking at what people actually do when they're on Facebook.

句子結構：_____

子句：_____

_____

_____

_____

5. One very important result of reasoning is that it enables animals to solve problems and respond to difficulties they encounter in their environment even when those difficulties are new to them.

句子結構：_____

子句：_____

6. If you did not have access to safe water, and therefore needed wood to boil drinking water so that you and your children would not get sick, would you worry about causing deforestation?

句子結構：＿＿＿＿＿＿＿＿＿＿＿＿＿＿＿

子句：＿＿＿＿＿＿＿＿＿＿＿＿＿＿＿＿＿

＿＿＿＿＿＿＿＿＿＿＿＿＿＿＿＿＿＿＿＿＿

＿＿＿＿＿＿＿＿＿＿＿＿＿＿＿＿＿＿＿＿＿

7. Everywhere Amelia Earhart, who had accomplished her own solo flight across the Atlantic in 1932, was greeted by people who admired her and were keeping track of her great adventure of attempting to fly with a co-pilot all the way around the world in 1937.

句子結構：＿＿＿＿＿＿＿＿＿＿＿＿＿＿＿

子句：＿＿＿＿＿＿＿＿＿＿＿＿＿＿＿＿＿

＿＿＿＿＿＿＿＿＿＿＿＿＿＿＿＿＿＿＿＿＿

＿＿＿＿＿＿＿＿＿＿＿＿＿＿＿＿＿＿＿＿＿

＿＿＿＿＿＿＿＿＿＿＿＿＿＿＿＿＿＿＿＿＿

8. The two horses had just lain down when a brood of ducklings, which had lost their mother, filed into the barn, cheeping feebly and wandering from side to side to find some place where

they would not be trodden on. (*Animal Farm*)

句子結構：＿＿＿＿＿＿＿＿＿＿＿＿＿＿＿＿

子句：＿＿＿＿＿＿＿＿＿＿＿＿＿＿＿＿＿＿

＿＿＿＿＿＿＿＿＿＿＿＿＿＿＿＿＿＿＿＿＿＿

＿＿＿＿＿＿＿＿＿＿＿＿＿＿＿＿＿＿＿＿＿＿

＿＿＿＿＿＿＿＿＿＿＿＿＿＿＿＿＿＿＿＿＿＿

9. Consumers increasingly believe that because farms and food companies have dramatically increased in size and are using technology they don't recognize or understand, the food system is likely to place profit ahead of public interest.

句子結構：＿＿＿＿＿＿＿＿＿＿＿＿＿＿＿＿

子句：＿＿＿＿＿＿＿＿＿＿＿＿＿＿＿＿＿＿

＿＿＿＿＿＿＿＿＿＿＿＿＿＿＿＿＿＿＿＿＿＿

＿＿＿＿＿＿＿＿＿＿＿＿＿＿＿＿＿＿＿＿＿＿

＿＿＿＿＿＿＿＿＿＿＿＿＿＿＿＿＿＿＿＿＿＿

10. Globalization is defined as a process that, based on international strategies, aims to expand business operations on a worldwide level, and was precipitated by the facilitation of global communications due to technological advancements, and socioeconomic, political and environmental developments.

句子結構：＿＿＿＿＿＿＿＿＿＿＿＿＿＿＿＿

子句：＿＿＿＿＿＿＿＿＿＿＿＿＿＿＿＿＿＿

＿＿＿＿＿＿＿＿＿＿＿＿＿＿＿＿＿＿＿＿＿＿

＿＿＿＿＿＿＿＿＿＿＿＿＿＿＿＿＿＿＿＿＿＿

8.9 複合句 (compound complex sentences)

　　到目前為止，我們已經學會如何運用對等連接詞來連接前後兩個獨立子句以形成合句，也學會如何使用從屬子句，包括名詞子句、副詞子句、以及形容詞子句，來跟獨立子句結合成為複句。接下來，我們要來學習如何完成一個複合句的結構。

　　複合句的構成，顧名思義，就是其中包含了合句跟複句的結構。如以下例句：

*Pamela's boss asked her to work extra hours yesterday for the new project, **but** she did not want to **because she already had other plans**.*

句子結構：獨立子句 + 對等連接詞 but + 獨立子句 + 副詞子句
　　　　　＝複合句

獨立子句：Pamela's boss asked her to work…. for the new project

獨立子句：she did not want to

副詞子句：because she already had other plans

***That the earth is round** is undeniable, **yet** today there are people **who believe that the earth is flat**.*

句子結構：獨立子句（內含名詞子句作為主詞）+ 對等連接詞
　　　　　yet + 獨立子句 + 形容詞子句 + 名詞子句（包含在

形容詞子句中作為受詞）＝複合句

獨立子句：名詞子句 + is undeniable

名詞子句：that the earth is round

獨立子句：today there are people + 限定形容詞子句

限定形容詞子句：who believe + 名詞子句

名詞子句：that the earth is flat

***Even though smartphones are very powerful and popu-
lar today***, *some elderly people* ***who are afraid of new
technologies*** *are reluctant to buy them,* ***and*** ***even when
they are given one***, *they may hesitate to activate the special functions of smartphones.*

句子結構：副詞子句 + 獨立子句（內含形容詞子句）+ 對等連
接詞 and + 副詞子句 + 獨立子句 = 複合句

副詞子句：even though smartphones are very powerful and
popular today

獨立子句：some elderly people + 限定形容詞子句

限定形容詞子句：who are afraid of new technologies

副詞子句：even when they are given one

獨立子句：*they are reluctant to activate the special functions of smartphones*

Students ***who study abroad*** *realize* ***that living and studying in a foreign country is very challenging***, *so they bring
domestic foods and snacks with them* ***when they leave their
own countries***.

句子結構：獨立子句（內含形容詞子句與名詞子句）+ 對等連

接詞 so + 獨立子句 + 副詞子句 = 複合句

獨立子句：students + 限定形容詞子句 realize + 名詞子句

限定形容詞子句：who study abroad

名詞子句：that living in a foreign country is very challenging

獨立子句：they bring domestic foods and snacks with them

副詞子句：when they leave their own countries

After Jason graduated from college, *he found a job in* *San Francisco*, **where the cost of living is one of the most** **expensive in the world**, **but** *he had no choice but to move* *there* **as it was the only good-paying job which he had** **landed**.

句子結構：副詞子句 + 獨立子句（內含形容詞子句）+ 對等連接詞 but + 獨立子句 + 副詞子句（內含形容詞子句）= 複合句

副詞子句：after Jason graduated from college

獨立子句：he found a job in San Francisco + 非限定形容詞子句

非限定形容詞子句：where the cost of living…most expensive in the world

獨立子句：he had no choice but to move there

副詞子句：as it was the only good-paying job + 限定形容詞子句

限定形容詞子句：which he had landed

Google Map, **which is a web mapping service**, *is very use-*

*ful in locating a place **to which the driver has never been**, **yet** sometimes it might plan a route **that would take the driver a much longer time to get to the destination**, or it might navigate the driver to follow a route **that leads to a dead end**.*

句子結構：獨立子句（內含非限定形容詞子句與限定形容詞子句）＋對等連接詞 yet＋獨立子句（內含限定形容詞子句）＋對等連接詞 or＋獨立子句（內含限定形容詞子句）

獨立子句：Google Map,＋非限定形容詞子句, is very⋯place＋限定形容詞子句

非限定形容詞子句：which is a web mapping service

限定形容詞子句：to which the driver had never been

獨立子句：sometimes it might plan a route＋限定形容詞子句

限定形容詞子句：that would take the driver a much⋯to the destinatoin

獨立子句：it might navigate the driver to follow a route

限定形容詞子句：that leads to a dead end

從以上的幾個複合句的例句，我們瞭解到英文句子可以很長，而其結構也可以是非常複雜的，複合句由**至少兩個獨立子句**及**至少一個從屬子句**互相結合而成，其中使用的子句越多，句子就越長，結構也更複雜。這樣又長又複雜的英文句子，就像路上的聯結車，不容易駕馭，必須先練好基本功，由小而大，由簡單而複雜，熟練所有子句的結構及用法，善用不同的對等連接詞、從屬連接詞、關係代名詞、關係副詞來串聯各種子句，

如此便能大展身手，正確地寫出複雜的複句和複合句了。

▶▶ 8.9.1 複合句與連接副詞的運用

　　為了避免句子太過冗長，造成讀者閱讀困難，或甚至寫出結構不合文法的句子，太長的複合句可以去掉對等連接詞，還原成兩個句子，再以連接副詞予以銜接，如此句子較為乾淨俐落，而使用連接副詞銜接兩個句子也維持了語氣的轉折。如下列例句：

At first, it appeared that the bees did avoid the food containing the pesticide, **yet** as individual bees increasingly experience the treated food, they develop a preference for it.

　　本句結構為：複句 + **對等連接詞 yet** + 複句 = 一個複合句
可以改寫成：

At first, it appeared that the bees did avoid the food containing the pesticide. **Nonetheless,** as individual bees increasingly experience the treated food, they develop a preference for it.

　　句子結構變成：複句 + **連接副詞 nonetheless** + 複句 = 兩個複句

Rising greenhouse gas emissions are steadily adding to the upward pressure on temperatures, **but** humans do not feel the change as a straight line because the effects are diminished or amplified by phases of natural variation.

　　本句結構為：簡單句 + **對等連接詞 but** + 複句 = 一個複合句
可以改寫成：

Rising greenhouse gas emissions are steadily adding to the upward pressure on temperatures. **However**, humans do not feel the change as a straight line because the effects are diminished or amplified by phases of natural variation.

句子結構變成：簡單句 + **連接副詞 however** + 複句 = 兩個句子

（有關連接副詞的運用詳細說明於第十一章）

▶▶ 8.9.2 複合句小試身手

分析下列句子結構以找出其中所包含的獨立子句與從屬子句。

示範：

She said that she would sign the contract, yet she denied it the next day.

句子結構：獨立子句（內含名詞子句）+ 對等連接詞 yet + 獨立
　　　　　子句

獨立子句：she said + 名詞子句

名詞子句：that she would sign the contract

獨立子句：she denied it the next day

---

1. When ants are attacked by an intruder, they send a chemical message to each other that acts as an alarm, and they rush to-ward the intruder to bite it and carry it away.

   句子結構：_____

   子句：

   _____

   _____

   _____

2. The earth's general weather patterns are responsible for the formation of the world's hot deserts, but in addition, there are

other things that keep moist air from reaching the areas that have become deserts.

句子結構：＿＿＿＿＿＿＿＿＿＿＿＿＿＿＿＿＿＿＿＿＿

子句：

＿＿＿＿＿＿＿＿＿＿＿＿＿＿＿＿＿＿＿＿＿＿＿＿＿

＿＿＿＿＿＿＿＿＿＿＿＿＿＿＿＿＿＿＿＿＿＿＿＿＿

＿＿＿＿＿＿＿＿＿＿＿＿＿＿＿＿＿＿＿＿＿＿＿＿＿

3. Romeo looked around the room, hoping to catch sight of Rosaline, but suddenly his eyes fell upon a girl so beautiful that all thoughts of Rosaline flew from his brain forever. (*Romeo and Juliet*)

句子結構：＿＿＿＿＿＿＿＿＿＿＿＿＿＿＿＿＿＿＿＿＿

子句：

＿＿＿＿＿＿＿＿＿＿＿＿＿＿＿＿＿＿＿＿＿＿＿＿＿

＿＿＿＿＿＿＿＿＿＿＿＿＿＿＿＿＿＿＿＿＿＿＿＿＿

＿＿＿＿＿＿＿＿＿＿＿＿＿＿＿＿＿＿＿＿＿＿＿＿＿

4. We want to learn about other people and have others learn about us, but through that very learning process we may start to resent both others' lives and the image of ourselves that we need to continuously maintain.

句子結構：＿＿＿＿＿＿＿＿＿＿＿＿＿＿＿＿＿＿＿＿＿

子句：

＿＿＿＿＿＿＿＿＿＿＿＿＿＿＿＿＿＿＿＿＿＿＿＿＿

＿＿＿＿＿＿＿＿＿＿＿＿＿＿＿＿＿＿＿＿＿＿＿＿＿

＿＿＿＿＿＿＿＿＿＿＿＿＿＿＿＿＿＿＿＿＿＿＿＿＿

5. Lieberman and his colleagues demonstrated that a painful

stimulus hurt less when a woman either held her boyfriend's hand or looked at his picture, and the pain-dulling effects of the picture were, in fact, twice as powerful as physical contact.

句子結構：_____

子句：

_____

_____

_____

_____

6. The Irish government is trying to revive activity with new tax breaks, but any recovery will take years when just under 8,500 house were built last year compared to the 23,000 built on average in the 1970s, when Ireland was a much poorer country.

句子結構：_____

子句：

_____

_____

_____

_____

7. Only a handful of his 60 classmates who graduated five years ago found work at home, and of the few others that remain, one owns a cake shop, while another designs mobile phone apps.

句子結構：_____

子句：

_____

8. Concussions occur when the brain bounces against the skull after someone's head is bumped or jolted, and these injuries are fairly common in contact sports, like football and hockey, which are popular in the United States.

句子結構：_____

子句：

_____

_____

_____

_____

9. Vincent Walsh, professor of human brain research at University College London, said people have become obsessed with sleeping only during the night, but he claims that humans have only adopted long night time sleep patterns since the industrial revolution and believes it may be damaging our ability to think creatively.

句子結構：_____

子句：

_____

_____

_____

_____

10. In 2009, the United States had an estimated 5.32 million people holding jobs that were either directly or indirectly involved in the production of goods or services sold to other countries, so for the United States, exports have become essential to economic stability and prosperity.

句子結構：＿＿＿＿＿＿＿＿＿＿＿＿＿＿＿＿＿＿

子句：

＿＿＿＿＿＿＿＿＿＿＿＿＿＿＿＿＿＿＿＿＿＿＿

＿＿＿＿＿＿＿＿＿＿＿＿＿＿＿＿＿＿＿＿＿＿＿

＿＿＿＿＿＿＿＿＿＿＿＿＿＿＿＿＿＿＿＿＿＿＿

＿＿＿＿＿＿＿＿＿＿＿＿＿＿＿＿＿＿＿＿＿＿＿

8.10 子句打通關

（一）寫出下列句子中獨立子句主詞與動詞的結構，（二）寫出從屬子句的連接詞／關係代名詞／關係副詞及主詞與動詞的結構以及其類別，（三）寫出整個句子的類型。

> 示範：
>
> *John Locke, an Englishman, was an Enlightenment philosopher of the 1600s who believed that people should be given as much freedom as possible.*
>
> 獨立子句：**John Locke was …**.
>
> 從屬子句：**1. who believed...** 形容詞子句
>
> **2. that people should be given...** 名詞子句
>
> 句子類型：**複句**

1. While he acknowledges that the virus isn't the sole cause of obesity, it may explain why some people struggle to lose weight.

   獨立子句：_____

   從屬子句：_____

   _____

   _____

   句子類型：_____

2. Because I couldn't bring myself to discard a gift, I decided to ask my in-laws to care for my pot plant while we were away.

   獨立子句：_____

   從屬子句：_____

   _____

   _____

   句子類型：_____

3. It symbolizes a change in me that occurred when I stopped listening to the voices around me and started to believe in myself.

   獨立子句：_____

   從屬子句：_____

   _____

   _____

   句子類型：_____

4. The beautiful rice paddies across three provinces are the result of five-month flood that leaves fertile land for planting without the need to apply any fertilizer.

   獨立子句：_____

從屬子句：_____

_____

_____

句子類型：_____

5. While traditional fishermen enjoy their catch, the brick makers quietly await for the water to recede, so they can resume brick production.

獨立子句：_____

從屬子句：_____

_____

_____

句子類型：_____

6. The French enjoy a diet of high saturated fat, but their low rate of cardiovascular disease has long baffled researchers.

獨立子句：_____

從屬子句：_____

_____

_____

句子類型：_____

7. In Japanese culture, emotions are often not openly expressed, and while it's possible to say "I love you," to many it just feels awkward.

獨立子句：_____

從屬子句：_____

_____

_____

句子類型：_____

8. As emerging news entities try to attract more users, traditional news organizations must adapt to the latest technologies to keep people interested in news.

　　獨立子句：＿＿＿＿＿＿＿＿＿＿＿＿＿＿＿＿＿

　　從屬子句：＿＿＿＿＿＿＿＿＿＿＿＿＿＿＿＿＿

　　　　　　　＿＿＿＿＿＿＿＿＿＿＿＿＿＿＿＿＿

　　　　　　　＿＿＿＿＿＿＿＿＿＿＿＿＿＿＿＿＿

　　句子類型：＿＿＿＿＿＿＿＿＿＿＿＿＿＿＿＿＿

9. This most certainly is the case for younger people, whose media behavior today is an indicator of what the news industry must learn to accommodate now and into the future.

　　獨立子句：＿＿＿＿＿＿＿＿＿＿＿＿＿＿＿＿＿

　　從屬子句：＿＿＿＿＿＿＿＿＿＿＿＿＿＿＿＿＿

　　　　　　　＿＿＿＿＿＿＿＿＿＿＿＿＿＿＿＿＿

　　　　　　　＿＿＿＿＿＿＿＿＿＿＿＿＿＿＿＿＿

　　句子類型：＿＿＿＿＿＿＿＿＿＿＿＿＿＿＿＿＿

10. While the results, which were published in Nature, are worrisome, they also hint at the possibility of treating concussions and lessening their harm.

　　獨立子句：＿＿＿＿＿＿＿＿＿＿＿＿＿＿＿＿＿

　　從屬子句：＿＿＿＿＿＿＿＿＿＿＿＿＿＿＿＿＿

　　　　　　　＿＿＿＿＿＿＿＿＿＿＿＿＿＿＿＿＿

　　　　　　　＿＿＿＿＿＿＿＿＿＿＿＿＿＿＿＿＿

　　句子類型：＿＿＿＿＿＿＿＿＿＿＿＿＿＿＿＿＿

11. Winning the Skytrax World's Best Airport Award for the fifth consecutive year is immense encouragement to our 50,000-strong airport community at Changi Airport, every

one of whom is passionate about delivering the most memorable airport experience to our passengers.

獨立子句：_____

從屬子句：_____

_____

_____

句子類型：_____

12. More than eight months have passed since Britain voted to leave the EU, but it's still not clear whether millions of EU migrants living in the U.K. will be permitted to stay.

獨立子句：_____

從屬子句：_____

_____

_____

句子類型：_____

13. Over the next 50 years, America would come to see magnificent bridges and other structures on which trains would run, awesome depots, ruthless rail magnates and the majesty of rail locomotives crossing the country.

獨立子句：_____

從屬子句：_____

_____

_____

句子類型：_____

14. After our conversation over the phone last night, I have reported the new ideas you presented to the head of our department, Mr. Huang, and he is concerned about the cost you

proposed since it is over our budget.

獨立子句：_____

從屬子句：_____

_____

_____

句子類型：_____

15. I understand that this five-year project emphasizes the long-term effect on the company's finance, but our past report indicates that investing so much money in this new line of products is somewhat risky.

獨立子句：_____

從屬子句：_____

_____

_____

句子類型：_____

8.11 子句挑戰題

使用複句或複合句的結構翻譯下列句子為英文（劃底線及框線內的部分要使用從屬子句）

1. 球隊老闆對於球隊未能贏得冠軍非常失望，所以他把教練解聘並且聘了一位曾經贏得兩次冠軍的新教練。（複合句）

_____

_____

2. 她上傳到 YouTube 介紹臺灣美食的影片已經吸引了超過百萬觀賞人數，並且她還打算要製作介紹臺灣熱門景點的影片。（複合句）

3. 剛剛才由 Tesla 發表的完全電動車 Model 3，是 2017 年備受期待的新車之一，而且公司也預期在 2017 年底每週生產五千輛的 Model 3。（複合句）

4. 身為馬里蘭大學正教授的 Martin Lo 博士，辭去他的教職以便他能以他在農業生產及食品加工的專長協助開發中國家的農民。（複句）

5. 多年前從臺灣遷移至中國為數不少的工廠如今正轉移到越南或印尼，在那裡勞力及土地成本低廉很多，並且外國政府歡迎那些工廠，因為它們將為當地人創造新的就業機會。（複合句）

6. 離臺中市區不遠的梧棲漁港，已經成為一處受到喜愛海鮮的人士歡迎的地點，因為它有一個 以低價販售各種新鮮海產的 魚市場。（複句）

7. Andrew Zimmern 是介紹世界各地古怪食物的電視影集主持人，已經嚐過很多不同種類的古怪食物，然而他認為榴槤是名列前三種難以下嚥的東西。（複合句）

_____

_____

8. 玉山為臺灣最高峰其山頂海拔 3,925 公尺，以其登山步道沿途令人屏息的景色著名，而身為國中英文老師的 Michelle，藉由登山上到玉山山頭來慶祝她的五十歲生日。（複合句）

_____

_____

9. 上個禮拜天我在公園打籃球時認識了 Peter Lai，他在在西雅圖上過五年的小學隨後跟著父母在去年回到臺灣，不過他還在適應臺灣又熱又溼的天氣，跟西雅圖的天氣非常不一樣。（複合句）

_____

_____

_____

10. 亞馬遜由 Jeff Bezos 於 1995 年在網路上推出，當時電子商務正要開始，如今已經成為全球最大的線上零售商，因為它以最低價錢出售每一樣東西，包括圖書、音樂、軟體、工具、玩具、運動用品、衣著、電子產品、電腦，甚至生鮮，而且它如何以令人高度滿意的服務對待客戶已使它成為當人們想要上網購物時的首選。（複合句）

_____

_____

8.12 從屬子句的被動語態

　　從屬子句與獨立子句一樣都會運用被動語態，其中，副詞子句是在獨立子句的開頭加上從屬連接詞所形成，其結構與獨立子句相同，不需另作討論。而名詞子句與形容詞的結構則與獨立子句有所不同，因此接下來我們要來探討名詞子句與形容詞子句中被動語態的句型變化。

▶▶ 8.12.1 名詞子句的被動語態

　　名詞子句的被動語態與獨立子句一樣，都具備了 be 動詞 + 過去分詞 的結構，名詞子句有以連接詞 that 開頭的，也有以疑問詞（what, who, when, why, how, where, which 等）開頭的，也有以 whether or not 或 if 開頭的，其後面所接的陳述句與獨立子句完全一樣，例如：

That women have been allowed to vote is being reported on TV.

The captain realized that the ship had been attacked.

Whether or not she will be admitted to the department is still unclear.

| How | the pyramid was built remains a mystery.

They will try to determine | why | customers are not satisfied with their services.

Do you remember | where | your car was parked?

The doctor won't disclose to the media | when | the patient will be released from the hospital.

但是以疑問詞開頭的名詞子句當中，**what 及 who 兩者是作為名詞子句的主詞**，這是唯一不同的地方。

例如：

| What | has been discovered by the archeologists in the village is significant.

Everyone in the company is speculating | who | will be promoted.

They have agreed to do | what | was suggested in the report.

▶▶ 8.12.2 小試身手

在空格中填入名詞子句開頭的連接詞或疑問詞，助動詞（如果需要的話），be 動詞，及過去分詞。

1. 研究人員正在努力釐清這個古城為什麼被遺棄。

The researchers are trying to figure out _____ the ancient city _____ _____ .

2. 我們新的辦公室到底坐落何處將在下禮拜的會議中決定。

_____ our new office _____ _____

_____ will be decided in the meeting next month.

3. 球員們心裡都在想這些規則是否可以改變。

The players are wondering _____ the rules _____

_____ _____ .

4. 全體工作同仁將要討論工作環境要如何可以進一步改善。

The staff will discuss _____ the working environment

_____ further _____ .

5. 修車師傅沒有把握多快車子可以修好。

The mechanic was not sure _____ _____ the

car _____ _____ _____ .

6. 文章中所描述的太難以置信了。

_____ _____ _____ in the article is un-

believable.

7. 市議會將要投票決定哪一個措施會予以採用來解決問題。

The city council will vote to decide _____ measures

_____ _____ _____ to solve the prob-

lem.

8. 大家心裡都在想這個困難的任務已經派給誰了。

We are all wondering _____ _____ _____

_____ the difficult task.

9. 這個新的體育館能夠蓋的多好取決於建築師與建築工人有多投
入。

_____ _____ the new stadium _____

_____ depends on _____ devoted

the architect and the workers _____ .

10. 新的規定在規範政府員工的表現要如何評估。

The new rules regulate ＿＿＿＿＿ the performances of government employees ＿＿＿＿＿ ＿＿＿＿＿ ＿＿＿＿＿ .

11. 明天將舉行會議來討論這個計畫的目標要如何達成。

A meeting ＿＿＿＿＿ ＿＿＿＿＿ ＿＿＿＿＿ to discuss ＿＿＿＿＿ the goal of the project ＿＿＿＿＿ ＿＿＿＿＿ ＿＿＿＿＿ .

12. 規律的健身有助於人們維持好心情正是這篇文章所確認的。

That working out regularly helps people maintain a good mood is ＿＿＿＿＿ ＿＿＿＿＿ ＿＿＿＿＿ in the paper.

13. 這本書真的是我們教授所極力推薦的嗎？

Is it true ＿＿＿＿＿ this book ＿＿＿＿＿ highly ＿＿＿＿＿ by our professor?

14. 這筆錢可以如何花用正是明天所要討論的。

＿＿＿＿＿ the money ＿＿＿＿＿ ＿＿＿＿＿ ＿＿＿＿＿ is ＿＿＿＿＿ ＿＿＿＿＿ ＿＿＿＿＿ tomorrow.

15. 這項研究揭露這條運河起初建造的時間和理由。

The study revealed ＿＿＿＿＿ and ＿＿＿＿＿ the canal ＿＿＿＿＿ initially ＿＿＿＿＿ .

▶▶ 8.12.3 形容詞子句的被動語態

　　形容詞子句的被動語態與獨立子句一樣，都具備了 be 動詞＋ 過去分詞 的結構，唯一不同的是形容詞子句的主詞為關係代名詞，主詞的單複數會支配 be 動詞的變化，而**關係代名詞的單複數是由其先行詞所決定的**，因此，形容詞子句使用被動語態時必須注意先行詞的單複數，才能使用正確的 be 動詞。

我們以下列例句說明：

The police officer who **was** **killed** in a rescue effort is being honored.

（形容詞子句關係代名詞為 who，其先行詞為 the police officer，屬於單數，因此 be 動詞為 was。）

People hunting animals that **are protected** by the laws will be severely punished.

（形容詞子句關係代名詞為 that，其先行詞為 animals，屬於複數，因此 be 動詞為 are。）

▶▶ 8.12.4 小試身手

在空格中填入被動語態形容詞子句的關係代名詞，be 動詞，及過去分詞。

1. 這部由世界最佳導演之一者所導的得獎電影是依據暢銷小說所拍的。

The award-winning film _____ _____ _____ by one of the greatest directors in the world is based on a best-selling novel.

2. 被這個醫療團隊醫好的病人以捐款來表達他們的謝意。

Patients _____ _____ _____ by the medical team showed their appreciation by donating money.

3. 已經獲頒年度最佳老師的林老師將於今天的會議與同仁分享其教學心得。

Mrs. Lin, _____ _____ _____ _____

Teacher of the Year, will share her teaching experience with the faculty in the meeting.

4. 由這家公司所製造的腳踏車已經賣出好幾百萬台了。

Bicylces _____ _____ _____ by the company _____ _____ in millions.

5. 延誤的這架班機已經重新調整時刻將於下午三點飛離。

The flight _____ _____ _____ has been rescheduled to leave at 3:00 p.m.

8.13 形容詞子句簡化為片語

　　英文句型變化需要運用許多技巧，例如副詞子句可以簡化為省略子句，而將形容詞子句簡化為片語也是英文寫作常用的一種技巧，**簡化形容詞子句可以將句子結構由複句簡化成為簡單句**，而不失原來的涵義。例如：

The company is developing a robot **that cooks like housewives**.（複句）

將限定形容詞子句 that cooks like housewives 簡化為現在分詞片語

→ The company is developing a robot **cooking like housewives**.（簡單句）

Taichung Train Station, **which was originally constructed by the Japanese between 1905 and 1908**, has been re-placed by the elevated station on October 16, 2016.（複句）
將非限定形容詞子句簡化爲過去分詞片語
→ Taichung Train Station, **originally constructed by the Japanese between 1905 and 1908**, has been replaced by the elevated station on October 16, 2016.（簡單句）

　　形容詞子句簡化爲片語的情況及方法不只上述例句的兩種變化，其簡化過程及結果依限定用法或非限定用法而有所不同，因此，以下分別就限定用法及非限定用法形容詞子句如何簡化爲片語來舉例說明。

8.13.1 限定用法形容詞子句簡化爲片語

　　限定用法形容詞子句可以簡化成爲
(1) 形容詞片語
(2) 現在分詞片語
(3) 過去分詞片語
(4) **with** 開頭的介系詞片語

(1) 限定用法形容詞子句簡化爲形容詞片語
　　限定用法形容詞子句的結構若是 **be 動詞後面接形容詞片語**，則可以把子句簡化成爲形容詞片語，如以下例子所示：

原來的句子是由**獨立子句和形容詞子句**結合而成的複句：
People **who are good at woodwork** can make a good living in this country.

將形容詞子句**簡化為形容詞片語**：

people **who are good at woodwork** → people **good at woodwork**（將子句中的關係代名詞及 be 動詞同時省略，留下來的就是形容詞片語了。）

句子的結構就由複句**簡化為簡單句**了：

People **good at woodwork** can make a good living in this country.

(2) 主動語態限定用法形容詞子句簡化為現在分詞片語

限定用法形容詞子句若是屬於**主動語態**，則可以簡化成為**現在分詞片語**，方法是**將關係代名詞省略**，並將**動詞改成現在分詞**；如以下例子所示：

例一：

原來的句子是由**獨立子句和形容詞子句結合而成的複句**：

The non-governmental organization is now recruiting students **who want to volunteer for community services**.

將**主動語態**的形容詞子句**簡化為現在分詞片語**：

students **who want to volunteer for community services**

→ students **wanting to volunteer for community services**

句子的結構就由複句**簡化為簡單句**了：

→ The non-governmental organization is now recruiting students **wanting to volunteer for community services**.

例二：

原來的句子是由**獨立子句和形容詞子句結合而成的複句**：

Civil servants **who have served for the country for over thirty years** will have the option to retire early.

將**主動語態**的形容詞子句**簡化爲現在分詞片語**：

civil servants **who have served for the country for over thirty years**

→ civil servants **having served for the country for over thirty years**

句子的結構就由複句**簡化爲簡單句**了：

Civil servants **having served for the country for over thirty years** will have the option to retire early.

(3) 被動語態限定用法形容詞子句簡化爲過去分詞片語

限定用法形容詞子句若是屬於**被動語態**，則可以簡化成爲**過去分詞片語**，方法是**將關係代名詞及 be 省略**，留下來的就是過去分詞片語了；如以下例子所示：

例如：

原來的句子是由**獨立子句和形容詞子句結合而成的複句**：

The house **that was sold yesterday** was worth more than one million dollars.

將**被動語態**的形容詞子句**簡化爲過去分詞片語**：

the house **that was sold yesterday** → the house **sold yesterday**

句子的結構就由複句**簡化為簡單句**了：

The house **sold yesterday** was worth more than one million dollars.

(4) 被動語態限定用法形容詞子句簡化為 with 開頭的介系詞片語

　　限定用法形容詞子句的動詞為 has 或 own 時，可以簡化為 with 開頭的介系詞片語。

　　例如：

A company **that has the ability to adapt to the changing market** is likely to excel.

→ A company |**with**| **the ability to adabp to the changing market** is likely to excel.

▶▶▶ 8.13.2 非限定用法形容詞子句簡化為片語

　　非限定用法形容詞子句依其不同句型可以分別簡化為：

(1) **名詞片語**

(2) **形容詞片語**

(3) **現在分詞片語**

(4) **過去分詞片語**

(1) 非限定用法形容詞子句簡化為名詞片語作為同位語

　　當非限定用法形容詞子句的**動詞為 be 動詞**，且其主詞補語為**名詞片語**時，可以將**關係代名詞及 be 動詞同時省略**，只留下名詞片語，作為獨立子句主詞的**同位語**。

　　例如：

原來的句子為**獨立子句結合非限定用法形容詞子句的複句**：

The Statue of Liberty, **which was a gift from the people of**

France to the United States, is a symbol of freedom and democracy.

將非限定用法形容詞子句**簡化為名詞片語**，作為**主詞的同位語**，於是句子就**由複句簡化為簡單句**了：

→ The Statue of Liberty, **a gift from the people of France to the United States**, is a symbol of freedom and democracy.

也可以將**名詞片語移到主詞前面**，並保留名詞片語後面的逗點：

→ **A gift from the people of France to the United States,** the Statue of Liberty is a symbol of freedom and democracy.

(2) 非限定用法形容詞子句簡化為形容詞片語

當非限定用法形容詞子句的**動詞為 be 動詞**，且其主詞補語為形容詞片語時，可以**將關係代名詞及 be 動詞同時省略**，只留下形容詞片語。例如：

原來的句子為**獨立子句結合非限定用法形容詞子句的複句**：

The Sydney Opera House, **which is famous for its distinctive building,** is an icon of Australia's creative and technical achievement.

將非限定用法形容詞子句**簡化為形容詞片語**，於是句子就**由複句簡化為簡單句**了：

→ The Sydney Opera House, **famous for its distinctive**

building, is an icon of Australia's creative and technical achievement.

形容詞片語也可以**移到句首**，也就是獨立子句主詞的前面，並保留形容詞片語後面的逗點：

→ **Famous for its distinctive building,** the Sydney Opera House is an icon of Australia's creative and technical achievement.

(3) 主動語態非限定用法形容詞子句簡化為現在分詞片語

非限定用法形容詞子句若是屬於**主動語態**，則可以簡化成為**現在分詞片語**，方法是**將關係代名詞省略**，並**將動詞改成現在分詞**；如以下例子所示：

原來的句子為**獨立子句結合非限定用法形容詞子句的複句**：

Usain Bolt, **who won three gold medals at three consecutive Olympic Games,** created history in Rio in 2016.

將**主動語態**非限定用法形容詞子句**簡化為現在分詞片語**，於是句子就**由複句簡化為簡單句**了：

→ Usain Bolt, **winning three gold medals at three consecutive Olympic Games,** created history in Rio in 2016.

現在分詞片語也可以**移到主詞的前面**，並保留現在分詞片語後面的逗點：

→ **Winning three gold medals at three consecutive Olympic Games,** Usain Bolt created history in Rio in 2016.

(4) 被動語態非限定用法形容詞子句簡化為過去分詞片語

　　非限定用法形容詞子句若是屬於**被動語態**，則可以簡化成為**過去分詞片語**，方法是**將關係代名詞及 be 省略**，留下來的就是過去分詞片語了。

　　例如：

　　以下的句子為<u>獨立子句結合非限定形容詞子句的複句</u>：

Dr. Scott Stevens, **who is appointed the director of the English Language Institute,** has been teaching foreign students English for over 20 years.

將被動語態非限定用法形容詞子句<u>簡化為過去分詞片語</u>，於是句子就<u>由複句簡化為簡單句</u>了：

→ Dr. Scott Stevens, **appointed the director of the English Language Institute,** has been teaching foreign students English for over 20 years.

過去分詞片語也可以<u>移到主詞前面</u>，並保留過去分詞片語後面的逗點：

→ **Appointed the director of the English Language Institute,** Dr. Scott Stevens has been teaching foreign students English for over 20 years.

8.13.3 小試身手

將劃底線的形容詞子句簡化爲適當的片語，從而將複句簡化爲簡單句。

1. The man who is playing basketball over there is my brother.

_____

2. Ms. Lin, who founded the company 45 years ago, is going to retire next month.

_____

3. Students who are good at sports are more likely to make friends with peers.

_____

4. The Art Museum, which is known for its amazing art collections, is located in Taichung.

_____

5. Sandy wants to make friends with foreign students who speak Spanish.

_____

6. The train that leaves for London is on schedule.

_____

7. The stadium that is built for the tournament will be completed in six months.

_____

8. Mount Ali, which is a hot tourist spot for viewing sunrise above the sea of clouds, is famous for growing high-mountain tea.

_____

9. Children <u>who are proud of themselves</u> are often more optimistic.

10. James Hudson Taylor, <u>who was a missionary from England,</u> set up numerous churches and schools during 51 years <u>that he worked in China.</u>

11. Many dentists are now making false teeth with top-notch 3D printing, <u>which has been developed at a fast pace and have influenced many industries in ways</u> <u>that were unthinkable before.</u>

12. All men are created equal, yet in reality those <u>who are born to parents</u> <u>who are in higher social status</u> may have more advantages in pursuing careers <u>that are chosen by themselves.</u>

13. A container ship, <u>which carries loaded 20-foot or 40-foot containers from one port to another,</u> is a major sea transportation <u>that ships cargos of assorted exporting goods</u> <u>that are manufactured domestically</u> to another country <u>that has demand for them.</u>

14. The trade war between the United States and China, which once focused on imposing higher tariffs on imports from both countries, has been extended to 5G and AI, which are at present the most advanced information technologies that have the highest potentials to control the world in every aspect in coming decades.

_____

_____

15. Nuclear power plants, which have caused serious damages to nearby residents and the surrounding environment when they are sabotaged by natural disasters or human errors, are gradually being replaced by other facilities that generate needed energy with different methods that are much safer but less cost-effective.

_____

_____

_____

▶▶ 8.13.4 小試身手

(1) 使用形容詞子句將劃底線部分翻成英文，以完成句子英譯；(2) 再將形容詞子句簡化為片語，將複句簡化為簡單句。

1. 銷售高檔電子產品的商店即將於下周六在這個由日本人所投資的百貨公司開幕。

(1)_____

_____

(2)_____

_____

2. 位於美國東岸的 Newark 將要以遊行來歡迎三十年來首度贏得冠軍的德拉瓦大學 (University of Delaware) 籃球隊。

(1)_____

_____

(2)_____

_____

3. 具備獎學金資格的學生必須在截止期限之前在網路上提出申請。

(1)_____

_____

(2)_____

_____

4. David Chen，身為業務經理，昨天與一家製造家電的多國企業簽下了一份價值五千萬美元的大合約。

(1)_____

_____

(2)_____

_____

5. 從各國邀請來的數十位專家學者將參與這個探討永續能源的研討會。

(1)_____

_____

(2)_____

_____

6. 這部在紐西蘭拍攝了三年的科幻電影 *The Black Hole* 獲得影評

及影迷的高度讚賞。

(1)_____

_____

(2)_____

_____

7. 快速時尚以速度與低價為特色，讓人們可以用負擔得起的價格買
到流行的服飾。（107 指考）

(1)_____

_____

(2)_____

_____

8. 然而，它所鼓勵的「快速消費」卻製造了大量的廢棄物，造成巨
大的汙染問題。（107 指考）

(1)_____

_____

(2)_____

_____

9. 玉山 (Jade Mountain) 在冬天常常覆蓋著厚厚的積雪，使整個山
頂閃耀如玉。（106 年學測）

(1)_____

_____

(2)_____

_____

10. 近年來，許多臺灣製作的影片已經受到國際的重視。（101 年
學測）

(1)_____

_____

(2)_____

_____

8.13.5 形容詞子句簡化為片語挑戰題

使用分詞片語翻譯劃底線的部分，並完成全句英譯。

1. 去年推出吸引國外投資的新政策，目前已經達成第一階段的目標，一共有十五家多國企業承諾要來臺灣投資。

_____,

the new policy _____,

with a total of fifteen multi-national corporations _____

_____.

2. 兩年前被地震所摧毀，這間學校已經重建完成，使得學生跟老師能夠在新的學期使用新的設施。

_____,

the school has been rebuilt, _____

_____.

3. 得到認證為綠建築，這棟新的市政府大樓將節省百分之三十的能源，為商業建築樹立了好榜樣。

_____, the new City Hall

will save energy by 30%, _____.

4. 用意在幫助低收入家庭，這個非政府組織派遣由自願醫師及護士組成的醫療團隊到偏遠地區的村落，提供免費健康檢查及醫療。

_____,

the Non-Governmental Organization are sending medical

teams _____ to villages in remote

areas _____.

第九章 分詞構句

　　分詞構句是英文寫作上經常運用的句型，也是必備的寫作技巧，其中分詞片語部分依 (1) **不同時式**、(2) **肯定或否定**、以及 (3) **主動或被動**而作變化，並暗藏陷阱，同學在使用上必須特別留意，避免犯錯。

　　在講解英文的分詞構句之前，我們先來看以下中翻英的例子：

　　她固定在健身房鍛練身體，健康狀況非常好。（中文主詞出現在**句首**）

　　這句中文可以翻成**兩個英文的簡單句**：
(1) *She works out in the fitness center regularly.*
(2) *She is in very good shape.*

　　或是翻成一個**合句**：
*She works out in the fitness center regularly, **so** she is in very good shape.*

　　或是翻成一個含有一個**副詞子句**的**複句**：
***Because she works out in the fitness center regularly**, she is in very good shape.*

　　或是翻成**分詞構句**：
***Working out in the fitness center regularly**, she is in very good shape.*（分詞構句英文主詞出現在**片語之後**）

（第一句英文的**主詞 she 已經省略**，而其**主動語態的動詞 works 也改成現在分詞**，因此第一句就簡化成**現在分詞片語**，並且與第二句英文形成了**分詞構句**。）

有趣的是，這個分詞構句的中文也可以寫成：

固定在健身房鍛練身體，她健康狀況非常好。（中文主詞出現在**片語之後**，與英文主詞位置相同。）

所以我們發現，**英文分詞構句的主詞**只會出現在**分詞片語之後**，而其所表達的**中文句子主詞**則可能出現**在句首**或**片語之後**。

9.1 分詞構句的結構

分詞構句為英文寫作常用的句子結構，分詞構句是由**一個分詞片語搭配一個簡單句所構成**，其形式分成兩種：(1) 現在分詞搭配簡單句構成**現在分詞構句**，或是 (2) 過去分詞搭配簡單句構成**過去分詞構句**。

例一：

Cindy 正在廚房煮咖啡。她不小心把咖啡壺掉落而打破了。

Cindy **was making** coffee in the kitchen. She accidentally dropped the pot and broke it.（兩個簡單句）

Cindy 正在廚房煮咖啡的時候不小心把咖啡壺掉落而打破了。

When Cindy **was making coffee in the kitchen**, she accidentally dropped the pot and broke it.（含有副詞子句的複句）

Cindy 正在廚房煮咖啡，不小心把咖啡壺掉落而打破了。

→**Making coffee in the kitchen**, Cindy accidentally dropped the pot and broke it.

（現在分詞構句）

例二：

他已經接受訓練成為特工。他負責保護總統。

He **has been trained** to be a special agent. He is responsible for protecting the President.（兩個簡單句）

因為他已經接受訓練成為特工，他負責保護總統。

Because he **has been trained to be a special agent**, he is responsible for protecting the President.（含有副詞子句的複句）

他已經接受訓練成為特工，負責保護總統。

已經接受訓練成為特工，他負責保護總統。

→**Having been trained to be a special agent**, he is responsible for protecting the President.

（過去分詞構句）

9.2 分詞構句如何產生

從以上的例子，我們瞭解到：使用分詞構句的前題是**前後兩個主詞必須是一致的**，如此，可以先將其中一個**表達時間、原因、**

條件或讓步的簡單句簡化成為分詞片語，再將分詞片語與維持不變的簡單句結合，形成分詞構句；或是以分詞片語取代複句中的副詞子句，從而將複句簡化為分詞構句的簡單句，而仍然表達相同的涵義。因此，分詞構句中的分詞片語具有隱藏的主詞，而這個隱藏的主詞必須與句子的主詞一致。

例如：

He works at a library. He has access to all kinds of books and journals.（兩個簡單句）

Because he works at a library, he has access to all kinds of books and journals.

（含有副詞子句的複句）

→ **Working at a library**, he has access to all kinds of books and journals.

（表達原因的現在分詞構句）

Virtual reality simulates the real world. It offers people a new way of playing video games.（兩個簡單句）

Because virtual reality simulates the real world, it offers people a new way of playing video games.（含有副詞子句的複句）

→ **Simulating the real world**, virtual reality offers people a new way of playing video games.

（表達原因的現在分詞構句）

The girl was walking to school. She came across a stray cat.（兩個簡單句）

When the girl was walking to school, she came across a stray cat.

（含有副詞子句的複句）

→ **Walking to school**, the girl came across a stray cat.

（表達**時間**的現在分詞構句）

She lived in the apartment by herself. She had to pay the full amount of the rent.

（兩個簡單句）

As she **lived in the apartment by herself**, she had to pay the full amount of the rent.

（含有副詞子句的複句）

→ **Living in the apartment by herself**, she had to pay the full amount of the rent.

（表達**原因**的現在分詞構句）

You open the box in the morning. You will find a precious gift left by Santa Claus.

（兩個簡單句）

If you **open the box in the morning**, you will find a precious gift left by Santa Claus.（含有副詞子句的複句）

→ **Opening the box in the morning**, you will find a precious gift left by Santa Claus.

（表達**條件**的現在分詞構句）

The food drive was organized by college students. It was very successful.

（兩個簡單句）

Because the food drive **was organized by college students**, it was very successful.

（含有副詞子句的複句）

→ **Organized by college students**, the food drive was very successful.

（表達原因的**過去分詞構句**）

The new model was released in 2015. It has become the best-selling car in Taiwan.

（兩個簡單句）

Since the new model **was released in 2015**, it has become the best-selling car in Taiwan.（含有副詞子句的複句）

→ **Released in 2015**, the new model has become the best-selling car in Taiwan.

（表達**時間**的**過去分詞構句**）

She is given the opportunity. She will do an outstanding job.（兩個簡單句）

If she **is given the opportunity**, she will do an outstanding job.

（含有副詞子句的複句）

→ **Given the opportunity**, she will do an outstanding job.
（表達**條件**的**過去分詞構句**）

The cathedral **was built** more than 100 years ago. It still looks magnificent.

（兩個簡單句）

Even though the cathedral **was built more than 100 years ago**, it still looks magnificent. （含有副詞子句的複句）

→ **Built more than 100 years ago**, the cathedral still looks magnificent.

（表達**讓步**的**過去分詞構句**）

貼心提醒

使用分詞構句的結構，**分詞片語與句子的主詞必須是一致的，否則就形成了不合文法的脫節修飾語**。（有關脫節修飾語，請詳讀該章說明。）

從以上的例子，我們瞭解到簡單句或從屬子句要簡化成為分詞片語有兩種情況，(1) 若簡單句或從屬子句是**主動語態**的句子，就將其簡化為**現在分詞片語**；(2) 若是**被動語態**，則要簡化為**過去分詞片語**。而在簡化過程中，依照 (1) **動詞時態**、(2) **肯定句或否定句**、(3) **動詞為 be 動詞**的不同情況，也會產生不同的變化。以下為現在分詞與過去分詞在不同情況下的變化列表，並以更多例子予以說明不同情況下分詞構句的形成過程。

9.2.1 主動語態的簡單句簡化為現在分詞片語

主動語態動詞轉換成現在分詞片語		
肯定 / 否定	句子或從屬子句動詞 （一般動詞 / be 動詞）	現在分詞片語
肯定句	簡單現在式 play/plays am/is/are	**playing** **being**
	簡單過去式 played was/were	**playing** **being**
	現在進行式 am/is/are playing am/is/are being	**playing** **being**
	過去進行式 was/were playing was/were being	**playing** **being**
	現在完成式 has/have played has/have been	**having played** **having been**
	過去完成式 had played had been	**having played** **having been**
	現在完成進行式 has/have been playing	**having been play-ing**
	過去完成進行式 had been playing	**having been play-ing**
否定句	簡單現在式 do not play/does not play am/is/are not	**not playing** **not being**
	簡單過去式 did not play was/were not	**not playing** **not being**
	現在進行式 am/is/are not playing am/is/are not being	**not playing** **not being**

主動語態動詞轉換成現在分詞片語		
肯定 / 否定	句子或從屬子句動詞 （一般動詞 / be 動詞）	現在分詞片語
否定句	過去進行式 was/were not playing was/were not being	**not playing** **not being**
	現在完成式 has/have not played has/have not been	**not having played** **not having been**
	過去完成式 had not played had not been	**not having played** **not having been**
	現在完成進行式 has/have not been playing	**not having been** **playing**
	過去完成進行式 had not been playing	**not having been** **playing**

1. 主動語態簡單現在式句子簡化爲現在分詞片語

(1) **The professor conducts** research on organic chemistry.（主
動語態 / 表達原因）

(2) **The professor** has published many research papers.

這兩個句子的**主詞相同**，都是 the professor（**這是分詞構句必
要的前提**），因爲句子 (1) 是**主動語態**，所以我們要把句子 (1)
簡化成爲**現在分詞片語**，然後將其與句子 (2) 結合，造出新的
句子。

步驟如下：

先把句子 (1) 的**主詞 the professor** 省略，再把主動語態動詞
conducts **改成現在分詞** conducting

~~The professor conducts~~ (conducting) research on organic chemistry.

→ **conducting** research on organic chemistry

如此一來，簡單句就搖身一變，成為現在分詞片語了。

接著再把現在分詞片語與句子 (2) 結合，就得到了**現在分詞構句**的新句子：

→ **Conducting research on organic chemistry**, the professor has published many research papers.

(3) If **he** keeps driving at this speed, **he** will get to the destination in less than an hour.（主動語態／表達條件）

這是含有副詞子句的複句，且副詞子句的主詞與主要子句的主詞一致，因此我們可以用現在分詞片語來取代主動語態的副詞子句，而把複句簡化成現在分詞構句的簡單句。

→ **Keeping driving at this speed**, he will get to the destination in less than an hour.

2. 主動語態簡單現在式句子（**動詞為 be**）簡化為現在分詞片語

(1) He is in a good mood.（**動詞為 be 動詞**／表達原因）

(2) He is taking his family out for a nice dinner.

先把句子 (1) 的**主詞 he 省略**，並把 **be 動詞改成 being**，即可簡化成**現在分詞片語**：He is (being) in a good mood.

→ being in a good mood

接著再把現在分詞片語與句子 (2) 結合，就得到了**現在分詞構**

句的新句子：

→ **Being in a good mood,** he is taking his family out for a nice dinner.

或是先把句子 (1) 改成副詞子句，與句子 (2) 結合成一個複句，再以現在分詞取代副詞子句，將複句簡化為分詞構句的簡單句。

→ Because he is in a good mood, he is taking his family out for a nice dinner.

→ Being in a good mood, he is taking his family out for a nice dinner.

3. 主動語態完成式句子簡化為現在分詞片語

(1) **The company has successfully tested the new product.**（現在完成式主動語態／表達先發生）

(2) **The company** will start selling it next month.

先把句子 (1) 的**主詞 the company** 省略，再把主動語態完成式**動詞** has successfully tested 改成**完成式現在分詞**：

~~The company~~ has successfully tested the new product.

→ **having successfully tested the new product**

再把現在分詞片語與句子 (2) 結合，即可構成**現在分詞構句**的新句子：

→ **Having successfully tested the new product**, the company will start selling it next month.

4. 主動語態簡單過去式否定句簡化為現在分詞片語

(1) **He did not pass the test.**（主動語態否定句／表達原因）

(2) **He** was very disappointed.

先把句子 (1) 的**主詞 he** 與**助動詞 did** 省略，保留否定詞 **not**，
再將**動詞 pass 改成現在分詞 passing**，即可簡化成**現在分詞片
語**：

He did not pass (passing) the test.

→ **not passing the test**

接著再把現在分詞片語與句子 (2) 結合，即可構成**現在分詞構
句**的新句子：

→ **Not passing the test**, he was very disappointed.

5. 主動語態簡單過去式否定句（動詞為 be）簡化爲現在分詞片語

(1) She was not able to carry out the project by herself.（主動
語態否定句 / 表達原因）

(2) She had to ask someone to work with her.

先把句子 (1) **主詞 she** 省略，**be 動詞 was 改成 being**，並把否
定詞 **no 移到 being 之前**，即可簡化成**現在分詞片語**：

She was not (being) able to carry out the project by herself.

→ not being able to carry out the project by herself

接著再把現在分詞片語與句子 (2) 結合，即可構成**現在分詞構
句**的新句子：

→ **Not being able to carry out the project by herself**, she
had to ask someone to work with her.

6. 主動語態完成式否定句簡化爲現在分詞片語

(1) He had not obtained the doctoral degree.（否定句 / 表達原
因）

(2) He continued to work really hard on his dissertation.

先把句子 (1) 的**主詞 he 省略**，**had 改成 having**，並把否定詞 **not 移到 having 之前**，即可把簡單句簡化成**否定的現在分詞片語**：

→ **not having obtained the doctoral degree**

接著再把現在分詞片語與句子 (2) 結合，即可構成**現在分詞構句**的新句子：

→ **Not having obtained the doctoral degree**, he continued to work really hard on his dissertation.

7. 主動語態簡單過去式從屬子句簡化成現在分詞片語

When the mother saw her injured son in the hospital, she stayed calm and comforted him.（由副詞子句搭配獨立子句的複句，從屬子句為主動語態／表達先發生）

先把句子 (1) 的**副詞子句的連接詞 when 與主詞 the mother 省略**，再把**動詞 saw 改成現在分詞 seeing**，如此一來，副詞子句就簡化為現在分詞片語，而整個複句也就簡化成現在**分詞構句**的簡單句了。

~~When the mother saw~~ (seeing) her injured son in the hospital

→ **Seeing her injured son in the hospital**, the mother stayed calm and comforted him.

8. 主動語態過去進行式從屬子句簡化成現在分詞片語

As she was talking on the phone in the restaurant, she did not notice someone had stolen her handbag from her seat.（由副詞子句搭配獨立子句的複句，從屬子句為主動語態／表達原因）

把副詞子句中的**連接詞 as、主詞 she、及 be 動詞 was 三者同時省略**，留下的即是現在分詞片語，而整個複句也就簡化成**分詞構句**了：

As she was talking on the phone in the restaurant, she did not notice someone had stolen her handbag from her seat.

→ **Talking on the phone in the restaurant**, she did not notice someone had stolen her handbag from her seat.

▶▶▶ 9.2.2 被動語態的簡單句簡化為過去分詞片語

被動語態動詞轉換成過去分詞片語		
肯定 / 否定	句子或從屬子句動詞	過去分詞片語
肯定句	簡單現在式 am/is/are played	**played**
	簡單過去式 was/were played	**played**
	現在進行式 am/is/are being played	**being played**
	過去進行式 was/were being played	**being played**
	現在完成式 has/have been played	**having been played**
	過去完成式 had been played	**having been played**
否定句	簡單現在式 am/is/are not played	**not played/not being played**
	簡單過去式 was/were not played	**not played/not being played**
	現在進行式 am/is/are not being played	**not being played**

被動語態動詞轉換成過去分詞片語		
肯定／否定	句子或從屬子句動詞	過去分詞片語
否定句	過去進行式 was/were not be-ing played	**not being played**
	現在完成式 has/have not been played	**not having been played**
	過去完成式 had not been played	**not having been played**

1. 被動語態簡單過去式的句子簡化爲過去分詞片語

(1) **She was saddened** by the news of the earthquake.（被動語態／表達原因）

(2) **She** donated money to help the victims of the earthquake.
這兩個句子的**主詞同樣都是** she（**這是分詞構句必要的前提**），因爲句子 (1) 是**被動語態**，所以我們要把句子 (1) 簡化成爲**過去分詞片語**，然後將其與句子 (2) 結合。

先把句子 (1) 的**主詞** she 與 be **動詞同時省略**，**留下過去分詞** saddened：
~~She was~~ saddened by the news of the earthquake.
→ **saddened by the news of the earthquake**
如此一來，簡單句就搖身一變，成爲**過去分詞片語**了。

接著再把過去分詞片語與句子 (2) 結合，就得到了以下**過去分詞構句**的新句子：→ **Saddened by the news of the earth-**

quake, she donated money to help the victims of the earth-quake.

2. 被動語態現在完成式的句子簡化為過去分詞片語

(1) **The old bridge** has been built for over 50 years.（完成式被動語態 / 表達先發生）

(2) **The old bridge** will be replaced by a new one.

先把句子 (1) 的**主詞** the old bridge **省略**，同時把**現在完成式被動語態動詞** has been built 改成**完成式過去分詞** having been built：

~~The old bridge has~~ (having) been built over 50 years.

→ **having been built for over 50 years**

如此一來，簡單句就搖身一變，成為**過去分詞片語**了。

接著再把過去分詞片語與句子 (2) 結合，即可構成**過去分詞構句**的新句子：

→ **Having been built for over 50 years**, the old bridge will be replaced by a new one.

3. 被動語態過去完成式的句子簡化為過去分詞片語

(1) **He had been laid off** by the company.（被動語態 / 表達原因）

(2) **He** had to look for a new job.

先把句子 (1) 的**主詞** he **省略**，同時把**過去完成式被動語態動詞** had been laid off **改成完成式過去分詞** having been laid off：

~~He had~~ (having) been laid off by the company.

→ **having been laid off**

如此一來，簡單句就搖身一變，成為**過去分詞片語**了。

接著再把過去分詞片語與句子 (2) 結合，即可構成**過去分詞構句**的新句子：

→ **Having been laid off by the company**, he had to look for a new job.

4. 被動語態現在進行式否定句簡化為過去分詞片語

(1) **The novel is not being sold** in Taiwan.（被動語態否定句／表達原因）

(2) **The novel** can only be purchased online from Amazon.

把句子 (1) 的**主詞 the novel 和 be 動詞 is 同時省略**，留下的部分就是**進行式的過去分詞片語**了。

~~The novel is~~ not being sold in Taiwan.

→ **not being sold in Taiwan**

接著再把過去分詞片語與句子 (2) 結合，即可構成**過去分詞構句**的新句子：

→ **Not being sold in Taiwan**, the novel can only be purchased online from Amazon.

5. 被動語態過去完成式否定句簡化為過去分詞片語

(1) **The patient had not been treated** properly in the clinic.（被動語態否定句／表達原因）

(2) **The patient** filed a lawsuit against the doctor.

先把句子 (1) 的主詞 the patient 省略，had 改成 having，並把 not 移到 having 之前，即可簡化成否定的完成式過去分詞片語。

~~The patient had~~ not (having) been treated properly in the clinic.

→ **not having been treated properly in the clinic**

接著再把過去分詞片語與句子 (2) 結合，即可構成**過去分詞構句**的新句子：

→ **Not having been treated properly in the clinic**, the patient filed a lawsuit against the doctor.

6. 被動語態簡單過去式從屬子句簡化成過去分詞片語

Since the customer was highly dissatisfied with the quality of the merchandise, he returned it to the store the next day.（由副詞子句搭配獨立子句形成的**複句**，從屬子句為被動語態／表達原因。）

把副詞子句子的**連接詞 since**、主詞 **the customer** 和 be 動詞 **was** 三者同時省略，即可簡化成**過去分詞片語**，而整個**複句**也就簡化成為分詞構句了：

~~Since the customer was~~ highly dissatisfied with the quality of the merchandise, he returned it to the store the next day.

→ **Highly dissatisfied with the quality of the merchandise**, he returned it to the store the next day.

7. 被動語態過去完成式從屬子句簡化成過去分詞片語

After the truck driver had finally finished his job, he went to a restaurant for a hot meal.（由副詞子句搭配獨立子句形成的**複句**，從屬子句為被動語態／表達先發生。）

把副詞子句的連接詞 after 與主詞 the truck driver 同時省略，並把 had 改成 having，即可簡化成過去分詞片語即可簡化成**過**

去分詞片語，而整個複句也就簡化成為分詞構句了：

After the trucker driver had (having) finally finished his job, he went to a restaurant for a hot meal.

→ **Having finally finished his job**, the trucker driver went to a restaurant for a hot meal.

8. 被動語態過去進行式從屬子句簡化成過去分詞片語

As she was being attacked, she quickly used the pepper spray to fend off the attacker. （由副詞子句搭配獨立子句形成的複句，從屬子句為被動語態 / 表達先發生。）

把副詞子句的**連接詞 as、主詞 she、與 be 動詞 was** 同時省略，即可簡化成**過去分詞片語**，而整個複句也就簡化為分詞構句了：

As she was being attacked, she quickly used the pepper spray to fend off the attacker.

→ **Being attacked**, she quickly used the pepper spray to fend off the attacker.

▶▶ 9.2.3 小試身手

將下列簡單句或副詞子句簡化成為<u>現在分詞片語</u>或<u>過去分詞片語</u>

示範：

The store opens 24 hours. → opening 24 hours

He was interviewed yesterday. → interviewed yesterday

---

1. They reached their final destination.

_____

2. He was saved by the rescuers.

_____

3. She is considered one of the best tennis players of all time.

_____

4. The song touched her heart.

_____

5. The car has been sold.

_____

6. She is frightened.

_____

7. The reporter took the photo.

_____

8. The photo was taken by the reporter.

_____

9. I sent the letter to the mayor.

_____

10. They were good friends.

_____

11. We have invited many guests.

_____

12. Many guests have been invited.

_____

13. Mary has been working for the company for over 25 years.

_____

14. She was not promoted.

_____

15. because the store was not open

_____

16. Timothy is the top student of his class.

_____

_____

17. Taiwan High Speed Rail was launched in 2007.

_____

18. The government has been implementing several major construction plans.

_____

19. The committee members are discussing the controversial issues.

_____

20. The controversial issues are being discussed by the committee members.

_____

21. After he was not convicted

_____

22. Jade Mountain is the highest mountain in Taiwan.

_____

23. The man delivers fresh vegetables to the store every morning.

_____

24. when the survivor is being sent to the hospital

_____

25. They had not been evaluated.

_____

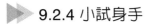 9.2.4 小試身手

將下列各題中劃底線的句子簡化為現在分詞片語或過去分詞片語，再與另外一句結合成為一個新的簡單句；或是將複句中的從屬子句簡化為分詞片語，進而將複句簡化成簡單句。

> 示範：*The tourist looks out the window. She sees the beautiful ocean.*
>
> → *Looking out the window, the tourist sees the beautiful ocean.*

1. Mrs. Chen is the most popular teacher in the school. Mrs. Chen has been named Teacher of the Year.

   _____

   _____

2. The woman had been saved by the firefighter. She sent a gift to him to express her gratitude.

   _____

   _____

3. The owner of the company profited more than fifty million dollars. The owner of the company donated 10% of his profit to a charitable organization.

   _____

   _____

4. The author was inspired by the little girl's true story. The author wrote a great novel.

   _____

5. She sold her 10-year-old car. She then bought a new SUV.

_____

6. After he had performed an incredible magic show on TV, he became famous overnight.

_____

7. The project began in 2001. The project has helped more than ten thousand people.

_____

_____

8. She had not been defeated by the failures. She kept trying hard until she finally succeeded.

_____

_____

9. He has been teaching for 40 years. He is retiring in two months.

_____

10. The giant blue-fin tuna was captured near the east coast of Taiwan. The giant blue-fin tuna weighed more than 250 kilograms.

_____

_____

11. Because she had lost so much weight after just 12 months, she was ready to have the excess skin removal surgery.

_____

_____

12. The machine did not function as it should. The machine had to be sent back to the factory for inspection.

13. He has saved enough money. He is planning to visit many different countries in Europe.

14. The boy solved the most difficult math problem. The boy won the math competition.

15. He made the final shot. He won the game for the team.

16. He was paid to do the job. He has finished it efficiently.

17. The car is powered by a turbo engine. The car is hot in the market.

18. Because it was not tainted, the food can still be sold in the store.

19. He was eager to learn how to make chocolate chip cookies. He downloaded the recipe from a website and bought the necessary materials.

20. She was being trained to be a professional dancer. She was on a strict diet.

_____

21. The girl had sailed around the world all by herself. The girl celebrated her 20-year-old birthday when returning to New York.

_____

_____

22. She has done a great deal for our country. She is commended by the President for her unselfish contribution.

_____

_____

23. Since he was not busy, he agreed to help his friend move to a new apartment.

_____

24. The contract had not been terminated. The contract still had to be honored by both sides.

_____

25. She went through a difficult time fighting cancer. She is going to share her story with us tonight.

_____

_____

將下列句子以分詞構句的句型翻成英文。

> **示範：**
> 受到父母的鼓勵，他決定要從軍。
> → Encouraged by his parents, he decided to join the army.

1. 對公司決策感到失望，他上禮拜辭職了。

2. 不受醜聞的影響，這位女市議員已經當選連任了。

3. 電視報導之後，這家牛排館生意已經增加了五成。

4. 在這個行業多年，她知道如何應付不同的客戶。

5. 不想要他妻子擔心，他絕口不提他公司的財務危機。

6. 不後悔其決定，她說她會信守她的承諾。

7. 出院了，他現在可以回去上班了。

8. 牛肉已經在冷凍庫冰了兩天，硬的跟石頭一樣。

9. 有些資深員工抗拒學習工作場所所需的新科技，只好被迫辭去工作。

_____

_____

10. 克服了懼高症，他設法走路穿越河上 30 公尺高的吊橋。

_____

11. 這個兩週的夏令營強調培養數位時代的創造力，吸引了數百位大學生來報名。

_____

12. 市長考量到事情的複雜性，已經決定要召開公聽會。

_____

_____

13. 很多通勤族沒有收到通知說大雨已經癱瘓了鐵路，依舊趕往火車站試圖搭上火車去上班。

_____

14. 明白沒有退路，他把他所有的時間和精力投注在兩千萬美金的人工智慧創業公司。

_____

15. 相信在澳洲可以挖到溫泉，他花了投資人三百萬美金歷經四年終於開發了澳洲第一個溫泉。

_____

_____

第十章 句型變換祕技：數個簡單句的結合

現在為止，我們已經學會了副詞子句與形容詞子句的結構與用法，也知道如何將副詞子句或形容詞子句簡化為不同種類的片語。因此接下來，我們要運用這些技巧，將**數個簡單句結合成為一個複合句或複句**，或是進一步**簡化成為一個合句或簡單句**。

10.1 數個簡單句的結合

底下我們以兩個例子說明其過程以及整合後可能產生的新的複句或簡單句。

例一：

(a) Kending National Park was established in 1982.

(b) Kending National Park was the first national park in Taiwan.

(c) Kending National Park now attracts millions of tourists annually.

以上三個簡單句，如果我們決定句子 (c) 是所要強調的重點而予以保留，那就可以將句子 (a) 和句子 (b) 加以變化，分別改成形容詞子句，或是進一步簡化成片語，然後再與所保留的句子 (c) 結合成為複句或甚至是簡單句。

以下的例子用來說明可能的幾種變化：

(a) Kending National Park was established in 1982.

可以將句子 (a) 改成**非限定用法形容詞子句**：

→ (a1) **which was established in 1982**

或是進一步將形容詞子句簡化爲**過去分詞片語**：

→ (a2) **established in 1982**

(b) Kending National Park was the first national park in Taiwan.

可以將句子 (b) 改成**非限定用法形容詞子句**：

→ (b1) **which was the first national park in Taiwan**

或是進一步將形容詞子句簡化爲**名詞片語**，作爲**同位語**：

→ (b2) **the first national park in Taiwan**

現在我們有**四種句型變化**的可能：

1. (a2) + (c) + (b1) = 過去分詞片語 + 獨立子句 + 形容詞子句 = **複句**
2. (b2) + (c) + (a1) = 名詞片語 + 獨立子句 + 形容詞子句 = **複句**
3. (a2) + (c) + (b2) = 過去分詞片語 + 獨立子句 + 名詞片語 = **簡單句**
4. (b2) + (c) + (a2) = 名詞片語 + 獨立子句 + 過去分詞片語 = **簡單句**

將句子 (a) 和句子 (b) 簡化爲形容詞子句或片語後，與維持不變的句子 (c) 重新組合構成的新句子，包括兩個複句和兩個簡單句，而所變化出來的四種不同結構的句子，所表達的涵義是一致的：

1. (a2) + (c) + (b1) = 過去分詞片語 + 獨立子句 + 形容詞子句 = **複句**：

Established in 1982, Kending National Park, **which was the first national park in Taiwan**, now attracts millions of tourists annually.

2. (b2) + (c) + (a1) = 名詞片語 + 獨立子句 + 形容詞子句 = **複句**

The first national park in Taiwan, Kending National Park, **which was established in 1982**, now attracts millions of tourists annually.

3. (a2) + (c) + (b2) = 過去分詞片語 + 獨立子句 + 名詞片語 = **簡單句**

Established in 1982, Kending National Park, **the first national park in Taiwan**, now attracts millions of tourists annually.

4. (b2) + (c) + (a2) = 名詞片語 + 獨立子句 + 過去分詞片語 = **簡單句**

The first national park in Taiwan, Kending National Park, **established in 1982**, now attracts millions of tourists annually.

例二：

(a) David had been on the injured list for over three months.
(b) He was activated yesterday before the game to start as the first baseman.
(c) He hit a walk-off home run to win the game.

以上三個簡單句，如果我們決定句子 (c) 是所要強調的重點而予以保留，那就可以將句子 (a) 和句子 (b) 加以變化，分別改成形容詞子句，或是進一步簡化成片語，然後再與所保留的句子 (c) 結合成為複句或甚至是簡單句。

以下的例子用來說明可能的幾種變化：

(a) David had been on the injured list for over three months.

可以將簡單句 (a) 改為**非限定用法形容詞子句**：

→ (a1) **who had been on the injured list for over three months**

或是進一步將主動語態形容詞子句簡化為**現在分詞片語**：

→ (a2) **having been on the injured list for over three months**

(b) He was activated yesterday before the game to start as the first baseman.

可以將簡單句 (a) 改為**非限定用法形容詞子句**：

→ (b1) **who was activated yesterday before the game to start as the first baseman**

或是進一步將被動語態形容詞子句簡化為**過去分詞片語**：

→ (b2) **activated yesterday before the game to start as the first baseman**

現在我們有**四種句型變化的可能**：

1. (a2) + (c) + (b1) = 現在分詞片語 + 獨立子句 + 形容詞子句 = **複句**
2. (b2) + (c) + (a1) = 過去分詞片語 + 獨立子句 + 形容詞子句 = **複句**
3. (a2) + (c) + (b2) = 現在分詞片語 + 獨立子句 + 過去分詞片語 = 簡單句
4. (b2) + (c) + (a2) = 過去分詞片語 + 獨立子句 + 現在分詞片語 = 簡單句

　　將句子 (a) 和句子 (b) 簡化為形容詞子句或片語之後，與維持不變的句子 (c) 重新組合構成的新句子，包括兩個複句和兩個簡單句，而所變化出來的四種不同結構的句子，所表達的涵義是一致的：

1. (a2) + (c) + (b1) = 現在分詞片語 + 獨立子句 + 形容詞子句 = **複句**

   Having been on the injured list for over three months, David, **who was activated yesterday before the game to start as the first baseman**, hit a walk-off home run to win the game.

2. (b2) + (c) + (a1) = 過去分詞片語 + 獨立子句 + 形容詞子句 = **複句**

   Activated yesterday before the game to start as the first baseman, David, **who had been on the injured list for over three months**, hit a walk-off home run to win the game.

3. (a2) + (c) + (b2) = 現在分詞片語 + 獨立子句 + 過去分詞片語 = 簡單句

   Having been on the injured list for over three months, David, **activated yesterday before the game to start as the first baseman**, hit a walk-off home run to win the game.

4. (b2) + (c) + (a2) = 過去分詞片語 + 獨立子句 + 現在分詞片語 = 簡單句

   Activated yesterday before the game to start as the first baseman, David, **having been on the injured list for over three months**, hit a walk-off home run to win the game.

例三：

(1) Pig farmers in China have been severely impacted by African swine fever.

(2) African swine fever has been spread to all provinces.

(3) It was first confirmed in a pig farm near the border of Russia.

(4) Pig farmers are struggling financially.

(5) It may take the government many years to control the epidemic.

(6) The epidemic has resulted in the culling or dying of up to 200 million pigs.

(7) The epidemic has thus caused huge disruption to the supply of pork in the country.

以上七個簡單句中，保留第四句跟第五句爲獨立子句，其餘的句子則改爲形容詞子句或副詞子句、或是進一步簡化爲分詞片語或省略子句：

(1) **Pig farmers in China have** been severely impacted by African swine fever.

改成現在分詞片語→ (1a) **having** been severely impacted by African swine fever

(2) **African swine fever** has been spread to all provinces.

改成非限定形容詞子句→ (2a) **which** has been spread to all provinces

再改成過去分詞片語 → (2b) **having been spread** to all provinces

(3) It was first confirmed in a pig farm near the border of Russia.

改成副詞子句 → (3a) **since** it was first confirmed in a pig farm near the border of Russia

再把副詞子句簡化成爲省略子句 → (3b) since **being** first **introduced** in a pig farm near the border of Russia

(6) **The epidemic** has resulted in the culling or dying of up to 200 million pigs.

改成非限定形容詞子句 → (6a) **which** has resulted in the culling or dying of up to 200 million pigs

再改成現在分詞片語 → (6b) **having resulted** in the culling or dying of up to 200 million pigs

(7) **The epidemic** has thus caused huge disruption to the supply of pork in the country.

改成非限定形容詞子句 → (7a) **which** has thus caused huge disruption to the supply of pork in the country

再改成現在分詞片語 → (7b) **having** thus **caused** huge disruption to the supply of pork in the country

(6a) + (7a) 結合成一個非限定形容詞子句

→ (8) **which** has resulted in the culling or dying of up to 200 million pigs and has thus caused huge disruption to the supply of pork in the country

或是 (6b) + (7b) 結合成一個現在分詞片語

→ (9) **having resulted** in the culling or dying of up to 200 million pigs and **having** thus **caused** huge disruption to the supply of pork in the country

完成以上步驟，接下來可以將七個簡單句組合成為一個**複合句**或是一個**合句**。

組成複合句

(1a) + (2a) + (3a) + 維持不變的 (4) 結合成為一個**複句**

→ (1a) Having been severely impacted by African swine fever, (2a) which has been spread to all provinces (3a) since it was first confirmed in a pig farm near the border of Russia, (4) pig farmers in China are struggling financially.

接著，維持不變的 (5) + 新的 (8) 結合成為另一個**複句**

→ (5) It may take the government many years to control the epidemic, (8) which has resulted in the culling or dying of up to 200 million pigs and has thus caused huge disruption to the supply of pork in the country.

最後，把兩個新的複句以對**等連接詞 and** 結合成為一個**複合句**：

→ Having been severely impacted by African swine fever, which has been spread to all provinces since it was first confirmed in a pig farm near the border of Russia, pig farmers in China are struggling financially, and it may take the government many years to control the epidemic, which has resulted in the culling or dying of up to 200 million pigs and has thus caused huge disruption to the supply of pork in the country.

組成合句

(1a) + (2b) + (3b) + (4) 結合成一個簡單句

→ Pig farmers in China, having been severely impacted by African swine fever, having been spread to all provinces since being first confirmed in a pig farm near the border of Russia, are struggling financially.

(5) + (9) 結合成另一個簡單句

→ It may take the government many years to control the epidemic, having resulted in the culling or dying of up to 200 million pigs and having thus caused huge disruption to the supply of pork in the country.

最後把兩個簡單句以**對等連接詞 and** 結合成一個合句

→ Pig farmers in China, having been severely impacted by African swine fever, having been spread to all provinces since being first confirmed in a pig farm near the border of Russia, are struggling financially, and it may take the government many years to control the epidemic, having resulted in the culling or dying of up to 200 million pigs and having thus caused huge disruption to the supply of pork in the country.

　　將下列各組句子中劃底線的句子維持不變，並將其他句子改成形容詞子句、省略子句或片語後，與所保留的句子結合成為 (1) 複合句或複句與 (2) 合句或簡單句。

示範：

Dr. Symonds is a famous scholar.

Dr. Symonds is specialized in urban planning.

Dr. Symonds will be giving a speech at our school tomorrow.

→ *(1) 複句（簡單句＋非限定用法形容詞子句）*

　　A famous scholar, Dr. Symonds, who is specialized in urban planning, will be giving a speech at our school tomorrow.

　　(2) 簡單句

　　A famous scholar, Dr. Symonds, specialized in urban planning, will be giving a speech at our school tomorrow.

　　或

　　Dr. Symonds, a famous scholar specialized in urban planning, will be giving a speech at our school tomorrow.

---

1. The restaurant across from the park serves excellent Italian food.

   The restaurant is open from 11:00 a.m. to 9:30 p.m.

   The restaurant is owned by a famous movie star.

   (1)（複句）＿＿＿＿＿＿＿＿＿＿＿＿＿＿＿＿＿＿

   ＿＿＿＿＿＿＿＿＿＿＿＿＿＿＿＿＿＿＿＿＿＿＿

   ＿＿＿＿＿＿＿＿＿＿＿＿＿＿＿＿＿＿＿＿＿＿＿

(2)（簡單句）＿＿＿＿＿＿＿＿＿＿＿＿＿＿＿

＿＿＿＿＿＿＿＿＿＿＿＿＿＿＿＿＿＿＿

＿＿＿＿＿＿＿＿＿＿＿＿＿＿＿＿＿＿＿

2. Scott Stevens is the Director of ELI at the University of Delaware.

He was excited to meet his good friend Sam.

Sam invited him to attend an international conference.

The conference was organized by the English Department at Feng Chia University.

(1)（複句）＿＿＿＿＿＿＿＿＿＿＿＿＿＿＿

＿＿＿＿＿＿＿＿＿＿＿＿＿＿＿＿＿＿＿

＿＿＿＿＿＿＿＿＿＿＿＿＿＿＿＿＿＿＿

(2)（簡單句）

＿＿＿＿＿＿＿＿＿＿＿＿＿＿＿＿＿＿＿

＿＿＿＿＿＿＿＿＿＿＿＿＿＿＿＿＿＿＿

＿＿＿＿＿＿＿＿＿＿＿＿＿＿＿＿＿＿＿

3. The archeologists unearthed an ancient grave yard in a hill near the village.

The archeologists are from three different countries.

They have been digging in the area for six months.

(1)（複句）＿＿＿＿＿＿＿＿＿＿＿＿＿＿＿

＿＿＿＿＿＿＿＿＿＿＿＿＿＿＿＿＿＿＿

＿＿＿＿＿＿＿＿＿＿＿＿＿＿＿＿＿＿＿

(2)（簡單句）＿＿＿＿＿＿＿＿＿＿＿＿＿＿

＿＿＿＿＿＿＿＿＿＿＿＿＿＿＿＿＿＿＿

＿＿＿＿＿＿＿＿＿＿＿＿＿＿＿＿＿＿＿

4. Joshua became a Christian at the age of 35.

He changed into a different person since then.

He quit his job as a pharmacist three years ago.

He is now a devoted missionary in India.

(1)（複句）_____

_____

_____

(2)（簡單句）_____

_____

_____

5. The Taiwan High Speed Rail was launched in 2007.

It connects major cities along the west coast of Taiwan.

It symbolizes the modernization of Taiwan's transportation system.

(1)（複句）_____

_____

_____

(2)（簡單句）_____

_____

_____

6. Timothy Lin is a certified accountant.

He has been working for a multi-national corporation for two decades.

The corporation is in the mining business.

He has been promoted to be the CFO of the corporation.

(1)（複句）_____

_____

_____

(2) （簡單句）_____

_____

_____

7. The iPhone was created by Steve Jobs.

Steve Jobs was the CEO of Apple Inc.

The iPhone was introduced in 2007.

The iPhone has attracted millions of users worldwide.

(1) （複句）_____

_____

_____

(2) （簡單句）_____

_____

_____

8. The bridge connects two major cities.

Two major cities are located in the east coast.

The bridge suddenly collapsed last month.

It caused many casualties of drivers and passengers in the cars.

The cars were crossing the bridge.

(1) （複句）_____

_____

_____

(2) （簡單句）_____

_____

_____

9. The National Taichung Theater is a new type of construction project.

The architecture of the National Taichung Theater consists of 58 individual curved-wall units.

The curved-wall units are part of a special construction technique.

The special construction technique uses steel reinforced bars to build a curved three-dimensional effect.

(1)（複句）_____

_____

_____

_____

_____

(2)（簡單句）_____

_____

_____

10. A drone is formally known as Unmanned Aerial Vehicle (UAV).

In addition to carrying out military missions, a drone is now also used in a wide variety of civilian roles.

The roles were unimaginable not long ago.

The roles range from surveying, inspection, security, aerial video and photography, delivery services to several other applications.

(1)（複句）_____

_____

_____

_____

_____

(2)（簡單句）_____

_____

_____

11. They were hiking in the deep woods at an altitude of 3,000 feet.（改成副詞子句）

The mountaineers unexpectedly spotted a Formosan black bear.

The Formosan black bear's population has been declining.

Their habitats are being diminished by severe exploitation by farmers.（改成副詞子句）

The farmers grow fruits and tea in the high mountains.

(1)（複句）_____

_____

_____

(2)（簡單句）_____

_____

_____

12. The trade war between the U.S. and China intensifies.（改成副詞子句）

Some of the top manufacturers in information technology industries were relocated from Taiwan to China years ago.

They are now moving back to set up new production lines to make products.

The products are exported to the U.S.

It creates thousands of new jobs and boosts the economy in Taiwan.

(1)（複句）_____

13. The insurance agent was determined to be more aggressive and competitive after she attended the seminar.

The seminar introduced new types of insurance.

The insurance agent employed an innovative approach to entice more clients to buy new insurance policies to cover a wider range of risks.

The innovative approach was just learned from a speaker at the seminar.

(1)（複句）＿＿＿＿＿＿＿＿＿＿＿＿＿＿＿＿＿＿＿＿

＿＿＿＿＿＿＿＿＿＿＿＿＿＿＿＿＿＿＿＿＿＿＿＿＿＿

＿＿＿＿＿＿＿＿＿＿＿＿＿＿＿＿＿＿＿＿＿＿＿＿＿＿

(2)（簡單句）＿＿＿＿＿＿＿＿＿＿＿＿＿＿＿＿＿＿＿＿

＿＿＿＿＿＿＿＿＿＿＿＿＿＿＿＿＿＿＿＿＿＿＿＿＿＿

＿＿＿＿＿＿＿＿＿＿＿＿＿＿＿＿＿＿＿＿＿＿＿＿＿＿

14. Grace was entrusted under a contract.

The contract was signed by a developer.

The developer recently acquired a suburban house.

The house was built in the 1970s.

Grace is an interior designer.

Grace has been working with a team.

The team specializes in home remodeling.

Grace plans to renovate the house in line with the contemporary style.

The contemporary style is more appealing to young couples.

(1)（複句）＿＿＿＿＿＿＿＿＿＿＿＿＿＿＿＿＿＿＿＿

(2)（簡單句）_____

15. Increasing drunk driving is involved in many deadly car accidents.

Increasing drunk driving has prompted the central government to revise the law to raise the penalties.

The law regulates such incidents.

The penalties are imposed on drunk drivers.

The Legislative Yuan has just passed the new version of the law.

The law is set to be enacted on July 1, 2019.

(1)（複合句）_____

_____

_____

(2)（合句）_____

_____

_____

▶▶ 10.1.2 句型變換挑戰題

　　將下列句子翻成英文的**複句（不含對等連接詞）**或複合句（含對等連接詞），劃底線部分爲主要子句。（*作法提示：先將中文翻成數個英文簡單句或複句，保留其中一句作爲主要子句，再運用簡單句轉換成從屬子句，以及副詞子句與形容詞子句簡化爲片語的技*

巧，然後將其結合成單一完整的複句；或是保留前後兩個簡單句爲主要子句，再運用簡單句轉換成從屬子句，以及副詞子句與形容詞子句簡化爲片語的技巧，最後以對等連接詞將其結合成單一完整的複合句。）

示範：

快樂寵物首先於 1988 在加州聖地牙哥開幕，於 2005 年出售給一位來自臺灣移民的新東家，在 2016 年擴大之後，已經變成當地最大的寵物店。（複句）

Happy Pets was first established in 1988 in San Diego, California.

It was sold in 2005 to a new owner.

The new owner was an immigrant from Taiwan.

It has now become the largest pet store there after it was expanded in 2016.

（保留劃底線的部分）

最後完成的英文複句爲：

(1) *Happy Pets, which was first established in 1988 in San Diego, California and was sold in 2005 to a new owner who was an immigrant from Taiwan, has now become the largest pet store there after it was expanded in 2016.*

(2) *Happy Pets, first established in 1988 in San Diego, California and sold in 2005 to a new owner who was an immigrant from Taiwan, has now become the largest pet store there after it was expanded in 2016.*

---

1. 有一位年輕人已經發明了一支特殊的手槍，需要擁有者或是得到擁有者授權的某人才能扣發扳機，這是設計來防止小孩誤用手槍。（複句）

_____

_____

2. 一家法國超市計畫在中國眾多快速發展的城市其中之一的蘇州開設一間大型超市，販售從歐洲進口的貨品與生鮮，將在那裡建造一座建築物，其二樓將會有 25 個單位的空間給當地的商家和餐廳加入其生意。（複句）

_____

_____

3. 去年九月身為一家在臺灣的高科技公司總經理的 David Wang，跟太太 Sharon 從臺北飛往舊金山與他們女兒 Vera 會合，然後一起搭乘遊輪去阿拉斯加，在那裡他們看到了景色絕美的冰河以及撼人心弦的北極光。（複句）

_____

_____

4. 十幾歲的 Ruth，其父親挑戰她獨自一人駕船航行世界一週，她認為這是瘋狂的主意，因為她從來沒有上過任何船隻，但是她後來決定接受挑戰並且完成這一趟不可思議的旅程，其間她差點在暴風中喪命。（複合句）

_____

5. 上大學之前，Henry 被深信教書是較好的職涯選擇的父親說服而放棄成為職業歌手的夢想，不過他在教書超過二十年也成為國中校長之後卻從未停止作曲與歌唱，而且他已經在一項大型歌唱比賽中贏得第二名的獎項，並且受邀在不同的場合演唱。（複合句）

第十一章 連接副詞 (Conjunctive Adverbs)

連接副詞屬於轉折語 (transitional expressions) 的用法，可以使用在單一句子中，出現的位置包括句首、句中、及句尾，例如：

(1) **In fact,** many people cannot live without smartphones.

(2) Many people, **in fact,** cannot live without smartphones.

(3) Many people cannot live without smartphones, **in fact**.

此外，有些連接副詞的作用類似對等連接詞，可以用來連接前後兩個句子，表達前後敘述內容的關聯性；在結構形式上，使用對等連接詞串聯兩個句子時結構是固定的，而使用連接副詞銜接前後兩個句子時，可以有不同的變化，例如使用**對等連接詞 so** 與**連接副詞 as a result**，要注意其**出現的位置**與所必須使用的**標點符號**有所不同，且其**句子結構**也相異。

(1) Many students need to earn money to support themselves financially, **so** they work part-time after school.（合句）

(2) Many students need to earn money to support themselves financially. **As a result,** they work part-time after school.（兩個簡單句）

(3) Many students need to earn money to support themselves financially. They, **as a result,** work part-time after school.（兩個簡單句）

(4) Many students need to earn money to support themselves financially. They work part-time after school, **as a result**.（兩個簡單句）

(5) Many students need to earn money to support themselves financially; **as a result**, they work part-time after school.（兩個簡單句）

　　連接副詞與對等連接詞相同，所銜接的兩個句子可以是**兩個簡單句、一個簡單句與一個複句、或是兩個複句**，並且兩個句子以連接副詞加以銜接並不會造成句子結構的變化，例如：

(1) She did not ask for help; **instead**, she accomplished the difficult task all by herself.（兩個簡單句）

(2) I saw a beautiful rainbow yesterday. **However**, it disappeared as soon as I took out my cellphone trying to take a picture of it.（一個簡單句與一個複句）

(3) Businesses in countries where the infrastructure is more advanced have a better chance to prosper; **on the contrary**, those in countries where the governments do not invest enough in the infrastructure find it more difficult to succeed.（兩個複句）

　　除此之外，連接副詞所可以表達的語氣轉折比對等連接詞更加豐富，更多變化，如 instead, for example, in fact, likewise, above all, on the other hand…等等所表達的語氣轉折是對等連接詞所沒有的。因此，同學若要把英文的句子寫的生動且富有變化，除了要學會活用對等連接詞及從屬連接詞之外，也必須熟練連接副詞的運用。

11.1 連接副詞與對等連接詞共有的語氣轉折

　　連接副詞中有些是具備與對等連接詞共有的語氣轉折，有些則是連接副詞特有的語氣轉折。我們先以下列例子來說明，使用對等連接詞 (**and, so, yet, but, or**) 和連接副詞銜接前後兩個句子所<u>共同表達的語氣轉折</u>，但在<u>結構上會出現的差異</u>。

▶▶ 11.1.1 對等連接詞 and 與連接副詞 additionally, moreover, besides, furthermore

這些用詞表達「加上」、「除此之外」、「尤有甚者」的涵義

(1) The store is promoting its merchandise with special discounts.

(2) It also offers a buy-one-get-one-free deal for many of the items.

　　句子 (2) 是對句子 (1) 敘述的追加，可以用對等連接詞 and 連接兩個簡單句，**成為一個合句**：

The store is promoting its merchandise with special discounts, **and** it offers a buy-one-get-one-free deal for many of the items.（合句）

　　或是用連接副詞 additionally, moreover, besides, furthermore 來連接這兩個句子，而連接之後句子的**結構仍然是兩個個別的句子**，可以有**兩種不同結構的變化**：

a. The store is promoting its merchandise with special discounts. **Additionally / Moreover / Besides / Furthermore,** it offers a buy-one-get-one-free deal for many of the items.（兩個簡單句）

b. The store is promoting its merchandise with special discounts; **additionally / moreover / besides / furthermore**, it offers a buy-one-get-one-free deal for many of the items.（兩個簡單句）

▶▶▶ 11.1.2 對等連接詞 so 與連接副詞 therefore, consequently, as a result

這些用詞表達「前因後果」的關係

(1) They bought a new house whose price is very affordable.

(2) They were very happy.

句子 (2) 是句子 (1) 所產生的結果，可以用對等連接詞 so 連接一個複句與一個簡單句，**成為一個複合句**：

They bought a new house whose price was very affordable, **so** they were very happy.（複合句）

或是用**連接副詞 therefore, consequently** 或 **as a result** 來銜接這兩個句子，而連接之後句子的**結構仍然是兩個個別的句子**，可以有**兩種不同結構的變化**：

a. They bought a new house whose price was very affordable. **Therefore / Consequently / As a result,** they were very happy.（複句與簡單句）

b. They bought a new house whose price was very affordable; **therefore / consequently / as a result,** they were very happy. （複句與簡單句）

11.1.3 對等連接詞 yet, but 與連接副詞 nonetheless, however, nevertheless

這些用詞表達「出人意料的結果」。

(1) They bought a new house.

(2) The wife was not very happy because it was a little too far from downtown.

句子 (2) 是句子 (1) 出人意料的結果，我們可以用**對等連接詞 yet 或 but** 連接一個簡單句與一個複句，**成為一個複合句**：

They bought a new house, **yet / but** the wife was not very happy because it was a little too far from downtown.（複合句）

或是用**連接副詞 nonetheless, however, 或 nevertheless** 來銜接這兩個句子，而連接之後句子的**結構仍然是兩個個別的句子**，可以有**兩種不同結構的變化**：

a. They bought a new house. **Nonetheless / However / Nevertheless**, the wife was not very happy because it was a little too far from downtown.（簡單句與複句）

b. They bought a new house; **nonetheless / however /nevertheless**, the wife was not very happy because it was a little too far from downtown.（簡單句與複句）

11.1.4 對等連接詞 or 與連接副詞 otherwise

這些用詞表達「否則」的涵義。

(1) Students going to study in a foreign country where it snows heavily in the winter must bring heavy coats with them.

(2) They will suffer from the freezing winter as the temperature

can drop to as low as 15 degrees Celsius below zero.

句子 (2) 所表達的意思是：如果句子 (1) 的條件沒有完成就會出現的後果。

我們可以用對等連接詞 **or** 連接兩個複句，**成爲一個複合句**：

Students going to study in a foreign country where it snows heavily in the winter must bring heavy coats with them, **or** they will suffer from the freezing winter as the temperature can drop to as low as 15 degrees Celsius below zero.（複合句）

或是用**連接副詞 otherwise** 來銜接這兩個複句，而銜接之後句子的**結構仍然是兩個個別句子**，可以有**兩種不同結構的變化**：

a. Students going to study in a foreign country where it snows heavily in the winter must bring heavy coats with them. **Otherwise**, they will suffer from the freezing winter as the temperature can drop to as low as 15 degrees Celsius below zero.（兩個複句）

b. Students going to study in a foreign country where it snows heavily in the winter must bring heavy coats with them; **otherwise**, they will suffer from the freezing winter as the temperature can drop to as low as 15 degrees Celsius below zero.（兩個複句）

11.2 連接副詞特有的語氣轉折

接下來，我們再看一些例子來說明**連接副詞特有的語氣轉折**運用：

| instead | 卻、反而

The mother of the victim did not hold a grudge against the drunk driver. **Instead**, she chose to forgive him just as God forgave those who crucified His only son, Jesus.

The mother of the victim did not hold grudge against the drunk driver; **instead**, she chose to forgive him just as God forgave those who crucified His only son, Jesus.

| for example / for instance | 舉例來說

There are many effective ways to deal with occasional depression in our lives. **For example / For instance**, one can certainly regain joy by reaching out to the disadvantaged.

There are many effective ways to deal with occasional depression in our lives; **for example / for instance**, one can certainly regain joy by reaching out to the disadvantaged.

| above all | 最重要地、尤其

The industrialized countries as well as developing countries need to work together to slow down global climate change. **Above all**, we need to replace fossil fuel with more green energy.

The industrialized countries as well as developing countries need to work together to slow down global climate change; **above all**, we need to replace fossil fuel with more green energy.

likewise / similarly 同樣地、類似地

Many college students have to work part-time to support themselves. **Likewise / similarly**, I work part-time in a fancy restaurant to earn my tuition.

Many college students have to work part-time to support themselves; **likewise / similarly**, I work part-time in a fancy restaurant to earn my tuition.

on the other hand 另一方面

Some of the professors in our department are very demanding in their courses. **On the other hand**, some of them are very generous in grading.

Some of the professors in our department are very demanding in their courses; **on the other hand**, some of them are very generous in grading.

on the contrary/conversely 反之

Almost everyone thought the project would fail. **On the contrary / conversely**, it worked.

Almost everyone thought the project would fail; **on the contrary / conversely**, it worked.

in fact 實際上

Jeremy is very good at investments. **In fact**, he has made handsome returns from investing heavily on the real estate market in the last three years.

Jeremy is very good at investments; **in fact**, he has made handsome returns from investing heavily on the real estate market in the last three years.

then 接著

She found a new job in Taipei. **Then**, she moved to a rented apartment there.

She found a new job in Taipei; **then**, she moved to a rented apartment there.

in conclusion 總之

Many issues were discussed and insightful suggestions were made during the three-hour meeting. **In conclusion**, it was a very fruitful meeting.

Many issues were discussed and insightful suggestions were made during the three-hour meeting; **in conclusion**, it was a very fruitful meeting.

meanwhile / in the meantime 同時

The debt of the giant apparel chain stores has greatly piled up since their some 1,500 foreign factory workers were found illegal. **Meanwhile / In the meantime**, they are on the brink of bankruptcy as their sales have failed to reach the target.

The debt of the giant apparel chain stores has greatly piled up since their some 1,500 foreign factory workers were found illegal; **meanwhile / in the meantime**, they are on the brink of bankruptcy as their sales have failed to reach the target.

indeed 確實

A new law has just been passed to further protect children from being abused. **Indeed**, they need more protection than others.

A new law has just been passed to further protect children from being abused; **indeed**, they need more protection than others.

11.3 連接副詞的涵義與作用一覽表

連接副詞	作用
also 還有；besides 並且、加之；moreover 並且、此外 in addition 此外、加之；furthermore 而且、此外	加上
thus 因此、於是；hence 由此；therefore 因此、於是 accordingly 因此、所以；as a result 因此、所以 as a consequence 因此、所以；consequently 因此、所以	前面敘述所造成的影響或結果
still 儘管如此，然而；however 然而；instead 反而、卻 nevertheless 然而；nonetheless 然而	後者非前者一般預期會有的結果
also 還有；likewise 同樣地；similarly 類似地	前後比較
on the other hand 另一方面；on the contrary 相反地 in contrast 相對照之下；conversely 相反地 in/by comparison 相較之下	前後對比
otherwise 否則	前面敘述的條件未達成時的後果

連接副詞	作用
for example 舉例來說；for instance 舉例來說	舉例說明
then 接著，然後；next 接著、然後；finally 最後 meanwhile 同時；subsequently 隨後，接著	時間順序
indeed 確實；that is 也就是	加強語氣或 再次陳述
in fact 實際上、事實上	以事實支持 前面的敘述
above all 最重要地、尤其；most importantly 最重要地 primarily 主要地	強調前面敘 述中最重要 的
all in all 總結來說；in brief 簡言之；in conclusion 總之 in short 總而言之；in summary 總結來說	作結論

11.4 小試身手

圈選恰當的連接副詞以連接前後兩個獨立子句

1. Most people have the impression that the founder of the company is a university graduate; _____, she did not even finish high school.

   (A. however   B. in conclusion   C. meanwhile   D. on the contrary)

2. We must get to the auditorium before seven o'clock tonight. _____, we will miss the concert.

   (A. Otherwise   B. Also   C. For instance   D. Thus)

3. Mr. Jiang is a full-time math teacher in our school; _____, he is the coach of our tennis team.

(A. hence   B. in addition   C. in brief   D. next)

4. The boutique did really well last year; _____, its revenue reached nearly three million dollars.

(A. finally   B. that is   C. indeed   D. for example)

5. The researchers have revealed how our diets affect our health. _____, eating too much sugar greatly increases risk of cancer.

(A. Likewise   B. Most importantly   C. Moreover   D. Accordingly)

6. When first meeting Albert, most people assume that he is a meat lover because of his big muscles; _____, he is a vegetarian.

(A. similarly   B. subsequently   C. on the contrary   D. nevertheless)

7. During the negotiation, the two parties discussed the terms, and each compromised a little; _____, the outcome of the negotiation was satisfactory to both sides.

(A. all in all   B. however   C. meanwhile   D. besides)

8. The law graduate has been trying to become a lawyer for several years; _____, she passed the bar examination last month.

(A. furthermore   B. finally   C. in short   D. instead)

9. They did not follow the speed limit while driving; _____, they would not have been fined for speeding.

(A. thus   B. above all   C. that is   D. otherwise)

10. Smartphones allow people to communicate with one another much easier than before; _____, fewer and fewer people are now writing letters to others.

(A. conversely   B. primarily   C. for example   D. hence)

11.5 小試身手

　　將下列各題的兩個獨立子句，依其涵義以連接副詞加以連接，以表現恰當的語氣轉折。

1. The game had been delayed. The crowd had to wait for the game to start.

_____

2. The couple have five children of their own. They agreed to adopt their neighbor's three children when she was diagnosed with terminal cancer.

_____

_____

3. They did not like to take the highway while traveling. They prefer taking local roads to enjoy the scenery along the way.

_____

_____

4. Living in urban areas is more convenient but stressful. Living in rural areas is more relaxing and healthy.

_____

_____

5. She seems to be well qualified for the job according to her résumé. The manager does not think she is a good fit for our company because of her personality.

_____

_____

6. The small house is very old. It has been sold for over two million dollars due to its invaluable location.

_____

_____

7. You must stop chewing beetle nuts. You will die from oral cancer sooner or later.

_____

8. My best friend is going to study abroad in Australia. She plans to get a part-time job there.

_____

9. William enjoys outdoor activities. His twin brother likes reading and playing the guitar.

_____

_____

10. He bought the used car and reconditioned it. He sold it to someone for a higher price.

_____

11. According to the trainer, the player has improved significantly. He still has a long way to go before fully recovering from the injury.

_____

_____

12. The tourists from France paid visits to many famous scenic spots in Taiwan. They went to Alishan and witnessed the spectacular sunrise and sea of clouds in the high mountains.

_____

_____

_____

13. The committee held a meeting to assess the positive and negative impacts of the new zoning project. They decided that it would bring substantial financial benefits to the city.

_____

_____

_____

14. Jobs fill your pocket. Adventures fill your soul.

_____

15. It seems the suspect has committed the crime. The prosecutor is skeptical about his conviction in the court due to the lack of hard evidence.

_____

_____

16. Classical music is favored by older people. Heavy metal music attracts more younger generations.

_____

_____

第十二章 誤置與脫節修飾語 (Misplaced and Dangling Modifiers)

　　英文的修飾語可能是一個字、一個片語或一個子句，在寫句子時，若是修飾語放錯位置，有可能造成語意上的模稜兩可，甚至文法上的錯誤，這是屬於修飾語的誤置或錯置。另外，如果修飾語所修飾的對象根本不在句子裡面，則是修飾語脫節。無論是修飾語的誤置、錯置或脫節，都是有問題的句子結構，我們在英文寫作時必須特別留意，避免犯錯。

12.1 誤置修飾語 (misplaced modifiers)

　　誤置修飾語可能導致的後果有二：(1) 造成語意上的模稜兩可，或是 (2) 造成語意上的誤解或結構上的錯誤，分別舉例說明如下。

▶▶ 12.1.1 誤置修飾語造成語意上的模稜兩可

例一：*Working out **quickly** improves one's health.*

說明：句子中的副詞 quickly 所修飾的對象可以是 working out，也可以是 improves，因此句子的涵義有可能是「快速健身會改善一個人健康」，或是「健身會快速改善一個人的健康」。

解決方法：爲了避免語意上模擬兩可，我們可以**將副詞 quickly 移到句尾**：

→ *Working out improves one's health **quickly**.*

如此一來，**quickly 所修飾的對象很清楚是 improves**，而不會是 working out 了。因此句子的涵義就是「**健身會快速改善一個人的健康**」。

例二：*He told me **on November 11** he was getting married.*

說明：句子中的介系詞片語 on November 所修飾的對象可以是 told，也可以是 getting married，因此句子的涵義有可能是「他在 11 月 11 日告訴我他要結婚了」，也可能是「他告訴我他要在 11 月 11 日結婚了」。

解決方法一：爲了避免語意上模稜兩可，我們可以**將介系詞片語 on November 11 移到句首**：

→ ***On November 11**, he told me he was getting married.*

如此一來，on November 11 所修飾的對象很清楚是 told，因此句子的涵義就是「**他在 11 月 11 日告訴我他要結婚了**」。

解決方法二：或是**將介系詞片語 on November 11 移到句尾**：

→ *He told me he was getting married **on November 11**.*

如此一來，on November 11 所修飾的對象很清楚是 getting married，因此句子的涵義就是「**他告訴我他要在 11 月 11 日結婚了**」。

改寫下列句子以避免模稜兩可的語意。

1. People who go online **regularly** buy things from online stores.

    (1)（**經常**上網的人會從網路商店購買東西。）

    _____

    (2)（上網的人**經常**從網路商店購買東西。）

    _____

2. The President vowed **after his reelection** to crack down on drug traffickers.

    (1)（總統宣誓他會**在連任之後**掃蕩毒品走私犯。）

    _____

    (2)（總統**在連任之後**宣誓他會掃蕩毒品走私犯。）

    _____

3. My friend in Australia sent me a text message **in summer** she would visit me in Taiwan.

    (1)（我在澳洲的朋友私訊我說她會**在暑假**來臺灣拜訪我。）

    _____

    (2)（我在澳洲的朋友**在暑假**私訊我說她會來臺灣拜訪我。）

    _____

4. Students who skip classes **frequently** upset the professor.

    (1)（**經常**蹺課的學生會惹惱教授。）

    _____

    (2)（蹺課的學生**經常**會惹惱教授。）

    _____

5. Employees who achieve monthly goals **often** got promoted.

(1)（達成每個月目標的員工**常常**會得到升遷。）

_____

(2)（**常常**達成每個月目標的員工會得到升遷。）

_____

6. The manager said **before the meeting ends** he would resign.
(1)（經理**在會議結束前**說他會辭職。）

_____

(2)（經理說他會**在會議結束前**辭職。）

_____

7. Cindy told me **when her husband returned** she would go shopping with me.
(1)（Cindy **在她先生回來的時候**告訴我說她會跟我去購物。）

_____

(2)（Cindy 告訴我說**她先生回來的時候**她會跟我去購物。）

_____

▶▶ 12.1.3 誤置修飾語造成語意上的誤解或結構上的錯誤

修飾語放錯位置，因而造成語意上的錯誤，這種情況不僅常出現在一般學生的英文寫作，就連資深的寫作人員都有可能犯此類的錯，不可不慎。修飾語之所以誤置，主要就是沒有將修飾語放在最靠近所修飾對象的位置，而造成讀者誤以為該修飾語在修飾另一個對象，而非筆者的原意。

1. only, just, nearly, almost 的誤置

only, just, nearly, 與 almost 都具有形容詞與副詞的功能，他們在句子中會因為放置的位置不同而扮演不同的功能，因此會表示不同的涵義。底下以例句分別說明 only, just, nearly, 與 almost 這

四個修飾語誤置的可能性：

(1) Only

Only Zack participated in the community service during winter break.（only 是形容詞，修飾 Zack）
只有 **Zack**（沒有其他人）在寒假期間參與了社區服務。

Zack only participated in the community service during winter break.（**only** 是副詞，修飾 participated）
Zack 在寒假期間**只做了一件事，就是參與了社區服務**。（這句話的涵義邏輯上不通）

Zack participated only in the community service during winter break.（**only** 是副詞，修飾 in the community service）
Zack 在寒假期間**只參與了一個活動，就是社區服務**。

Zack participated in the community service only during winter break.（**only** 是副詞，修飾 during winter break）
Zack **只有在寒假期間**參與社區服務。

(2) just

Just Sophia was picked to compete in the speech contest.（**Just** 是形容詞，修飾 Sophia）
只有 **Sophia** 被挑選參加演講比賽。

Sophia was just picked to compete in the speech contest.（**just** 是副詞，修飾 picked）

Sophia **剛剛被挑選**參加演講比賽。

Sophia was picked to compete **just** in the speech contest.
（**just** 是副詞，修飾 in the speech contest.）
Sophia 被挑選**僅僅參加演講比賽**。

(3) nearly

An experienced Mahjong player, her mother **nearly** lost NT\$2,000 on Lunar New Year's Eve.（**nearly** 是副詞，修飾 lost）

身為經驗老到的麻將高手，她母親**差一點就**在農曆除夕夜**輸了**兩千元。因為 nearly 所修飾的是 lost，所以意思是她母親有可能沒輸半毛錢，或是有輸錢，但是不知道輸了多少錢。

An experienced Mahjong player, her mother lost **nearly** NT\$2,000 on Lunar New Year's Eve.（**nearly** 是形容詞，修飾 NT\$2,000）

身為經驗老到的麻將高手，她母親在農曆除夕夜輸了**將近兩千元**。

(4) almost

William **almost** earned NT\$50,000 in the stock market yesterday.（**almost** 是副詞，修飾 earned）
William 昨天**差一點**就在股票市場**賺到**五萬元。意思是可能沒賺到，也可能有賺到，但是賺到多少不知道。

William earned **almost** NT\$50,000 yesterday.（**almost** 是形

容詞，修飾 NT$50,000）

William 昨天在股票市場賺了將近五萬元。

2. 其他修飾語的誤置

例一：

Mike ate a **cold** piece of pizza for lunch.

本句中的形容詞 cold 所修飾的對象應該是 pizza，而非 piece，形成**文法上的錯誤**，正確的寫法應該如下：

→ Mike ate a piece of **cold** pizza for lunch.

例二：

The teacher was strict on students **giving quizzes every week**.

本句中的分詞片語 giving quizzes every week 原意是要修飾 teacher，但該分詞片語卻放置在 students 之後，而非放在 teacher 之後或之前，因此造成**語意上的誤解**。

正確的寫法應該如下：

→ The teacher **giving quizzes every week** was strict on students.

→ **Giving quizzes every week**, the teacher was strict on students.

例三：

Frank recently presented a paper at a conference **titled "Exploring Effective Strategies for Learning English Vocabulary."**

本句中的過去分詞片語 titled "Exploring Effective Strategies

for Learning English Vocabulary" 原意是要修飾 a paper，但因該修飾語放在 a conference 之後，而非放在 a paper 之後，因此造成語意上的誤解。

正確的寫法應該如下：

Recently at a conference, Frank presented a paper titled **"Exploring Effective Strategies for Learning English Vocabulary."**

例四：

The parents bought a puppy for their daughter **they called Spotty**.

本句中的形容詞子句 they called Spotty 原意要修飾的對象應是 a puppy，但該子句卻放置在 their daughter 之後，因此造成語意上的誤解。

正確的寫法應該如下：

→ The parents bought their daughter a puppy **they called Spotty**.

從以上的幾個例子，我們瞭解到要避免修飾語的誤置，唯一之道就是要將修飾語放置在最靠近所修飾對象的位置，如下列句子的改寫：

*I **only** have two weeks to finish writing my research paper.

→ I have **only** two weeks to finish writing my research paper.

（形容詞 only 所修飾的對象是 two weeks，而非 have）

* They did their home assignments **assisted by online friends**.

→ **Assisted by online friends**, they did their home assignments.

* The sofa looks great **in the furniture store**.

→ The sofa **in the furniture store** looks great.

（介系詞片語 in the furniture store 所修飾的對象是 the sofa，而非 looks）

▶▶ 12.1.4 小試身手

改正下列句子中的誤置修飾語

1. After jogging for over an hour, she drank an icy-cold bottle of cola.

   _____

2. The shirt was just too small for me in the store.

   _____

3. The robot amazed everyone cooking food.

   _____

4. I almost ate the entire extra-large pizza myself.

   _____

5. He said that he only played basketball for two hours this afternoon.

   _____

6. Nowadays people can order a meal delivered to them through a cellphone app.

   _____

7. She read a science fiction, *When You Reach Me*, a story about sacrificing one's life by returning to the past with a time machine by Rebecca Stead.

---

8. She gave an Apple Watch to her boyfriend she purchased from Apple Website.

---

9. With the deal sealed, she was happy that she nearly bought the house for $500,000.

---

10. My father is a big fan of Michael Jordan, who taught me how to play basketball.

12.2 脫節／虛懸修飾語 (dangling modifiers)

　　脫節修飾語屬於廣義的誤置修飾語的一種，與其他誤置修飾語的區別在於：(1) 脫節修飾語出現的位置在句子的開頭，而其他誤置修飾語則可能出現在句子的任何位置；(2) 脫節修飾語所修飾的對象不在句子中。脫節修飾語之所以出現，在於原來的兩個句子的主詞不同，卻將其中一個句子簡化為片語，從而造成**修飾語懸吊在半空中，無法與主詞連結，而找不到修飾的對象**。因此，這樣的修飾語就稱為**脫節**或**虛懸修飾語**。

▶▶ 12.2.1 脫節修飾語的類型

脫節修飾語的類型包括：

(1) 脫節現在分詞片語

(2) 脫節過去分詞片語

(3) 脫節不定詞片語

(4) 脫節介系詞片語

(5) 脫節同位語

(6) 脫節省略子句

1. 脫節現在分詞片語

臺灣的學生在使用分詞構句時容易出錯，原因在於中文的結構與英文不一樣，如下列例子：

從窗戶往外看，山上覆蓋著白雪。

這一句中文的涵義是「**有人**」從窗戶往外看，「**看見**」山頂覆蓋著白雪。但是臺灣的學生有可能會翻成：

Looking out the window, the mountain is covered with snow.

問題是 the mountain 不會往外看，不能當 looking out 的主詞，往外看的是人而不是山，因此這句英文乍看之下似乎正確，其實是**不合文法**的。

正確的寫法應該是：

He looked out the window. → looking out the window

He saw the mountain is covered with snow.

兩個句子的主詞一致，因此第一句可以簡化成現在分詞片語。

然後再與第二句結合：

→ ***Looking out the window***, *he saw the mountain is covered with snow.*

第二個例子：

大學畢業了，他爸爸鼓勵 Mark 去念碩士。
這一句中文的涵義是「Mark 大學畢業了，他爸爸鼓勵 Mark 去唸碩士。」但是臺灣的學生有可能按照中文字面的結構而翻成：
*Having graduated from college, **his father** encourages Mark to pursue a master's degree.*
但是這句英文的涵義卻是 " <u>爸爸</u>大學畢業了 "，而不是原來中文的涵義 "Mark 大學畢業了。
仔細分析，原來這一句翻出來的英文是由兩個句子合併而來：
His father has graduated from college. (1)
His father encourages Mark to pursue a master's degree. (2)
這兩個句子<u>**主詞相同**</u>，這是分詞構句的重要前提，因此可以將第一句簡化為現在分詞片語，再與第二句合併：
His father has graduated from college.
→ 簡化為現在分詞片語 having graduated from college
→ 與第二句合併 Having graduated from college, **his father** encourages Mark to pursue a master's degree.
如此一來，反而是爸爸大學畢業了，而不是 Mark 大學畢業了。

因此，<u>**正確的寫法**</u>應該是：
Mark has graduated from college.

His father encourages him to pursue a master's degree.

兩個句子主詞不同，所以不能將第一句簡化為現在分詞片語，只能以對等連接詞將兩個簡單句結合成為一個合句：

→ *Mark has graduated from college, so his father encourages him to pursue a master's degree.*

或是將第一句改成副詞子句，再與第二句結合成為複句：

→ *As Mark has graduated from college, his father encourages him to pursue a master's degree.*

如果一定要使用**分詞構句**，則必須將第二句改成被動語態，主詞變成 **Mark**，使兩個句子的主詞一致：

Mark has graduated from college. → having graduated from college

Mark is encouraged by his father to pursue a master's degree.

→ *Having graduated from college, Mark is encouraged by his father to pursue a master's degree.*

2. 脫節過去分詞片語

我們以下列中文句子的英譯說明脫節過去分詞片語：

兩個月前開始執行，工廠員工已經使用新的規定改善了效率。

如果按照中文字面結構直接翻成英文，有可能出現以下錯誤的句子：

*Implemented two months ago, **the factory workers** have improved their efficiency with the new protocols.*

仔細分析，我們發現過去分詞 implemented two months ago 所隱藏的主詞是 the new protocols，而主要子句的主詞卻是 the factory workers，**兩者並不一致**，因而造成脫節過去分詞 的句子結構錯誤。

改正的方法就是把**主要子句的主詞換成過去分詞片語所隱藏的 主詞** the new protocols，如下列句子所示：
→ *Implemented two months ago, the new protocols have improved the efficiency of the factory workers.*

3. 脫節不定詞片語

我們以下列中文句子的英譯說明脫節不定詞片語：

要成為飛行員，飛行訓練課程是絕對需要的。
如果按照中文字面結構直接翻成英文，有可能出現以下錯誤的 句子：
*To become a pilot, **a flight training program** is absolutely needed.*
仔細分析，這個句子的不定詞片語 to be a pilot 所隱藏的主詞 是某人，而主要子句的之詞卻是 a flight training program，兩者並不一致，因此造成脫節不定詞片語的句子結構錯誤。

改正的方法就是把**主要子句的主詞換成過去分詞片語所隱藏的 主詞** one，如下列句子所示：
→ *To become a pilot, **one** absolutely needs to take a flight training program.*

4. 脫節介系詞片語

我們以下列中文句子的英譯說明脫節介系詞片語：

一注意到有急迫的危險，他的雙手迅速抓起小孩逃離現場。

如果按照中文字面結構直接翻成英文，有可能出現以下錯誤的句子：

*Upon noticing the imminent danger, **his hands** quickly grabbed the child to escape from the scene.*

仔細分析，這個句子的介系詞片語 upon noticing the imminent danger 所隱藏的主詞是 he，而主要子句的主詞卻是 his hands，兩者顯然並不一致。

改正方法就是把**主要子句的主詞換成過去分詞片語所隱藏的主詞** he，如下列句子所示：

→ *Upon noticing the imminent danger, he quickly grabbed the child with his hands to escape form the scene.*

5. 脫節同位語

我們以下列中文句子的英譯說明脫節同位語：

一座建造於1800年代初期富麗堂皇的建築物，入侵的軍隊使用這座大教堂當作軍事醫院。

如果按照中文字面結構直接翻成英文，有可能出現以下錯誤的句子：

A magnificent architecture built in the early 1800s, the invading army used the cathedral as a military hospital.

仔細分析，這個句子的同位語片語 a magnificent architecture

所隱藏的主詞是 the cathedral，而主要子句的主詞卻是 the invading army，兩者顯然並不一致。

改正方法就是把<u>主要子句的主詞換成同位語片語所隱藏的主詞</u> the cathedral，如下列句子所示：
→ *A magnificent architecture built in the early 1800s, the cathedral was used as a military hospital.*

6. 脫節省略子句

我們以下列中文句子的英譯說明脫節省略子句：

在網路上訂機票時，航空公司提供 Paul 來回票的特別折扣。
如果按照中文字面直接翻成英文，有可能出現以下錯誤的句子：
When booking a plane ticket online, the airline offered Paul a special discount for a round-trip ticket.
仔細分析，這個句子的省略子句 when booking a plane ticket online 所隱藏的主詞是 Paul，而主要子句的主詞卻是 the airlines，兩者顯然並不一致。

改正方法就是把<u>主要子句的主詞換成省略子句所隱藏的主詞</u> Paul，如下列句子所示：
→ *When booking a plane ticket online, Paul was offered by the airline a special discount for a round-trip ticket.*

改正下列使用了脫節修飾語的句子。（<u>將主要子句的主詞改正</u><u>並作適當改寫</u>，或是<u>把脫節修飾語改成從屬子句</u>。）

例如：

Watching the game on TV, my phone rang.

→ Watching the game on TV, **I heard my phone ring**.

→ **While I was watching the game on TV**, my phone rang.

1. Sitting on the porch, the view of the open space made her joyful.

_____

_____

2. When 48, her dream finally came true.

_____

_____

3. If lost, people can always replace traveler's checks.

_____

_____

4. Riding in a train, what he saw was pretty farm houses and golden wheat fields.

_____

_____

5. After sitting in our seats for over an hour, the plane finally took off.

_____

_____

6. Bought 10 years ago, we now sell the car for $5,000.

_____

_____

7. Since joining the baseball team, the team has won many games with Peter as a powerful starting pitcher.

_____

_____

8. Walking in the night market, many stands were selling different kinds of local delicacies.

_____

_____

9. While working on his presentation slides, his cat interrupted him jumping on the keyboard.

_____

_____

10. To play tennis well, practicing regularly with a coach is necessary.

_____

_____

11. Married with kids, the life seems wonderful for Lisa.

_____

_____

12. Although a high school student, her younger brother and sister need her to take care of them since their parents are gone.

_____

_____

12.2.3 脫節修飾語挑戰題

中翻英（劃底線的部分要使用片語或省略子句，並注意避免造成脫節修飾語錯誤。）

示範：

她一邊開著車，沿途都是美麗的農舍和麥田。

→ **While driving, she saw beautiful farm houses and wheat fields**.

（如果翻成 While driving, there were beautiful farm houses and wheat fields along the way. 這樣的句子就是使用了脫節修飾語。若是把脫節修飾語 while driving 改成從屬子句，而寫成 While she was driving, there were beautiful farm houses and wheat fields along the way. 這樣也是正確的句子結構。）

---

1. 儘管身為富有經驗的警探，這個可怕的犯罪現場也把他嚇到了。

   Although _____ ,

   _____

2. 獨自一人時，聽古典音樂是她的最愛。

   When _____ ,

3. 從嫌犯的手提電腦取出，調查人員將以該份檔案呈給法官作為證據。

   _____

   _____

4. 為了減重，一臺跑步機就安裝在地下室。

   _____

   _____

5. 設立於 100 年前，市政府已經將該所廢棄學校轉換成社區活動中心了。

_____

_____

6. 贏了樂透三千萬美金，舊房子跟舊車子都立刻被她賣掉了。

_____

_____

7. 辛苦工作了一整天，一餐熱食就足以讓我感恩了。

_____

_____

8. 如果選上了總統，他的承諾不一定會完全實現。

_____

_____

9. 安裝了新的冷氣機，整個夏天我們都覺得在房子裏好涼爽。

_____

_____

10. 自從 1970 年代以來廣泛使用下，環保人士目前估計全世界一年至少生產五千億的塑膠袋。

_____

_____

特殊句式篇 |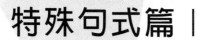

喜樂的心，乃是良藥；憂傷的靈，使骨枯乾。

（聖經 箴言 17:22）

A cheerful heart is good medicine, but a crushed spirit dries up the bones.

(Proverbs 17:22)

第十三章 條件句與假設語氣 (Conditional Sentences)

　　條件句可以分成兩種情況，一種是條件有可能滿足，另一種是條件不可能滿足。**條件不可能滿足的條件句又稱為假設語氣或虛擬語氣**。英文的假設語氣句型的變化豐富，這類的句型在中文裡面並沒有，因此，臺灣的學生在使用假設語氣時難免感到困擾而容易出錯。本章就假設語氣在不同情況下所必須適用的動詞與助動詞的變化，以例句作詳細的解說與比較，並提供同學密集的練習題，以掌握其細微的變化差異，而能在寫作上純熟地運用假設語氣。

13.1 條件句的結構與句型變化

　　英文條件句的結構與句型變化包括：(1) 四種基本類型的結構與句型，(2) 混合類型假設語氣的結構與句型，以及 (3) 其他條件句的結構與句型（例如 wish）；另外，我們也會學習第二類型與第三類型結果子句中的助動詞的使用，以及條件句的結構、條件子句與結果子句前後的調動變化，與條件子句的倒裝句型。

▶▶ 13.1.1 四種基本類型的結構與句型
　　首先來看下列中文句子要如何翻成英文：

1. 如果他（將來）托福分數夠高，他就有資格申請美國大學研究所了。　（引申的涵義是：現在他的托福分數也許不夠高，但是將來如果考到夠高的分數，他就有資格申請美國大學研究所了）

2. 如果他（現在）托福分數夠高，他就有資格申請美國大學研究所了。（引申的涵義是：可惜他現在托福分數不夠高，否則他就有資格申請美國大學研究所了。）

　　第一句的情境是：**將來如果**他滿足了托福分數夠高條件，他就可以得到後面的結果：「有資格申請美國大學研究所」。這個句子所表達的是：**將來有可能滿足這樣的條件**，而條件一旦滿足，自然就會帶來後面的結果。

　　反觀第二句的情境則是：若是他**現在**就具備了托福分數夠高的條件，他就可以得到後面的結果：「有資格申請美國大學研究所」。但可惜的是**他目前的托福分數不夠高**，因此他也就沒有資格申請美國大學研究所了。換句話說，**第二句所表達的是與現實不符合的虛擬語氣**，而**第一句所表達的是將來可能實現的條件**，是兩種不同的情況，因此在英文必須用**兩種不同的句型**加以表達。

1. If he **has** a high enough TOEFL score, he **will be** eligible to apply to a graduate school in the US.
   （**條件子句**的時式為**簡單現在式**，而**結果子句**則為**簡單未來式**。）
   如果他（將來）托福分數夠高，他就有資格申請美國大學研究所了。

2. If he **had** a high enough TOEFL score, he **would be** eligible to apply to a graduate school in the US.
   （**條件子句**的時式為**簡單過去式**，而**結果子句**的動詞結構則是**would/could/might/should + 原型動詞**。）
   如果他（現在）托福分數夠高，他就有資格申請美國大學研究所了。

說明：

1. 這兩種句型都屬於條件句 (conditional sentences)，而條件句的結構包含兩個子句：含有 if 的條件子句，以及結果子句。條件子句是從屬子句 (dependent clauses)，而結果子句則是獨立子句 (independent clauses) 或稱主要子句 (main clauses)，而兩個子句必須以逗點 (commas) 隔開。

2. 第一句所表達的是將來某一個條件的滿足會帶來某一個結果，其條件子句的動詞時式是簡單現在式，而結果子句的動詞則是簡單未來式。這一類的條件句屬於**第一類型**。

3. 第二句所表達的是與現況不符的條件與結果，其條件子句的動詞時式是簡單過去式，而結果子句的動詞則是**過去式助動詞加上原型動詞**。這一類的條件句屬於**第二類型**。

4. 第二類型的條件句所**引申的事實即是原來句子的相反**。例如前面的第二句

   If he **had** a high enough TOEFL score, he **would be** eligible to apply to a graduate school in the US.

   所**引申的事實**即是：

   He **does not have** a high enough TOEFL score, so he **is not** eligible to apply to a graduate school in the US.

5. 另外，第二類型的條件句也可以用來表達建議或不同的作法，例如：

   A：What **would** you **do** if you **were** me?（換作是你，你會怎麼做？）

B：If I **were** you, I **would accept** the invitation.（換作是我的話，我會接受邀請。）

條件句	條件子句／副詞子句	結果子句／主要子句
第一類型 未來可能發生	簡單現在式 If she **invites** me,	簡單未來式 I **will go** to the party.
第二類型 與現在事實不符	簡單過去式 If she **invited** me, If it **were** not raining, (be 動詞一律用 were)	would/could/might/should ＋原型動詞 I **would go** to the party. I **would go** hiking.

接下來看下一句跟前面的兩個條件句有何不同：

如果你把冰塊放進飲料，冰塊就會融化。

乍看之下，這一句似乎和第一類型的條件句相同；但仔細分辨，二者並不相同。冰塊放進飲料會融化所表達的是一項**恆為真的事實**，因此這一類的句子另外歸類為 **第零類型 (Type Zero)** 的條件句，不過其句型與第一類型一致。

其英文翻譯為：

If you **put** the ice cube in the drink, it **will melt**.

接下來這一句所表達的則是**過去恆為真的事實**：

If I **came** home late, my mother **always spared** some food for me.

（我若是晚回家，母親都會幫我留些菜。）

於是，我們要在表格裡面增加一個類型，就是**第零類型**：

條件句	條件子句／副詞子句	結果子句／主要子句
第零類型 現在或過去恆為 真的事實	**恆為真**：簡單現在式 If you **drop** the glass, **過去恆為真**：簡單過去式 If he went camping,	簡單未來式 it **will break**. 簡單過去式 he brought a Swiss Army knife with him.
第一類型 未來可能發生	簡單現在式 If she **invites** me,	簡單未來式 I **will go** to the party.
第二類型 與現在事實不符	簡單過去式 If she **invited** me, If it **were** not raining, (be 動詞一律用 were)	would/could/might/should ＋原型動詞 I **would go** to the party. I **would go** hiking.

接著，我們再進一步看下一句與前面三種條件句有何不同：

他最後一投如果進了，昨天的比賽我們就贏了。

這一句所表達的是對於昨天比賽的結果感到扼腕，也就是說他最後一投並沒投進，而比賽也輸了。這是與過去已經發生的事實不符的虛擬語氣，屬於第三類條件句，其句型與其他類型的條件句都不相同：

條件子句的時式為過去完成式 (had + p.p.)，而結果子句則為 (would, could, should, might) + have + 過去分詞。

其英文翻譯為：

If he **had made** the final shot, we **would have won** the game yesterday.

而這個與過去事實不符的條件句所**引申的事實**為：

He **did not make** the final shot, so we **did not win** the game yesterday.

　　總結起來，英文的條件句一共有四種基本類型，分別以不同的時式和助動詞表達不同的情境與涵義，而**第二類型**的條件句又稱為**與現在事實不符的虛擬／假設語氣**，第三類型的條件句又稱為<u>**與過去事實不符的虛擬／假設語氣**</u>；詳如下表。

四種基本類型條件句的結構與句型

條件句	條件子句／副詞子句	結果子句／主要子句
第零類型 現在或過去恆為真的事實	**恆為真**：簡單現在式 If you **drop** the glass, **過去恆為真**：簡單過去式 If I **made** a mistake,	簡單未來式 it **will break**. 簡單過去式 my father **corrected** me.
第一類型 未來可能發生	簡單現在式 If she **invites** me,	簡單未來式 I **will go** to the party.
第二類型 與現在事實不符的虛擬／假設語氣	簡單過去式 If she **invited** me, If it **were** not raining, (be 動詞一律用 were)	would/could/might/should + 原型動詞 I **would go** to the party. I **would go** hiking.

條件句	條件子句／副詞子句	結果子句／主要子句
第三類型 與過去事實不符 的虛擬／假設語 氣	過去完成式 If she **had invited** me,	would/could/might/should + have + 過去分詞 I **would have gone** to the party.

▶▶ 13.1.2 小試身手

一、將下列句子翻成英文的條件句

1. 如果她現在有足夠的錢，她就會買新車了。（事實上她沒有足夠
   的錢）

   If she _____ enough money, she _____ _____
   a new car.

2. 如果她（將來）有足夠的錢，她就會買新車。

   If she _____ enough money, she _____ _____
   a new car.

3. 如果她去年就有足夠的錢，她早就買新車了。

   If she _____ _____ enough money last year, she
   _____ _____ _____ a new car.

4. 換做我是她的話，我不會買中古車。

   If I _____ she, I _____ _____ _____ a
   used car.

5. 我若是需要加班，我都會打電話告訴我太太。

   If I _____ to work over time, I _____ _____
   my wife.

6. 昨天要不是他沒趕上高鐵，我們就會一起吃晚餐了。

If he _____ _____ _____ the High Speed Rail yesterday, we _____ _____ _____ dinner to-gether.

7. 你若是把門打開，警報就會響了。

The alarm _____ _____ if you _____ the door.

二、將下列虛擬／假設語氣的句子改寫成所引申的事實

1. If the boy were not old enough, he wouldn't be allowed to watch the movie in the theater.

_____

_____

2. He would have missed the plane if he had not left the house earlier.

_____

3. They would have canceled the concert in the square if it had rained last night.

_____

4. If he had heard the announcement, he would not have missed the meeting.

_____

三、將下列的事實陳述改寫成與現在或過去事實不符合的虛擬／假設語氣的句子

1. His mother is not alive. Otherwise, his mother will be proud of him now.

_____

2. He did not work hard enough. He did not get good grades last semester.

_____

3. She was not in the building. She was not injured in the earthquake.

_____

▶▶ **13.1.3** 混合類型假設語氣的結構與句型

前面所介紹的都是單純類型的條件句，在英文中可以依情境的需要，將第二類型（與現在事實不符）和第三類型（與過去事實不符）的條件句混合搭配，構成混合類型的虛擬／假設語氣條件句。舉例說明如下：

If he **had invested** in the real estate market, he **would be** a rich man now.

(**The truth**: He **did not invest** in the real estate market, and he **is not** a rich man now.)

這個句子中的**條件子句屬於第三類型**，而其**結果子句則是第二類型**，所表達的涵義是他之前要是有投資房地產，現在他就是有錢人了。換句話說，他過去沒有投資房地產，而且現在也不是有錢人。

再來看下一句：

If the government **had not built** the High Speed Rail, we **would not be** able to enjoy the fast and convenient land travel along the west coast of Taiwan.

(**The truth**: The government **built** the High Speed Rail, and we **are able** to enjoy the fast and convenient land travel along the west coast of Taiwan.)

與前一句相同，這一句也是由**第三類型的條件子句**搭配**第二類型的結果子句**所構成，而其引申的涵義則是：政府蓋了高速鐵路，我們現在才能享受這麼便捷的陸上交通，往來於臺灣的西岸。

▶▶ 13.1.4 小試身手

將下列句子翻成英文

1. 如果上個月沒下雨的話，我們現在就受苦於缺水了。

   If it _____ _____ _____ last month, we _____ _____ from water shortage now.

2. 他要是上學期認真念書的話，現在他也不會重修經濟學了。

   If he _____ _____ hard enough last year, he _____ _____ be _____ Economics for the second time now.

3. 要是去年冬天沒有那麼冷的話，今年的蔬菜和水果也不會那麼貴了。

   The prices of vegetables and fruits _____ _____ _____ so expensive this year if it _____ _____ _____ so severely cold last winter.

▶▶ 13.1.5 第二類型與第三類型結果子句中的助動詞的使用

第二類型與第三類型的虛擬／假設語氣條件句，其中的結果子句可以使用不同的助動詞 (would, could, should, might) 來表達不同的情境和涵義。以下說明各個助動詞所表達的不同的情境與涵義。

我們來比較下列各組的兩個句子：

1. would and could

(1) If your best friend were here, he **would** take you home.
　　如果你最要好的朋友這裡的話，他**就會**帶你回家了。
　　（這一句的 "would" 表達的是**一定會發生**的結果）

(2) If your best friend were here, he **could** take you home.
　　如果你最要好的朋友這裡的話，他**就可以**帶你回家了。
　　（這一句的 "could" 表達的是主詞**能力所及**的結果）

上列兩句都是表達與現在事實不符的條件句，兩者的差別僅在於結果子句中所使用的助動詞，第一句是 "**would**"，而第二句則是 "**could**"；前者一定會發生，後者則是主詞**能力所及**的結果。

2. would and should

(1) If the weather had turned bad, they **would** have cancelled the show.
　　如果天氣變壞了，他們**就會**取消表演。
　　（這一句的 "would" 表達的是**一定會**發生的結果）

(2) If the weather had turned bad, they **should** have cancelled the show.

如果天氣變壞了，他們**就應該**取消表演。

（這一句的 "should" 表達的是**應該**發生的結果）

　　上列兩句都是表達與現在事實不符的條件句，兩者的差別僅在於結果子句中所使用的助動詞，第一句是 **"would"**，而第二句則是 **"should"**；前者一定**會**發生，後者則是**應該**發生。

3. would and might

(1) If the teacher **saw** you cheat in the exam, she **would** inform your parents.

如果老師看見你考試作弊，他就會通知你父母。

（這一句的 "would" 表達的是**一定會發生**的結果）

(2) If the teacher **saw** you cheat in the exam, she **might** inform your parents.

如果老師看見你考試作弊，他有可能會通知你父母。

（這一句的 "might" 表達的是**可能會發生**的結果）

　　上列兩句都是表達與現在事實不符的條件句，兩者的差別僅在於結果子句中所使用的助動詞，第一句是 **"would"**，而第二句則是 **"might"**；前者一定會發生，後者則是有可能發生。

▶▶ 13.1.6 小試身手

將下列虛擬語氣句子翻成英文

1. 當初要簽合約的時候要不是她聽從律師的建議，今天可能就無法保護她法律上的權利了。

If she ＿＿＿＿＿＿ ＿＿＿＿＿＿ ＿＿＿＿＿＿ the lawyer's advice when signing the contract, she ＿＿＿＿＿ ＿＿＿＿＿ ＿＿＿＿＿

able to protect her legal rights today.

2. 如果十年前公司的生產系統沒有電腦化的話，現在我們應該就無法滿足國外客戶的不斷增加的需求了。

If the company's production system _____ _____
_____ _____ 10 years ago, we _____ _____
_____ able to meet the _____ demand from the foreign clients now.

3. 當初我要是沒趕上火車而錯過面試的話，我的職業生涯會完全不同，而我太太可能會嫁給別人了。

If I _____ _____ _____ the train and _____
_____ the interview, my career _____ _____
_____ completely different, and my wife _____
_____ _____ to someone else.

4. 如果他沒有把中古的機車賣給那個美國老師，他不會有機會去美國念到碩士，今天也不會在大學教英文了。

If he _____ _____ _____ the used motorcycle
to the American teacher, he _____ _____ _____
_____ the opportunity to obtain a master's degree in the
US, and he _____ _____ be _____ English in a
university now.

13.2 條件句的結構變化

▶ 13.2.1 條件子句與結果子句的前後順序調動

條件句中的條件子句與結果子句的前後順序可以互換，也就是說可以把結果子句放在句首，條件子句則放在句尾，如下列句子：

The ice cube will melt **if** you put it in the drink.

He will have the opportunity to play in the NBA **if** he grows to 210cm tall.

He would have the opportunity to play in the NBA **if** he were 210cm tall.

We would have won the game yesterday **if** he had made the final shot.

注意：當結果子句放在句首時，原先用來隔開條件子句和結果子句的逗點就不需要了。

▶▶ 13.2.2 第二類型與第三類型條件子句的倒裝

第二類型與第三類型條件子句可以作如下的倒裝變化：

If he **were** 210cm tall, he might have the opportunity to play in the NBA.

→ **Were** he 210cm tall, he might have the opportunity to play in the NBA.

→ He might have the opportunity to play in the NBA **were** he 210cm tall.

（在倒裝的第二類型條件子句，其中原有的 "if" 省略了，而 be 動詞 "were" 則移到句首；結果子句維持不變）

If he **had** made the final shot, we would have won the game yesterday.

→ **Had** he made the final shot, we would have won the

game yesterday.

→ We would have won the game yesterday **had** he made the final shot.

（在倒裝的第三類型條件子句，其中原有的 "if" 省略了，而助動詞 "had" 則移到句首；結果子句則維持不變）

13.3 條件句的被動語態

(1) 未來可能發生的條件句

學生如果違反了規定，學校會給予處罰。

If any student breaches the rule, the school will discipline him.

→ If the rule **is breached** by any student, he **will be disciplined** by the school.

承包商如果依照合約完成工作，政府會支付所同意的金額。

If the contractor carries out the tasks according to the contract, the government will pay the agreed-upon amount of money.

→ If the tasks **are carried out** by the contractor according to the contract, the agreed-upon amount of money **will be paid** by the government.

(2) 與現在事實不符的條件句

若是現在沒有下雨的話，他們也不會將比賽延後舉行了。

If it were not raining, they would not postpone the game.

→ If it were not raining, the game **would not be postponed**.

如果不是當地的小孩深深觸動她的心，他們也不會招募她去第三世界國家擔任志工了。

They would not recruit her to be a volunteer in a Third World country if the children there did not deeply touch her heart.

→ She **would not be recruited** to be a volunteer in a Third World country if her heart **were not** deeply **touched** by the children there.

(3) 與過去事實不符的條件句

若是他們那時候按照步驟一步一步來，他們就可以達成他們的目標了。

If they had followed the procedures step by step, they would have accomplished their goals.

→ If the procedures **had been followed** step by step, their goals **would have been accomplished**.

若是有關單位早一點發出警告，民眾可能就可以避免這場悲劇了。

Had the authorities sent the alarm earlier, people could have avoided the tragedy.

→ **Had** the alarm **been sent** by the authorities earlier, the tragedy **could have been avoided**.

▶▶ **13.3.1 小試身手**

填入適當的字以完成被動語態條件句

A. 未來可能發生的條件句

1. If the machine _____ _____ (use) improperly, it will not _____ _____ (damage).

2. The customer agreed that if the car _____ _____ (fix) by the mechanic immediately, an extra amount of US$100 will _____ _____ (pay).

B. 與現在事實不符的條件句

1. If the price _____ _____ (lower) by the shopkeeper, the ring would _____ _____ (buy) by the husband for his wife.

2. If I _____ (be) the owner of the house, the offer would _____ _____ (accept).

3. If it _____ (be) not raining, the game would not _____ _____ (postpone).

4. If the budget _____ _____ (pass) by the city council, a new park would _____ _____ (develop).

5. We _____ _____ (need) a bigger house for the family if we _____ (have) more children than now.

C. 與過去事實不符的條件句

1. If the villagers _____ _____ _____ (give) warnings earlier by the government, such a disaster _____ not _____ _____ _____ (cause) by the storm.

2. If the candidate's scandal _____ not _____ _____ (report), he would _____ _____ _____ _____ (elect) the new mayor.

3. If the firefighters had not arrived at the scene soon enough, the people in the house _____ not _____ _____ _____ (save) from the fire.

4. If the final shot _____ not _____ _____ (miss) by the star player at the buzzer, the game _____ _____ _____ (win) by the defending team.

5. If the assembly line _____ not _____ _____ (design) by Henry Ford to build Model-T automobiles, they _____ not _____ _____ _____ (sell) at such an affordable price.

6. If the refrigerator _____ not _____ _____ (invent) for households, cold drinks _____ not _____ _____ _____ (enjoy) so conveniently.

▶▶ **13.3.2 小試身手**

條件句被動語態中翻英填充

1. 如果其最新款式比它的對手早一步推出的話，這家公司會獲得更多的市佔率。

   More market share _____ (gain) by the company if its latest model _____ (roll out) earlier than its opponent's.

2. 如果指派的工作在截止日前完成的話，妳就會獲得獎勵。

   If the assignment _____ (finish) before the deadline, you _____ (reward).

3. 如果房子是登記在他名下，它就可以設定抵押給銀行來向其貸款。（但事實上房子不是登記在他名下）

If the house _____ (list) under his name, it _____ (mortgage) to a bank for a loan.

4. 若不是航班誤點，我們會及時抵達在倫敦的研討會。

We would have arrived at the conference in London in time if the flight _____ (delay).

5. 如果當時三個月之前購買的股票晚幾天再賣的話，我們會賺的更多。

If the stocks that _____ (purchase) three months earlier _____ (sell) a few days later, we would have made more profit.

13.4 其他條件句的結構與句型

英文的條件句除了以 if 開頭的副詞子句來表達，還有以其他動詞或連接詞或助動詞所連用的條件句。這裡所要介紹其他條件句的句型使用不同的詞彙來表達，包括 **wish, should, were to, without, if only, as if / as though,** 以及 **provided**。分別說明如下。

13.5 wish 條件句

使用 wish 條件句可以用來
(1) 表達與現在、過去、未來事實不符的願望

(2) 表達未來可能實現的願望

 13.5.1 使用 "wish" 來表達與事實不符的願望

wish + 名詞子句（表達與事實不符的願望）		
	事實	**願望**
表達 與現在事實 不符的願望	He does not know how to ride a scooter.	He wishes (that) he **knew** how to ride a scooter.（子句中的動詞用過去式）
	She is not a musician.	She wishes (that) she **were** a musician.（子句中的 be 動詞一律用 were）
表達 與過去事實 不符的願望	The school did not build a new auditorium.	The students wish the school **had built** a new auditorium.（子句中的動詞用過去完成式）
表達 與未來事實 不符的願望	The family will move to another city.	He wishes his family **would** not **move** to a new city.（子句中的動詞用 would 加上原型動詞）

例句：

The little boy wishes he **didn't have** to go to school.

現在的事實：The little boy **has to** go to school.

Martin wishes that he **had chosen** to attend college when he was young.

過去的事實：Martin **did not choose** to attend college when he was young.

Cindy wishes her best friend **could come** to her birthday party tomorrow night.

未來的事實：Unfortunately, her best friend **is not feeling** well and **won't be** able to show up in her birthday party tomorrow night.

▶▶ 13.5.2 wish 練習填充

1. My family is taking a vacation in southern Taiwan this summer. I wish we ＿＿＿＿＿ ＿＿＿＿＿ a vacation in Japan instead.

2. Lisa is not a famous singer. She wishes she ＿＿＿＿＿ a famous singer.

3. Tiffany did not learn how to ride a scooter when she was in college. She wishes she ＿＿＿＿＿ ＿＿＿＿＿ how to ride a scooter then.

4. The doctor does not have the medicine to cure the disease. The doctor wishes she ＿＿＿＿＿ the medicine to cure the disease.

5. The manager regrets that he did not adopt the new marketing strategy. The manager now wishes he ＿＿＿＿＿ ＿＿＿＿＿ the new marketing strategy.

6. The school will not have the budget to build a new auditorium. The students wish the school ＿＿＿＿＿ ＿＿＿＿＿ the budget to build a new auditorium.

7. The tourists forgot to make reservations for the hotel room. They wish they ＿＿＿＿＿ ＿＿＿＿＿ reservations for the

hotel room.

8. They failed to get the tickets to the NBA game. They won't be able to watch the game in the stadium. They wish they _____ watch the game in the stadium.

9. The government passed a law to legalize mercy killing. Many opponents wish the government _____ _____ _____ such a law.

13.5.3 使用 "wish" 表達未來可能實現的願望

使用 **"wish"** 表達未來可能實現的願望	
事實	未來可能實現的願望
It's raining now. It may or may not stop soon.	I wish the rain **would** stop soon
She is inviting people to her wedding. She may or may not invite me.	I wish she **would** invite me to her wedding.

句型解說

使用 "wish" 來表達 (1) 未來可能實現的願望或是 (2) 未來不可能實現的願望,兩者的句型是一樣的,都是在名詞子句裡以 "would" 加上原型動詞來表現。

13.6 should 條件句

　　"should" 條件句所表達涵義是雖然未來有可能發生，但是發生的機會很小，中文可以翻成「萬一」。我們來比較以下的例句，就可以瞭解 "should" 條件句的使用情境了。

例一：

(1) If you see the book in the store, please buy it for me.

（如果你在店裡看到這本書，請幫我買下來。所表達的意思是：**說話的人認為那家店應該有那本書，所以有機會在店裡看到那本書。**）

(2) If you **should** see the book in the store, please buy it for me.

（萬一你在店裡看到這本書，請幫我買下來。所表達的意思是：**說話的人認為那家店應該沒有那本書，所以要在店裡看到那本書的機會很小。**）

> "should" 條件句也可以倒裝如下：
>
> **Should** you see the book in the store, please buy it for me.

例二：

(1) If the flight is delayed, we will have more time to buy souveniors at duty-free shops.

（如果飛機誤點，我們就有更多時間在免稅商店買紀念品了。所表達的意思是**說話的人認為飛機有機會誤點。**）

(2) If the flight **should** be delayed, we will have more time to buy souveniors at duty-free shops.

（萬一飛機誤點，我們就有更多時間在免稅商店買紀念品了。所表達的意思是**說話的人認為飛機不太可能誤點**。）

13.7 were to 條件句（僅用於 if 子句）

時間	表達的狀況	句型
現在	目前某種極不可能或難以想像的可怕狀況	If... **were to** 原型動詞 ..., S + **would** 原型動詞 ...
未來	未來某種極不可能或難以想像的可怕狀況	If... **were to** 原型動詞 ..., S + **would** 原型動詞 ...
過去	過去某種難以想像的可怕狀況	If... **were to have** + **p.p.** ..., S + **would have** + **p.p.** ...

(a) "were to" 用於**現在**的情況時，所表達的是目前某種極不可能或難以想像的可怕的狀況。

例如：

If he **were to be** a billionaire, he **would be** hard to please.（*他極不可能是億萬富翁，但他要真的是億萬富翁的話，一定很難取悅。*）

If she **were to be** my wife, my life **would be** miserable.（*她真要是我老婆的話，我一定會生不如死。想到若是有這樣的老婆就感到恐怖！*）

(b) "were to" 用於**未來**的情況時，所表達的是未來某種極不可能或難以想像的可怕狀況。

例如：

If her family **were to move** to another city, she **would have** a hard time making new friends. (她們家將來要搬家到另一個都市的可能性微乎其微)

If he **were to retire** early, he **would work** as a volunteer at a hospital. (他極不可能提早退休)

If he **were to lose his high-paying job**, he **would not be** able to pay back the loan and **would lose** his house in the end. (失去這份高薪的工作是很難以想像的可怕狀況)

(c) "were to" 用於<u>過去</u>的情況是，所表達的是過去某種難以想像的可怕狀況。

例如：

If they **were to have stayed** in the area near the epicenter for another day, they **would have lost** their lives in the earthquake. (幸好他們沒有多停留一天，否則後果難以想像的可怕。)

If the plane **were to have failed** to land safely, it **would have crashed** and many passengers **would have died or seriously injured**. (幸好飛機安全降落，否則後果難以想像的可怕。)

▶▶ 13.7.1 were to 練習填充

1. As the typhoon is coming, the captain of the fishing boat decides to stay at the harbor. If the fishing boat _____ _____ _____ (leave) the harbor to fish in such a bad weather, it _____ _____ (be) too risky.

2. The bridge collapsed just seconds before the car went on it. If the car _____ _____ _____ _____ (reach) the bridge seconds sooner, it _____ _____ _____ (fall) into the river.

3. The city is a dangerous place for tourists to visit at night. If I _____ _____ _____ (visit) the city, I _____ _____ (avoid) going out at night in the city.

13.8 without 條件句

比較下列句子所表達的事實和假設的情境：

現在的事實 ：

The country produces a lot of oil. The country is very wealthy.

假設的相反情境與後果：

If the country **did not produce** a lot of oil, it **would not be** very wealthy.

Without producing a lot of oil, the country **would not be** very wealthy.

過去的事實：

Because of your generous financial support, he succeeded in his business.

假設的相反情境與後果：

If it **had not been** your generous financial support, he **would not have succeeded** in his business.

Without your generous financial support, he **would not have succeeded** in his business.

> **句型解說**：由上面的例子，我們發現 **if 子句**可以改寫成由 "**without**" 引導的片語，結果子句的部分維持不變。換句話說，原來的**複句**已經簡化為**簡單句**了。

▶▶ 13.8.1 without 練習填充

1. Fortunately I applied sunscreen lotion at the beach. Without ＿＿＿＿＿ (apply) sunscreen lotion, I ＿＿＿＿＿ ＿＿＿＿＿ ＿＿＿＿＿ (get) sunburn.

2. God helped the mother overcome her predicament. Without God's help, the mother ＿＿＿＿＿ ＿＿＿＿＿ ＿＿＿＿＿ (give up) on herself.

13.9 if only 條件句

"**if only**" 用來表達**與現在事實不符的願望**，也可用來表達**未來可能成就的願望**，或是用來表達**與過去事實不符的願望或後悔**，其用法與 "wish" 相同，但語氣較為強烈。

句型	作用
"if only" + 簡單過去式	表達與現在事實不符的願望
"if only" + would + 原型動詞	表達未來可能成就的願望
"if only" + had + p.p.	表達與過去事實不符的願望或後悔

(a) **"if only"** + 簡單過去式 用來表達 <u>與現在事實不符的願望</u>

例如：

If only I **knew** how to drive a car.（我現在不會開車，但我真的很希望我會。）

If only we **were** parents.（我們現在不是為人父母，但我們真的很希望我們有兒女。）

(b) <u>**"if only"** + would + 原型動詞</u> 用來表達 <u>未來可能成就的願望</u>

例如：

If only the city council **would approve** the budget for our research project.（衷心希望預算能夠通過）

If only they **would sell** their house to me.（衷心希望他們會把房子賣給我）

(c) **"if only"** + **had** + **p.p.** 用來表達 <u>與過去事實不符的願望或後悔</u>

例如：

If only we **had invested** our money in the stock market.（可惜之前沒有把錢投資在股票，不然的話⋯⋯）

If only the doctor **had not treated** the patient improperly.（眞希望當時醫生沒有給病患不當的治療）

▶▶ 13.9.1 if only 練習填充

1. I really like the house, but the price is beyond my budget. If only I _____ (have) the money to buy it.

2. She regrets that she didn't follow her parents' advice. She said to her parents, "If only I _____ _____ (listen) to you."

3. Jerry, a sales representative at a big company, needs to do business with Japanese. However, Jerry did not take the Japanese course in college. He said to his colleagues, "If only I _____ _____ (learn) Japanese when in college."

4. We are living in a small town. The life here is kind of boring. If only we _____ _____ (move) to a big city to enjoy a more exciting life.

13.10 as if (as though) 條件句

英文 as if / as though 所表達的涵義爲「彷彿、好像…一樣」，在**寫作上**，as if / as though 往往用來表達與現在或過去事實相反的假設語氣，這種句型的條件子句的動詞時態就必須作特殊的變化；另外在**口語或非正式用法上**，as if / as though 可以用來表達純粹推測某人事實上的感受，或某事物事實上看起來的樣子，通常接在動詞爲 look 或 seem 的主要子句之後，這種情況的條件子句爲直述句，其動詞時態不需作特殊的變化，如以下不同情況的例句：

as if 條件子句的用法	
與現在或當時事實相反的假設語氣	She is only twelve, but she acts as if she **were** an adult.
	The thief was caught at the scene, yet he behaved as if he **were** innocent.
與過去事實相反的假設語氣	She didn't watch the movie; however, she talked as if she **had watched** it.
純粹推測	The grapes look as if they **are** ready to be picked.

　　as if 條件子句表達假設語氣時，動詞時態必須作變化：(1) 以**簡單過去式**表達與**現在或當時事實相反**的假設語氣，或是 (2) 以**過去完成式**表達與**過去事實相反**的假設語氣。

▶▶ **13.10.1** as if 條件子句表達與現在或當時事實相反的假設語氣

　　在動詞時態變化上，以 as if 來達與現在或當時事實相反的假設語氣時，句子的主要子句有可能是簡單現在式、現在進行式、簡單過去式、過去進行式；**無論主要子句為現在式或過去式，只要 as if 條件子句所指的時間與其相同**，可能是**現在**，也可能是**當時**，as if 條件子句**一律使用簡單過去式**。如下表所示：

as if 條件子句以簡單過去式表達與現在或當時事實相反的假設語氣	
主要子句	**as if** 條件子句 簡單過去式（**be** 動詞一律用 **were**）
She acts（簡單現在式）	as if she were an adult. （事實上她不是大人）
She is telling a story（現在進行式）	as if it were real. （事實上故事是虛構的）
She talked（簡單過去式）	as if she owned the store. （事實上她不是店主）
She was singing（過去進行式）	as if she were a famous singer. （事實上她不是歌手）

▶▶ 13.10.2 as if 條件子句表達與過去事實相反的假設語氣

在動詞時態變化上，若是 **as if 條件子句所指的時間早於主要子句發生的時間**，則 as if 條件子句以**過去完成式**來達**與過去事實相反**的假設語氣，而句子的主要子句有可能是簡單現在式、現在進行式、簡單過去式、或過去進行式，而如下表所示：

as if 條件子句以過去完成式表達與過去事實相反的假設語氣	
主要子句	**as if** 條件子句（過去完成式）
He talks（簡單現在式）	as if he **had been** to France. （事實上他沒去過法國）
He is acting（現在進行式）	as if nothing **had happened**. （事實上有發生了某件事）
He spent money（簡單過去式）	as if he **had won** the lottery. （事實上他並未中樂透）

as if 條件子句以過去完成式表達與過去事實相反的假設語氣	
主要子句	as if 條件子句（過去完成式）
He was eating（過去進行式）	as if he **had not eaten** for several days.（事實上他並非好幾天沒吃飯）

▶▶ 13.10.3 as if 練習：填入適當的動詞時式以完成句子。

1. He hasn't read the book, yet he talks as if he _____ (read) it.

2. He is married, but he acted as if he _____ (be) single.

3. She slept for eight hours last night, yet she looks as if she _____ (sleep) at all.

4. After winning the game, the kids celebrated as if they _____ (win) the world championship.

5. The thief was caught at the scene, yet he behaved as if he _____ (be) innocent.

6. She was not making much money; however, she was living her life as if she _____ (be) rich.

13.11 provided (that) 條件句

"provided that" 所表達的意思相當於 "on the condition that"（在……的條件下）

例如：

You **may go** to the movies **provided (that)** you **finish** your homework before noon.

The Admission Committee **agreed** to interview the applicant **provided (that)** she **submitted** her application before
the deadline.

（"that" 可以省略）

句型分析

"provided that" 引導出一個名詞子句，子句中的動詞時態須
配合主要子句的動詞時態。主要子句動詞為簡單現在式，名詞子句
的動詞時式則為簡單現在式；若是主要子句動詞為簡單過去式，名
詞子句的動詞時態則為簡單過去式。

主要子句	provided (that) + 名詞子句
S + 簡單現在式動詞 You **may go** to the movies	S + 簡單現在式動詞 provided (that) you **finish** your homework before noon.
S + 簡單過去式動詞 The Admission Committee **agreed** to interview the applicant	S + 簡單過去式動詞 provided (that) she **submitted** her application by Friday.

13.12 條件句及假設語氣打通關

一、將下列的事實陳述改寫成與事實不符合的虛擬語氣條件句

1. The driver took the wrong turn, and he got lost in the strange
   city.

2. My secretary didn't remind me, so I forgot about the appointment with my client.

_____

3. He is not on our team. He can't help us.

_____

4. She switched the mode of her cellphone to mute, so she didn't hear my call.

_____

5. This item is not on sale. I won't buy it.

_____

6. She was sick on the day of the competition. She may win the prize.

_____

7. Tom hit a walk-off home run. His team won the game at the bottom of the 12th inning.

_____

8. I passed the certification test. I am now qualified for the job.

_____

9. She didn't sign the contract. She can be a famous singer today.

_____

10. He sold the house too early. He didn't make more profit.

_____

二、假設語氣中翻英填充

1. 我要是忘了擦防曬油，我昨天在海灘就曬傷了。

   I _____ _____ sunburned if I _____

   _____ to apply sunscreen lotion yesterday.

2. 若非家人的鼓勵和支持，她或許早就放棄了。

   _____ her family's encouragement and support, she

   _____ _____ _____ up long time ago.

3. 當初如果已經有這個藥來治療她的病，她今天應該還健在。

   If there _____ _____ the medicine to treat her dis-

   ease, she _____ still _____ alive today.

4. 當初教練要是讓他放棄訓練，他現在也不會是出名的運動員了。

   He _____ _____ _____ a famous athlete now if

   the coach _____ _____ him _____ training.

5. 如果他不是好朋友，他今天可能不會借你錢吧。

   If he _____ _____ your good friend, he _____

   _____ _____ you money.

6. 如果他們有遵守規定的話，昨天晚上發生的悲劇應該可以避免的。

   If they _____ _____ the rules, the disaster last night

   _____ _____ _____ _____ _____.

7. 換作他是你的話，他也會為你犧牲的。

   He _____ _____ for you if he _____ _____.

8. 換作我是財務長的話，我或許會修改上禮拜所提出的拓展計畫。

   If I _____ _____ the CFO, I _____ _____

   _____ the expansion plan _____ last week.

9. The oil company found natural gas in the farm that had belonged to Terry's father. Once Terry learned that, he said to

his wife,「要是我爸爸沒有賣掉那個農場該有多好啊！我們就會賺進數百萬美金了！」

"If _____ my father _____ not _____ the farm!
We _____ _____ _____ millions of dollars!"

10. 沒有電腦的發明，我們今天的生活會完全不一樣。

    Our lives _____ _____ completely different _____
    the _____ of the computer.

11. 這棟公寓大樓若不是設計錯誤也不會倒塌了。

    The condominium _____ _____ _____ _____
    had it _____ _____ falsely _____.

12. 公司再不推出新產品的話，市場佔有率就會大幅縮減了。

    If the company _____ _____ launch new products,
    its market _____ _____ _____ sharply.

13. Tina's parents said to her,「你可以養小貓，只要妳負起全責照顧牠。」

    "You may keep a kitten _____ that you _____ full
    _____ of taking care of it."

14. 當初她要是沒有堅持下去的話，她今天就不會是知名的藝術家了。

    Had she _____ _____, she _____ _____
    _____ a renowned artist today.

15. 若非日本在第二次世界大戰戰敗，臺灣今天仍然是由日本所統治。

    Taiwan _____ still _____ _____ by Japan to-
    day if Japan _____ _____ _____ _____
    in World War II.

16. 她要是年幼的時候沒有被外國父母領養，她可能沒有機會上大學讀書。

If she _____ _____ _____ by for-

eign parents, she _____ _____ _____ _____

the _____ to go to college.

17. 昨天的籃球比賽，他最後一投要是進的話，我們就贏了。

We _____ _____ _____ yesterday's basketball

game if he _____ _____ the final shot.

18. 他但願當初 921 大地震後有投資房地產，今天就不必那麼辛苦地工作了。

He wished that he _____ _____ in the real estate

market after the 921 Earthquake, so he _____ _____

need to be _____ so hard today.

19. 如果沒有他朋友給予財務支援，他的公司早就破產了。

His company _____ _____ _____ _____

if his friend _____ _____ _____ him _____.

20. 美洲野牛若是沒有政府的保護，應該早已經滅絕了。

American bisons _____ _____ _____ _____

without the government's _____.

第十四章 比較句型 (Comparison)

比較的句型在英文寫作中經常使用，有些句型較簡單，容易掌握，例如：

She is **younger than** my sister.

He is **less motivated than** she.

He runs much **faster than** anyone else in the team.

I love you **more than** he loves you.

有些則較複雜，容易混淆出錯，例如：

There are **not more than** 15 students in the class. 班上 至多 有 15 位學生。

There are **no more than** 15 students in the class. 班上 僅有 15 位學生。

"not more than" 表達的是 至多 的涵義，而 "no more than" 所表達的則是 僅有 的涵義。一字之差，語氣完全不同，使用時不可不慎。

另外有一種**雙重比較級**的句型，例如：

The harder you work, the better chance you will succeed.

接下來我們一一介紹英文中常用來作比較的句型，包括簡單易懂、容易混淆出錯的句型，以及雙重比較級的句型。

簡單易懂的比較句型

$\boxed{\textbf{more} + \text{形容詞或副詞} + \textbf{than}}$ 或是 $\boxed{\text{比較級形容詞} + \textbf{than}}$ 表示勝於；比較多

$\boxed{\textbf{less} + \text{形容詞或副詞} + \textbf{than}}$ 表示不如；比較少

$\boxed{\textbf{as} + \text{形容詞或副詞} + \textbf{as}}$ 表示如同；一樣

$\boxed{\textbf{not as/so} + \text{形容詞或副詞} + \textbf{as}}$ 表示不如

$\boxed{\text{倍數} + \textbf{as} + \text{形容詞或副詞} + \textbf{as}}$ 表示前者是後者的幾倍

這些用來作比較的句型，雖然簡單易懂，但在使用時仍<u>須避免語意上的模稜兩可</u>。

▶▶ 14.1.1 兩者之間作比較

英文兩者之間作比較的情況包括：(1) more + 形容詞或副詞 + than，(2) less + 形容詞或副詞 + than，(3) as + 形容詞或副詞 + as，以及 (4) 倍數 + 形容詞或副詞 + as 四種句型，底下分別以例句詳細說明。

1. $\boxed{\textbf{more} + \text{形容詞或副詞} + \textbf{than}}$

我們先看底下兩個例句：

She likes playing piano more than I.

她比我更喜歡彈鋼琴。

She likes playing piano more than sports.
她喜歡彈鋼琴勝於打球。

以上兩個例句的涵義都很清楚，不會造成模稜兩可的情況。
再來看下面的例句：
She admires the movie star more than her father.

這句話有兩種可能的涵義：(1) 她比她父親更崇拜那個影星（父親是主詞），或是 (2) 她崇拜那個影星勝於崇拜她父親（父親是受詞）。

為了避免句義的模稜兩可，我們可以作以下的修改：
(1) 如果要表達的涵義是*她比她父親更崇拜那個影星*，句子就寫成
    She admires the movie star **more than her father does** .
(2) 如果要表達的涵義是*她崇拜那個影星勝於崇拜她父親*，句子就寫成
    She admires the movie star **more than she does her father** .

也就是在句子中適當的位置加上助動詞 does，代替原來的動詞 admires，就可以分別清楚 her father 到底是主詞還是受詞，若是主詞就是跟前面的主詞 she 作比較，若是受詞就是跟前面的受詞 her father 作比較了。

再舉一例：
Paul helped Jamie more than Cindy.

這個句子也是模稜兩可，需要改寫成：

(1) Paul helped Jamie **more than Cindy did** . Paul 比 Cindy 幫助 Jamie 更多。

（Cindy 為主詞，跟前面的主詞 Paul 作比較）

(2) Paul helped Jamie **more than he did Cindy** . Paul 幫助 Jamie 比幫助 Cindy 多。

（Cindy 為受詞，跟前面的受詞 Jamie 作比較）

再舉一例：

Peter is more interested in teaching children than Olivia.

這個句子也是模稜兩可，需要改寫成：

(1) Peter is more interested in teaching children **than Olivia is** .

（在 Olivia 後面加上 be 動詞 is，表明 Olivia 是主詞，語意就清楚了。）

Peter 對教小孩子的興趣比 Olivia 高，也就是 Peter 比 Olivia 較有興趣教小孩子。

(2) Peter is more interested in teaching children **than in teaching Olivia**.（在 than 後面加上 in teaching，表明 Olivia 是受詞，語意就清楚了。）

Peter 對教小孩子比教 Olivia 興趣高。

再舉一例：

He pays more attention to his daughter than his wife.

這個句子也是模稜兩可，需要改寫成：

(1) He pays more attention to his daughter **than his wife does** .

（在 wife 後面加上助動詞 does，表明 his wife 是主詞，語意就清楚了。）

他比他老婆更關注他女兒。

(2) He pays more attention to his daughter **than** **to** **his wife** .（在 than 後面加上介系詞 to，表明 his wife 是受詞，語意就清楚了。）

他關注他女兒比關注他老婆還多。

2. **less + 形容詞或副詞 + than**

在作比較時，我們用 **less + 形容詞或副詞 + than** 來表達<u>不如</u>、<u>比較不</u>的意思，如以下例句：

Working as a register at the counter in a supermarket is less challenging than a computer programmer.

這個句子中在 than 後面的 a computer programmer 應該是 as 的受詞，無法跟前面的主詞 working 作比較，必須在 a computer programmer 前面補上介系詞 as，而修正為：

Working as a register at the counter in a supermarket is **less challenging than** **as** **a computer programmer** .

在超市擔任櫃臺收銀員的工作<u>不如</u>擔任電腦程式設計師的工作具有挑戰性。

再舉一例：

The air in the rural areas is normally less polluted than the urban areas.

同樣的，這個句子中在 than 後面的 the urban areas 應該是 in

的受詞，無法跟前面的主詞 the air 作比較，必須在 the urban areas 前面補上介系詞 in，而修正為：

The air in the rural areas is normally **less polluted than in the urban areas**.

在鄉下地區的空氣通常<u>比</u>在都會地區的<u>較</u>不受汙染。

3. as + 形容詞或副詞 + as

另外，**兩者相比較是一樣的**，我們用 as + 形容詞或副詞 + as 來表達**如同、一樣**的意思，如以下例句：

Hiking is **as good** for one's health **as** working out in the gym is.（as 後面接**形容詞**）

健行對於人的健康跟在體育館裡健身是一樣好的。

When playing baseball, Jerry swings the bat **as hard as** he can, hoping to hit a home run.（as 後面接**副詞**）

打棒球時，Jerry 盡他全力揮棒，希望能打出全壘打。

或是**兩者比較，一方不如另一方時**，我們用 not as/so + 形容詞或副詞 + as 來表達**不如**的意思，如以下例句：

The results of the study were **not so convincing as** we had expected.

研究的結果不如我們原來預期的令人信服。（so 後面接**形容詞**）

The newly hired employees are **not** working **as efficiently as** original workers are.

新聘員工工作不如原有員工有效率。（as 後面接**副詞**）

4. 倍數 + as + 形容詞或副詞 + as

兩者作比較，前者是後者的幾倍時，我們用 倍數 + as + 形容詞或副詞 + as 來加以表示，如以下例句：

Your car is **twice as expensive as** his.
你的車是他的車的兩倍貴。（as 後面接**形容詞**）

He earns nearly **three times as much as** I do.
他賺的幾乎是我賺的三倍之多。（as 後面接**副詞**）

14.1.2 群體中的一個成員與其他所有成員作比較

我們要把群體中的一個成員與其他所有成員作比較時，英文可以有不同的表達方式如下：

He is **more athletic than any other student** in the class.
He is **more athletic than all other students** in the class.
He is **more athletic than anyone else** in the class.
He is **the most athletic** student in the class.

這四句英文都清楚的表明他是班上最有運動細胞的學生。

但如果寫成下面的句子就**不合文法**了：
*He is more athletic than any student in the class. (any student in the class 包括他自己，而自己比自己受人喜歡，邏輯不通，所以作比較時必須把自己排除在群體之外，因此要寫成 **any other student** 或 **all other students**。）

再舉一例：

The outlet store sells sneakers at **lower prices than any other store** in the entire state.

The outlet store sells sneakers at **lower prices than all other stores** in the entire state.

The outlet store sells sneakers at **the lowest prices** among all stores in the entire state.

這家工廠直營商店（暢貨中心）銷售球鞋的價格比全州其他任何商店都要低。

再舉一例：

Though she is **not so good looking as many other children**, she is **as unique and precious as any other child** in God's eyes.

Though she is **not so good looking as many other children**, she is **as unique and precious as all other children** in God's eyes.

Though she is **not so good looking as many other children**, she is **as unique and precious as anyone else** in God's eyes.

雖然她不如其他很多小孩長的好看，在上帝眼中她跟其他孩子都是一樣獨特與珍貴的。

14.2 容易混淆的比較句型

英文容易涵義的比較句型包括：(1) not more than vs. no more than，(2) not less than vs. no less than，(3) The 比較

級……，the 比較級…，(4) no more than vs. not any more than，
(5) no less than vs. not any less than，以及 (6) all the + 比較級，
一共六種不同的變化。

▶▶ 14.2.1 Not More Than vs. No More Than

not more than + 名詞 表示至多的意思，相當於 at most

It will cost you **not more than** NT$600 to have your car
washed.
洗車至多花你 600 元臺幣。

Professors are allowed to teach **not more than** 12 hours a
week.
教授一週只容許授課至多 12 小時。

no more than + 名詞 表示僅有、只有的意思，相當於 only。
如以下例句：

My favorite football team performed so well that it lost **no
more than** three games in the whole season.
我最喜歡的足球隊表現好到整個球季一共只輸了三場。

The tourists from Japan spent **no more than** five days
sightseeing in eastern part of Taiwan.
來自日本的觀光客花了僅僅五天時間欣賞臺灣東部風景。

▶▶ 14.2.2 Not Less Than vs. No Less Than

not less than + 名詞 表示至少的意思，相當於 at least。
如以下例句：

It took the carpenters **not less than** eight months to build the cabin by the lake.

蓋這座湖邊小木屋花了木匠們至少八個月的時間。

no less than + 名詞 表示**多達、不少於**的意思，通常含有驚訝的意思；相當於 **as much as**（接不可數名詞）或 **as many as**（接可數名詞）。

如以下例句：

The philanthropist donated no less than US$7,000,000 to several different charities last year.

這位慈善家去年捐贈了**多達**七百萬美金給數個慈善機構。

No less than 300 protestors were arrested during a protest that turned violent last night.

昨晚在一場轉趨暴力的示威活動中**多達** 300 位示威者遭到逮捕。

▶▶▶ 14.2.3 The 比較級⋯，the 比較級⋯（越⋯，就越⋯）

The more convenient online shopping becomes, **the more consumers will place orders online**.

線上購物變的越方便，消費者就越多在線上下訂單。

The newer and **bigger** the house is, **the higher** the price is usually asked.

房子越新越大，通常求售的價格就越高。

The less time people are exposed to sunshine, **the less** likely they will be healthy.

人越少曝露在日光下，就越不可能身體健康。

The more time parents spend with their children, **the better** relationships they will develop.

14.2.4 No More Than vs. Not Any More Than

no more than 或 **not any more than** 強調兩者都否定的意思，用來表示**兩者（人或事物）所不具備的特質或屬性**，或是**同一個人都不具備的兩種特質或屬性**。

例如：

Since you have been in this business for less than six months, **you are no more experienced than I am**.

Since you have been in this business for less than six months, **you are not any more experienced than I am**.

既然你在這一行工作不到半年，你跟我一樣都是<u>沒</u>什麼經驗的。（你和我<u>同時否定</u>相同的特質）

Unlike 20 years ago, students' parents nowadays are **no more respectful** to the teachers **than** the students are.

Unlike 20 years ago, students' parents nowadays are **not any more respectful** to the teachers **than** the students are.

不若 20 年前，現在的<u>家長與學生一樣</u>都<u>不尊重</u>老師了。（<u>家長與學生同時否定</u>相同的特質）

The councilman is **no more innocent than** his wife in the bribery scandal.

The councilman is **not any more innocent than** his wife in the bribery scandal.

這次的賄賂醜聞，議員和他太太<u>兩個都不是無辜的</u>。（<u>議員和他太太同時否定</u>相同的特質）

Tina's mother is **no more generous than** Tina is **diligent**.

Tina's mother is **not any more generous than** Tina is **dili-gent**.

Tina 的母親**不慷慨**，Tina **也不勤奮**。（母親和 **Tina** 同時否定 不同的特質 ）

My father is **no more strict than boring**.

My father is **not any more strict than boring**.

我父親**既不嚴厲也不會無趣**。（本身的特質兩者同時否定）

Deserting soldiers are **no more brave than patriotic**.

Deserting soldiers are **not any more brave than patriotic**.

逃兵**既不勇敢也不愛國**。（本身的特質兩者同時否定）

▶▶ 14.2.5 No Less Than vs. Not Any Less Than

no less than 或 not any less than 強調兩者都肯定的意思，用來表示**兩者（人或事物）所具備的特質或屬性**，或是**同一個人同時具備的兩種特質或屬性**。

例如：

The delicacies in Taiwan are **no less attractive than** the **scenic spots** to foreign tourists.

The delicacies in Taiwan are **not any less attractive than** the **scenic spots** to foreign tourists.

臺灣的**美食跟風景區**對外國遊客**同樣有吸引力**。（美食和風景區同時肯定 相同的特質 ）

In modern history, Winston Churchill was **no less a great leader than** Ronald Reagan was.

In modern history, Winston Churchill was **not any less a great leader than** Ronald Reagan.

在現代歷史上，邱吉爾跟雷根**同樣是**偉大的領袖。（兩者同時肯定 相同的特質）

The coach is **no less smart than** the players are **skillful**.

The coach is **not any less smart than** the players are **skillful**.

教練的**聰明不亞於**球員的**球技精湛**。 同時肯定 教練和球員 不同的特質

The new CEO is **no less resourceful than charismatic**.

The new CEO is **not any less resourceful than charismatic**.

新的執行長**既足智多謀且具領袖魅力**。（本身的特質兩者同時肯定）

▶▶ 14.2.6 all the + 比較級 （更加…）

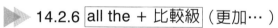

例如：

With chili in the pizza, it tastes **all the better**.
披薩加了辣椒，嚐起來味道<u>更加好</u>。

After she won the English speech contest and was praised by her instructor, she loves studying English **all the more**.
她贏得英語演講比賽，又被老師稱讚，她就<u>更加喜歡讀英文了</u>。

The fact that he has mastered Spanish and Japanese without going abroad makes it **all the more** incredible.

他精通西班牙文和日文，卻從來沒有出過國，這更加令人稱奇。

▶▶ 14.2.7 比較句型打通關

中翻英填空（一格填一個單字）

1. 目前大學所提供的線上課程數量是六年前的兩倍之多。

   The number of online courses offered by universities now are _____ _____ _____ six years ago.

2. 我太太做菜跟我媽媽做的一樣好吃。

   The dishes my wife cooks taste _____ _____ _____ those my mom does.

3. 夏天雨下的越少，西瓜就長的越甜。

   _____ _____ it rains in the summer, _____ the watermelons will _____.

4. 作為全職家庭主婦跟全職工作者是一樣不簡單。

   It is _____ _____ _____ to be a full-time housewife than to be a full-time worker.

5. 我朋友問我借錢，我說我至多能借他 50,000 臺幣。

   My friend asked me to lend him some money, and I said I could loan him _____ _____ _____ NT$50,000.

6. 她是公司裡面最有企圖心的員工，因為她每天都比其他人早到公司，工作的表現也比其他人優秀。

   She is more ambitious _____ any _____ in the company as she arrives at the office _____ than anyone _____ and outperforms all _____.

7. 這家超市賣的食品沒有另外一家新鮮。

The foods _____ in this supermarket is _____ _____ fresh as _____ in another _____.

8. 你在工作中投入越多努力，你就越覺得自豪。

_____ _____ _____ you put into your work, _____ _____ you feel _____ _____ yourself.

9. 她們家很有錢，她擁有多達四部奢華進口車。

She comes from a wealthy family, and she owns _____ _____ _____ four luxurious _____ cars.

10. 當飛機駕駛在強烈雷陣雨下成功完成緊急降落時，機上旅客跟機組人員一樣都鬆了一口氣。

The passengers were _____ any _____ than the crew when the pilot made a successful _____ landing during a severe thunderstorm.

11. 想要精通英文寫作，經常不斷的練習跟澈底瞭解英文文法一樣重要。

To master English writing, _____ practicing is _____ _____ _____ than thorough understanding of English grammar.

12. 身為經驗老道的登山者，Joshua 已經登過的臺灣高山比我認識的其他任何人更多。

Joshua, an _____ mountain hiker, has climbed _____ high mountains in Taiwan than _____ _____ I know.

13. 由於這位球星捐助了一大筆驚人的慷慨善款，要幫助至少兩千個小孩上大學，球迷們就更加喜歡他了！

The fans like the sports star _____ the _____ for his incredibly generous charity _____ that will help _____

_____ than two thousand kids attend college.

14. 受面試的越是吹噓他的技術和經驗，面試者對其印象就越差。

_____ _____ the _____ boasts about his skills

and experiences, _____ _____ the _____ is

impressed.

15. 你在法庭的論證跟任何傑出律師的論證一樣高明。

Your _____ in the court are _____ brilliant _____

any _____ outstanding _____ can be.

16. 這所私立大學的學費是國立大學的三倍貴。

The tuition of this private university is _____ _____

_____ _____ _____ that of a national univer-

sity.

17. 農夫用的殺蟲劑越多，農作物對我們健康的威脅就更嚴重。

_____ _____ _____ the farmers use, _____

_____ _____ the crops will pose to our health.

18. 遊覽巴士的司機不僅幽默而且又專注。

The tour bus driver is _____ any _____

than _____.

19. 她不誠實，而她先生也不謙遜。

She is _____ more _____ _____ her husband

is _____.

20. 政府做的基礎建設越多，就有越多的國外投資會被吸引過來。

_____ _____ _____ the government builds, _____

_____ foreign _____ will be lured.

21. 軍事無人機能夠跟任何先進的戰鬥機一樣精準地發射飛彈。

The military _____ can fire missiles _____

_____ _____ any _____ jet fighter.

22. Daniel 才九歲大，然而他運球神乎其技如職業籃球員一般。

Daniel is only nine years old, _____ he dribbles the ball _____ fantastically _____ professional basketball players _____.

23. 機器人組裝汽車比人工有效率的多。

The robots _____ the cars _____ _____ _____ than human workers _____.

24. 你一旦能夠像你父親一樣把生意經營好，他就會把生意交給你然後退休了。

Once you are able to _____ the business _____ _____ _____ your father _____, he will _____ over the business to you and retire.

25. 汽車製造廠新推出的跑車跑的比世界上任何跑車都快。

The sports car newly _____ by the car _____ runs _____ than _____ _____ in the whole world.

26. 歷史學家眼中，漢朝跟羅馬帝國一樣都是偉大的政權。

In historians' eyes, the Han Dynasty was not _____ _____ a great regime _____ the Roman Empire _____.

27. 今年的年終獎金高達六個月的薪水，這家銀行每一位員工都超級興奮。

Every _____ of the bank is super excited that the year-end _____ this year is _____ less _____ six months' pay.

28. 古董的傢俱越老舊，就變的越有價值。

_____ _____ the antique furniture gets, the more _____ it will _____.

29. 背叛朋友的人既不受尊重也不值得信任。

People _____ _____ their friends are no _____ respected _____ _____.

30. 聖雄甘地跟小馬丁路德一樣都是偉大的國家英雄。

Mahatma Gandhi was _____ _____ a great national hero _____ Martin Luther King Jr. _____.

31. 一個人越有錢，所能擁有的真實好友就越少。

The _____ one gets, the _____ true friends one can have.

32. 腐敗貪汙的政客跟強盜和殺人犯一樣都很邪惡。

_____ politicians are _____ any _____ evil than robbers and murderers _____.

33. 她用錢節儉因為她一個月只賺 32,000 臺幣，同時又住在臺北市，也是全臺灣最貴的城市。

She is thrifty because she makes _____ _____ NT$32,000 a month while living in Taipei, the _____ _____ city in Taiwan.

34. 你父親並不像大家所認為的那樣固執，事實上，他跟任何其他愛護兒女的父親一樣好商量。

Your father is _____ so _____ _____ people think he _____; actually, he is _____ flexible as _____ other father _____ cares for his children.

14.3 雙重比較級

雙重比較級是英文的特殊句型，用來表達**前半句的原因或條件**和**後半句的影響與結果**兩者的連動關係。其前後的兩個獨立子句皆**是將比較級的形容詞或副詞或名詞移到句首的特殊結構**，前者表達**原因或條件**，後者表達結果與影響。

例如：

The more time learners are exposed to a foreign language, the more quickly they will master it.

依照正規的英文句子結構，兩個獨立子句必須以對等連接詞或分號加以結合，或是將第一個表達原因或條件的獨立子句變換成副詞子句，再與第二個維持不變的獨立子句結合成為複句。然而，**雙重比較級前後兩個獨立子句卻是以逗點 (comma) 相連結而構成完整的句子**，若是在非雙重比較級的情況，以逗點連接兩個獨立子句即形成不合文法的連寫句 (run-on sentences)。

例如：

教授越幽默有趣，就越受歡迎。

句子若是翻成以下的英文：

* *A professor is more humorous* , *he/she is more popular*.
（前後兩個獨立子句以逗點連接，形成**不合文法**的**連寫句**）

若是改成以下的句型，則是**合乎文法**的句子：

*A professor is more humorous, **and** he/she is more popular.*
（合句）

***If** a professor is more humorous, he/she is more popular.*（複句）

When *a professor is more humorous, he/she is more popu-*
lar.（複句）

若是改成以下的句型，則是**結構完整的雙重比較級句型**：

The more humorous *a professor is* ， ***the more popular*** *he/*
she is.（**雙重比較級**）

14.3.1 雙重比較級與其他句型表達相同的涵義

　　雙重比較級的結構是兩個獨立子句以逗點結合成為一個完整的句子，所表達是**前半句的原因或條件**和**後半句的影響與結果**兩者的連動關係，若是要表達與雙重比較級句子相同的涵義，也可以運用合句或複句的結構來表達，如以下例句：

　　挑戰越大，有領袖魅力的領導人就變的越有動力。

The greater the challenge is, **the more** motivated a charis-matic leader becomes.

The challenge is greater, **and** a charismatic leader becomes more motivated.

If the challenge is greater, a charismatic leader becomes more motivated.

When the challenge is greater, a charismatic leader becomes more motivated.

　　你越學習英文文法，你就能寫出更好的英文文章。

The more you study English grammar, **the better** English essays you will write.

You study English grammar more, **and** you will write better English essays.

If you study English grammar more, you will write better English essays.

When you study English grammar more, you will write better English essays.

我們攝取越多的糖，我們的體重就越增加。

The more sugar we consume, **the more weight** we gain.

We consume more sugar, **and** we gain more weight.

If we consume more sugar, we gain more weight.

When we consume more sugar, we gain more weight.

▶▶ **14.3.2 雙重比較級的句型結構與用法**

要瞭解雙重比較級的句型結構與用法，我們先來看以下的中英對照的句子：

多運動，身體越健康。

The more one works out , *the healthier* one becomes .
（前面副詞比較級；後面形容詞比較級）

組織越小，越有彈性；組織越大，越不容易改變。

The smaller an organization is , *the more* flexible it is .
The bigger an organization is , *the more difficult* for it to make changes .
（前後都是形容詞比較級）

公司僱用的員工越多，就要付越多的薪水。

The more employees _a company hires_, **_the more salaries_** _it pays._
（前後都是 more + 名詞）

每周工作時數越少，我們越開心。

The fewer hours _we work every week_, **_the happier_** _we are_.
（前面 fewer + 名詞；後面形容詞比較級）

從以上的例句，我們歸納出英文的雙重比較級的句型結構有三類：
（一）**前後兩個獨立子句的開頭都是 the + 形容詞或副詞的比較級**

（二）**前後兩個獨立子句的開頭都是 the + more/fewer/less + 名詞**

（三）混合結構，也就是前後兩個獨立子句其中一個的開頭為
　　　the + 形容詞／副詞比較級，另一個的開頭為 **the + more/**
　　　fewer/less + 名詞
（提醒：**fewer + 可數名詞；less + 不可數名詞**）

(一) 前後兩個獨立子句的開頭都是 **the + 形容詞或副詞的比較級**
　The + 形容詞／副詞比較級 + 主詞 + 動詞, the + 形容詞／副詞比較級 + 主詞 + 動詞

　　這樣的句型結構又依動詞是否為連綴動詞再分成三種句型：
　　(1) 前後動詞均為連綴動詞
　　(2) 前後動詞其中一個為連綴動詞
　　(3) 前後動詞均非連綴動詞

(1) 前後動詞均爲連綴動詞 (be, become, get, feel, remain)

The fresher the food **is**, **the healthier** it **is**.

（前後兩個獨立子句都是**形容詞比較級**）

The more optimistic a leader **is**, **the more popular** he **is**.

（前後兩個獨立子句都是**形容詞比較級**）

The less populated **an area** is, the better **the natural environment** gets.

（前後兩個獨立子句都是**形容詞比較級**，並且前後兩個獨立子句的**主詞不一樣**）

(2) 前後動詞其中一個爲連綴動詞

The less nervous players **feel**, **the better** they perform in the game.

（前面獨立子句爲**形容詞比較級**，後面獨立子句則是**副詞比較級**。）

The less people desire, **the happier** they are.

（前面獨立子句爲**副詞比較級**，後面獨立子句則是**形容詞比較級**。）

(3) 前後動詞均非連綴動詞

The more we **understand** our clients, **the more easily** we **sell** them our products.

（前後兩個獨立子句都是**副詞比較級**）

The more hastily you do a job, **the more easily** you make mistakes.

（前後兩個獨立子句都是**副詞比較級**）

(二) 前後兩個獨立子句的開頭都是 **the** + **more/less/fewer** + 名詞

The **more/less/fewer** + 名詞 + 主詞 + 動詞 , **the more/less/fewer** + 名詞 + 主詞 + 動詞

例如：

The more books we read, **the more knowledge** we gain.

The fewer challenges one encounters, **the fewer lessons** one learns.

(三) 混合句型結構：前後兩個獨立子句其中一個的開頭為 **the** + 形容詞／副詞比較級，另一個的開頭為 **the** + **more/less** + 名詞

(1) *The* + 形容詞／副詞比較級 + 主詞 + 動詞, **the more/less/fewer** + 名詞 + 主詞 + 動詞

例如：

The richer a person is, **the more privileges** he/she enjoys.

The more exciting a movie is, **the more audience** it attracts.

(2) **The more/less/fewer** + 名詞 + 主詞 + 動詞 , *the* + 形容詞／副詞比較級 + 主詞 + 動詞

例如：

The more time the husband spends with his wife, **the happier** his wife is.

The less money you make, **the harder** your life is.

The more roads the government builds, **the more conveniently** we travel from one place to another.

The fewer factories there are in the area, **the fresher** the air is.

▶▶ 14.3.3 雙重比較級的省略

雙重比較級的句型在某些條件下可以：

（一）將連綴動詞省略

（二）將動詞與主詞同時省略

仍然表達相同的涵義，而達到句子簡潔有力的效果。

(一) 雙重比較級連綴動詞的省略

例一：

The more trees we grow, the better the environment **becomes**.

可以將第二個獨立子句的連綴動詞 **becomes** 省略，全句成為：

→ *The more trees we grow, the better the environment.*

例二：

The less generous an employer **is**, the less loyal the employees **are**.

可以將句子中的**兩個連綴動詞 is 和 are 同時省略**，全句成為：

→ *The less generous an employer, the less loyal the employees.*

例三：

The harder the task **is**, the sweeter the accomplishment **is**.

可以將句子中的**兩個連綴動詞 is 同時省略**，全句成為：

→ *The harder the task, the sweeter the accomplishment.*

(二) 雙重比較級主詞與動詞的省略

1. 當雙重比較級的前後兩個獨立子句的主詞相同，且第二個獨立子句的動詞為連綴動詞時，可以將第二個獨立子句的主詞與動詞同時省略，仍然表達相同的涵義。

例一：

（一個人）讀的書越多，就越有知識。

The more books **one** reads, the more knowledgeable **one becomes**.

前後主詞相同，且後面獨立子句的**動詞 becomes** 為連綴動詞，可以將第二個獨立子句的主詞與動詞同時省略，全句成為：

→ *The more books one reads, the more knowledgeable.*

例二：

我們的孩子越多，我們就越幸福。

The more children **we** have, the happier **we are**.

前後主詞相同，且後面獨立子句的**動詞 are** 為連綴動詞，可以將第二個獨立子句的主詞與動詞同時省略，全句成為：

→ *The more children we have, the happier.*

2. 當雙重比較級的前後兩個獨立子句的主詞相同，且第二個獨立子句的動詞為連綴動詞時，將第二個獨立子句的主詞與動詞同時省略之後，可以更進一步，在不影響語意的前提下，將第一個獨立子句的主詞與動詞同時省略，以作更簡潔的表達。

例一：

The more children **we** have, the happier **we are**.

先將第二個獨立子句的主詞與動詞同時省略，全句成為：

→ *The more children we have, the happier.*

再進一步把第一個獨立子句的主詞與動詞同時省略，全句成爲：
→ *The more children, the happier.*

例二：
男孩子長的越高，（他）就越有自信心。
The taller **a boy** grows, the more self-confident **he is**.
將第二個獨立子句的主詞與動詞同時省略，全句成爲：
→ *The taller a boy grows, the more self-confident.*
再進一步把第一個獨立子句的主詞與動詞同時省略，全句成爲：
→ *The taller, the more self-confident.*

3. 當第二個獨立子句的主詞爲**虛主詞 it**，動詞爲連綴動詞時，可以**將 it 與連綴動詞同時省略**，仍然表達相同的涵義。
   例如：
   （你）開的越快，就越危險。
   The faster you drive, the more dangerous **it is**.
   將 **it 與連綴動詞同時省略**，全句成爲：
   → *The faster you drive, the more dangerous.*

4. 當獨立子句的結構爲 **there is/are** 時，可以將 **there is/are 同時省略**，仍然表達相同的涵義。
   例一：
   賓客越多，（我們）就要準備更多食物。
   The more guests **there are**, the more food we need to prepare.
   將 **there are 同時省略**，全句成爲：
   → *The more guests, the more food we need to prepare.*

例二：

競標的人越多，就會越刺激。

The more bidders **there are**, the more exciting **it is**.

將 **there are** 以及 **it is** 同時省略，全句成為：

→ *The more bidders, the more exciting.*

（前後獨立子句都簡化為片語。）

 14.3.4 小試身手

將下列句子改寫成雙重比較級的結構

1. If a business owner is less generous, the employees are less loyal.

   _____

2. When the professors are younger, they tend to be more energetic and enthusiastic.

   _____

3. If you expect more, you may get less satisfied.

   _____

4. When the products we sell are more diverse, we can entice more varieties of buyers.

   _____

5. If the players feel more comfortable in a competition, they will perform better.

   _____

6. If fewer students are in a class, the teacher can pay more attention to individual students.

   _____

7. When the land is located farther away from the urban area, it gets cheaper.

_____

8. If we walk closer with God, we will be stronger when faced with adversity.

_____

9. When a person is less responsible, he will less likely succeed in anything he does.

_____

10. If a city provides less public transport, the air pollution produced by motor vehicles will be more serious.

_____

▶▶ 14.3.5 雙重比較級挑戰題

使用雙重比較級將下列句子翻成英文

1. 走訪的國家越多，越能欣賞 (appreciate) 不同的文化。

_____

2. 人工智慧越進步 (advanced)，對產業越有助益 (benefit)。

_____

3. 食物越新鮮，嚐起來越好吃。

_____

4. 身體健康檢查越澈底，要價就越高。

_____

5. 古董越古老，越有價值。

_____

6. 越低度開發的國家，生活費越低。

_____

7. 事情越複雜，越難解決。

_____

8. 研究人員使用越少的樣本做統計分析，結論就越不能令人信服。

_____

_____

9. 我們由於工業開發而失去的雨林越多，全球的生態就變的越糟糕。

_____

_____

10. 任務期間我們越保持專注，我們越有可能成功地將其完成。

_____

_____

11. 製造過程越是自動化 (automated)，就越有效率 (it is)。

_____

12. 有 (there are) 越多的觀眾在體育館看比賽，球員就打的越賣力，並且兩支球隊就賺越多。

_____

_____

第十五章 直接引述與間接引述 (Quoted / Reported Speech)

　　當我們要引述別人說過的話，有兩種引述的方式：一種是直接引述，另一種是間接引述。直接引述就是用雙引號將別人說的話一字不差的轉述給第三者聽，而間接引述則是將雙引號內的句子加以改變，包括句子結構、人稱、時態、代名詞、時間及地點，然後轉述給他人聽。例如：

直接引述：Henry said, "I will play basketball with you tomorrow."

說明：在雙引號內直接引述的句子是當時 Henry 親口所說出的話，一字不漏的照說，完全沒有變動；在格式上，(1) 直接引述的動詞後面要加逗點，(2) 雙引號內的句子第一個字母要大寫，(3) 在動詞 said 的後面要加逗點，以及 (4) 句子最後的標點符號則要放在第二個雙引號之前。）

改成**間接引述**：Henry said (that) **he would** play basketball with **me the next day**.

說明：改成間接引述之後，改變的部分包括：(1) 間接引述動詞後面的逗點去掉，(2) 雙引號去掉，(3) 雙引號內的句子變成名詞子句，(4) 人稱由 I 變成 he，(5) 人稱 you 變成 me，(6) 動詞時態由簡單未來式 will play 變成 would play，(7) 時間由 tomorrow 變成 the next day

在這一篇我們將學會直接引述和間接引述的句型結構，以及兩種引述句型如何互換。

15.1 直接引述轉換成間接引述

將直接引述改成間接引述有三種類型：

1. 直接引述雙引號內的**直述句** (statements) 改成間接引述
2. 直接引述雙引號內的**疑問句** (questions) 改成間接引述
3. 直接引述雙引號內的**祈使句** (requests) 改成間接引述

▶▶ **15.1.1 直述句之直接引述如何改成間接引述**

將直接引述改成間接引述時，原來雙引號內的**直述句要改寫成名詞子句**，並作其他部分的變化，如以下例句：

直接引述：Julia said, "**I want to buy a pizza.**"

→改成**間接引述**：Julia said **(that) she wanted to buy a pizza.**

其中的變化包括：

(1) 直接引述**動詞後面的逗點去掉**
(2) **雙引號去掉**
(3) 雙引號內的 直述句改寫成由 **that** 引導的名詞子句（**that** 可以省略）
(4) 直述句的**主詞 I 改寫成 she**
(5) 間接引述的**動詞時態配合 said** 由現在式 **want** 改寫成過去式 **wanted**

直接引述中雙引號內的句子為直述句，在改為間接述句時，必須注意的變化除了上述例句中 (1) **代名詞與指示代名詞**及 (2) **動詞時態**的改寫，另外，還涉及到 (3) **時間**與 (4) **地點**的改寫，分別以例句及表格說明如下：

▶▶ 15.1.2 代名詞在直接引述改成間接引述時如何改寫

代名詞在引述句改成間接引述時，要**依其所指稱的對象來決定改寫成哪一個代名詞**，例如：

*Jasmine says, "**My** brother is getting married."*

→ Jasmine says (that) **her** brother is getting married.（直接引述中的 My 指稱的是 Jasmine，而 Jasmine 是女生，改成間接引述時，代名詞就要改寫成 her。）

*My friends said, "**We** are having a party."*

→ My friends said (that) **they** were having a party.（直接引述中的 We 指稱的是 my friends，改成間接引述時，代名詞就要改寫成 they。）

*Peter said, "**My** father bought **me** a new bike."*

→ Peter said (that) **his** father had bought **him** a new bike.（直接引述中的 My 指稱的是 Peter，而 Peter 是男生，改成間接引述時，代名詞就要改寫成 his 及 him。）

代名詞及指示代名詞從直接引述改為間接引述時的改寫

直接引述	間接引述
代名詞	*代名詞*
I / you (subject)	→**she / he**
we / you (subject)	→**they**
me / you (object)	→**him / her**
us / you (object)	→**them**
指示代名詞	*指示代名詞*
my / your	→**his / her**
mine / yours	→**his / hers**
our / your	→**their**
ours / yours	→**theirs**
指示代名詞	*指示代名詞*
this	→**that**
these	→**those**

更多例句如下：

直接引述：*Julia said to **me**, "**I will** buy **you** a pizza."*

→ 間接引述：Julia said to me (that) **she would** buy **me** a pizza.

（主詞 "I" 改成 "she," 代名詞 "you" 改成 "me." 動詞時式由 "will" 改成 "would"。）

直接引述：*Julia said to **my brother**, "**I will** buy **you** a pizza."*

→ 間接引述：Julia said to my brother (that) **she would** buy **him** a pizza.

（代名詞 "you" 指稱的是 "my brother"，改成 "him"。）

直接引述：*Julia said to **her parents**, "**I will** buy **you** a pizza."*

→ 間接引述：Julia said to her parents (that) **she would** buy **them** a pizza.

（代名詞 "you" 指稱的是 "her parents"，改成 "them"。）

直接引述：*Julia said, "**My** sister and **I are** going to buy a piz-za."*

→ 間接引述：Julia said (that) **her** sister and **she were** going to buy a pizza.

（代名詞 "my" 改成 "her," "I" 改成 "she." 動詞時態改成過去式 "were"。）

▶▶ 15.1.3 動詞時態在直接引述改成間接引述時如何改寫

動詞時態在直接引述改成間接引述時，其改寫分兩種情況：(1) 原句的引述動詞時態為現在式，及 (2) 原句的引述動詞時態為過去式。

(a) 原句的引述動詞時態為現在式

直接引述原句的主要動詞時態為**現在式**時，直接引述改成間接引述時，其**動詞時態維持不變**。

例如：

*Brian **says**, "My father **is** an architect."*（直接引述原句的引述動詞時態為現在式 says）

→ Brian **says** (that) his father **is** an architect.（間接引述中的動詞時態與原句中的直接引述動詞時態維持不變，仍然是 is。）

(b) 直接引述原句的引述動詞時態為過去式

直接引述原句的引述動詞時態為**過去式**時，直接引述改成間接引述時，其**動詞時態要向後推遲**，也就是現在式的改成過去式，過去式改成過去完成式，而原來是過去完成式的維持不變：

(1) 簡單現在式要改成簡單過去式 (play → played)

(2) 現在進行式要改成過去進行式 (is/am/are playing → was/were playing)

(3) 簡單過去式及現在完成式要改成過去完成式 (played or have/has played → had played)

(4) 現在完成進行式要改成過去完成進行式 (have/has been playing → had been playing)

(5) 過去完成式及過去完成進行式維持不變 (had played → had played; had been playing → had been playing)

(6) 簡單未來式 be going to 改成 was/were going to

(7) 簡單未來式 will 要改成 would

(8) 現在式助動詞 can, may, have to 要改成過去式助動詞 could, might, had to

(9) must 及過去式助動詞 would, should, could, might, ought to 維持不變。

直接引述改成間接引述時動詞時態的後推

直接引述	間接引述
簡單現在式 She said, "I cook dinner."	→ 簡單過去式 **She said (that) she cooked dinner**
現在進行式 She said, "I am cooking dinner."	→ 過去進行式 **She said (that) she was cooking dinner.**
簡單過去式 She said, "I cooked dinner."	→ 過去完成式 **She said (that) she had cooked dinner.**
現在完成式 She said, "I have cooked dinner."	→ 過去完成式 **She said (that) she had cooked dinner.**
過去完成式 She said, "I had cooked dinner."	→ 過去完成式 **She said (that) she had cooked dinner.**
過去進行式 She said, "I was cooking dinner."	→ 過去完成進行式 **She said (that) she had been cooking dinner.**
現在完成進行式 She said, "I have been cooking dinner."	→ 過去完成進行式 **She said (that) she had been cooking dinner.**
過去完成進行式 She said, "I had been cooking dinner."	→ 過去完成進行式 **She said (that) she had been cooking dinner.**

直接引述	間接引述
簡單未來式 (be going to) She said, "I am going to cook dinner."	→ was / were going to She said (that) she was going to cook dinner.
簡單未來式 (will) She said, "I will cook dinner."	→ would She said (that) she would cook dinner.
條件句 (would) She said, "I would cook dinner."	→ would She said (that) she would cook dinner.
助動詞 can She said, "I can cook dinner."	→ could She said (that) she could cook dinner.
助動詞 may She said, "I may cook dinner."	→ might She said (that) she might cook dinner.
助動詞 must / have to She said, "I must cook dinner." She said, "I have to cook dinner."	→ must / had to She said (that) she must (or had to) cook dinner. She said (that) she had to cook dinner.
過去式助動詞 should She said, "I should cook dinner."	→ should She said (that) she should cook dinner.
過去式助動詞 ought to She said, "I ought to cook dinner."	→ ought to She said (that) she ought to cook dinner.

直接引述本句的主詞和動詞也可以放在第二個雙引號之後，但是原來**雙引號內的句點必須改寫成逗點**，例如：

She said, "*I will buy a pizza for you.*"

→ "I will buy a pizza for you," **she said.**

（直接引述的主詞和動詞移到雙引號後面，原來第二個雙引號前面的句點要改寫成逗點，而句點則是出現在直接引述動詞的後面了。）

或是移動到雙引號之後的主詞和動詞也可以倒裝，將動詞移到主詞前面，例如：

"*I will buy you a pizza,*" ***said she***.（**動詞 said 移到主詞 she 前面**）

而主詞和動詞放在雙引號後面的情況，當其改寫成間接引述時，仍然要將該主詞及動詞移動到句子前面，例如：

"*I will buy a pizza for you,*" ***she said***.

或是 "*I will buy a pizza for you,*" ***said she***.

→ **She said** (that) she would buy me a pizza.

▶▶ 15.1.4 小試身手

將下列直接引述改成間接引述

1. Julia said, "I like the song."

→ Julia said (that) _____.

2. He said, "I bought a new shirt."

   → He said (that) _____.

3. The boy said, "I am working on my homework."

   → The boy said (that) _____.

4. His wife said, "My husband will be home soon."

   → His wife said (that) _____.

5. They said, "We have been playing video games for over four hours."

   → They said (that) _____.

6. Mary said, "My sister and I are going to visit our uncle."

   → Mary said (that) _____.

7. John's mother said, "I must go to pick up your sister."

   → John's mother said (that) _____.

8. Our English teacher said, "You may work with your partners on the assignment."

   → Our English teacher said (that)

   _____.

9. The players said to the coach, "We have been practicing since you came in at six."

   → The players told the coach (that) _____.

10. Her brother said to her, "I can take you to the party to meet with some of my good friends."

   → Her brother told her (that)

   _____.

▶▶▶ 15.1.5 時間及地點在直接引述改成間接引述時如何改寫

時間及地點在從直接引述改寫成間接引述時會出現兩種情況：
(1) 間接引述的**時間或地點**與直接引述發生的時間或地點<u>相同</u>，或
(2) 間接引述的**時間或地點**與直接引述發生的時間或地點<u>不相同</u>。
依時間或地點的相同與否有兩種不同的改寫。

例如：

直接引述：*Cindy said, "I will buy a turkey **tomorrow**."*

(1) → 間接引述：Cindy said (that) she would buy a *turkey* **to-morrow**.
（間接引述與直接引述<u>發生在同一天</u>，則**tomorrow 維持不便**。）

(2) → 間接引述：Cindy said (that) she would buy a *turkey* **the next day**.
（間接引述與直接引述**非發生在同一天**，則 tomorrow 要改寫成 **the next day**。）

直接引述：*Cindy said, "I will buy a turkey **here**."*

(1) → 間接引述：Cindy said (that) she would buy a turkey **here**.
（間接引述與直接引述**發生在同一地點**，則 **here 維持不便**。）

(2) → 間接引述：Cindy said (that) she would buy a turkey **there**.
（間接引述與直接引述**發生在不同地點**，則 **here 要改成 there**。）

時間及地點從直接引述改為間接引述時的變化

直接引述	間接引述
today / tonight	→that day / that night
now	→then
yesterday	→the day before
yesterday morning	→the morning before / the previous morning
yesterday afternoon	→the afternoon before / the previous afternoon
yesterday evening	→the evening before / the previous evening
last night	→the night before / the previous night
the day before yesterday	→two days before
... days ago	→... days before
tomorrow	→the next day / the following day
tomorrow morning	→the next morning / the following morning
tomorrow afternoon	→the next afternoon / the following afternoon
tomorrow evening	→the next evening / the following evening
the day after tomorrow	→in two days' time / two days later
this week	→that week
last week	→the week before
next week	→the following week
this month	→that month
last month	→the month before / the previous month

直接引述	間接引述
next month	→**the following month**
this year	→**that year**
next year	→**the following year**
here	→**there**
this (place)	→**that (place)**

▶▶ 15.1.6 小試身手

將下列直接引述改寫成<u>間接引述</u>（兩者發生的時間及地點不相同）

1. Philip's mother said to him, "Your teacher called you tonight."

   → Philip's mother told him (that) _____.

2. The lawyer advised him, "You should accept the deal now."

   → The lawyer advised him (that) _____.

3. Karen said, "My brother will have dinner with his girlfriend in this restaurant the day after tomorrow."

   → Karen said (that) _____

   _____.

4. The sales manager said to the gentleman, "We will deliver the sofa to your place tomorrow.

   → The sales manager told the gentleman (that) _____

   _____.

5. She said on the phone, "I shipped the item three days ago, and it shall arrive next Monday."

   → She said on the phone (that) _____

   _____.

6. My colleague said to me, "You left your cellphone here last

night."

→ My colleague told me (that) _____.

7. The famous female marathon runner said to the media, "I won the gold medal last week, and I am going to retire next year."

→ The famous female marathon runner told the media (that)

_____

_____.

8. The rich woman announced, "I donated three million dollars to victims of the storm the day before yesterday, and I am considering donating another two million dollars to an orphanage next month."

→ The rich woman announced (that)

_____

_____.

 15.1.7 疑問句之直接引述如何改寫成間接引述

　　直接引述雙引號內的句子為疑問句要改寫成間接引述時有兩種情況：

1. 雙引號內的句子為 WH 疑問句

2. 雙引號內的句子為 Yes/No 疑問句

1. WH 疑問句之直接引述改寫成間接引述

　　例如：

直接引述： Timothy asked , "Where is she?"

說明：直接引述雙引號內的 WH 疑問句，第一個字母要大寫，疑問句後有問號，而且問號要放在第二個雙引號前面。

→間接引述：Timothy asked **where she was.**

說明：改成間接引述後，**去掉雙引號**，**WH 疑問句改寫成名詞子句**，本句**間接引述為直述句**，因此，**問號也去掉**了，而句子最後的**標點符號為句點**。另外，還要依情況需要改寫代名詞、動詞時態、時間、地點等等。

再舉一個例子：

直接引述：**Did she asked** , "*Where* **will Sarah meet me to-night?**"

說明：直接引述雙引號內的 WH 疑問句，第一個字母要大寫，疑問句後有問號，而且問號要放在第二個雙引號前面。

→間接引述：**Did she asked** where **Sarah would meet her tonight/that night?**

說明：改成間接引述後，**去掉雙引號**，**WH 疑問句改寫成名詞子句**，本句間接引述為**疑問句**，因此句子最後的**標點符號為問號**。另外，還要依情況需要改寫代名詞、動詞時態、時間、地點等等。

▶▶ 15.1.8 小試身手

將下列 WH 疑問句之直接引述改寫成間接引述

1. Timothy asked me, "Who has been teaching you how to play badminton?"

   → Timothy asked me _____

2. Timothy asked his sister, "When will you arrive tomorrow?"

   → Timothy asked his sister _____

3. Did Timothy ask the audience, "How do you like my song?"

   → Did Timothy ask the audience _____

4. Did Timothy ask Kyle, "How much did you pay for the dinner last night?"

   → Did Timothy ask Kyle _____

5. Timothy asked Janet, "Why didn't you come to my birthday party last Saturday?"

   → Timothy asked Janet _____

▶▶ 15.1.9 小試身手

將下列 WH 疑問句之間接引述改寫成<u>直接引述</u>

1. He asked her where she came from.

   → He asked her, _____

2. His mother asked who was playing tennis with him then.

   → His mother asked, _____

3. The teacher asked the students which place they wanted to visit for the field trip the following month.

   → The teacher asked the students, _____

   _____

4. She asked the clerk how much the watch cost.

   → She asked the clerk, _____

5. Mary asked her father when he had made reservations of the hotel for their family's vacation.

   → Mary asked her father, _____

   _____

2. Yes/No 疑問句之直接引述改寫成間接引述

例如：

直接引述：*Timothy asked, "**Does Sam play basketball here tonight?**"*

說明：直接引述 **雙引號內為 Yes/No 疑問句，第一個字母要大寫**，疑問句的**問號要放在第二個雙引號之前。**）

→ 間接引述：Timothy asked **whether (or not) Sam played basketball there that night.**

→ 間接引述：Timothy asked **if Sam played basketball there that night.**

說明：改成間接引述後，**去掉雙引號**，Yes/No 疑問句要改寫成 **whether 或 if 所引導的名詞子句**；本句間接引述為**直述句**，因此，**問號也去掉了**，句子最後的**標點符號為句點**。另外，還要依情況需要改寫代名詞、動詞時態、時間、地點等等。

再舉兩個例子：

*Timothy asked, "**Is Sam playing** basketball **here tonight?**"*

→ Timothy asked **whether (or not)** Sam **was playing** basketball **there that night**.

→ Timothy asked **if** Sam **was playing** basketball **there that night**.

說明：去掉雙引號，Yes/No 疑問句要改寫成 **whether 或 if 所引導的名詞子句**，動詞時態由現在進行式改成過去進行式 was playing，here 改成 there，tonight 改成 that night。

*Did Timothy ask, "**Will** Sam **play** basketball **tomorrow**?"*

→ Did Timothy ask **whether (or not)** Sam **would play** bas-ketball **the next day**?

→ Did Timothy ask **if** Sam **would play** basketball **the next day**?

說明：去掉雙引號，Yes/No 疑問句要改寫成 **whether 或 if** 所引導的名詞子句，動詞時態由未來式改成 would play，to-morrow 改成 the next day。

▶▶ 15.1.10 小試身手

將下列 Yes/No 疑問句之直接引述改寫成間接引述

1. Dora asked Kevin, "Did Sam play basketball with you and my brother?"

   → Dora asked Kevin _____

2. Dora asked Lisa, "Have you been playing video games this af-ternoon?"

   → Dora asked Lisa _____

3. My mother asked me, "Did you invite your best friend to the party yesterday?"

   → My mother asked me _____

4. Did you ask your sister, "Can you show me how to write a book report this weekend?"

   → Did you ask your sister _____

5. My father asked me, "Have you seen my sunglasses?"

   → My father asked me _____

6. She asked me, "Will you sign up for the community service next week?"

$\rightarrow$ She asked me _____

7. The waitress asked us, "Are you enjoying the meal tonight?"

    $\rightarrow$ The waitress asked us _____

▶▶ **15.1.11 小試身手**

將下列 Yes/No 之間接引述改寫成直接引述

1. The lawyer asked the judge whether she was allowed to call another witness the following week.

    $\rightarrow$ The lawyer asked the judge, _____

    _____

2. Peter asked his wife whether she could pick up their daughter for him because his car had had a flat tire.

    $\rightarrow$ Peter asked his wife, _____

    _____

3. The police officer asked the driver if he had been driving under influence that night.

    $\rightarrow$ The police officer asked the driver, _____

4. The athlete asked his coach whether he had broken the record that morning.

    $\rightarrow$ The athlete asked his coach, _____

5. My mother asked me if I had forgotten to pay the bill the previous day.

    $\rightarrow$ My mother asked me, _____

6. Did Katie asked Nina if she would join them in that night club to celebrate?

    $\rightarrow$ Did Katie asked Nina, _____

7. Did the boss ask Ethan if he was willing to be sent to Singapore the following month?

→ Did the boss ask Ethan, _____

15.1.12 祈使句之直接引述改寫成間接引述

雙引號內的句子為祈使句時，其直接引述改成間接引述的變化如下例：

直接引述：*My mother **said**, "**Finish** your homework."*

這個直接引述句子要改寫成間接引述時有**兩種改法**：

(1) → 間接引述：**My mother asked me to finish my homework.**
（1. 句子的**動詞 said** 改成 **asked**，2. 祈使句的**原型動詞 finish** 改成不定詞 **to finish**）

(2) → 間接引述：**My mother told me to finish my homework.**
（1. 句子的**動詞 said** 改成 **told**，2. 祈使句的**原型動詞 finish** 改成不定詞 **to finish**)

底下再舉兩個例子：

*She **said to** her daughter, "**Come** back before ten."*
→ She **asked** her daughter **to come** back before ten. （**said to** 改成 **asked, come** 改成 **to come**）
→ She **told** her daughter **to come** back before ten. （**said to** 改成 **told, come** 改成 **to come**）

特殊例子：

*Peter **said**, "**Give me** the statistics **tomorrow**, Sarah."*

這個句子中的直接引述要改寫成間接引述時，會因引述的人是否為 Sarah 本人而有兩種不同的寫法。

(1) → Peter **asked/told me to give him** the statistics **the next day**.

說明：引述的人是 **Sarah**, asked/told 後面要接 me；而 give me 要改成 to give him, 因為 give me 的 me 指的是 Peter；另外 tomorrow 要改成 the next day

(2) → Peter **asked/told Sarah to give him** the statistics **the next day**.

說明：引述的人不是 **Sarah**，而是第三者，則 **asked/told** 後面要接 **Sarah**

▶▶ 15.1.13 小試身手

將下列祈使句之直接引述改寫成間接引述

1. The police officer said, "Show me your driver's license."

   _____

2. Jeremy said to his brother, "Return the car to me this week-end."

   _____

3. Cindy said to her husband, "Remember to pick up our grand-son this afternoon."

   _____

4. The professor said to the class, "Hand in your reports to my assistant no later than next Friday"

   _____

5. Rosa said, "Buy me a breakfast tomorrow morning, Paul."

_____

▶▶ 15.1.14 小試身手

將下列祈使句之間接引述改寫成<u>直接引述</u>

1. My father told me to turn down the music.

_____

2. Zana asked her friend Robert to lend her his bike the following morning.

_____

3. She asked her children to share their toys with their friends.

_____

4. The coach told the players to shoot 100 times before going home that night.

_____

5. The manager asked the sales representatives to submit their reports the following week.

_____

▶▶ 15.1.15 否定式祈使句之直接引述改寫成間接引述

否定式祈使句之直接引述若要改寫成間接引述，需要改變的有：(1)**said to** 改成 **asked** 或 **told**，(2) 去掉雙引號，(3) 把 **Don't + V** 改成 **not to + V**，(4) 代名詞，及 (5) 時間。說明如下例：

The teacher **said to** the class, "**Don't forget** to sign up for the trip **tomorrow**."

→ The teacher **asked** the class **not to forget** to sign up for the trip **the next day**.

→ The teacher **told** the class **not to forget** to sign up for the trip **the next day**.

（**said to** 改成 **asked** 或 **told**，**Don't forget** 改成 **not to for-get**，**tomorrow** 改成 **the next day**）

 15.1.16 小試身手

將下列否定式祈使句之直接引述改寫成間接引述

1. She said to the children, "Don't open the gifts until tomorrow morning."

_____

2. The doctor said to the patient, "Do not eat any food the night before the operation."

_____

3. She said to her husband, "Please don't forget to water the plants for me."

_____

4. He said, "Don't tell your parents what happened here tonight."

_____

5. The police said to the reporters, "Don't enter the crime scene or you will be arrested."

_____

15.1.17 小試身手

將下列否定式祈使句之間接引述改寫成直接引述

1. She told me not to tell my brother when she would come to my house.

_____

2. He asked the investors not to sell their stocks until the following week.

_____

3. She asked her teacher to please not to tell her parents she had been punished that day.

_____

4. He asked Nancy not to forget to feed his dog when he was away the following weekend.

_____

5. The supervisor told Peter not to be late for the meeting the following afternoon.

_____

15.1.18 直接引述與間接引述打通關

I. 將下列直接引述改寫成間接引述

1. The detective said to the eyewitness, "What does the suspect look like?"

_____

2. The new president said, "I will do my best to solve problems our country is faced with."

_____

3. The doctor said to Victoria, "Your father is recovering from the surgery last night."

_____

4. Jack said to Tina, "I will wait for you here tomorrow afternoon."

_____

5. The professor said to the students, "Who wants to help me with the experiment next week?"

_____

_____

6. Jane's father said to her, "I will take you and your brother to Disney World if I get promoted next month."

_____

_____

7. The judge said to the female lawyer, "Do you have any more questions for the witness?"

_____

_____

8. The coach said to the players, "Don't forget to come to practice tomorrow at six."

_____

9. The saleswoman said to the manager, "I sold two cars last week, and I will try to sell more cars next week."

_____

_____

10. The customer said to the street vender, "Are you selling sandwiches here every morning?"

11. Eric said to Mary on the phone, "John is having lunch with me now. Do you want to join us?"

_____

_____

12. The police said to Mr. Wang, "Your stolen car has been found last night."

_____

13. The mother said to the child, "Where is my cellphone?"

_____

14. The policeman said to the fugitive, "Surrender or you will be shot."

_____

15. Jesus said to his followers, "Forgive those who offend you."

_____

16. The students said to the teacher, "We have finished our assignments. Can we take a break now?"

_____

_____

17. Karen said, "The purse is my sister's, not mine."

_____

18. The clerk said to Peter, "The item you ordered has been shipped to you two days ago."

_____

19. The mechanic said to me on the phone, "Your father's car has been repaired and you can pick it up today."

20. She said to my brother, "I heard that you are moving to Taic-hung next month."

21. My colleague said to me in disbelief, "Are you being as-signed to Hong Kong next week?"

22. Did Mary's doctor said to her parents, "How long have you been feeding her this kind of food?"

23. In the supermarket, a woman said to the clerk, "Where can I find blenders?"

24. The manager said to her, "Your application has been ap-proved."

25. The reporter asked the successful businessman, "How did you overcome difficulties and succeed?"

II. 將下列間接引述改寫成直接引述

1. He said that his boss had assigned him a new task.

2. They asked the professor when they were required to submit the term report.

3. The pilot told the passengers that they would arrive at the destination soon.

4. The taxi driver asked me where I wanted to go.

5. The clerk at the liquor store asked the girl if she was 21 or older.

6. My friend asked me whether I had seen his girlfriend the previous night.

7. Tom's brother asked me whether I would play basketball with his brother the next day.

8. The instructor told the students not to cheat in the exam or they would be punished.

9. At the end of the interview, the manager told the lady that she seemed to be a good fit for their company.

10. Excitedly, Jerry told his parents that he had been hired and would start working the following week.

11. My sister told me that she would try her best to come to my

commencement the following month.

_____
_____

12. The police spokesman said the two suspects had been arrested the night before and would be charged soon.

_____
_____

13. Lillian told me that she would be presenting her paper in that conference.

_____

14. Sam asked Jane whether she had seen his student ID the day before.

_____

15. The general said that they had saved the hostages and would send them home in two days' time.

_____
_____

16. The plumber said that the toilet had been repaired and he would charge me $150.

_____

17. The patient said that she wanted to cancel the appointment with the dentist scheduled the following afternoon because her daughter was sick.

_____
_____

18. The lawyer told me not to sign the contract before I was fully advised.

19. Did the young child ask the magician how she had done the trick?

20. The wife told her husband she was not feeling well and asked him if he could fix dinner that night.

第十六章 代名詞 it 的用法

英文的代名詞 it 神通廣大，神出鬼沒，扮演多重角色，可以用來指稱時間、日期、天氣、溫度、距離、長度、情況等等，這樣的用法與句子的結構無關，純粹是以 it 來代替所指稱的東西。另一類的用法更是巧妙，與句子的結構有關，可以用來代替真正的主詞，受詞，或是用來強調句子中的某一個重點。這樣的用法也使得英文的句型更有變化，是英文寫作必備的技巧。以下就這兩類用法分別以例句加以解說：

16.1 it 用來指稱時間、日期、天氣、溫度、距離、長度、情況等等

(1) it 用來指稱時間與日期

It's 10:30 when you called me.

It's getting late, and you had better go home.

It's been over 10 years since I last saw you.

Everyone is happy because it's Friday.

(2) it 用來指稱天氣與溫度

It's raining today.

It was a sunny day yesterday.

It's November, yet it hasn't snowed yet.

It was 5 degrees below zero last night.

It gets dark after 5:30 in the afternoon during the winter.

(3) it 用來指稱距離長度

It's about five kilometers from our place to the church.

(4) it 用來指稱某種情況

It's the best scenario we can expect.

The best of it is that with a smartphone you can have access to the Internet.

It is under our control.

16.2 與句子結構有關的 it 用法

英文的代名詞 it 在句子結構上所扮演的角色包括：

(1) 作為虛主詞

(2) 作為虛受詞

(3) 強調用法（分裂句 cleft sentences）

分別以例句說明如下。

▶▶ 16.2.1 it 作為虛主詞來代替真正的主詞

句子真正的主詞如果是**不定詞片語**，**動名詞片語**，或**名詞子句**，由於 (1) 這三類均為抽象名詞，因此我們可以用結構上的 it 來代替，而以 it 作為句子的虛主詞；或是 (2) 作為主詞的不定詞片語，動名詞片語，或名詞子句過長，放在句首作為主詞，使得整個句子頭重腳輕，而導致閱讀理解困難，因此需要以 it 來加以取代，放在句首作為虛主詞，好讓讀者容易理解句子涵義。

例如：

To take our children to visit the Science Museum to

learn how to protect our environment is a good idea.（不定詞片語爲句子的主詞，放在句首，句子明顯地頭重腳輕。）

→It is a good idea **to take our children to visit the Science Museum to learn how to protect our environment**.

（以 it 替代不定詞片語作爲句子的虛主詞，同時將眞正主詞移置句子後面，句子就容易理解了。）

(a) it 代替不定詞片語

> **It** was so nice **to hear from you**.
> **It** cost me $600 **to buy the ring**.
> **It** takes about 50 minutes **to go from Taichung to Taipei by High Speed Rail**.
> **It** was very kind of her **to offer the homeless hot meals on Thanksgiving**.

(b) it 代替動名詞片語

> **It** was exciting **watching the motorcycle racing**.
> **It** was fun **pretending we were hiding in a cave**.
> **It** is not safe **walking alone at night in that neighborhood**.

(c) it 代替名詞子句

> **It** occurred to me **that I had left my watch in the hotel**.
> **It** was unbelievable **that he made that kind of shot at the buzzer to win the game**.

> **It** was during the summer vacation **that I realized how much our children had grown**.
>
> **It** was a miracle **that the two little kids were saved by him from a car crash**.
>
> **It** is not easy to tell **whether they can make it or not**.

(d) 據說 / 據信 / 根據報導 / 據估計 …（**It** + **be** + 過去分詞 + 名詞子句）

> **It is said** that eating too much sugar is harmful to one's health.
>
> **It is believed** that more and more factory workers will be replaced by robots.
>
> **It was reported** that the police had arrested the suspect of the terrorist attack.
>
> **It was estimated** that the property could be worth more than 15 million dollars.
>
> **It is highly expected** that the team will win the championship this season.
>
> **It is rumored** that the two movie stars are getting divorced again.

16.2.2 it 作為虛受詞

He finds **it** hard **to learn math**.

People take **it** for granted **for children to acquire their first language**.

The mother made **it** clear **that everyone in the family must help with housekeeping**.

They regard **it** very fortunate **to be awarded the prize**.

16.2.3 強調用法（分裂句 cleft sentences）

在分裂句中，我們會利用 **it** 來強調句子中的某一個重點，可能是名詞片語或動名詞片語、介系詞片語、副詞或副詞片語，或不定詞片語。改寫後的所強調的重點如果是**指稱人的名詞片語**，其後面會接 **who** 所引導的名詞子句；如果是**指稱時間**的片語，其後會接 **when** 所引導的名詞子句；如果是**指稱物或地點或目的**的片語，其後會接 **that** 所引導的名詞子句。that/who/when 所接的子句內容通常是前文已經提過、已知的內容。

例一：

Jane opened a Taiwanese restaurant in New York in May.
為了強調句子中的某一個重點，這個句子可以改寫成以下四個句子：

It was **Jane** who opened a Taiwanese restaurant in New York in May.

It was **a Taiwanese restaurant** that Jane opened in New York in May.

> **It** was **in New York** | that | Jane opened a Taiwanese restaurant in May.
>
> **It** was **in May** | when | Jane opened a Taiwanese restaurant in New York.

例二：

> *Jerry's parents* *bought* | *a new car* | *for Jerry* | *last week* | *to celebrate his 20th birthday*.

為了強調不同重點，這個句子可以改寫成以下五個句子：

> **It** was **Jerry's parents** | who | bought a new car for Jerry last week to celebrate his 20th birthday.
>
> **It** was **a new car** | that | Jerry's parents bought for Jerry last week to celebrate his 20th birthday.
>
> **It** was **for Jerry** | that | Jerry's parents bought a new car last week to celebrate his 20th birthday.
>
> **It** was **last week** | when | Jerry's parents bought a new car for Jerry to celebrate his 20th birthday.
>
> **It** was **to celebrate his 20th birthday** | that | Jerry's parents bought a new car for Jerry last week.

▶▶ 16.2.4 小試身手

使用結構性的 it 來改寫下列句子。

1. To meet the new boss for the first time made her nervous.

2. Reading the news stories of current international events allows people to keep up with what is going on in the world.

_____

_____

3. That the young prodigy got admitted to the prestigious university to major in Physics was not surprising at all.

_____

_____

4. He found studying in a foreign country is very challenging in terms of language and culture.

_____

_____

5. How you accomplish the goals is more significant than the end results.

_____

6. For him to marry the beautiful young lady is nearly impossible.

_____

7. They left when to resume the negotiation undecided.

_____

8. When he will return to his hometown is hard to predict.

_____

9. To work in a multi-national corporation like that is many college graduates' top choice.

_____

10. Whether the trainees will be ready to perform their jobs properly in six months is the trainer's biggest concern.

11. Who made the rule that no one is allowed to enter the kitchen after midnight?

_____

12. For college students to work part-time is now very common.

_____

▶▶ 16.2.5 小試身手

將下列句子改爲分裂句來強調劃底線的重點

1. **The firefighters** bravely saved the children from the fire.

_____

2. They donated money to the charity **for the underprivileged school children**.

_____

3. **Who** gave the order to arrest the celebrity?

_____

4. **The victims of the earthquake** needed food and shelters the most.

_____

5. The victims of the earthquake needed **food and shelters** the most.

_____

6. The company spent **more than five million dollars** in developing new products last year.

_____

7. The company spent more than five million dollars **in developing new products** last year.

_____

_____

8. Peter was appointed **the new district attorney** last week.

_____

9. Peter was appointed the new district attorney **last week**.

_____

10. The Mayor commended the pastor **to show appreciation** for what he had done for the community.

_____

_____

11. **What the evidence shows** matters to the jury in a trial.

_____

12. **Whether or not the new cellphone app will become popular** depends on its effectiveness.

_____

_____

▶▶ 16.2.6 it 句型挑戰題

使用結構性的 it 來翻譯下列句子。

1. 大學生**必須修滿 128 個學分**才能取得學士學位。

It is _____ for college students to _____ 128 _____

_____ to obtain a bachelor's degree.

2. **在體育館看籃球賽**比在看電視轉播**要刺激多了**。

It is _____ more _____ _____ the game in the

_____ than doing it live on TV at home.

3. 一直到她母親過世，**她才明白她母親為了家庭作了多少犧牲**。

It was not _____ her mother passed away that she _____

_____ much her mother had _____ for the family.

4. 在調查期間，**警方意外發現嫌犯犯了多年前的一件富商綁架案**。

It was _____ the investigation _____ the police

found out that the _____ _____ _____

the _____ of a wealthy businessman many years before.

5. 一位臺灣高中生精通三種外國語言，**最近被哈佛大學率取一事**令人佩服。

It is impressive that a high school student in Taiwan _____

is _____ in three foreign languages has _____ _____

to Harvard University recently.

6. 根據昨天電視新聞報導，**有數個新品種魚類被研究海洋動物科學家發現了**。

It was reported in the TV news yesterday that several new

_____ of fish had _____ _____ by scientists

_____ ocean animals.

7. **連接臺北市和桃園國際機場的捷運於 2017 年終於啟用**。

It _____ _____ _____ when the Mass _____

_____ (MRT) _____ Taipei and Taoyuan Airport was

finally _____.

8. **涉及賄賂醜聞的政客否認指控一事**並不令人意外。

It was not surprising that the politician _____ in a brib-

ery _____ has _____ the allegation.

9. 是我們所完成的事，而非我們所擁有的**決定我們的人生是否值得**。

It is _____ we _____, not _____ we possess,

_____ decides _____ or not our lives count.

10.是 Bill Hewlett, 也就是 HP 兩位創辦人之一，**提供 12 歲的 Steve Jobs 一份暑期工作**讓他可以學習公司經營之道。

It _____ Bill Hewlett, one of the two _____ of HP,

_____ _____ the 12-year-old Steve Jobs a summer

Job _____ allowed him to learn _____ to _____

a company.

第十七章 倒裝句

在寫作技巧上，爲了（一）**強調句子中的某一部分**、或是（二）**文法上的要求**、或是（三）**讓句型更有變化**，英文句子會以倒裝的形式出現。而不同情況所構成的倒裝句，其所倒裝的部分與方式也有所不同。

（一）**出於強調**的倒裝有四種方式：

(1) 獨立子句或主要子句需要**倒裝成爲疑問句**的形式，又分成兩種情況：

    (a) 表達否定或限制的單一副詞或副詞片語移至句首，例如：*Never **had I** been so encouraged by a speech.*（前倒裝），與 *Not until the rain stopped **did the game** resumed.*（後倒裝），以及

    (b) "so + 形容詞" 或是 "such + 名詞" 移至句首，例如：*So fun **was the trip** to the island that we hated to end it.*；

(2) **動詞與主詞互換位置**的倒裝，例如：*On the bench **sits a boy** eating a sandwich.*；

(3) **be 動詞或助動詞與主詞互換位置**的倒裝，例如：*Sympathetic **is the woman** who regularly feeds stray dogs.*；以及

（二）**出於文法上的要求**而必須倒裝時，獨立子句本身要**倒裝成爲疑問句**的形式，例如：*He speaks fluent English, and **so does** his sister.*。

（三）出於**句型變化**的倒裝，則是假設語氣中的 if 子句，其 **be 動詞或助動詞與主詞互換位置**的倒裝，例如：***Were I in her shoes, I would handle the issue differently.***

英文倒裝句的使用時機與句型變化

倒裝原因	倒裝時機	倒裝方式
強調	表達否定或限制的副詞片語移至句首	獨立子句或複句中在前的主要子句倒裝成為疑問句（複句前倒裝）
	表達否定或限制的副詞片語或連接詞同時與副詞子句移至句首	複句中在後的主要子句倒裝成為疑問句（複句後倒裝）
	"so + 形容詞" 或是 "such + 名詞" 移至句首	獨立子句或主要子句倒裝成為疑問句
	表達位置或方向的副詞或副詞片語移至句首	非代名詞的主詞與動詞互換位置
	主詞補詞移至句首	be 動詞或 be 動詞之前的助動詞與主詞互換位置
文法要求	neither, nor, so, as, than, such 開頭的獨立子句	獨立子句倒裝成為疑問句
句型變化	省略連接詞 if	假設語氣中的 if 子句，其 be 動詞或助動詞與主詞互換位置

17.1 出於強調的倒裝

出於強調的倒裝有五種情況：

一、表達否定或限制的副詞片語移至句首（見 17.1.1 的說明）

二、複句的後倒裝（見 17.1.3 的說明）

三、"so + 形容詞" 或是 "such + 名詞" 移至句首（見 17.1.4 的說明）

四、表達位置或方向的副詞或副詞片語移至句首（見 17.1.5 的說明）

五、主詞補語移至句首的倒裝。（見 17.1.6 的說明）

底下分節詳細說明其用法。

▶▶ 17.1.1 表達否定或限制的副詞片語移至句首的倒裝

當句子中用來表達否定或限制的副詞或副詞片語移至句首引導句子，句子的**獨立子句或主要子句必須以疑問句的形式呈現倒裝**。

簡單句的倒裝

> **例一（簡單句的倒裝）：**
> *無論如何他絕不會背叛朋友。（簡單句）*
> 原句：He **will** betray his friends **under no circumstances**.
> **倒裝 → Under no circumstances will** he betray his friends.
> （獨立子句構成的簡單句，倒裝成為疑問句的形式。）

複句的 前倒裝 ：複句中的**主要子句出現在句子前端**，主要子句要作倒裝。

例二（複句前倒裝）：
當我父親獲知我贏得金牌時從來沒有如此以我爲榮。（複句）
原句：My father **had never** been so proud of me when he
learned that I had won a gold medal.

倒裝 → **Never had** my father been so proud of me when he
learned that I had won a gold medal.
（**主要子句在前，並倒裝成爲疑問句的形式**，屬於**前倒裝**。）

　　爲了強調的效果，而將否定或限制的副詞或副詞片語移至句首，於是獨立子句構成的簡單句或是出現在前的主要子句，必須倒裝成爲疑問句的形式，而複句在這一種情形的倒裝屬於前倒裝。

　　這一類的倒裝一共有六類用來表達否定或限制的副詞或副詞片語會移到句首：

(1) never 從來未曾、一定不會；rarely 幾乎不；seldom 幾乎不

(2) hardly...when, barely...when, scarcely...when, no sooner...than
　　"一…，就…"

(3) in no way, by no means, on no account, under no circum-
　　stances 無論如何絕不，nowhere 任何地方都不，no longer 再
　　也不

(4) little 幾乎沒有

(5) not only..., but also 不僅…，還有…

(6) only then 只在那時候；only in this way 唯獨以此方式；only

by 唯有藉由

(1) | **never 從來未曾、一定不會、rarely 幾乎不、seldom 幾乎不** |

例一：

車禍受傷的駕駛一定不會忘記有位陌生人是如何幫他的。

原句：The driver injured in the car accident **will never forget** how a stranger helped him.

倒裝 → **Never will** the driver injured in the car accident **forget** how a stranger helped him.（倒裝成為疑問句的形式）

例二：

這位單親媽媽幾乎不曾抱怨要獨自撫養三個小孩的辛苦。

原句：**The single mother seldom complains** about the hardship of raising three children all by herself.

倒裝 → **Seldom does the single mother complain** about the hardship of raising three children all by herself.（倒裝成為疑問句的形式）

例三：

高中畢業前她幾乎從來沒跳過舞。

原句：**She had rarely danced** before graduating from high school.

倒裝 → **Rarely had she danced** before graduating from high school.

（倒裝成為疑問句的形式）

(2)

> **hardly...when, barely...when; scarcely...when ; no sooner...than**
>
> " 一…，緊接著就…"

　　這些句型所描述的情境是連續的兩件事發生在過去，而且前一件事剛一結束，緊接著下一件事就發生了。中文的用詞就是" 一…，緊接著就…"。因為兩件事都發生在過去，因此較早發生的動詞必須用過去完成式，而稍微晚一點發生的動詞則用簡單過去式。

例一：

他們剛一踏出體育館，火災警報就響了。

原句：They **had scarcely** stepped out of the stadium **when** the
　　　fire alarm sounded.

倒裝 → $\boxed{\text{Scarcely}}$ had they stepped out of the stadium **when** the
fire alarm sounded.

（倒裝成為疑問句的形式）

例二：

他一把他的積蓄投資在股票，股市隨即就崩盤了。

原句：**He had hardly invested** his savings in the stocks **when**
　　　the stock market crashed.

倒裝 → $\boxed{\text{Hardly}}$ had he invested his savings in the stocks **when**
the stock market crashed.

（倒裝成為疑問句的形式）

例三：

我們剛吃完晚餐，地震就來了。

原句：**We had barely finished** our dinner **when** the earthquake hit.

倒裝 → **Barely** **had we finished** our dinner **when** the earth-quake hit.

（倒裝成為疑問句的形式）

例四：

他們才剛大學畢業，戰爭就爆發了。

原句：**They had no sooner graduated** from college **than** the war broke out.

倒裝 → **No sooner** **had they graduated** from college **than** the war broke out.

（倒裝成為疑問句的形式；**No sooner** 必須跟 **than** 連用，而非 when。）

(3)

> **in no way** 一點也不，一點也沒有；相當於 not at all
> **by no means** 絕不，不可能
> **on no account** 無論如何絕不
> **under no circumstances** 無論如何絕不
> **nowhere** 任何地方都不
> **no longer** 再也不

例一：

他無論如何也不會辭掉他的高收入的工作。

原句：**He will quit** his high-paying job **under no circumstances**.

倒裝 → Under no circumstances **will** **he quit** his high-paying job.

（倒裝成為疑問句的形式）

例二：

任何學生都不可能一個禮拜內就背下來一千個英文單字。

By no means **can** any students memorize one thousand English words within a week.

（倒裝成為疑問句的形式）

例三：

無論如何他們都不會把他們祖先留下來的土地賣掉。

原句：They will **under no circumstances** sell the land left behind by their ancestors.

倒裝 → Under no circumstances **will** they sell the land left behind by their ancestors.

（倒裝成為疑問句的形式）

例四：

他們找不到他們從前跟幼稚園朋友玩耍的公園。

原句：**They could nowhere** find the park where they used to play with their kindergarten friends.

倒裝 → Nowhere **could they find the park** where they used to play with their kindergarten friends.

（倒裝成為疑問句的形式）

(4) little（“little” 一詞爲否定的含義。）

例一：

在讀聖經之前，我對於上帝創造宇宙與地球上萬物的奧妙一無所知

原句：I **had realized little** the wonder of God's creation of the universe and everything on the Earth before I read the Bible.

倒裝 → **Little** **had I realized** the wonder of God's creation of the universe and everything on the Earth before I read the Bible.

（倒裝成爲疑問句的形式）

例二：

醫生警告她之前，她不知道攝取太多糖分對健康的潛在風險。

原句：**She had understood little** the potential health risk of taking too much sugar before she was cautioned by the doctor.

倒裝 → **Little** **had she understood** the potential health risk of taking too much sugar before she was cautioned by the doctor.

（倒裝成爲疑問句的形式）

(5) Not only..., but also 不僅…，並且也…

例一：

他不但熱愛玩滑板，也擅長滑雪。

原句：**He not only loves** skateboarding, but he is also good at skiing.

倒裝 → **Not only** **does he love** skateboarding, but he is also good at skiing.

（倒裝成爲疑問句的形式）

例二：

她不僅率取進入醫學院，而且也獲得提供獎學金。

原句：**She has not only been admitted** to the medical school,
　　　but she has also been offered a scholarship.

倒裝 → |**Not only**| **has she been admitted** to the medical school,
but she has also been offered a scholarship.
（倒裝成為疑問句的形式）

(6)

> **only then** 只在那時候
> **only in this way** 唯獨以此方式
> **only by** 唯有藉由

例一：

在那個時候我才瞭解問題所在。

原句：**I only understood** the problem then.

倒裝 → |**Only then**| **did I understand** the problem.
（倒裝成為疑問句的形式）

例二：

他唯有以此方式才能賺取足夠的錢以求生存。

原句：**He could earn** enough money **only in this way** to survive.

倒裝 → |**Only in this way**| **could he earn** enough money to survive.
（倒裝成為疑問句的形式）

例三：

我們唯有藉著不斷練習才能改進我們的寫作能力。

原句：We **will** improve our writing ability **only by constant practicing**.

倒裝 → **Only by** constant practicing **will** we improve our writing ability.

 17.1.2 小試身手

將下列句子改寫成倒裝句。

示範：

He played little tennis when he was young.

→ Little did he play tennis when he was young.

1. As a diligent student, Jessica rarely missed classes when in college.

   _____

2. They will not sell their father's art collections under any circumstances.

   _____

3. The team could win the game only in this way.

   _____

4. Barry had barely finished his term paper on the computer when the power went out.

   _____

5. The organization will survive only by cutting down its expenses substantially.

   _____

6. She not only was awarded Outstanding Instructor of 2018, but she was also promoted to be an associate professor.

7. After the terrifying accident, she will no longer ride a scooter.

8. He seldom made public speeches as a student, yet he has become one of the most famous motivational speakers in Taiwan.

9. The trainee had no sooner completed her task than the time was up.

10. She never saw such a fascinating singing performance by a young child.

▶▶ 17.1.3 複句的後倒裝

　　複句中的副詞子句移至句首，而主要子句的否定詞也移至副詞子句開頭；或是限制性的連接詞所引導的副詞子句移至句首，從而形成副詞子句在前，而主要子句在後的結構，這種情形主要子句的倒裝屬於後倒裝。

　　這一類的否定詞有：**not⋯until, not⋯since**；而限制性的連接詞則有：**only after, only when, only if**

　　複句的 後倒裝 之一：主要子句的否定詞隨著副詞子句移到句首，而主要子句位置在後，主要子句要倒裝。

* 複句後倒裝之一：

嫌犯一直到檢察官提出直接證據後才認罪。（複句）

原句：The suspect **did not** plead guilty **until** the prosecutor presented the hard evidence.

倒裝 → **Not until** the prosecutor presented the hard evidence **did** the suspect plead guilty.

（副詞子句移到句首，且主要子句內的否定詞也移至副詞子句之前，形成主要子句位置在後，並**倒裝成為疑問句的形式**，屬於後倒裝。）

　　　　複句的 後倒裝 之二：限制性的連接詞所引導的副詞子句移至句首，而主要子句位置在後，主要子句要作倒裝。

* 複句後倒裝之二：

他只有在達成公司設定的目標條件下才會獲得升遷。（複句）

原句：He will be promoted **only if** he reaches the goals set by the company.

倒裝 → **Only if** he reaches the goals set by the company **will he be** promoted.

（限制性的連接詞所引導的副詞子句移至句首，形成主要子句位置在後，並**倒裝成為疑問句的形式**，屬於後倒裝。）

底下以兩個例子說明句子倒裝的過程。

例一：複句中的副詞子句移至句首，而主要子句的否定詞也移至副詞子句開頭

他們直到看見他展現他天生的歌唱技巧才確信不疑。

| They were **not** convinced | | **until** they saw him display his natural singing skills | .

| 他們無法確信 | | 直到他們看見他展現他天生的歌唱技巧 | 。

| 否定的主要子句 | + | 副詞子句 |

倒裝前置步驟：**將副詞子句移到句首（這個步驟還不需要倒裝）**

| **Until** they saw him display his natural singing skills | , | they were **not** convinced | .

| 副詞子句 | + | 否定的主要子句 |

進行倒裝步驟：**將主要子句中的否定詞 not 移到副詞子句開頭位置，並將主要子句改成疑問句的形式**，完成倒裝。

倒裝 → **Not until** they saw him display his natural singing skills **were they convinced**.

例二：限制性的連接詞所引導的副詞子句移至句首

| 唯獨在親身經歷神蹟之後 | ， | 她才相信了上帝 | 。

| 副詞子句 | + | 主要子句 |

可以使用兩種結構翻成英文：

(1) | 主要子句 | + | 副詞子句 | （主要子句在前，不必倒裝）

　　She believed in God **only after** she had experienced the miracle herself.

(2) 副詞子句 + 主要子句（主要子句在後，必須倒裝）

倒裝 → **Only after** she had experienced the miracle herself **did** she believe in God.

▶▶ **17.1.4** "so ＋ 形容詞" 或是 "such ＋ 名詞" 由句中移至句首

若是將 "**so** ＋形容詞" 或是 "**such** ＋名詞" 由句中移至句首，則句子必須**以疑問句的形式呈現倒裝**。

例如：

原句：The girl **is so naive** that she thinks everyone in the world speaks the same language.

倒裝 → **So naive** is the girl that she thinks everyone in the world speaks the same language.

原句：She **is such a naive girl** that she thinks everyone in the world speaks the same language.

倒裝 → **Such a naive girl** is she that she thinks everyone in the world speaks the same language.

▶▶ **17.1.5** 句子中用來表達位置或方向的副詞或副詞片語移至句首的倒裝

當句子中用來表達位置或方向的副詞或副詞片語移至句首時，則形成非代名詞的主詞與動詞互換位置的倒裝。

例一：

原句：The newly bought silverware sets **are on the table**.

倒裝 → **On the table** **are** the newly bought silverware sets.

例二：

原句：The young couple **walked toward the beach** to appreciate the sunset.

倒裝：**Toward the beach** **walked the young couple** to appreciate the sunset.

▶▶ 17.1.6 主詞補語移至句首的倒裝

當主詞補語移至句首時，則形成 **be** 動詞或 **be** 動詞之前的助動詞與主詞互換位置的倒裝。

例一：

原句：The audience who saw the incredible skills performed by the gymnasts **was deeply impressed**.

將主詞補語 **deeply impressed** 移至句首，形成 **be** 動詞與主詞互換位置的倒裝：

→ **Deeply impressed** **was** **the audience** who saw the incredible skills preformed by the gymnasts.

例二：

原句：The interviewees **must be nervous** when they are asked questions during the job interview.

將主詞補語 **nervous** 移至句首，形成 **be** 動詞之前的助動詞與主詞互換位置的倒裝：

→ **Nervous** **must** the interviewees **be** when they are asked questions during the job interview.

例三：

原句：**We are in the same position** when it comes to how children should be raised.

將主詞補語 in the same position 移至句首，形成 be 動詞與主詞互換位置的倒裝：

→ **In the same position** **are** **we** when it comes to how children should be raised.

▶▶ 17.1.7 小試身手

將下列句子改寫成倒裝句。

示範：

His wife was excited to hear that he had been promoted.

→ Excited was his wife to hear that he had been promoted.

1. Tourists will not be allowed to enter the National Park until the snow storm stops.

   _____

2. The job is so lucrative that many young people are applying for it.

   _____

3. The lifeguard jumped into the pool to rescue the drowning girl.

   _____

4. The landlord will rent the apartment to you only if your monthly income exceeds US$3,000.

   _____

5. The audience was emotional when the sad movie ended.

_____

6. She will marry him only after he buys a house.

_____

7. *The Old Man and the Sea* is such a popular novel that many people have read it.

_____

8. The dog will fully recover from the injury only if it is properly treated by a veterinarian.

_____

_____

9. When the judge sentenced the murder suspect to life in prison, the prosecutor was calm and relieved.

_____

_____

10. He can drive the car only after he gets the driver's license.

_____

17.2 出於文法上的要求

由 **neither, nor, so, as, than, such** 開頭的獨立子句必須以疑問句的形式呈現倒裝。

例一：

原句：My wife doesn't like cold weather, and I **don't like it either**.

倒裝 → My wife doesn't like cold weather, and $\boxed{\text{neither}}$ do I.

例二：

原句：Susan is a big fan of football, and **I am, too**.

倒裝：Susan is a big fan of football, and $\boxed{\text{so}}$ **am** I.

例三：

原句：Jack does not like Chinese food, and **he does not like** Indian food, either.

倒裝：Jack does not like Chinese food, $\boxed{\text{nor}}$ **does he like** Indian food.

17.3 出於句型的變化

　　假設語氣中 **if** 子句的 **be** 動詞或助動詞與主詞交換位置，移至句首，則 **if** 必須省略，結果子句／主要子句維持不變。（屬於非強調性質的倒裝）

例如：

If he **were** the president, he would focus more on economic development of the nation.

倒裝 → **Were** he the president, he would focus more on economic development of the nation.

If she **had** majored in another field, her career would have been different.

倒裝 → **Had** she majored in another field, her career would have been different.

17.4 倒裝句打通關

中翻英：使用倒裝句翻譯下列句子

1. 我不但喜歡吃日本料理，我也去日本觀光過好幾次。

_____

_____

2. _Secret Daughter_ 是一本很精彩的小說因此每一個英文系學生都應該讀它。

_____

_____

3. 他讀高中的時候很少從圖書館借書。

_____

4. 昨天晚上他們才剛唱完生日快樂歌，她父母就回到家了。（no sooner… ）

_____

_____

5. 唯有在看完學生的簡報之後老師才作出評論。

_____

6. 這個測驗非常困難以致學生至少要花一年準備。

_____

7. 我們在臺北從來沒吃過如此美味又便宜的牛肉麵。

_____

8. 這些年輕的業務代表有強烈的動機因為他們得到公司承諾他們會拿到高額的佣金。

_____

9. 這個高中生組成的團隊怎麼樣也不可能贏得程式設計比賽首獎。
(in no way)

_____

_____

10. 直到她 15 歲她才被父母告知她是被領養的。

_____

11. 我們不但應該參與國際性的活動，並且應該展現我們自己的文化特色。（94 年指考）

_____

_____

12. 這個職業籃球選手唯有通過身體檢查才能跟球隊簽約。

_____

_____

13. 無論在什麼情況下他都不會考慮搬去大城市因為他的朋友都住在他的家鄉。

_____

_____

14. 由於受憂鬱症所苦這位電視明星再也不會演戲了。

_____

15. 希望以低價買到新鮮的魚，廚師每天凌晨三點開車<u>去魚市場</u>。
(to the fish market)

_____

_____

16. 乘客們一離開發生車禍的遊覽車，遊覽車就燒起來了。

_____

習題解答 |

▶▶ 1.4.4 小試身手

1. After a day's hard work, the farmer felt exhausted.

2. These dishes taste so good.

3. Junk food is not good for health.

4. They don't seem very happy.

5. Some of the guests did not leave until midnight.

6. She stayed calm during the test (or exam).

7. The deer disappeared in the woods.

8. He has become an outstanding photographer.

9. Hamburgers have always been my favorite meal in the summer.

10. Countries in Southeast Asia is prospering because of foreign investments.

▶▶ 1.4.7 小試身手

1. Twenty years ago, he established the company.

2. The revenue of the company reached five hundred million dollars for the first time last year.

3. The employer appreciates all of the employees for their efforts this past year.

4. She has made / earned over three hundred thousand dollars from the stock market this year.

5. The professor is conducting a study on online shopping.

▶▶ 1.4.10 小試身手

1. Playing sports / Doing exercises makes people happy.

2. She named her cat Tiger.

3. The law firm offers her a job.

4. Have you sent the check to them?

   Have you sent them the check?

5. The difference between them makes communication difficult.

6. Everyone considers him the most creative leader.

7. She handed the receipt to the customer.

   She handed the customer the receipt.

8. The company gave me a round-trip ticket to Spain.

9. They appointed her the new CEO.

10. The accident cost him NT$50,000.

▶ 1.5 英文句子的構成打通關

1. The English teacher from Australia bought his girlfriend a new watch .
   授與動詞 + 間接受詞 + 直接受詞 (Vt. + O2 + O1)

2. To buy merchandise from online stores is more convenient and less time-consuming .
   不完全不及物動詞 + 主詞補語 (Vi. + S.C.)

3. Playing video games too much may harm one's eyes .
   完全及物動詞 + 受詞 (Vt. + O.)

4. A man with a cellphone in his hand carelessly walked into a fountain.
   完全不及物動詞 (Vi.)

5. Watching the funny skit made the kids sitting in front of the stage laugh wildly .
   不不完全及物動詞 + 受詞 + 受詞補語 (Vt. + O. + O.C.)

6. A lion escaping from the zoo looked hungry and angry .
   不完全不及物動詞 + 主詞補語 (Vi. + SC.)

7. Dora sent her friend in Paris a birthday present purchased in Italy .
   授與動詞 + 間接受詞 + 直接受詞 (Vt. + O2 + O1)

8. Not getting sufficient exercise seems common among young people .
   不完全不及物動詞 + 主詞補語 (Vi. + S.C.)

9. To win the championship takes a lot of painful training and endeavors.
完全及物動詞 + 受詞 (Vt. + O.)

10. Getting injured without health insurance can cost one a fortune .
不完全及物動詞 + 受詞 + 受詞補語 (Vt. + O. + O.C.)

11. People singing in the karaoke consider themselves the happiest in the world .
不完全及物動詞 + 受詞 + 受詞補語 (Vt. + O. + O.C.)

12. College students rarely borrow books from the library .
完全及物動詞 + 受詞 (Vt. + O.)

13. The woman in a purple dress hesitated in front of the ATM .
完全不及物動詞 (Vi.)

14. The jewelry displayed in the window seems expensive .
不完全不及物動詞 + 主詞補語 (Vi. + S.C.)

15. The bridge connecting the two cities suddenly collapsed last week
完全不及物動詞 (Vi.)

第二章

▶▶ **2.11 英文單字的種類與功能打通關**

1. (1) 不完全不及物動詞 (2) 形容詞 / 主詞補語 (3) 現在分詞 / 修飾 mother

2. (1) 副詞 / 修飾 seemed (2) 不完全不及物動詞 (3) 形容詞 / 主詞補語

3. (1) 助動詞 / 表達現在完成式 (2) 副詞 / 修飾 advanced (3) 形容詞 / 修飾 decade

4. (1) 名詞 / 句子主詞 (2) 形容詞 / 修飾 performances

5. (1) 疑問副詞 (2) 副詞 / 修飾 go (3) 完全不及物動詞

6. (1) 助動詞 / 表達過去式 (2) 主格代名詞 / 主詞 (3) 連接詞 / 連接前後兩個名詞

7. (1) 完全及物動詞 (2) 不定詞 / 動詞的受詞

8. (1) 助動詞 / 表達應該 (2) 完全不及物動詞 (3) 副詞 / 修飾 stay

9. (1) 疑問副詞 (2) 完全不及物動詞

10. (1) 動名詞 / 句子主詞 (2) 副詞 / 修飾 relaxing (3) 現在分詞 / 主詞補語

11. (1) 形容詞 / 修飾 girl (2) 完全不及物動詞 (3) 副詞 / 修飾 runs

12. (1) 完全及物動詞 (2) 名詞 / 動詞的受詞 (3) 動名詞 / 介系詞 of 的受詞

13. (1) 疑問代名詞 (2) 授與動詞 (3) 受格代名詞 / 介系詞 for 的受詞

14. (1) 完全及物動詞 (2) 形容詞 / 修飾 rent (3) 名詞 / 介系詞 for 的受詞

15. (1) 助動詞 / 表達現在完成式 (2) 完全不及物動詞 (3) 形容詞 / 修飾 hours

16. (1) 疑問代名詞 / 句子主詞 (2) 助動詞 / 表達過去式 (3) 名詞所有格 / 修飾 branch

17. (1) 助動詞 / 表達能力 (2) 介系詞 (3) 副詞 / 修飾 come

18. (1) 不完全不及物動詞 (2) 形容詞 / 主詞補語

19. (1) 疑問副詞 (2) 連接詞 / 連接前後兩個名詞

20. (1) 過去分詞 / 修飾 car (2) 不完全及物動詞 (3) 形容詞 / 修飾 US$2,000

21. (1) 名詞 / 句子主詞 (2) 副詞 / 修飾 won (3) 完全及物動詞

22. (1) 疑問副詞 (2) 副詞 / 修飾 many (3) 形容詞 / 主詞補語

23. (1) 助動詞 / 表達可能 (2) 不定詞 / 修飾 lawyer

24. (1) 副詞 / 修飾 much (2) 形容詞 / 修飾 sugar (3) 完全及物動詞

25. (1) 動名詞 / 介系詞 of 的受詞 (2) 不完全不及物動詞 (3) 副詞 / 修飾 expensive

26. (1) 授與動詞 (2) 現在分詞 / 修飾 job (3) 過去分詞 / 修飾 store

27. (1) 過去分詞 / 修飾 store (2) 完全及物動詞 (3) 所有格代名詞 / 修飾 services

28. (1) 主格代名詞 / 句子主詞 (2) 動名詞 / 介系詞 in 的受詞 (3) 助動詞 / 表達可能

29. (1) 現在分詞／修飾 man (2) 不完全不及物動詞
30. (1) 形容詞／修飾 patients (2) 名詞／need 的受詞 (3) 不定詞／修飾 care

第三章

▶▶ **3.4 小試身手**

1. 現在分詞　　　　　　　　　2. 動詞進行式
3. 動名詞　　　　　　　　　　4. 現在分詞
5. 動名詞　　　　　　　　　　6. 現在分詞
7. 動名詞　　　　　　　　　　8. 現在分詞
9. 動名詞　　　　　　　　　　10. 動名詞
11. 現在分詞　　　　　　　　　12. (1) 動詞進行式 (2) 動名詞
13. (1) 動詞進行式 (2) 動名詞　　14. (1) 現在分詞 (2) 動名詞
15. (1) 動名詞 (2) 動詞進行式

▶▶ **3.7 小試身手**

1. a redefined program 重新定義的計畫
2. the surrounding area 周遭區域
3. recalled vehicles 召回的車輛
4. blinding light 刺眼的光線
5. the promised land 應許之地
6. uplifting news 振奮人心的新聞
7. encouraging words 鼓勵人的言詞
8. a destroyed city 遭毀滅的城市
9. convincing evidence 令人信服的證據
10. uploaded files 已上傳的檔案

11. an unsolved case 未破的案子

12. a suspended driver's license 吊銷的駕照

13. refreshing activities 恢復精神的活動

14. unexplored issues 尚未探討的議題

15. hidden treasure 隱藏的寶物

16. overwhelming pressure 招架不住的壓力

17. a certified accountant 有執照的會計師

18. organized crimes 黑道集團犯罪

19. amazing grace 奇異恩典

20. a delayed flight 延遲的班機

21. sharpened skills 熟練的技術

22. a calculated plan 精心策劃的計畫

23. classified files 機密文件

24. fallen leaves 落葉

25. an amusing story 有趣的故事

26. an activated software 已啟動的軟體

27. an unnoticed event 未受注意的事件

28. a pleasing personality 討人喜歡的個性

29. civilized people 文明人

30. a deteriorating condition 惡化中的狀態

31. upgraded equipment 升級的配備

32. a misleading argument 誤導的論證

33. qualified applicants 符合資格的應徵者

34. unexpected guests 不請自來的客人

35. an overhauled engine 大修過的引擎

36. an undefeated team 零敗的球隊

37. the unfolded truth 揭露的真相

38. accumulated rainfall 累積雨量

39. an inviting dessert 誘人的甜點

40. <u>deafening</u> music 震耳欲聾的音樂

41. <u>stolen</u> items 失竊物品

42. an <u>appealing</u> résumé 引人注目的履歷

43. a <u>proven</u> theory 經過證實的理論

44. <u>integrated</u> marketing 整合的行銷

45. a <u>tempting</u> offer 誘人的出價

46. an <u>enlarged</u> picture 放大的圖片

47. a <u>worried</u> mother 憂心的母親

48. <u>enhanced</u> security 加強的保全

49. <u>deceiving</u> looks 會令人受騙的外觀

50. <u>endangered</u> species 瀕臨危險的物種

▶▶ 3.8 動狀詞打通關

1. The store is selling bicycles to students at a <u>reduced</u> price.

2. At the age of 62, Grace is now attending a ballroom <u>dancing</u> class every Wednesday.

3. The kids are looking forward to the <u>coming</u> of the Christmas.

4. Many companies are testing self-<u>driving</u> vehicles.

5. The <u>traveling</u> time from Taipei to Los Angeles by plane is about 12 hours.

6. <u>Empowering</u> words are always helpful in <u>boosting</u> employees' morale.

7. As a <u>satisfied</u> customer, she sent a card to the company to show her appreciation.

8. The new rules <u>regulating</u> the use of cellphones on campus will take effect next month.

9. The businessman was betrayed by his most <u>trusted</u> friend.

10. As a <u>forgiving</u> mother, Sarah never hesitates <u>to help</u> her rebellious son.

11. The prosecutor submitted the <u>convincing</u> evidence to the jury and the judge.

12. She is lucky to be hired by a promising company.

13. The devastated parents mourned over the tragic loss of their baby.

14. His mission is to set the suppressed people free.

15. Homeschooling can be demanding for parents.

16. The inspiring speech sparked surprising reforms of the country.

17. Her colleagues consider Mary a hardworking but sometimes intimidating supervisor.

18. When she comes home from work, she likes to listen to comforting music.

19. She had her boring room repainted.

20. The fast growing population in the urban area is a threatening problem in housing.

21. To shoot / Shooting the basketball 300 times a day is exhausting.

22. The church can be a stabilizing force in a troubled society.

23. The little girl doesn't mind doing all the housework for her disabled mother.

24. The missing antique car was found abandoned in a parking lot.

25. We want to obtain the desired outcomes of the exciting experiment.

26. When her husband went down with illness, she got plenty help from the supporting group.

27. The more time people spent browsing the Web site, the more envious they felt.

28. After the boy went missing, the police searched the surrounding areas thoroughly, but he was nowhere to be found.

29. Dr. Newby, a well-trained physician from the United States, is committed to offering medical services to indigenous people in Taiwan.

30. It can be challenging to cheer up an irritated baby, but one mom has found the secret for brightening her daughter's mood: Katy Perry!

第四章

▶▶ 4.3 小試身手

1. (1) 介片 / 形片 修飾 scientists (2) 動片 作為述部

2. (1) 過分片 / 形片 修飾 the truck driver (2) 不片 作為 decided 的受詞

3. (1) 動名片 作為句子主詞 (2) 動名片 作為 to 的受詞

4. (1) 不片 作為句子主詞 (2) 名片 作為主詞補語

5. (1) 不片 作為 fail 的受詞 (2) 過分片 / 形片 修飾 promises

6. (1) 過分片 / 形片 修飾 the new law (2) 介片 / 形片 修飾 two days off

7. (1) 現分片 / 形片 修飾 the young musician (2) 動片 作為述部

8. (1) 現分片 / 形片 修飾 players (2) 名片 作為 trying 的受詞

9. (1) 動片 (2) 現分片 / 形片 修飾 candidates

10. (1) 過分片 / 形片 修飾 the car (2) 介片 / 形片 作為主詞補語

11. (1) 過分片 / 形片 修飾 the theory (2) 動片 作為述部

12. (1) 名片 作為主詞 (2) 名片 作為 pass 的受詞

13. (1) 過分片 / 形片 修飾 the amusement park (2) 名片 作為 attracting 的受詞

14. (1) 副片 修飾 excited (2) 不片 作為 excited 的補語

15. (1) 副片 修飾 renovated (2) 名片 作為 offers 的 (直接) 受詞

16. (1) 介片 / 形片 修飾 the next step (2) 現分片 / 形片 修飾 a job

17. (1) 過分片 / 形片 修飾 the canned food (2) 介片 / 副片 修飾 sold

18. (1) 介片 / 副片 修飾 gathered (2) 不片 / 副片 修飾 gathered (3) 過分片 / 形片 修飾 agenda

19. (1) 動名片 作為 avoid 的受詞 (2) 介片 / 副片 修飾 using (3) 不片 / 副片 修飾 to avoid

20. (1) 動名片 作為 before 的受詞 (2) 不片 受詞 her friend 的補語 (3) 副片 修飾 to feed

▶▶ 4.4 片語組合練習

1. The mobile app developed by the city government provides passengers via cellphones with an estimated arrival time to every stop of all city buses.

2. The farmers growing mangos in southern Taiwan made considerable profits this year due to suitable weather.

3. The mechanic is very efficient spending just half an hour identifying the defected part and replacing it with a new one.

4. Sushi, a common Japanese food popular among foreigners nowadays, is actually not difficult to make in your own kitchen with the right ingredients and tools.

5. In addition to the expertise in the field, to get a high-paying job requires creativity and communication skills.

6. As a working mother, she is very happy to receive a card with sweet words from her eight-year-old daughter on Mother's Day.

7. Tourists from all over the world are attracted to view the Grand Canyon from the Skywalk at Eagle Point, a glass bridge extending 70 feet out over the rim of the Canyon.

8. The apparel company producing garments for the youth has made bold changes in their fashion design to stay competitive in the market.

9. After going through a difficult time, she has finally overcome the grief and regained passion for life.

10. Products manufactured by workers at sweatshops make tremendously high profits for the company in the global market.

第五章

▶▶ **5.1.1 小試身手**

1. The owner of the land built several cabins for people to rent to stay for vacations.

2. Students taking the demanding course of Calculus spent many hours preparing for its final exam.

3. Tina, one of my best friends, texted me a message last night inviting me to her birthday party next Saturday.

4. People allergic to peanuts must avoid eating food containing such ingredient.

5. The powerful multi-national corporations have been influencing government's policies in many developing countries to expand their businesses in the global market.

6. The old lady running a restaurant selling traditional Taiwanese noodles to college students at low prices is actually losing money over the business every month.

7. Light pollution in populated modern cities is very serious with many different kinds of lights turned on during the night.

8. The bullet train connecting Tokyo and Osaka built by Japanese is the prototype of Taiwan High Speed Rail, officially launched in 2007.

9. David's boss assigned him a challenging job to lead a group composed of 30 computer specialists to implement an AI project.

10. After long-hour discussions in numerous meetings in the past few months, the two sides finally agreed to collaborate in developing the land near the capital of the country.

▶▶▶ 5.1.2 小試身手

1. The man living across the street works in a Japanese restaurant as a chef to support his family.

2. The excited young couple from Canada named their baby girl Angel before its birth.

3. Mrs./Miss./Ms. Hu, our English teacher, gave us an assignment to speak English with native-speakers during the weekend.
   （**提醒**：英文稱呼已婚未婚女老師為 **Mrs. XXX**，未婚女老師 **Miss XXX**，婚姻狀態不確定者為 **Ms. XXX**；稱呼男老師為 **Mr. XXX**；中文則通稱為**胡老師**。臺灣兒童英美語班的學童都被錯誤地教導，稱呼老師為 Teacher XXX，這是不正確且不禮貌的。）

4. Many factories in different industries are using technologies, including big data and Internet of Things, to effectively improve their production to stay competitive in the global market.

5. The birthday cake prepared by my mother last night for my 20-year-old sister looked pretty and delicious.

▶▶▶ 5.3 簡單句內部擴充挑戰題

1. The victim trapped in the collapsed building in the earthquake maintained / kept calm in the dark and tried to send out signals for help by knocking on the wall.

2. Dr. Richardson, a famous expert on child education, established the school developing children's potentials through various learning activities.

3. After attaining a master's degree in Hotel Management in Vancouver, she stayed there to work in a hotel as an assistant to the sales manager to start her career.

4. Seth, an aspiring young chef working at a French restaurant in Taipei, is planning to open a high-end / high-class restaurant in Shanghai with another chef one day.

5. Privatized twenty years ago, the once state-run brewery now produces one of the best beer in the world with annual sales of 700 million dollars.

6. To adapt to American culture, the cheer leader from Japan dancing for an NBA team deliberately dressed like Americans and tried her best to improve her English.

7. The newly built sports center, located across the biggest park of the city, provides city residents with three indoor basketball courts and a swimming pool for practicing or competitions at low prices.

第六章

▶▶ **6.1.1** 小試身手
1. (C) 2. (A) 3. (A) 4. (C) 5. (C) 6. (A) 7. (A) 8. (B) 9. (D) 10. (D)

▶▶ **6.1.2** 小試身手
1. Every citizen should abide by the law.
2. The police quickly responded to the emergency.
3. The car accident resulted from the bad weather.
4. The questionnaire exploring/investigating the best strategies for learning English consists of twenty questions.
5. The mother of the suspect interfered with the police investigation.
6. The majority of the residents in Penghu object to the establishment of casinos.
7. Jesus sympathized with the poor and the sick for their suffering.
8. The tenants of the apartment often complain about the increasing monthly rent.

9. Most college students are concentrating on preparing for the final exam near the end of the semester.

10. Companies or individuals should not dispose of toxic waste.

11. Exercising regularly and eating properly <u>can / may</u> insure against health problems.

12. Every member of the research team contributes to the outstanding achievements of the project.

13. Constantly reading English novels will naturally lead to significant improvement on one's English proficiency.

14. The conflict between parents and their children usually result from insufficient communication and different values.

15. The experienced <u>eye doctor / ophthalmologist</u> specializes in laser eye surgery.

▶ **6.2.1 小試身手**

1. <u>**as**</u>　　2. <u>**of**</u>　　3. <u>**with**</u>　　4. <u>**of**</u>　　5. <u>**of**</u>

▶ **6.2.2 小試身手**

1. Her mother, the CEO (Chief Executive Officer) of a construction company, always regards challenges as opportunities.

2. The story of an outstanding teacher reminds / reminded me of my English teacher in junior high school.

3. A new rule made last year prevents players from getting injured.

4. We should attribute the victory of the team to the coach.

5. The chemistry teacher divided the students of the class into groups of five to do experiments.

6. The tour guide leads / led the tourists to the museum famous for its collections of modern artworks.

7. The missionary nurse from Canada dedicated her life to people in Taiwan.

8. Will the new regulations deprive blue-collar workers of voluntarily working overtime?

▶▶ 6.3.1 小試身手

1. He got his hair cut before the interview.
2. We keep the air-conditioner running before going to bed.
3. The company has its employees wear formal clothing to work.
4. The invention of the refrigerator allows us to enjoy fresh and cold food any time.
5. Nowadays in some countries, poverty still forces children to work to earn money.
6. Her lawyer got her to sign the contract/agreement with the publishing company to sell her new novel.
7. My boss convinced me to take leaves for a whole week.
   My boss convinced me to take a whole week off.
8. She had her new car washed yesterday for the coming of Lunar New Year.
9. His success story motivated many underprivileged students to work harder.
10. The football/soccer coach makes/made the players trained in the rain to prepare for the games of the next season.
11. The realtor persuaded the retired engineer to buy a house with a swimming pool.
12. The professor got his proposal approved by the Ministry of Education.
13. His innovative idea got him promoted.
14. The failure of the experiment caused the researchers to try new methods.
15. The DNA evidence enabled the judge to convict the accused/defendant.

16. The low/cheap ticket fare lets more young people attend the concert.

17. The police had the crime scene thoroughly searched.

18. The zoo keeper lets the lions be released from the cage every morning.

19. The doctor had the patient checked with X-rays.

20. His fitness trainer makes him do 50 push-ups and 50 sit-ups every day.

▶▶ 6.4.1 小試身手

1. After smoking for 30 years, he has finally quit smoking.

2. She denied accepting a job offer to work in Shanghai.

3. She regrets / regretted not going abroad to study for a master's degree.

4. Most (of the) employees do not mind working overtime.

5. Loyal patrons keep returning to the pastry shop for its delicious pies.

6. The illegal foreign workers cannot stand / bear being exploited by their employers anymore.

7. They are risking losing money to develop new products.

8. She cannot stop missing her daughter working in Japan.

9. The corrupt mayor admitted taking bribes from the construction company.

10. The owner of the pet shop is considering opening a new shop to meet the demand.

11. The earthquake survivor appreciated being rescued from the collapsed building.

12. The successful entrepreneur mentioned being fearless despite the severe challenges.

13. The ambitious student fancies himself / herself being a CEO of a

multi-national corporation.

14. The professional cyclist practices riding the bicycle 100 kilometers a day.

15. The celebrity dislikes being in a hostile environment.

▶▶ 6.5.3 小試身手

1. The security guard urged the residents to leave the building immediately because of the fire alarm.

2. The school teachers threatened to go on strike.

3. His parents persuaded him to take over their family business.

4. The professor warns her students not to cheat in the test / exam.

5. The tough boy refused to give up during the tug of war.

6. He proposed to hire a Spanish teacher to train our staff.

7. His college classmate running a furniture factory in Vietnam invited him to have a sightseeing tour there.

8. They forbid their children to go to the Internet cafe.

9. The doctor instructed the taxi driver over the phone to help the pregnant woman deliver the baby in the car.

10. Has your husband promised to take you to the Caribbean to celebrate your twentieth anniversary?

▶▶ 6.6.4 小試身手

1. James has not seen his best friend in high school for over 35 years. Yesterday they finally got together. They must have a lot to **catch up**.

2. The authorities have to **call off** the football game due to security concern. They will reschedule the game to next week.

3. She drove her car to the gas station just in time before it **ran out of** gas.

4. The president of the car company vowed to **roll out** a completely

new model next year to attract younger buyers.

5. Interestingly, the son looks just like the mother while the daughter **takes after** the father.

6. Before Lunar New Year, people in Taiwan **get rid of** old clothes and buy new ones for good luck.

7. After viewing the footage of the surveillance camera, the detective immediately **figured out** the identity of the intruder.

8. The professor asked his students not to **let** her **down** in the final exam. After all, she has taught them everything they needed to know.

9. The university offered Cindy a scholarship, but she **turned** it **down** because she didn't like the cold weather there.

10. The air pollution was so bad that they could not **put up with** it anymore. They decided to move to another city for health sake.

11. They **went over** the wedding procedure in the church yesterday before the wedding day to make sure it would be perfect.

12. The school will have to **cut down on** their annual budget as the number of students is decreasing.

13. The coach asked his assistant to **take over** his job training the players for a few days because he was sick.

14. The police officer eventually **talked** the suspect's mother **into** giving her son's whereabouts by promising not to harm him.

15. The boss didn't like my monthly report. I had to **do** it **over**.

16. People need to **fill out** the forms online to apply for a job nowadays.

17. They had to **put off** the meeting until next week because of the approaching typhoon.

18. Our neighbor downstairs was playing music too loud. I went to knock on his door and asked him to **turn down** the volume.

19. The cyclist is going so fast that no one could **keep up with** him. He certainly will be the winner of the game.

20. This is a good program, and we need to hire some experts to **carry** it **out**.

▶▶ 6.7 動詞句型打通關

1. The new President did not appoint her the ambassador to Germany.

2. She translated the English document / file into Japanese.

3. Did / Does the company regard the promotion as very successful?
   Did / Does the company consider the promotion very successful?

4. The NGO is recruiting volunteers to take care of the elderly.

5. The professor specializes in analyzing consumer behavior.

6. To find a better job, he is considering learning Spanish.

7. She mistook the car of the same model for her husband's.

8. The seat belt protects the driver and the passengers from serious injuries.

9. The opposing party accuses / accused the president of abusing his power.

10. The old vacuum cleaner broke down.

11. He prefers drinking black coffee in the morning.

12. The teacher asked / asks the students to avoid making the same mistakes.
    The teacher asked / asks the students not to make the same mistakes.

13. Several satellite factories supply / provide the car manufacturer with different parts.

14. The committee consists of eleven members.

15. The transfer student from Taipei gets along with his / her classmates.

16. I got tired after studying English for an hour.

17. Scientists associate the phenomenon with climate change.

18. He always stands by his teammates.

19. His lack of patience resulted in the failure of his plan.

20. The job offers him a good opportunity to apply his expertise.

21. Deforestation deprives wild animals of their habitats.

22. The online search engine allows us to quickly acquire / get different kinds of information.

23. The wrong decision cost the company a huge loss.

24. The library is giving away old magazines.

25. They attribute the success to his creative strategy.

26. Will the school's new measures prevent students from missing the class?

27. During the war, the mother entrusted her sick baby to the nurse next door.

28. After the earthquake, the government provides victims with shelters, food, and medical care.

29. The labeling of our products conforms to the government's regulations.

30. They are looking forward to watching an intense game between the two basketball teams.

31. She filled up the gas tank before driving to Hualian.

32. My boss instructed me to deliver the flowers to the customer before noon.

33. His misconduct got him fired by the company.

34. The university decided to incorporate the two departments into a new one.

35. The job content involves taking phone calls in the office and visiting potential customers.

第七章

▶▶ **7.2.2** 小試身手

1. The suspect **has been identified** by the eyewitness.

2. **Has** mercy killing **been legalized** in Taiwan?

3. The contract **has to be signed** by the end of the month.

4. The program **is sponsored** by our company.

5. **Has** the baseball game **been delayed** due to the rain?

6. **Is** the accounting system **being computerized**?

7. Last night, eight dancers **were chosen / selected / picked** to perform in the ceremony.

8. The patient **was diagnosed** with dementia last week.

9. Her application **had been approved** before she made the call to inquire.

10. How many projects **were proposed** by the Task Force?

11. Millions of refugees **have been accepted** by several countries in Europe.

12. Christmas presents **are being prepared** by everyone before the Christmas Eve.

13. Many different vegetables **are grown** in this organic farm.

14. More doctors and nurses **have been sent** to the towns hardest hit by the strong earthquake.

▶▶ **7.2.4** 小試身手

1. Many kinds of free services **are offered** by Google.

2. The lady **sent** an instant message to her boss.

3. The new marketing strategies **have been announced** by the company.

4. The game **will be postponed** if it rains tomorrow night.

5. The injured passengers of the crashed bus **are** now **being treated** in the Emergency Room by doctors and nurses.

6. Many grammatical errors in her paper **were corrected** by the professor.

7. What he has done for the people in this city **will** always **be remembered** by them.

8. Europeans **had not discovered** America until Christopher Columbus first reached the New World in 1492.

9. The government **has assigned** five scientists to carry out the research.

10. The committee members **are** now hotly **debating** the proposed budget before voting.

▶▶ **7.3.1 小試身手**

1. People should not **be exposed to** the sunlight too much in the summer.

2. Parents **are annoyed with** the government's new tuition policy.

3. College graduates majoring in English **are qualified for** this position.

4. Professor Chen **is devoted to** developing new computer technologies.

5. The father **is concerned about** his son's academic progress as he has been working part-time since entering the college.

6. The largest shopping mall in the nation **is located in** our city.

7. Mr. and Mrs. Johnson **are** now **accustomed to** the loud noise produced by the airplanes.

8. The auditorium **was crowded with** students as a concert was going on in there.

9. The committee **is composed of** seven members.

10. The children **are worried about** the lost dog.

11. **Are** you **done with** your home assignment?

12. Tina **was dressed in** her finest clothes when she attended the party last night.

13. Research has revealed that learners' reading ability **is related to** their vocabulary size.

14. Timothy **is excited about** the field trip.

15. The table **is covered with** all kinds of delicious foods.

16. On her birthday Julia received a box that **was filled with** presents.

17. After many days' work, the team **was** finally **finished with** the experiment.

18. Weeks after the disastrous earthquake, people **are / were** still **frightened of** the aftershocks.

19. Jessica **was involved with** several student clubs when she was in college.

20. The main dishes served in this restaurant **are limited to** beef and chicken.

21. In Taiwan most computers **are connected to** the Internet.

22. Everyone except the manager **is opposed to** the new business model.

23. She **is married to** a movie star.

24. The car **is equipped with** a sunroof and the cruise control.

25. The teacher **is / was** very **pleased with** the outcome of the test.

26. Investors **are satisfied with** the company's profit gained last year.

27. The group **is committed to** environmental protection.

28. She likes to wear pants that **are made of** natural fabrics such as cotton or wool.

29. Kending **is known for** its beautiful sand beaches.

30. The fans **were disappointed at** the game results because their favorite team had been defeated.

7.4.1 小試身手

1. **Being nominated** the best female singer of the annual singing award makes her proud.
2. No one likes **to be bullied** by the peers.
3. Products **to be examined** are placed here.
4. Hard-working employees enjoy **being rewarded** for their contributions.
5. **To be promoted** after working for just six months is a recognition of his talent and performance.

   Having been promoted after working for just six months is a recognition of his talent and performance.
6. The producer of TV program is disappointed at **being criticized** by the audience.
7. **Being called weak** annoys the professional football player.
8. Students went excitedly crazy to **have been informed** to leave school earlier due to the fast approaching typhoon.
9. **Having been admitted** to Harvard University, Patrick immediately called his parents and high school teacher about the wonderful news.
10. The proposal **to be modified** will be discussed in the meeting this afternoon.

7.5 被動語態打通關

1. **What will be served** on the table tonight?
2. No one likes **to be betrayed** by their **trusted** friends.
3. **Being defeated** in a game is **disappointing**.
4. Tourists **are warned not to feed** the wild animals.
5. The kids really enjoyed **being treated** to the amusement park.
6. **Being praised** by the teacher encourages students **to learn**.
7. Shoes **made / manufactured** in Taiwan **are sold** in many countries.
8. The artworks **created by modern artists** will **be exhibited** next

week.

9. A team of five scientists **from** different **fields has been assigned** to **carry out** the preservation project.

10. Many department stores across the United States **are being shut down** due to fast **declining** profits.

▶▶ 7.6 被動語態挑戰題

1. The new marketing strategy was announced by the CEO in the meeting last Friday and will be implemented next season.

2. Passengers injured in the accident are being treated by doctors in the Emergency Room.

3. Vegetables must be washed to be cooked / before being cooked.

4. The sales representative with the best performance by the end of the year will be promoted to be the manager.

5. The song before the game last night was sung by a famous singer invited by the owner of the home team.

6. Ms. Zhang, the best of the applicants, will be hired by the company.

7. The mayor serving the city for eight years will always be remembered by the citizens.

8. Hunting animals protected by the authorities may / can be severely punished.

9. The library designed by a famous architect has been certified as a green building.

10. All the foods processed in the factories must be inspected by the government to be sold / before being sold in the market.

第八章

▶▶ 8.2.4 小試身手

1. Her bike was stolen, **so** she had to walk home from the park.

2. The budget was not approved, **yet** they would not drop the proposed project.

3. He did not invest in the stock market, **nor** did he invest in the real estate.

4. She is on a diet, **yet** she really wants to eat ice cream.

5. They recycle almost everything, **for** doing so can help protect the environment.

6. She loves sports, **and** she plays badminton every week.

7. The earthquake destroyed their house, **but / yet** they did not give up on themselves.

8. The employees can choose to work from 9:00 to 18:00, **or** they can choose to work from 8:00 to 17:00.

9. The workers were hoping for a pay raise, **but** the results of the ne-gotiation between the factory owner and the union were disappoint-ing.

10. We are moving to Taipei, **for** my father has found a new job there.

11. The research team has not found any evidence to support the theo-ry, **yet** the researchers insist on their theory.

12. The citizens are fleeing their country, **for** a civil war has broken out between the government and the rebels.

13. The new smartphones have been sold out, **so / and** they have to or-der more.

14. She likes drinking coffee every morning, **and** she prefers it black.

15. Children have never been very good at listening to their elders, **but**

they have never failed to imitate them. (*James A. Baldwin*)

▶▶ 8.2.5 合句中翻英

1. Technologies make our lives more comfortable, **yet** / **but** they are also used for committing crimes.

2. Humans have limited knowledge about the outer space, **but** / **yet** we have long been very interested in it.

3. Reading is <u>good</u> / <u>beneficial</u> for children, **so** teachers should encourage students to check out books from the library.

4. The birth rate of our country has dropped rapidly in the past twenty years, **and** it may <u>lead to</u> / <u>result in</u> serious shortage of our human resources in the future.

5. Experts warns us not to take low food prices for granted, **for** global food crisis has caused serious social problems in many <u>parts</u> / <u>areas</u> of the world.

▶▶ 8.3.3 小試身手

1. She had found a better job, **so** she quit her current job.

2. The new immigrants are taking English language classes, **for** English is not their native language.

3. Several companies had made offers to buy the patent, **but** / **yet** the young inventor turned them down.

4. The basketball player had a severe cold, **yet** he played an incredible game by scoring 40 points.

5. They did not buy new furniture, **nor did** they buy a new refrigerator.

6. The tourists have packed their luggage, **so** / **and** they are ready to check out.

7. She likes to work out, **and** she spends two hours a day in the fitness center.

8. He is now driving an electric car, **for** it is good for the environment.

9. The old man wanted to withdraw money from his bank account at an ATM, **but** he forgot the password.

10. The university wanted to recruit elite students to its graduate programs, **so** it offers them full scholarships.

▶▶ 8.5.5 小試身手

（一）名詞子句作爲主詞

1. **How**
2. **What**
3. **Why**
4. **How**
5. **What**
6. **That**
7. **How**
8. **Whether (or not)**

（二）名詞子句作爲受詞或補語

1. **when**
2. **whether**
3. **whether**
4. **which**
5. **whether**
6. **that**
7. **how**
8. **where**
9. **that**
10. **how**
11. **whether, what**
12. **that**
13. **whether**
14. **that**
15. **whether**

▶▶ 8.5.6 名詞子句打通關

1. The results of the study reveal **that lack of sleep may lead to serious illnesses**.

2. Julia was sad **that she lost her newly bought smartphone**.

3. The city government will decide **whether the project is feasible with the limited budget**.

4. We may not fully realize **what price parents are willing to pay for their children**.

5. **That globalization may result in / lead to a greater discrepancy between industrialized countries and developing countries** is now a hot topic.

6. Are you questioning **whether / if she will make / become a good leader in the army**?

7. **Whether a new international airport should be built** is a major issue for the new government.

8. **Whether the research project can achieve its goals / objectives** depends on the efforts and collabration of the research team.

9. Her greatest achievement is **that she earned / acquired a Ph.D. in Computer Science after many years' efforts / hard work.**

10. **Whether the surgery is necessary** is still in discussion.

11. **How the development of a new business district may affect / impact the environment** will be the focus of the hearing.

12. Were they surprised to hear **how expensive an old apartment's rent was in Taipei?**

13. They are looking into **whether changing diets can help cure cancer**.

14. After visiting the orphanage last week, they realized **how fortunate they were to have their own families** and **what they could do for the orphans**.

15. In the advanced writing class, **students will learn what a research paper is and how they should conduct research**.

▶▶ 8.5.7 名詞子句挑戰題

1. Will the weather condition decide when the construction of the new stadium will be completed / finished?

2. The government is considering whether / if mandatory labeling of genetically modified foods should be regulated by law.

3. What we learn from the textbooks is only / just a small part of human knowledge, but what we learn from the experiences of our lives is more precious.

4. How the plane crashed is still under investigation.

5. Whether we will allow the employees to work on flexible hours will be discussed and decided by voting in the meeting next week.

6. Graduating college students expressed that they appreciated the professors of the department very much for what they had taught them in the class in the past four years.

7. Is whether she needs to / has to work part-time during her postgraduate study her major concern?

8. Robots are really incredible / amazing that they are much more efficient than workers in assembling cars, so whether robots are going to / will replace human workers in other manufacturing industries is not hard to predict.

9. That becoming a professional pilot working for international airlines is very difficult does not stop him from pursuing his dream of flying airplanes.

10. The price and the quality will decide whether / if a new product will survive in a competitive market.

11. The researchers are concentrating on whether the new approach will lead to the desired / expected outcome / results.

12. That the ability to acquire human languages simply by being exposed to them is built in our brains is really amazing.

13. Knowing that smart home appliances will be hot items on the market, the company has invested a tremendous amount of money in developing such products.

14. Proving that the theory is correct requires conducting properly designed experiments.

15. Forecasting that the torrential rain will continue for a few more days, the Weather Bureau warns that residents by the riverside should watch out for flash floods.

1. The **candidate** running for Mayor **estimates** that the **election** will **cost** her at least NT$30,000,000.

2. The new **principal** of the high school **promised** the parents that under his **leadership** the school would **excel**.

3. The **nutritionist recommends / suggests** (**recommended / suggested**) that she **eat** less **deep fried** food.

4. The researchers **claim** that they have **found / identified** the **cause** of **dementia**.

5. An **expert** in food science **reveals** that certain foods will **boost** our **immune system**.

6. The coach of the basketball team **demanded** the players **report** to the basketball **court on time** to **practice**.

7. **Meteorologists warned** that **greenhouse effect** would **cause** the sea level to **rise** and inundate cities in **coastal** areas.

8. The psychiatrist **advised** the **patient** that he **take** the **prescribed** medications on a daily **basis**.

9. The **findings** of the study **indicate** that **exposing** to **electronic** devices may have a **negative** impact **on** children.

10. During the debate yesterday, the **opponent(s) argued** that **globalization benefited** multinational **corporations** more than the **individuals** in the **developing** countries.

▶▶ **8.5.10** 引述名詞子句挑戰題

1. Experts assert that Tesla's electric cars will soon seriously threaten the traditional automobile industry.

2. The driver was caught speeding, yet he argued that he was in a hurry taking his wife to the hospital.

3. After three days' search, the rescue team confirmed over the radio that they had found the missing hiker alive but weak.

4. The architect insists that all materials (used) for building the hotel conform to the government's regulations.

5. The factory workers are complaining that the poor working condition is leading to inefficiency.

   The factory workers are complaining that the poor working condition has led to inefficiency.

6. During the consultation, the professor advises / advised him that he continue to pursue a doctoral degree in the field of biochemistry.

7. The protesters demand / demanded that the government immediately release the political leader of the opposition party arrested last month.

8. The new evidence from the DNA test reveals that the suspect did not commit the crime.

9. After an impressive presentation, the advertisement agency convinced the soft drink manufacturer that it could produce for their new products the most creative advertising on TV and the Internet.

10. In the meeting yesterday, the financial analyst proposed that the company merge with its major competitor in the market, but she also reminded everyone that there were risks in the merging.

▶▶ 8.6.2 小試身手

1. B. When
2. A. as
3. A. once
4. C. if
5. A. While
6. D. since
7. C. Even if
8. C. While
9. A. Since
10. C. unless
11. D. like
12. B. until
13. B. Now that
14. C. until
15. B. Whereas
16. A. although
17. (1) D. When (2) A. in case
18. C. because
19. (1) D. so that (2) B. whenever

20. B. as soon as   21. D. While   22. C. when

23. A. because   24. D. If   25. C. Since

▶ 8.6.4 小試身手

1. Even though simple in its lyrics and melody, the song has become very popular.

2. When first introduced, the new model did not attract many buyers.

3. Although the only eyewitness, she refused to testify in the court.

4. After having obtained the certificate, he asked for a raise.

5. Unless proven guilty, a person is assumed innocent.

6. The car will be parked in the evidence garage after being impounded.

7. Before becoming a Christian, he had been leading a miserable life.

8. Don't hesitate to express your opinions if in a meeting with your colleagues.

9. She runs marathons several times a year though no longer young.

10. Before writing the bestselling novel, she had been a school teacher.

11. Tourists won't miss visiting the National Palace Museum when in Taipei.

12. Tom will be promoted after having been successfully trained in the program.

13. She would not easily give up when determined to do something.

14. Since quitting her job, she has managed to open an online store selling frozen dumplings.

15. While hiking, they found a wounded rabbit.

▶ 8.6.5 副詞子句挑戰題

1. Once a mosquito / mosquitoes bites / bite a patient with a certain infectious disease, it / they may pass the virus to other people.

2. Most students are not accustomed to solving problems by them-

selves as / since / in that / because they always expect teachers to provide them with standard answers.

3. If we just live for ourselves, we will not feel truly happy.

4. As long as we keep working hard, we will learn to speak a foreign language fluently.

5. Though / Even though the rule of prohibiting indoor smoking is objected by many smokers, it is indeed / actually good news for non-smokers.

6. The puppies will be euthanized unless they are adopted this week.
   Unless they are adopted this week, the puppies will be euthanized.

7. While the polar bears are hunting for food during the cold winter, the brown bears are hibernating to wait / waiting for the spring.

8. The factory workers will not stop striking until the employer agrees to raise their wages and improve the working environment.

9. Whether you are convinced or not, you must accept the results of the investigation.

10. Everyday thousands of Mexicans cross the border to enter the United States illegally so that they can live a better life there.

▶ 8.7.5 小試身手

1. **who / that** have participated in the community services

2. **which** they have participated **in**
   in which they have participated

3. **who / that** have agreed to the deal

4. **which** the two sides have agreed **to**
   to which the two sides have agreed

5. **where** the conference is taking place

6. **that / which** is chasing a scooter

7. **that / which** the dog is chasing

8. **for which** the family decided to move to Australia

why the family decided to move to Australia

9. **whose** assistant is taking online courses to develop more business skills

10. **which / that** the manager's assistant is taking to develop more business skills

11. **which / that** the manager's assistant is taking online courses to develop

12. **who / whom** the doctor saved by transplanting a man's kidney

13. **which / that** the government will give to innovative inventors

14. **where** Barry proposed to his girlfriend

15. **whom** the government will give grants to

    to whom the government will give grants

16. **who** speak English and Spanish

17. **which** the new nurse in the emergency room coped **with** professionally

    with which the new nurse in the emergency room cope professionally

18. **when / on which** people in Taiwan have barbecues everywhere

19. **which / that** applicants speak

20. **whose** hair is orange

▶▶ **8.7.8 小試身手**

1. James is the only one in our office **whose** mother tongue is not English.

2. Mary is the kindergarten teacher from **whom** the children hear funny stories.

3. She is the professor **who / whom** the Computer Science Department has just hired.

4. They can also send messages pointing out problems **that / which** need to be addressed, such as a streetlight **that / which** is not work-

ing.

5. She didn't tell her friends the reason **why** she broke up with her boyfriend.

6. His parents asked the teacher not feed any food **which** he is allergic to.

7. This is the laptop from **which** we retrieved the files **that / which** will serve as hard evidence.

8. It was a Sunday afternoon **when** we had a yard sale before we moved out of the old house.

9. A great leader is someone **who / that** can inspire people **who / that** follow him.

10. This is the restaurant **where** I met my wife for the first time.

11. He finally got to interview the author **whose** novel had sold more than two million copies.

12. Not everything **that / which** can be counted counts, and not every-thing **that / which** counts can be counted. – *Albert Einstein*

13. This is the miracle **that / which** happens every time to those **who / that** really love; the more they give, the more they possess. – *Rainer Maria Rilke*

▶▶ **8.7.9 小試身手**

一、將下列各題中劃底線的簡單句改成限定用法形容詞子句,再與另一 個簡單句結合成為複句。

1. The couple is looking to rent an apartment whose monthly rent is around NT$25,000.

2. Researchers are conducting a survey to find out the challenges that / which foreign students may face when studying abroad.

3. The NGO is recruiting young people who / that are willing to spend at least three years in poor countries helping children.

4. He is the programmer who / that developed the popular app for

smartphones.

5. The number of vehicles that / which run across the suspension bridge has exceeded 10 million a year.

6. As a daughter of a wealthy father, Sarah wants to marry to someone who / that has the same family background.

7. The airlines overbooked and offered cash as compensation for passengers who were willing to take the next flight.

8. The Department of Architecture is hiring a young scholar whose research focuses on green buildings.

9. The female applicant who / whom the manager interviewed last week will report to the research and development department.

10. She remembers that it was a rainy day when she bought her first computer.

二、中翻英

1. Scientists are looking for green energy that is safe, clean, and inexpensive to meet our needs of electricity.

2. Some of the packaged food (that / which) we think is safe may contain ingredients that / which are harmful to the human body.

3. Locations where these movies were filmed have also become hot spots for sightseeing.

4. The aim of the project is to send graduate students who / that have performed extraordinarily to one of the top 100 universities in the world to pursue a doctoral degree.

5. The newly established airline is recruiting young people whose aptitude and English language skills are suitable to be trained to become pilots.

▶▶ **8.7.11** 限定用法形容詞子句挑戰題

1. (1) We are considering buying the house because there is a park near the neighborhood.

(2) Our kids can play with their friends there.

(1)+(2) We are considering buying the house because there is a park near the neighborhood where our kids can play with their friends.

2. (1) To organize the event, we are looking for a hotel near an international airport with a spacious conference hall.

(2) The conference hall can accommodate 200 people and offers western meals.

(1)+(2) To organize the event, we are looking for a hotel near an international airport with a spacious conference hall that can accommodate 200 people and offers western meals.

3. (1) The church set up an after-school program for the under-achieving students.

(2) These under-achieving students have gradually improved their academic performance.

(1)+(2) These under-achieving students for whom the church set up an after-school program have gradually improved their academic performance.

4. (1) Our company donated two ambulances to the hospital.

(2) The hospital offers free medical care for underprivileged patients.

(1)+(2) The hospital to which our company donated two ambulances offers free medical care for underprivileged patients.

5. (1) The master's program is famous for its innovative and practical curriculum / courses.

(2) Many college graduates are applying to the master's program.

(1)+(2) The master's program to which many college graduates are applying is famous for its innovative and practical curriculum / courses.

6. (1) Yesterday I went to watch a game in a stadium.

(2) My favorite NBA team had won three championships in a row there.

(1)+(2) Yesterday I went to watch a game in a stadium where my favorite NBA team had won three championships in a row.

7. (1) The rescue team saved a tourist this afternoon.

(2) The tourist had been trapped under a huge rock for several hours.

(1)+(2) The tourist who / whom the rescue team saved this afternoon had been trapped under a huge rock for several hours.

8. (1) The rich woman is actually an undercover angel.

(2) Her company makes five million dollars a year.

(3) She wants to build several schools for children in remote villages in Africa.

(1)+(2)+(3) The rich woman whose company makes five million dollars a year is actually an undercover angel who wants to build several schools for children in remote villages in Africa.

9. (1) The famous master baker helps failing bakeries with his expertise.

(2) These failing bakeries have all successfully turned their businesses around.

(1)+(2) These failing bakeries that / which the famous master baker helps with his expertise have all successfully turned their businesses around.

10. (1) Making our company more competitive is crucial to our future business.

(2) This is the reason why our company is being reorganized / restructured.

(1)+(2) That making our company more competitive is crucial to our future business is the reason why our company is being reorganized / restructured.

▶▶ **8.7.16 小試身手**

1. **whose**	2. **which**	3. **who**
4. **which**	5. **which**	6. **where**
7. **whose**	8. **which**	9. **when**
10. **whom**	11. **which**	12. **who**

▶▶ **8.7.19 小試身手**

1. The young couple is looking for an apartment **whose** monthly rent is around NT$25,000.

2. Tina has read 20 books during the summer break, one of which is "*Kira, Kira,*" **which** is a novel written by a Japanese American author.

   Tina has read 20 books during the summer break, and one of **them** is "*Kira, Kira,*" **which** is a novel written by a Japanese American author.

3. Steven Curry, **who** shoots sharply from three-point range, has created many new records in the NBA.

4. The Taiwan High Speed Rail, **which** connects the major cities in the west coast of Taiwan, represents the new era of Taiwan's transportation system.

5. The hunters are trying to figure out the reason **why** the boar escaped from the trap.

6. Donald Trump, **who** is the President of the United States, holds a strong stance against illegal immigrants.

7. Kending National Park, **which** is the first national park in Taiwan, was established in 1982.

8. Brain **is** a successful businessman who is specialized in creative marketing, has just published a new book.

Brain, **who** is a successful businessman specialized in creative marketing, has just published a new book.

▶▶▶ 8.7.20 小試身手

1. Dr. Huang, who graduated from the University of Delaware, is now a renowned professor at a prestigious university in Taiwan.

2. She has read eight books during this semester, one of which is "*When You Reach Me,*" a novel about making sacrifices for friends.

3. A virtual reality headset, which allows people to experience a three dimensional, computer generated environment when playing games, can cost as much as $800.

4. A new shopping mall which / that the city council initiated the plan to build will be located in the outskirts of the city.

5. The Moon Festival, when / on which family members in Taiwan gather together for reunion, is celebrated on the fifteenth day of August on the lunar calendar.

6. The two-year study lead by Dr. White, of which the results will be released next year, is aimed at finding out the key factors contributing to the fast economic growth of the country in recent years.

7. The teacher invited the students who participated in community services during the winter break to a dinner party at her house.

8. The engine oil of my car, which has been running over 5,000 kilometers since its last maintenance, needs to be changed.

9. Nathan, to whose unique vision the amazing success of this corporation is attributed, is the new CEO of this multinational corporation operating in Taipei.

10. People in Taiwan like to shop at Costco, where a large variety of imported American foods are available.

8.7.21 小試身手

1. Jennifer's father, who migrated from Taiwan to California with his parents in the 1970s, is now a famous physician in Los Angeles.

2. Working for the high-tech company is an opportunity (that / which) he has been dreaming of.

3. With a master's degree in physical therapy, Tony is looking for a job that / which is closely related to his expertise.

4. A lady who was one of the people interviewed by the manager yesterday was a perfect match for the company.

5. In Taiwan, every class in a grade school has its own classroom where students take almost all of the courses.

6. Children who are exposed to an environment where two languages are spoken will acquire the two languages naturally.
   Children who are exposed to a bilingual environment will acquire the two languages naturally.

7. Online stores provide a very convenient way of shopping for consumers who do not go out often or who live in remote areas.

8. We will exchange presents that /which cost no less than NT$1,000 in the Christmas party this year.
   We will exchange presents whose prices are no less than NT$1,000 in the Christmas party this year.

9. To entice / attract foreign investors, the government must create a friendly environment that is safe, corruption-free, and low in taxation.

10. Killer whales, which are the largest predators in the world, work together to hunt for prey.

11. People / Those who speak two foreign languages have much better chances of finding high paying jobs than people / those who speak only one foreign language.

12. Master Lee, who has been working in the pop music industry for years, is the writer of several movie theme songs.

13. Parents who spend time with their children and often go on family vacations together develop better relationships with them.

14. Weiyin Chen, who used to play professional baseball in Japan, is now a starting pitcher in the Major League in the United States.

15. Sandra Bullock, a famous movie star who won the Academy Award for Best Actress in 2010, will be the director of the new film.

▶▶ **8.7.22** 形容詞子句挑戰題

1. (1) Climate change <u>results mainly from</u> / <u>is mainly due to</u> the consumption of fossil fuels.

(2) Farmers suffer from climate change the most.

(1)+(2) Climate change, from which farmers suffer the most, <u>results mainly from</u> / <u>is mainly due to</u> the consumption of fossil fuels.

2. (1) Paul is proficient in English and Spanish.

(2) He is the head of a department.

(3) The department is <u>responsible for</u> / <u>in charge of</u> developing overseas / international markets.

(1)+(2)+(3) Paul, who is proficient in English and Spanish, is the head of a department that / which is <u>responsible for</u> / <u>in charge of</u> developing overseas / international markets.

3. (1) Organic foods are produced <u>according to</u> / <u>following</u> the standards of organic farming.

(2) Organic foods are becoming / getting more and more popular among consumers.

(1)+(2) Organic foods, which are produced <u>according to</u> / <u>following</u> the standards of organic farming, are becoming / getting more and more popular among consumers.

4. (1) The Universiade is a major international sports and cultural

event.

(2) The Universiade is hosted by different cities every two years.

(1)+(2) The Universiade, which is a major international sports and cultural event, is hosted by a different city every two years.

5. (1) Under a fast-changing global economic system, a company needs to constantly organize workshops and on-site training programs for its employees to upgrade their professional knowledge and skills.

(2) The company depends on / upon its employees' professional knowledge and skills to enhance / improve its productiveness and competitiveness.

(1)+(2) In a fast-changing global economic system, a company needs to organize workshops and on-site training programs for its employees to upgrade their professional knowledge and skills which the company depends on / upon to enhance / improve its productiveness and competitiveness.

6. (1) The multimillion-dollar medical research project is financed / sponsored / funded by a major pharmaceutical company.

(2) The research project is recruiting scholars and researchers.

(3) These scholars and researchers are specialized in the field of biotechnology.

(1)+(2)+(3) The multimillion-dollar medical research project, which is financed / sponsored / funded by a major pharmaceutical company, is recruiting scholars and researchers who / that are specialized in the field of biotechnology.

7. (1) After many years of construction, in 1914 the United States finally completed and opened the Panama Canal.

(2) It connected the Atlantic Ocean and the Pacific Ocean and greatly reduced the time.

(3) Ships spend time (in) traveling between the two Oceans.

(1)+(2) After many years of construction, in 1914 the United States finally completed and opened the Panama Canal, which connected the Atlantic Ocean and the Pacific Ocean and greatly reduced the time (that / which) ships spend (in) traveling between the two Oceans.

8. (1) Their grandmother was celebrating her eightieth birthday yesterday.

(2) They had secretly recorded a video clip / film to congratulate her.

(3) When she watched the video clip / film, she smiled very happily.

(1)+(2)+(3)

When their grandmother, who was celebrating her eightieth birthday yesterday, watched the video clip / film that / which they had secretly recorded to congratulate her, she smiled very happily.

9. (1) Dakeng attracts numerous hikers every day.

(2) A group of young chefs used to work at different restaurants.

(3) They have opened a new restaurant in Dakeng.

(4) Hikers can enjoy seafood at the restaurant.

(5) The seafood is delivered from Penghu by plane daily.

(1)+(2)+(3)+(4)+(5) In Dakeng, which attracts numerous hikers every day, a group of young chefs who used to work at different restaurants have opened a new restaurant where / in which hikers can enjoy seafood that / which is delivered from Penghu by plane daily.

▶▶ 8.8.1 複句小試身手

1. 句子結構：獨立子句（內含非限定形容詞子句與限定形容詞子句）

   獨立子句：Germs, + 非限定形容詞子句 are actually very small organism + 限定形容詞子句

   非限定形容詞子句：which scientists call microbes

   限定形容詞子句：that can be seen only under a microscope

2. 句子結構：獨立子句（內含限定形容詞子句）＋副詞子句

獨立子句：Even in areas ＋限定形容詞子句, deserts can form

限定形容詞子句：where winds blow from the sea onto land

副詞子句：if there is a mountain range between these lands and the sea

3. 句子結構：獨立子句（內含非限定形容詞子句、名詞子句）（名詞子句內含限定形容詞子句）

獨立子句：A very important feature of DNA, ＋非限定形容詞子句, is ＋名詞子句＋形容詞子句（名詞子句作為主詞補語）

非限定形容詞子句：which determines the complexity of the organism

名詞子句：that the instructions ＋限定形容詞子句＋can be duplicated and passed to offspring

限定形容詞子句：it contains（省略了關係代名詞 which）

4. 句子結構：獨立子句（內含三個名詞子句與副詞子句）

獨立子句：The key to understanding ＋名詞子句＋名詞子句＋may be in simply looking at ＋名詞子句＋副詞子句

名詞子句一：why reputable studies are…on the question of ＋名詞子句二

名詞子句二：what Facebook does to our emotional state

名詞子句三：what people actually do ＋副詞子句

副詞子句：when they're on Facebook

5. 句子結構：獨立子句（內含名詞子句）（名詞子句內含限定形容詞子句）＋副詞子句

獨立子句：One very…of reasoning is ＋名詞子句＋限定形容詞子句

名詞子句：that it enables animals…respond to difficulties ＋限定形容詞子句

限定形容詞子句：they encounter…environment（省略了關係代名詞 which）

副詞子句：even when those difficulties are new to them

6. 句子結構：副詞子句 + 副詞子句 + 獨立子句

副詞子句：if you did not have access to safe water, and...drinking water

副詞子句：so that you and your children would not get sick

獨立子句：would you worry about causing deforestation?

7. 句子結構：獨立子句（內含非限定形容詞子句與限定形容詞子句）

獨立子句：Everywhere Amelia Earhart, + 非限定形容詞子句 was greeted by people + 限定形容詞子句

非限定形容詞子句：who had accomplished...across the Atlantic in 1932

限定形容詞子句：who admired her and were...around the world in 1937

8. 句子結構：獨立子句 + 副詞子句（內含非限定形容詞子句與限定形容詞子句）

獨立子句：The two horses had just lain down

副詞子句：when a brood of ducklings, + 非限定形容詞子句, filed into the barn...some place + 限定形容詞子句

非限定形容詞子句：which had lost their mother

限定形容詞子句：where they would not be trodden on

9. 句子結構：獨立子句（內含名詞子句作為受詞，而名詞子句則內含副詞子句與限定形容詞子句）

獨立子句：consumers increasingly believe + 名詞子句 + 副詞子句 + 限定形容詞子句

名詞子句：that + 副詞子句 + 限定形容詞子句, the food system is likely to place profit ahead of public interest

副詞子句：because farms...and are using technology + 限定形容詞子句

限定形容詞子句：they don't recognize or understand（省略了關係代名詞 which）

10. 句子結構：獨立子句（內含限定形容詞子句）

獨立子句：globalization is defined as a process + 限定形容詞子句

限定形容詞子句：that, based on international...environmental developments

▶▶ 8.9.2 複合句小試身手

1. 句子結構：副詞子句 + 獨立子句（內含限定形容詞子句）+ 對等連接詞 and + 獨立子句

副詞子句：when ants are attacked by an intruder

獨立子句：they send a chemical message to each other + 限定形容詞子句

限定形容詞子句：that acts as an alarm

獨立子句：they rush toward the intruder to bite it and carry it away

2. 句子結構：獨立子句 + 對等連接詞 but + 獨立子句（內含限定形容詞子句一，而限定形容詞子句一又內含限定形容詞子句二）

獨立子句：the earth's general weather patterns…of the world's hot deserts

獨立子句：in addition, there are other things + 限定形容詞子句一

限定形容詞子句一：that keep…reaching the areas + 限定形容詞子句二

限定形容詞子句二：that have become deserts

3. 句子結構：獨立子句 + 對等連接詞 but + 獨立子句 + 副詞子句

獨立子句：Romeo looked around the room, hoping to catch sight of Rosaline

獨立子句：suddenly his eyes fell upon a girl so beautiful

副詞子句：that all thoughts of Rosaline flew from his brain forever

4. 句子結構：獨立子句 + 對等連接詞 but + 獨立子句（內含限定形容詞子句）

獨立子句：we want to learn about other people and have others learn about us

獨立子句：through that very learning...of ourselves + 限定形容詞子句

限定形容詞子句：that we need to continuously maintain

5. 句子結構：獨立子句（內含名詞子句，而名詞子句又內含副詞子句）+ 對等連接詞 and + 獨立子句

獨立子句：Lieberman and his colleagues demonstrated + 名詞子句

名詞子句：that a painful stimulus hurt less + 副詞子句

副詞子句：when a woman either held...or looked at his picture

獨立子句：the pain-dulling effects of...powerful as physical contact

6. 句子結構：獨立子句 + 對等連接詞 but + 獨立子句 + 副詞子句（內含非限定形容詞子句）

獨立子句：the Irish government is trying to revive activity with new tax breaks

獨立子句：any recovery will take years

副詞子句：when just under 8,500 house...in the 1970s + 非限定形容詞子句

非限定形容詞子句：when Ireland was a much poorer country

7. 句子結構：獨立子句（內含限定形容詞子句）+ 對等連接詞 and + 獨立子句（內含限定形容詞子句）+ 副詞子句

獨立子句：Only a handful of his 60 classmates + 限定形容詞子句 + found work at home

限定形容詞子句：who graduated five years ago

獨立子句：of the few others + 限定形容詞子句 , one owns a cake shop

限定形容詞子句：that remain

副詞子句：while another designs mobile phone apps

8. 句子結構：獨立子句 + 副詞子句 + 副詞子句 + 對等連接詞 and + 獨立子句 + 非限定形容詞子句

獨立子句：concussions occur

副詞子句：when the brain bounces against the skull

副詞子句：after someone's head is bumped or jolted

獨立子句：these injuries are fairly...contact sports, like football and hockey

非限定形容詞子句：which are popular in the United States

9. 句子結構：獨立子句（內含名詞子句一）＋ 對等連接詞 but ＋ 獨立子句（內含名詞子句二與名詞子句三）

獨立子句：Vincent Walsh, professor...College London, said ＋ 名詞子句

名詞子句一：people have become obsessed with sleeping only during the night

獨立子句：he claims ＋ 名詞子句二 and believes ＋ 名詞子句三

名詞子句二：that humans have only adopted long night time sleep patterns

名詞子句三：it may be damaging our ability to think creatively

10. 句子結構：獨立子句（內含限定形容詞子句）＋ 對等連接詞 so ＋ 獨立子句

獨立子句：in 2009, the United States had...holding jobs ＋ 限定形容詞子句

限定形容詞子句：that were either directly...or services sold to other countries

獨立子句：for the United States, exports...economic stability and prosperity.

▶▶ 8.10 子句打通關

1. 獨立子句：it may explain

從屬子句：1. while he acknowledged 副詞子句

　　　　　2. that the virus isn't 名詞子句

　　　　　3. why some people struggle 名詞子句

句子類型：複句

2. 獨立子句：I decided

　從屬子句：1. because I couldn't bring 副詞子句

　　　　　　2. while we were away 副詞子句

　句子類型：複句

3. 獨立子句：it symbolizes

　從屬子句：1. that occurred 限定形容詞子句

　　　　　　2. when I stopped…and started 副詞子句

　句子類型：複句

4. 獨立子句：the beautiful rice paddies…are

　從屬子句：that leaves 限定形容詞子句

　句子類型：複句

5. 獨立子句：1. the brick makers quietly await for

　　　　　　2. they can resume

　從屬子句：while traditional fishermen enjoy 副詞子句

　句子類型：複合句

6. 獨立子句：1. the French enjoy

　　　　　　2. their low rate of cardiovascular disease has long baffled

　從屬子句：None

　句子類型：合句

7. 獨立子句：1. emotions are often not openly expressed

　　　　　　2. it just feels

　從屬子句：1. while it's possible 副詞子句

　　　　　　2. I love 名詞子句

　句子類型：複合句

8. 獨立子句：traditional news organizations must adapt

　從屬子句：as emerging news entities try 副詞子句

　句子類型：複句

9. 獨立子句：this most certainly is

　從屬子句：1. whose media behavior today is 非限定形容詞子句

2. what the news industry must learn 名詞子句

　　句子類型：複句

10. 獨立子句：they also hint at

　　從屬子句：1. while the results are 副詞子句

　　　　　　　2. which were published 非限定形容詞子句

　　句子類型：複句

11. 獨立子句：winning the Skytrax Word's Best Airpoet⋯is

　　從屬子句：everyone of whom is 非限定形容詞子句

　　句子類型：複句

12. 獨立子句：1. more than eight months have passed

　　　　　　　2. it's not clear

　　從屬子句：1. since Britain voted 副詞子句

　　　　　　　2. whether millions of EU migrants...will be permitted
　　　　　　　　 名詞子句

　　句子類型：複合句

13. 獨立子句：America would come

　　從屬子句：on which trains would run 限定形容詞子句

　　句子類型：複句

14. 獨立子句：1. I have reported

　　　　　　　2. he is concerned

　　從屬子句：1. you presented 限定形容詞子句

　　　　　　　2. you proposed 限定形容詞子句

　　　　　　　3. since it is 副詞子句

　　句子類型：複合句

15. 獨立子句：1. I understand

　　　　　　　2. our past report indicates

　　從屬子句：1. that this five-year project emphasizes 名詞子句

　　　　　　　2. that investing so much⋯is 名詞子句

　　句子類型：複合句

▶▶ 8.11 子句挑戰題

1. The owner of the team was very disappointed that the team failed to win the championship, so he fired the coach and hired a new one who had won the championship twice before.

2. The video / film (which / that) she uploaded to YouTube that / which introduces delicacies in Taiwan has attracted millions of viewers, and she is planning to produce a video / film that introduces tourist hot spots / attractions in Taiwan.

3. The fully electric car Model 3, which has just been released by Tesla, is one of the most anticipated new cars of 2017, and the company expects to produce 5,000 Model 3 per week at the end of 2017.

4. Dr. Martin Lo, who was a full professor at the University of Maryland, quit his teaching job so that he could help farmers in developing countries with his expertise in agricultural production and food processing.

5. Many factories that / which moved from Taiwan to China years ago are now relocating to Vietnam or Indonesia, where the cost of labor and land is much cheaper, and the foreign governments welcome those factories because they will create new jobs for local people.

6. Wuqi Fishing Port, which is not far from downtown Taichung, has become a popular place for people who like seafood because it has a fish market that sells all kinds of fresh seafood at low prices.

7. Andrew Zimmern, who is the host of television series that introduce bizarre foods all over the world, has tasted many different kinds of bizarre foods, yet he thinks that durians are among the top three things that are hard to swallow.

8. Jade Mountain, which is the highest mountain in Taiwan with its peak at 3,925 meters above the sea level, is known for its breathtaking scenery along the hiking trail, and Michelle, who is an English

teacher at a junior high school, celebrated her 50th birthday by hiking to the top of Jade Mountain.

9. When I was playing basketball in the park last Sunday, I met Peter Lai, who had attended schools in Seattle for five years before returning to Taiwan with his parents last year, but he is still adjusting to the hot and humid weather in Taiwan, which is very different from that in Seattle.

10. Amazon, which was launched online by Jeff Bezos in 1995, when the era of e-commerce has just begun, has now become the biggest online retailer on Earth because it sells everything that includes books, music, software, tools, toys, sporting goods, clothing, electronics, computers, and even groceries at lowest prices, and how the company treats the customers with highly satisfying service has made it the top choice when people want to purchase online.

▶▶ 8.12.2 小試身手

1. The researchers are trying to figure out **why** the ancient city **was abandoned**.

2. **Where** our new office **will be located** will be decided in the meeting next month.

3. The players are wondering **whether** the rules **can be changed**.

4. The staff will discuss **how** the working environment **can be** further **improved**.

5. The mechanic was not sure **how soon** the car **could be fixed**.

6. **What is described** in the article is unbelievable.

7. The city council will vote to decide **which** measures **will be adopted / used** to solve the problem.

8. We are all wondering **who has been assigned** the difficult task.

9. **How well** the new stadium **will be built** depends on **how** devoted the architect and the workers **are**.

10. The new rules regulate **how** the performances of government employees **will be evaluated / assessed**.

11. A meeting **will be held** to discuss **how** the goal of the project **will be achieved**.

12. That working out regularly helps people maintain a good mood is **what is confirmed** in the paper.

13. Is it true **that** this book **is** highly **recommended** by our professor?

14. **How** the money **can be spent** is **what will be discussed** tomorrow.

15. The study revealed **when** and **why** the canal **was** initially **constructed / built**.

▶▶ 8.12.4 小試身手

1. The award-winning film **that / which is directed** by one of the greatest directors in the world is based on a best-selling novel.

2. Patients **who / that had been cured** by the medical team showed their appreciation by donating money.

3. Mrs. Lin, **who has been awarded** Teacher of the Year, will share her teaching experience with the faculty in the meeting.

4. Bicycles **that / which are made / manufactured** by the company **have been sold** in millions.

5. The flight **that / which was delayed** has been rescheduled to leave at 3:00 p.m.

▶▶ 8.13.3 小試身手

1. The man playing basketball over there is my brother.

2. Ms. Lin, founding the company 45 years ago, is going to retire next month.

3. Students good at sports are more likely to make friends with peers.

4. The Art Museum, known for its amazing art collections, is located in Taichung.

5. Sandy wants to make friends with students <u>speaking Spanish</u>.

6. The train <u>leaving for London</u> is on schedule.

7. The stadium <u>built for the tournament</u> will be completed in six months.

8. Mount Ali, <u>a hot tourist spot for viewing sunrise above the sea of clouds</u>, is famous for growing high-mountain tea.

9. Children <u>proud of themselves</u> are often more optimistic.

10. James Hudson Taylor, <u>a missionary from England</u>, set up numerous churches and schools during 51 years <u>working in China</u>.

11. Many dentists are now making false teeth with top-notch 3D printing, <u>having been developed at a fast pace</u> and <u>having influenced many industries in ways</u> unthinkable before.

12. All men are created equal, yet in reality those <u>born to parents in higher social status</u> may have more advantages in pursuing careers <u>chosen by themselves</u>.

13. A container ship, <u>carrying loaded 20-foot or 40-foot containers from one port to another</u>, is a major sea transportation <u>shipping cargos of assorted exporting goods</u> <u>manufactured domestically</u> to another country <u>having/with demand for them</u>.

14. The trade war between the United States and China, <u>once focusing on imposing higher tariffs on imports from both countries</u>, has been extended to 5G and AI, <u>(being) at present the most advanced information technologies</u> <u>having/with the highest potentials to control the world in every aspect in coming decades</u>.

15. Nuclear power plants, <u>having caused serious damages to nearby residents and the surrounding environment</u> when (they are) <u>sabotaged by natural disasters or human errors</u>, are gradually being replaced by other facilities <u>generating needed energy with different methods</u> much safer but less cost-effective.

1. (1) A store that / which sells high-end electronic products will be opening next Saturday in the department store that is invested by Japanese.

   (2) A store selling high-end electronic products will be opening next Saturday in a department store invested by Japanese.

2. (1) Newark, which is located in the East Coast of the United States, is going to have a parade to welcome the basketball team of the University of Delaware, who has won their first championship in thirty years.

   (2) Newark, located in the East Coast of the United States, is going to have a parade to welcome the basketball team of the University of Delaware, having won their first championship in thirty years.

3. (1) Students who are eligible / qualified for scholarships must file applications online before the deadline.

   (2) Students eligible / qualified for scholarships must file applications online before the deadline.

4. (1) David Chen, who is the sales manager, signed a big contract that / which is worth fifty million dollars with a multinational corporation that / which produces / manufactures home appliances.

   (2) David Chen, the sales manager, signed a big contract worth fifty million dollars with a multinational corporation producing / manufacturing home appliances.

5. (1) Dozens of experts and scholars who are invited from different countries will participate in the symposium / forum that / which explores sustainable energy.

   (2) Dozens of experts and scholars invited from different countries will participate in the symposium / forum exploring sustainable energy.

6. (1) The science fiction (sci-fi) movie *The Black Hole*, which has been filmed in New Zealand for three years, is highly praised by the movie / film critics and fans.

(2) The science fiction (sci-fi) movie *The Black Hole*, having been filmed in New Zealand for three years, is highly praised by the movie / film critics and fans.

Having been filmed in New Zealand for three years, the science fiction (sci-fi) movie *The Black Hole* is highly praised by the movie / film critics and fans.

7. (1) Fast fashion features / is characterized by speed and the low price, which allows people to purchase / buy fashionable clothing / garments / clothes at affordable prices.

(2) Fast fashion features / is characterized by speed and the low price, allowing people to purchase / buy fashionable clothing / garments / clothes at affordable prices.

8. (1) Nevertheless / However, the "fast consumption" it encourages has created / produced / yielded a massive / tremendous /enormous / great amount of waste / wastes, which has caused / lead to / resulted in huge / serious / major pollution problems.

(2) Nevertheless / However, the "fast consumption" it encourages has created / produced / yielded a massive / tremendous /enormous / great amount of waste / wastes, having caused / lead to / resulted in huge / serious / major pollution problems.

9. (1) Jade Mountain is usually covered with heavy snow during the winter, which makes the top of the mountain shine / sparkle like jade.

(2) Jade Mountain is usually covered with heavy snow during the winter, making the top of the mountain shine / sparkle like jade.

10. (1) In recent years, many movies that / which are produced by Tai-

wan have been highly regarded internationally.

(2) In recent years, many movies produced by Taiwan have been highly regarded internationally.

▶▶ 8.13.5 形容詞子句簡化爲片語挑戰題

1. Introduced last year to entice / lure / attract foreign investments, the new policy has now reached the goal of the first phase, with a total of fifteen multi-national corporations promising to invest in different industries in Taiwan.

2. Destroyed by the earthquake two years ago, the school has been rebuilt, allowing students and teachers to use the new facilities in the new semester.

3. Certified as a green building, the new City Hall will save energy by 30%, setting up a good example for commercial buildings.

4. Intended to help low-income families, the Non-Governmental Organization are sending medical teams consisting of volunteer doctors and nurses to villages in remote areas offering free medical check-ups and medical care.

第九章

▶▶ 9.2.3 小試身手

1. reaching their final destination

2. saved by the rescuers

3. considered one of the best tennis players of all time

4. touching her heart

5. having been sold

6. frightened

7. taking the photo

8. taken by the reporter

9. sending the letter to the mayor

10. being good friends

11. having invited many guests

12. having been invited

13. having been working for the company for over 25 years

14. not being promoted / not promoted

15. not being open

16. being the top students of his class

17. launched in 2007

18. having been implementing several major construction plans

19. discussing the controversial issues

20. being discussed by the committee members

21. not being convicted / not convicted

22. being the highest mountain in Taiwan

23. delivering fresh vegetables to the store every morning

24. being sent to the hospital

25. not having been evaluated

▶▶ 9.2.4 小試身手

1. Being the most popular teacher in the school, Mrs. Chen has been named Teacher of the Year.

2. Having been saved by the firefighter, she sent a gift to him to express her gratitude.

3. Profiting more than fifty million dollars, the owner of the company donated 10% of his profit to a charitable organization.

4. Inspired by the little girl's true story, the author wrote a great novel.

5. Selling her 10-year-old car, she then bought a new SUV.

6. Having performed an incredible magic show on TV, he became famous overnight.

7. Beginning in 2001, the project has helped more than ten thousand people.

8. Not having been defeated by the failures, she kept trying hard until she finally succeeded.

9. Having been teaching for 40 years, he is retiring in two months.

10. Captured near the east coast of Taiwan, the giant blue-fin tuna weighed more than 250 kilograms.

11. Having lost so much weight after just 12 months, she was ready to have the excess skin removal surgery.

12. Not functioning as it should, the machine had to be sent back to the factory for inspection.

13. Having saved enough money, he is planning to visit many different countries in Europe.

14. Solving the most difficult math problem, the boy won the math competition.

15. Making the final shot, he won the game for the team.

16. Paid to do the job, he has finished it efficiently.

17. Powered by a turbo engine, the car is hot in the market.

18. Not being tainted, the food can still be sold in the store.

19. Being eager to learn how to make chocolate chip cookies, he downloaded the recipe from a website and bought the necessary materials.

20. Being trained to be a professional dancer, she was on a strict diet.

21. Having sailed around the world all by herself, the girl celebrated her 20-year-old birthday when returning to New York.

22. Having done a great deal for our country, she is commended by the President for her unselfish contribution.

23. Not being busy, he agreed to help his friend move to a new apartment.

24. Not having been terminated, the contract still had to be honored by both sides.

25. Going through a difficult time fighting cancer, she is going to share her story with us tonight.

▶▶ 9.2.5 分詞構句挑戰題

1. Disappointed at the company's decision, he resigned last week.

2. Unaffected by the scandal, the councilwoman has been reelected.

3. Having been reported by TV, the steak restaurant has increased its business by fifty percent.

4. Being in the business for years, she knows how to cope with different clients.
   Having been in the business for years, she knew how to cope with different clients.

5. Not wanting his wife to be worried, he said nothing about the financial crisis of his company.

6. Not having regretted about her decision, she said she would keep her promise.

7. Released from the hospital, he can now go back to work.

8. Having been frozen in the freezer for two days, the beef was as hard as a rock.

9. Resisting to learn new technologies needed in the workplace, some of the senior workers were forced to quit their jobs.

10. Overcoming acrophobia / the fear of heights, he managed to walk through the suspension bridge thirty meters above the river.

11. Emphasizing developing creativity in the digital era, the two-week summer camp attracted hundreds of college students to sign up.

12. Considering the complexity of the issue, the mayor has decided to

call for a public hearing.

13. Not having been informed that the heavy rain had paralyzed the railroad, many commuters still rushed to the train station trying to catch the train to work.

14. Realizing that there was no turning back, he devoted all of his time and energy to the Artificial Intelligence startup of twenty million dollars.

15. Believing that hot springs can be drilled in Australia, he spent three million dollars of the investors and four years to finally develop the first hot spring in Australia.

第十章

▶▶▶ **10.1.1** 小試身手

1.

(1-1) Open from 11:00 a.m. to 9:30 p.m., the restaurant across from the park, which is owned by a famous movie star, serves excellent Italian food.

(1-2) Owned by a famous movie star, the restaurant across from the park, which is open from 11:00 a.m. to 9:30 p.m., serves excellent Italian food.

(2-1) Open from 11:00 a.m. to 9:30 p.m., the restaurant across from the park, owned by a famous movie star, serves excellent Italian food.

(2-2) Owned by a famous movie star, the restaurant across from the park, open from 11:00 a.m. to 9:30 p.m., serves excellent Italian food.

2.

(1) Scott Stevens, (who is) the Director of ELI at the University of Delaware, was excited to meet his good friend Sam, who invited him to attend an international conference (that / which was) organized by the English Department at Feng Chia University.

(2) Scott Stevens, the Director of ELI at the University of Delaware, was excited to meet his good friend Sam, inviting him to attend an international conference organized by the English Department at Feng Chia University.

3.

(1) The archeologists from three different countries who have been digging in the area for six months unearthed an ancient grave yard in a hill near the village.

(2) Having been digging in the area for six months, the archeologists from three different countries unearthed an ancient grave yard in a hill near the village.

4.

(1) Becoming a Christian at the age of 35, Joshua, who changed into a different person since then and quit his job as a pharmacist three years ago, is now a devoted missionary in India.

(2) Becoming a Christian at the age of 35, Joshua, changing into a different person since then and quitting his job as a pharmacist three years ago, is now a devoted missionary in India.

5.

(1) Launched in 2007, the Taiwan High Speed Rail, which connects major cities along the west coast of Taiwan, symbolizes the modernization of Taiwan's transportation system.

(2) Launched in 2007, the Taiwan High Speed Rail, connecting major cities along the west coast of Taiwan, symbolizes the moderniza-

tion of Taiwan's transportation system.

6.

(1) Timothy Lin, who has been working for a multi-national corporation in the mining business for two decades, has been promoted to be the CFO of the corporation.

(2) Timothy Lin, having been working for a multi-national corporation in the mining business for two decades, has been promoted to be the CFO of the corporation.

7.

(1) Introduced in 2007, the iPhone, which was created by Steve Jobs, (who was) the CEO of Apple Inc., has attracted millions of users worldwide.

(2) Introduced in 2007, the iPhone, created by Steve Jobs, the CEO of Apple Inc., has attracted millions of users worldwide.

8.

(1) The bridge which / that connects two major cities which / that are located in the east coast suddenly collapsed last month, which caused many casualties to drivers and passengers in the cars which / that were crossing the bridge.

(2) The bridge connecting two major cities located in the east coast suddenly collapsed last month, causing many casualties of drivers and passengers in the cars crossing the bridge.

9.

(1) The architecture of the National Taichung Theater, which is a new type of construction project, consists of 58 individual curved-wall units which / that are part of a special construction technique which / that uses steel reinforced bars to build a curved three-dimensional effect.

(2) The architecture of the National Taichung Theater, a new type

of construction project, consists of 58 individual curved-wall units being part of a special construction technique using steel reinforced bars to build a curved three-dimensional effect.

10.

(1) In addition to carrying out military missions, a drone, which is formally known as Unmanned Aerial Vehicle (UAV), is now also used in a wide variety of civilian roles that were unimaginable not long ago ranging from surveying, inspection, security, aerial video and photography, delivery services to several other applications.

(2) In addition to carrying out military missions, a drone, known as Unmanned Aerial Vehicle (UAV), is now also used in a wide variety of civilian roles unimaginable not long ago ranging from surveying, inspection, security, aerial video and photography, delivery services to several other applications.

11.

(1) When (they were) hiking in the deep woods at an altitude of 3,000 feet, the mountaineers unexpectedly spotted a Formosan black bear, whose population has been declining after their habitats are being diminished by severe exploitation by farmers who grow fruits and tea in the high mountains.

(2) When hiking in the deep woods at an altitude of 3,000 feet, the mountaineers unexpectedly spotted a Formosan black bear, whose population having been declining after their habitats being diminished by severe exploitation by farmers growing fruits and tea in the high mountains.

12.

(1-1) As the trade war between the U.S. and China intensifies, some of the top manufacturers in information technology industries that were relocated from Taiwan to China years ago are now moving back to set up new production lines to make products that are exported to the U.S., which creates thousands of new jobs and boosts the economy in Taiwan.

(1-2) As the trade war between the U.S. and China intensifies, some of the top manufacturers in information technology industries relocated from Taiwan to China years ago are now moving back to set up new production lines to make products exported to the U.S., creating thousands of new jobs and boosting the economy in Taiwan.

13.

(1) Being determined to be more aggressive and competitive after she attended the seminar that introduced new types of insurance, the insurance agent employed an innovative approach that was just learned from a speaker at the seminar to entice more clients to buy new insurance policies to cover a wider range of risks.

(2) Being determined to be more aggressive and competitive after attending the seminar introducing new types of insurance, the insurance agent employed an innovative approach learned from a speaker at the seminar to entice more clients to buy new insurance policies to cover a wider range of risks.

14.

(1) Entrusted under a contract that was signed by a developer who recently acquired a suburban house that was built in the 1970s, Grace, (who is) an interior designer who has been working with a team that specializes in home remodeling, plans to renovate the house in line with the contemporary style, which is more appealing to young couples.

(2) Entrusted under a contract signed by a developer recently acquiring a suburban house built in the 1970s, Grace, an interior

designer having been working with a team specializing in home remodeling, plans to renovate the house in line with the contemporary style, more appealing to young couples.

15.

(1) Increasing drunk driving, which is involved in many deadly car accidents, has prompted the central government to revise the law that regulates such incidents to raise the penalties that are imposed on drunk drivers, and the Legislative Yuan has just passed the new version of the law, which is set to be enacted on July 1 2019.

(2) Increasing drunk driving, involved in many deadly car accidents, has prompted the central government to revise the law regulating such incidents to raise the penalties imposed on drunk drivers, and the Legislative Yuan has just passed the new version of the law, set to be enacted on July 1 2019.

▶▶ 10.1.2 句型變換挑戰題

1. A young man has invented a special handgun that requires the fingerprint of the owner or someone who is authorized by the owner to pull the trigger, which is designed to prevent kids from misusing the handgun.

2. A French supermarket that is planning to open a hypermarket selling goods and groceries imported from France and other European countries in Suzhou, one of the many fast-developing cities in China, will build a structure there whose second floor will have a space of 25 units for local stores and restaurants to join its business.

3. Last September, David Wang, who is the general manager of a high-tech company in Taiwan, flied with his wife, Sharon, to San Francisco to meet with their daughter, Vera, before taking a cruise together to Alaska, where they saw the magnificent glacier and the thrilling northern lights.

4. Ruth, a teenager whose father challenged her to sail around the world all by herself, thought it was an insane idea because she had never been aboard any boat, but later she decided to take the challenge and completed the incredible journey during which she almost lost her life in a storm.

5. Before entering college, Henry was persuaded by his father, who believed that teaching was a better career choice, to give up his dream of becoming a professional singer, yet after teaching over twenty years and becoming a principal in a junior high school, he never stopped composing and singing songs, and he has won the second-place prize in a major singing contest and has been invited to sing in different occasions.

第十一章

▶ 11.4 小試身手

1. D. on the contrary   2. A. Otherwise   3. B. in addition

4. C. indeed   5. B. Most importantly   6. C. on the contrary

7. A. all in all   8. B. finally   9. D. otherwise

10. D. hence

▶ 11.5 小試身手

1. The game had been delayed; therefore / hence / consequently, the crowd had to wait for the game to start.

2. The couple have five children of their own; still / however/ nonetheless / nevertheless, they agreed to adopt their neighbor's three chil-

dren when she was diagnosed with terminal cancer.

3. They did not like to take the highway while traveling; instead, they prefer taking local roads to enjoy the scenery along the way.

4. Living in urban areas is more convenient but stressful; on the other hand / conversely / in contrast, living in rural areas is more relaxing and healthy.

5. She seems to be well qualified for the job according to her resume; however/ nonetheless / nevertheless, the manager does not think she is a good fit for our company because of her personality.

6. The small house is very old; still / however/ nonetheless / nevertheless, it has been sold for over two million dollars due to its invaluable location.

7. You must stop chewing beetle nuts; otherwise, you will die from oral cancer sooner or later.

8. My best friend is going to study abroad in Australia; also / besides / in addition / moreover / furthermore, she plans to get a part-time job there.

9. William enjoys outdoor activities; on the other hand / in contrast / in comparison, his twin brother likes reading and playing the guitar.

10. He bought the used car and reconditioned it; then, he sold it to someone for a higher price.

11. According to the trainer, the player has improved significantly; still / however/ nonetheless / nevertheless, he still has a long way to go before fully recovering from the injury.

12. The tourists from France paid visits to many famous scenic spots in Taiwan; for example, they went to Alishan and witnessed the spectacular sunrise and sea of clouds in the high mountains.

13. The committee held a meeting to assess the positive and negative impacts of the new zoning project; in conclusion / in summary,

they decided that it would bring substantial financial benefits to the city.

14. Jobs fill your pocked; on the other hand / in contrast / conversely, adventures fill your soul.

15. It seems the suspect has committed the crime; still / however/ nonetheless / nevertheless, the prosecutor is skeptical about his conviction in the court due to the lack of hard evidence.

16. Classical music is favored by older people; on the other hand / in contrast / in comparison /conversely, heavy metal music attracts more younger generations.

第十二章

▶▶ **12.1.2** 小試身手

1. (1) People who **regularly** go online buy things from online stores.

   (2) People who go online buy things from online stores **regularly**.

2. (1) The President vowed to crack down on drug traffickers **after his reelection**.

   (2) **After his reelection**, the President vowed to crack down on drug traffickers.

3. (1) My friend in Australia sent me a text message she would visit me in Taiwan **in summer**.

   (2) **In summer**, my friend in Australia sent me a text message she would visit me in Taiwan.

   My friend in Australia **in summer** sent me a text message she would visit me in Taiwan.

   My friend in Australia sent me **in summer** a text message she would visit me in Taiwan.

4. (1) Students who **frequently** skip classes upset the professor.

   (2) Students who skip classes upset the professor **frequently**.

5. (1) Employees who achieve monthly goals got promoted **often**.

   (2) Employees who **often** achieve monthly goals got promoted.

6. (1) **Before the meeting ends**, the manager said he would resign.

   (2) The manager said he would resign **before the meeting ends**.

7. (1) **When her husband returned**, Cindy told me she would go shopping with me.

   (2) Cindy told me she would go shopping with me **when her husband returned**.

▶▶▶ 12.1.4 小試身手

1. After jogging for over an hour, she drank a bottle of icy-cold cola.

2. The shirt in the store was just too small for me.

3. The robot cooking food amazed everyone.

4. I ate almost the entire extra-large pizza myself.

5. He said that he played basketball for only two hours this afternoon.

6. Nowadays people can order a meal through a cellphone App delivered to them.

7. She read a science fiction, *When You Reach Me*, a story by Rebecca Stead about sacrificing one's life by returning to the past with a time machine.

8. She gave an Apple Watch she purchased from Apple Website to her boyfriend.

9. With the deal sealed, she was happy that she bought the house for nearly $500,000.

10. My father, who taught me how to play basketball, is a big fan of Michael Jordan.

▶▶ 12.2.2 小試身手

1. → Sitting on the porch, she enjoyed the view of the open space.

   → When she was sitting in the porch, the view of the open space made her joyful.

2. → When she was 48, her dream finally came true.

3. → If lost, traveler's checks can always be replaced.

   → If people lose their traveler's checks, they can always replace them.

4. → Riding in a train, he saw pretty farm houses and golden wheat fields.

5. → After we had sit in our seats for over an hour, the plane finally took off.

6. → Bought 10 years ago, the car is now sold for $5,000 by us.

7. → Since joining the baseball team, Peter has won many games for the team as a powerful starting pitcher.

   → Since Peter joined the baseball team, the team has won many games with Peter as a powerful starting pitcher.

8. → Walking in the night market, we / tourists / people saw many stands (were) selling different kinds of local delicacies.

   → When we / tourists / people walked in the night market, many stands were selling different kinds of local delicacies.

9. → While working on his presentation slides, he was interrupted by his cat jumping on the keyboard.

   → While he was working on his presentation, his cat interrupted him jumping on the keyboard.

10. → To play tennis well, one needs to practice regularly with a coach.

11. → Married with kids, Lisa seems to lead a wonderful life.

12. → Although a high school student, she needs to take care of her

younger brother and sister since their parents are gone.

→ Although she is a high school student, her younger brother and sister need her to take care of them since their parents are gone.

▶▶ 12.2.3 脫節修飾語挑戰題

1. Although an experienced detective, he was horrified / shocked by the terrifying crime scene.

2. When alone, she enjoys classical music most.

3. Retrieved from the suspect's notebook / laptop computer, the file will be submitted to the judge as evidence by the investigators.

4. To lose weight, I (or any human subject) installed a running machine / treadmill in the basement.

5. Established 100 years ago, an abandoned school has been transformed into a community center by the City Government.

6. Having won / Winning the $30,000,000 lottery, she immediately sold the old car and the old house.

7. Having worked all day, I am grateful for merely having a hot meal.

8. If elected president, he may not fully keep / fulfill his promises.

9. With a new air conditioner being installed, we felt so cool in the house all summer.

10. Having been widely used since the 1970s, at least 500 billion plastic bags are estimated by environmentalists to be produced in a year in the whole world at present.

第十三章

▶▶ **13.1.2 小試身手**

一、將下列句子翻成英文的條件句

1. If she **had** enough money, she **would buy** a new car.

2. If she **has** enough money, she **will buy** a new car.

3. If she **had had** enough money last year, she **would have bought** a new car.

4. If I **were** she, I **would not buy** a used car.

5. If I **need** to work over time, I **will call** my wife.

6. If he **had not missed** the High Speed Rail yesterday, we **would have had** dinner together.

7. The alarm **will sound** if you **open** the door.

二、將下列虛擬／假設語氣的句子改寫成所引申的事實

1. The boy is old enough. He was allowed to watch the movie in the theater.

2. He left the house earlier. He didn't miss the plane.

3. It didn't rain last night. They didn't cancel the concert in the square.

4. He did not hear the announcement. He missed the meeting.

三、將下列的事實陳述改寫成與現在或過去事實不符合的虛擬／假設語氣的句子

1. If his mother were alive, she would be proud of him now.

2. If had worked hard enough, he would have gotten good grades last semester.

3. If she had been in the building, she would have been injured in the earthquake.

▶▶ 13.1.4 小試身手

1. If it **had not rained** last month, we **would suffer** from water shortage now.

2. If he **had studied** hard enough last year, he **would not** be **taking** Economics for the second time now.

3. The prices of vegetables and fruits **would not be** so expensive this year if it **had not been** so severely cold last winter.

▶▶ 13.1.6 小試身手

1. If she **had not followed** the lawyer's advice when signing the contract, she **might not be** able to protect her legal rights today.

2. If the company's production system **had not been computerized** 10 years ago, we **should not be** able to meet the **increasing** demand from the foreign clients now.

3. If I **had not caught** the train and **had missed** the interview, my career **would have been** completely different, and my wife **could have married** to someone else.

4. If Sam **had not sold** the used motorcycle to the American teacher, he **would not have had** the opportunity to obtain a master's degree in the US, and he **would not** be **teaching** English in a university now.

▶▶ 13.3.1 小試身手

A. 未來可能發生的條件句

1. If the machine **is used** improperly, it will not **be damaged**.

2. The customer agreed that if the car **is fixed** by the mechanic immediately, an extra amount of US$100 will **be paid**.

B. 與現在事實不符的條件句

1. If the price **were lowered** by the shopkeeper, the ring would **be bought** by the husband for his wife.

2. If I **were** the owner of the house, the offer would **be accepted**.

3. If it **were** not raining, the game would not **be postponed**.

4. If the budget **were passed** by the city council, a new park would **be developed**.

5. We **would need** a bigger house for the family if we **had** more children than now.

C. 與過去事實不符的條件句

1. If the villagers **had been given** warnings earlier by the government, such a disaster **would** not **have been caused** by the storm.

2. If the candidate's scandal **had** not **been reported**, he would **have been elected** the new mayor.

3. If the firefighters had not arrived at the scene soon enough, the people in the house **would** not **have been saved** from the fire.

4. If the final shot **had** not **been missed** by the star player at the buzzer, the game **would have been won** by the defending team.

5. If the assembly line **had** not **been designed** by Henry Ford to build Model-T automobiles, they **would** not **have been sold** at such an affordable price.

6. If the refrigerator **had** not **been invented** for households, cold drinks **would** not **have been enjoyed** so conveniently.

▶▶▶ **13.3.2 小試身手**

1. More market share **would have been gained** by the company if its latest model **had been rolled out** earlier than its opponent's.

2. If the assignment **is finished** before the deadline, you **will be rewarded**.

3. If the house **were listed** under his name, it **could be mortgaged** to a bank for a loan.

4. We would have arrived at the conference in London in time if the flight **had not been delayed**.

5. If the stocks that **had been purchased** three months earlier **had been sold** a few days later, we would have made more profit.

▶ 13.5.2 [wish] 練習填充

1. My family is taking a vacation in Southern Taiwan this summer. I wish we **would take** a vacation in Japan instead.

2. Lisa is not a famous singer. She wishes she **were** a famous singer.

3. Tiffany did not learn how to ride a scooter when she was in college. She wishes she **had learned** how to ride a scooter then.

4. The doctor does not have the medicine to cure the disease. The doctor wishes she **had** the medicine to cure the disease.

5. The manager regrets that he did not adopt the new marketing strategy. The manager now wishes he **had adpoted** the new marketing strategy.

6. The school will not have the budget to build a new stadium. The students wish the school **would have** the budget to build a new auditorium.

7. The tourists forgot to make reservations for the hotel room. They wish they **had made** reservations for the hotel room.

8. They failed to get the tickets for the NBA game. They won't be able to watch the game in the stadium. They wish they **could** watch the game in the stadium.

9. The government passed a law to legalize mercy killing. Many opponents wish the government **had not passed** such a law.

▶ 13.7.1 [were to] 練習填充

1. As the typhoon is coming, the captain of the fishing boat decides to stay at the harbor. If the fishing boat **were to leave** the harbor to fish in such a bad weather, it **would be** too risky.

2. The bridge collapsed just seconds before the car went on it. If the

car **were to have reached** the bridge seconds sooner, it **would have fallen** into the river.

3. The city is a dangerous place for tourists to visit at night. If I **were to visit** the city, I **would avoid** going out at night in the city.

▶▶ 13.8.1 without 練習填充

1. Fortunately I applied sunscreen lotion at the beach. Without **applying** sunscreen lotion, I **would have gotten** sunburn.

2. God helped the mother overcome her predicament. Without God's help, the mother **would have given up** on herself.

▶▶ 13.9.1 if only 練習填充

1. I really like the house, but the price is beyond my budget. If only I **had** the money to buy it.

2. She regrets that she didn't follow her parents' advice. She said to her parents, "If only I **had listened** to you."

3. Jerry, a sales representative at a big company, needs to do business with Japanese. However, Jerry did not take the Japanese course in college. He said to his colleagues, "If only I **had learned** Japanese when in college."

4. We are living in a small town. The life here is kind of boring. If only we **could move** to a big city to enjoy a more exciting life.

▶▶ 13.10.3 as if 練習

1. He hasn't read the book, yet he talks as if he **had read** it.

2. He is married, but he acted as if he **were** single.

3. She slept for eight hours last night, yet she looks as if she **had not slept** (sleep) at all.

4. After winning the game, the kids celebrated as if they **had won** the world championship.

5. The thief was caught at the scene, yet he behaved as if he **were** innocent.

6. She was not making much money; however, she was living her life as if she **were** rich.

▶▶ 13.12 條件句及假設語氣打通關

一、將下列的事實陳述改寫成與事實不符合的虛擬語氣條件句

1. If the driver had not taken the wrong the turn, he would not have gotten lost in the strange city.

2. If my secretary had reminded me, I would not have forgotten about the appointment with my client.

3. If he were on our team, he could help us.

4. If she had not switched the mode of her cellphone to mute, she would have heard my call.

5. If the item were on sale, I would buy it.

6. If she had not been sick on the day of the competition, she might have won the prize.

7. If Tom had not hit a walk-off home run, his team would not have won the game at the bottom of the 12th inning.

8. If I had not passed the certification test, I would not be qualified for the job.

9. If she had signed the contract, she could be a famous singer today.

10. If he had not sold the house too early, he would have made more profit.

二、假設語氣中翻英填充

1. I **would have gotten** sunburned if I **had forgotten** to apply sunscreen lotion yesterday.

2. **Without** her family's encouragement and support, she **might have given** up long time ago.

3. If there **had been** the medicine to treat her disease, she **should** still

be alive today.

4. He **would not be** a famous athlete now if the coach **had let** him **quit** training.

5. If he **were not** your good friend, he **might not lend** you money.

6. If they **had followed** the rules, the disaster last night **should have been avoided**.

7. He **would sacrifice** for you if he **were you**.

8. If I **had been** the CFO, I **might have modified / revised** the expansion plan **proposed** last week.

9. The oil company found natural gas in the farm that had belonged to Terry's father. Once Terry learned that, he said to his wife, "If **only** my father **had** not **sold** the farm! We **would have made** millions of dollars!"

10. Our lives **would be** completely different **without** the **invention** of the computer.

11. The condominium **would not have collapsed** had it **not been** falsely **designed**.

12. If the company **does not** launch new products, its market **share will decrease / shrink** sharply.

13. Tina's parents said to her, "You may keep a kitten **provided** that you **take** full **responsibility** of taking care of it."

14. Had she **not persisted**, she **would not be** a renowned artist today.

15. Taiwan **would** still **be ruled** by Japan today if Japan **had not been defeated** in World War II.

16. If she **had not been adopted** by foreign parents, she **might not have had** the **opportunity** to go to college.

17. We **would have won** yesterday's basketball game if he **had made** the final shot.

18. He wished that he **had invested** in the real estate after the 921

Earthquake, so he **would not** need to be **working** so hard today.

19. His company **would have gone bankrupt** if his friend **had not supported** him **financially**.

20. American bisons **should have gone / become extinct** without the government's **protection**.

第十四章

▶▶ **14.2.7 比較句型打通關**

1. The number of online courses offered by universities now are **twice as many as** six years ago.

2. The dishes my wife cooks taste **as delicious as** those my mom does.

3. **The less** it rains in the summer, **the sweeter** the watermelons will **grow**.

4. It is **no less easy** to be a full-time housekeeper than to be a full-time worker.

5. My friend asked me to lend him some money, and I said I could loan him **not more than** NT$50,000.

6. She is more ambitious **than** any **other employee** in the company as she arrives at the office **earlier** than anyone **else** and outperforms all **others**.

7. The foods **sold** in this supermarket is **not so / as** fresh as **those** in another **one**.

8. **The more efforts** you put into your work, **the more** you feel **proud of** yourself.

9. She comes from a wealthy family, and she owns **no less than** four luxurious **imported** cars.

10. The passengers were **not** any **less relieved** than the crew when the pilot made a successful **emergency** landing during a severe thunderstorm.

11. To master English writing, **constant** practicing is **no less important** than thorough understanding of English grammar.

12. Joshua, an **experienced** mountain hiker, has climbed **more** high mountains in Taiwan than **anyone else** I know.

13. The fans like the sports star **all** the **more** for his incredibly generous charity **donations** that will help **not less** than two thousand kids attend college.

14. **The more** the **interviewee** boasts about his skills and experiences, **the less** the **interviewer** is impressed.

15. Your **arguments** in the court are **as** brilliant **as** any **other** outstanding **lawyer's** can be.

16. The tuition of this private university is **three times as expensive as** that of a national university.

17. **The more pesticides** the farmers use, **the more threats** the crops will pose to our health.

18. The tour bus driver is **not** any **less humorous** than **focused**.

19. She is **no** more **honest than** her husband is **humble**.

20. **The more infrastructure** the government builds, **the more** foreign **investments** will be lured.

21. The military **drone** can fire missiles **as accurately as** any **advanced** jet fighter.

22. Daniel is only nine years old, **yet** he dribbles the ball **as** fantastically **as** professional basketball players **do**.

23. The robots **assemble** the cars **much more efficient** than human workers **do**.

24. Once you are able to **run** the business **as well as** your father **does**,

he will **hand** over the business to you and retire.

25. The sports car newly **released** by the car **manufacturer** runs **fast-er** than **any other one** in the whole world.

26. In historians' eyes, the Han Dynasty was not **any less** a great regime **than** the Roman Empire **was**.

27. Every **employee** of the bank is super excited that the year-end **bonus** this year is **no** less **than** six months' pay.

28. **The older** the antique furniture is, the more **valuable** it will **become**.

29. People **who betray** their friends are no **more** respected **than trust-worthy**.

30. Mahatma Gandhi was **no less** a great national hero **than** Martin Luther King Jr. **was**.

31. The **richer / wealthier** one gets, the **less** true friends one can have.

32. **Corrupt** politicians are **not** any **less** evil than robbers and murderers **are**.

33. She is thrifty because she makes **no more than** NT$32,000 a month while living in Taipei, the **most expensive** city in Taiwan.

34. Your father is **not** so **stubborn as** people think he **is**; actually, he is **as** flexible as **any** other father **who** cares for his children.

▶▶ **14.3.4 小試身手**

1. The less generous a business owner is, the less loyal the employees are.

2. The younger the professors are, the more energetic and enthusiastic they tend to be.

3. The more you expect, the less satisfied you may get.

4. The more diverse the products we sell are, the more varieties of buyers we can entice.

5. The more comfortable the players feel in a competition, the better

they will perform.

6. The fewer students are in a class, the more attention the teacher can pay to individual students.

7. The farther away from the urban area the land is located, the cheaper it gets.

8. The closer we walk with God, the stronger we will be when faced with adversity.

9. The less responsible a person is, the less likely he will succeed in anything he does.

10. The less public transport a city provides, the more serious the air pollution produced by motor vehicles will be.

▶▶ **14.3.5 雙重比較級挑戰題**

1. The more countries one visits, the more one appreciates different cultures.

2. The more advanced AI becomes, the more it can benefit the industry.

3. The fresher the food (is), the better it tastes.

4. The more thorough the physical examination is, the more it costs.
   The more thorough the physical examination is, the more expensive it is.

5. The more ancient an antique (is), the more valuable (it is).

6. The less developed a country (is), the lower the cost of living (is).

7. The more complicated the issue (is), the harder/more difficult for it to get resolved.

8. The fewer samples researchers use for statistical analysis, the less convincing the conclusion (is).

9. The more rainforests we lose due to industrial development, the worse the global ecology (becomes).

10. The more focused we keep during a mission, the more likely we

carry it out successfully.

11. The more automated the manufacturing process (is), the more efficient (it is).

12. The more audience (there are) watching the game in the stadium, the harder the players play, and the more money the two teams make.

第十五章

▶▶ 15.1.4 小試身手

1. Julia said (that) she liked the song.

2. He said (that) he had bought a new shirt.

3. The boy said (that) he was working on his homework.

4. His wife said (that) her husband would be home soon.

5. They said (that) they had been playing video games for over four hours.

6. Mary said (that) her sister and she were going to visit their uncle.

7. John's mother said (that) she must go to pick up his sister.

8. Our English teacher said (that) we might work with our partners on the assignment.

9. The players told the coach (that) they had been practicing since he / she came in at six.

10. Her brother told her (that) he could take her to the party to meet with some of his good friends.

▶▶ 15.1.6 小試身手

1. Philip's mother told him (that) his teacher had called him that night.

2. The lawyer advised him (that) he should accept the deal then.

3. Karen said (that) her brother would have dinner with his girlfriend in that restaurant two days later / in two days' time.

4. The sales manager told the gentleman (that) they would deliver the sofa to his place the next day.

5. She said on the phone (that) she had shipped the item three days before, and it should arrive the following Monday.

6. My colleague told me (that) I had left my cellphone there the night before / the previous night.

7. The famous female marathon runner told the media (that) she had won the gold medal the previous week / the week before, and she was going to retire the following year.

8. The rich woman announced (that) she had donated three million dollars to victims of the storm two days before, and she was considering donating another two million dollars to an orphanage the following month.

▶▶ 15.1.8 小試身手

1. Timothy asked me **who had been teaching me how to play badminton.**

2. Timothy asked his sister **when she would arrive the next day.**

3. Did Timothy ask the audience **how they liked his song?**

4. Did Timothy ask Kyle **how much he had paid for the dinner the previous night / the night before?**

5. Timothy asked Janet **why she hadn't come to his birthday party the previous Saturday.**

▶▶ 15.1.9 小試身手

1. He asked her, "**Where do you come from?**"

2. His mother asked, "**Who is playing tennis with you now?**"

3. The teacher asked the students, "**Which place do you want to visit for the field trip next month?**"

4. She asked the clerk, "**How much does the watch cost?**"

5. Mary asked her father, "**When did you make reservations of the hotel for our family's vacation?**"

▶▶ **15.1.10** 小試身手

1. Dora asked Kevin **whether (or not) Sam had played basketball with him and her brother.**

2. Dora asked Lisa **whether (or not) she had been playing video games that afternoon.**

3. My mother asked me **whether (or not) I had invited my best friend to the party the day before / the previous day.**

4. Did you ask your sister **whether (or not) she could show you how to write a book report that weekend?**

5. My father asked me **whether (or not) I had seen his sunglasses.**

6. She asked me **whether (or not) I would sign up for the community service the following week.**

7. The waitress asked us **whether (or not) we were enjoying the meal that night.**

▶▶ **15.1.11** 小試身手

1. The lawyer asked the judge, "**Am I allowed to call another witness next week?**"

2. Peter asked his wife, "**Can you pick up our daughter for me because my car had a flat tire?**"

3. The police officer asked the driver, "**Have you been driving under influence tonight?**"

4. The athlete asked his coach, "**Did I break the record this morning?**"

5. My mother asked me, "**Did you forget to pay the bill yesterday?**"

6. Did Katie asked Nina, "**Will you join us in this night club to celebrate?**"

7. Did the boss asked Ethan, "**Are you willing to be sent to Singapore next month?**"

▶▶ **15.1.13** 小試身手

1. The police officer asked / told me to show him / her my driver's license.

2. Jeremy asked / told his brother to return the car to him that weekend.

3. Cindy asked / told her husband to remember to pick up their grandson that afternoon.

4. The professor asked / told the class to hand their reports to his / her assistant no later than the following Friday.

5. Rosa asked / told Paul to buy her a breakfast the following morning.

▶▶ **15.1.14** 小試身手

1. My father said to me, "Turn down the music."

2. Zana said to her friend Robert, "Please lend me your bike tomorrow morning."

3. She said to her children, "Share your toys with your friends."

4. The coach said to the players, "Shoot 100 times before going home tonight."

5. The manager said to the sales representatives, "Please submit your reports next week."

▶▶ **15.1.16** 小試身手

1. She asked / told the children not to open the gifts until the following morning.

2. The doctor asked / told the patient not to eat any food the night before the operation.

3. She asked / told her husband (to please) not to forget to water the plants for her.

4. He asked me not to tell my parents what had happened there that night.

5. The police asked / told the reporters not to enter the crime scene or they would be arrested.

▶▶ 15.1.17 小試身手

1. She said to me, "Don't tell your brother when I will come to your house."

2. He said to the investors, "Don't sell your stocks until next week."

3. She said to her teacher, "Please don't tell my parents I have been punished today."

4. He said to Nancy, "Don't forget to feed my dog when I am away next weekend."

   He said, "Nancy, don't forget to feed my dog when I am away next weekend."

5. The supervisor said to Peter, "Don't be late for the meeting tomorrow afternoon."

   The supervisor said, "Don't be late for the meeting tomorrow afternoon, Peter."

▶▶ 15.1.18 直接引述與間接引述打通關

I. 將下列直接引述改寫成間接引述

1. The detective asked the eyewitness what the suspect looked like.

2. The new president said (that) he / she would do his / her best to solve problems our / their country is faced with.

3. The doctor told Victoria (that) her father was recovering from the

surgery the previous night / the night before.

4. Jack told Tina (that) he would wait for her there the following / next afternoon.

5. The professor asked the students who wanted to help him / her with the experiment the following week.

6. Jane's father told her (that) he would take her and her brother to Disney World if he got promoted the following month.

7. The judge asked the female lawyer if / whether (or not) she had any more questions for the witness.

8. The coach told the players not to forget to come to practice the next day at six.

9. The saleswoman told the manager (that) she had sold two cars the previous week, and she would try to sell more cars the following week.

10. The customer asked the street vender if / whether (or not) he / she was selling sandwiches there every morning.

11. Eric told Mary on the phone (that) John was having lunch with him then and asked her if / whether (or not) she wanted to join them.

12. The police told Mr. Wang (that) his stolen car had been found the night before / the previous night.

13. The mother asked the child where her cellphone was.

14. The policeman told the fugitive to surrender or he / she would be shot.

15. Jesus told his followers to forgive those who offeded them.

16. The students told the teacher they had finished their assignments and asked him / her whether (or not) / if they could take a break then.

17. Karen said (that) the purse was her sister's, not hers.

18. The clerk told Peter (that) the item he had ordered had been shipped to him two days before.

19. The mechanic told me on the phone (that) my father's car had been repaired and I could pick it up that day.

20. She told my brother (that) she had heard that he was moving to Taichung the following month.

21. My colleague asked me in disbelief whether (or not) / if I was being assigned to Hong Kong the following week.

22. Did Mary's doctor asked her parents how long they had been feeding her that kind of food?

23. In the supermarket, a woman asked the clerk where she could find blenders.

24. The manager told her (that) her application had been approved.

25. The reporter asked the successful businessman how he had overcome difficulties and succeeded.

II. 將下列間接引述改寫成直接引述

1. He said, "My boss (has) assigned me a new task."

2. They said to the professor, "When are we required to submit the term report?"

3. The pilot said to the passengers, "We will arrive at the destination soon."

4. The taxi driver said to me, "Where do you want to go?"

5. The clerk at the liquor store said to the girl, "Are you 21 or older?"

6. My friend said to me, "Did you see my girlfriend last night?"

7. Tom's brother said to me, "Will you play basketball with my brother tomorrow?"

8. The instructor said to the students, "Do not cheat in the exam or you will be punished."

9. At the end of the interview, the manager said to the lady, "You seem to be a good fit for our company."

10. Excitedly, Jerry said to his parents, "I have been hired and will

start working next week."

11. My sister said to me, "I will try my best to come to your commencement next month."

12. The police spokesman said, "The two suspects have been arrested last night and will be charged soon."

13. Lillian said to me, "I will be presenting my paper in this conference."

14. Sam said to Jane, "Did you see my student ID yesterday?"

15. The general said, "We have saved the hostages and will send them home the day after tomorrow."

16. The plumber said, "The toilet has been repaired, and I will charge you $150."

17. The patient said, "I want to cancel the appointment with the dentist scheduled tomorrow afternoon because my daughter is sick."

18. The lawyer said to me, "Don't sign the contract before you are fully advised."

19. Did the young child ask the magician, "How did you do the trick?"

20. The wife said to her husband, "I am not feeling well. Can you fix dinner tonight?"

第十六章

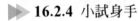 **16.2.4 小試身手**

1. It made her nervous to meet the new boss for the first time.

2. It allows people to keep up with what is going on in the world reading the news stories of current international events.

3. It was not surprising at all that the young prodigy got admitted to

the prestigious university to major in Physics.

4. He found it very challenging in terms of language and culture studying in a foreign country.

5. It is more significant how you accomplish the goals than the end results.

6. It is nearly impossible for him to marry the beautiful young lady.

7. They left it undecided when to resume the negotiation.

8. It is hard to predict when he will return to his hometown.

9. It is many college graduates' top choice to work in a multi-national corporation like that.

10. It is the trainer's biggest concern whether the trainees will be ready to perform their jobs properly in six months.

11. Who made it a rule that no one is allowed to enter the kitchen after midnight?

12. It is now very common for college students to work part-time.

▶▶ 16.2.5 小試身手

1. It was the firefighters who bravely saved the children from the fire.

2. It was for the underprivileged school children that they donated money to the charity.

3. Who was it that gave the order to arrest the celebrity?

4. It was the victims of the earthquake who needed food and shelters the most.

5. It was food and shelters that the victims of the earthquake needed the most.

6. It was more than five million dollars that the company spent in developing new products last year.

7. It was in developing new products that the company spent more than five million dollars last year.

8. It was the new district attorney that Peter was appointed last week.

9. It was last week when Peter was appointed the new district attorney.

10. It was to show appreciation that the Mayor commended the pastor for what he had done for the community.

11. It matters to the jury in a trial what the evidence shows.

12. It depends on its effectiveness whether the new cellphone app will become popular.

▶▶ 16.2.6 it 句型挑戰題

1. It is **required** for college students to **finish** 128 **credit hours** to obtain a bachelor's degree.

2. It is **much** more **exciting watching** the game in the **stadium** than doing it live on TV at home.

3. It was not **until** her mother passed away that she **realized / understood how** much her mother had **sacrificed** for the family.

4. It was **during** the investigation **that** the police **accidentally** found out that the **suspect had committed** the **kidnapping / abduction** of a wealthy businessman many years before.

5. It is impressive that a high school student in Taiwan **who** is **proficient** in three foreign languages has **been admitted** to Harvard University recently.

6. It was reported in the TV news yesterday that several new **species** of fish had **been discovered** by scientists **studying / researching** ocean animals.

7. It **was in 2017** when the Mass **Rapid Transit** (MRT) **connecting** Taipei and Taoyuan Airport was finally **launched**.

8. It was not surprising that the politician **involved** in a bribery **scandal** has **denied** the allegation.

9. It is **what** we **achieve**, not **what** we possess, **that** decides **whether** or not our lives count.

10. It **was** Bill Hewlett, one of the two **founders** of HP, **who offered**

the 12-year-old Steve Jobs a summer Job **that** allowed him to learn **how** to **run** a company.

第十七章

▶▶ 17.1.2 小試身手

1. As a diligent student, rarely did Jessica miss classes when in college.
2. Under no circumstances will they sell their father's art collections.
3. Only in this way could the team win the game.
4. Barely had Barry finished his term paper on the computer when the power went out.
5. Only by cutting down its expenses substantially will the organization survive.
6. Not only was she awarded Outstanding Instructor of 2018, but she was also promoted to be an associate professor.
7. After the terrifying accident, no longer will she ride a scooter.
8. Seldom did he made public speeches as a student, yet he has become one of the most famous motivational speakers in Taiwan.
9. No sooner had the trainee completed her task than the time was up.
10. Never did she see such a fascinating singing performance by a young child.

▶▶ 17.1.7 小試身手

1. Not until the snow storm stops will tourists be allowed to enter the National Park.
2. So lucrative is the job that many young people are applying for it.

3. Into the pool jumped the lifeguard to rescue the drowning girl.

4. Only if your monthly income exceeds US$3,000 will the landlord rent the apartment to you.

5. Emotional was the audience when the sad movie ended.

6. Only after he buys a house will she marry him.

7. Such a popular novel is *The Old Man and the Sea* that many people have read it.

8. Only if it is properly treated by a veterinary will the dog fully recover from the injury.

9. Calm and relieved was the prosecuter when the judge sentenced the murder suspect to life in prison.
   When the judge sentenced the murder suspect to life in prison, calm and relieved was the prosecutor.

10. Only after he gets the driver's license can he drive the car.

▶▶ 17.4 倒裝句打通關

1. Not only do I like Japanese food, but I have also been to Japan for sightseeing several times.

2. Such an excellent / a wonderful / a brilliant novel is *Secret Daughter* that every student in the English department should read it.

3. Rarely / Seldom did he borrow books from the library when in high school.

4. No sooner had they finished singing the birthday song last night than her parents came back home.

5. Only after watching students' presentations will the teacher make comments.

6. So difficult / hard is the test that students need to spend at least one year to prepare for it.

7. Never have we eaten such delicious and inexpensive beef noodles in Taipei.

8. Strongly motivated were the young sales representatives as they were promised by the company that they would get large amounts of commissions.

9. In no way will the team composed / consisting of high school students win the first prize of the programming contest.

10. Not until she was 15 was she told by her parents that she had been adopted.

11. Not only should we participate in / take part in international events, but we should also demonstrate / show the unique features of our own culture.

12. Only if the professional basketball player passes the physical examination can he sign the contract with the team.

13. Under no circumstances will he consider moving to a big city because all his friends live in his hometown.

14. Due to suffering from depression, no longer will the TV star act.
No longer will the TV star act due to suffering from depression.

15. Hoping to buy fresh fish at low prices, to the fish market drives the chef at three (o'clock) every morning.

16. Hardly had the passengers escaped from the tour bus (involved) in a car accident when it started to burn.

國家圖書館出版品預行編目資料

談笑用兵 英文句型全攻略／林羨峯著. --
初版. -- 臺北市：五南，2019.09
　　面；　公分
　　ISBN 978-957-763-653-9（平裝）

1.英語　2.句法

805.169　　　　　　　　　108015064

1X7L

談笑用兵　英文句型全攻略

作　　者 ― 林羨峯（118.5）

發 行 人 ― 楊榮川

總 經 理 ― 楊士清

總 編 輯 ― 楊秀麗

副總編輯 ― 黃文瓊

責任編輯 ― 吳雨潔

封面設計 ― 姚孝慈

美術設計 ― 吳佳臻

出 版 者 ― 五南圖書出版股份有限公司

地　　址：106台北市大安區和平東路二段339號4樓

電　　話：(02)2705-5066　　傳　　真：(02)2706-6100

網　　址：http://www.wunan.com.tw

電子郵件：wunan@wunan.com.tw

劃撥帳號：01068953

戶　　名：五南圖書出版股份有限公司

法律顧問　林勝安律師事務所　林勝安律師

出版日期　2019年9月初版一刷
　　　　　2020年6月初版二刷

定　　價　新臺幣780元

經典永恆・名著常在

五十週年的獻禮——經典名著文庫

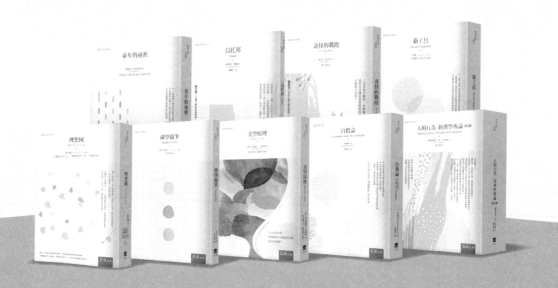

五南，五十年了，半個世紀，人生旅程的一大半，走過來了。

思索著，邁向百年的未來歷程，能為知識界、文化學術界作些什麼？

在速食文化的生態下，有什麼值得讓人雋永品味的？

歷代經典・當今名著，經過時間的洗禮，千錘百鍊，流傳至今，光芒耀人；

不僅使我們能領悟前人的智慧，同時也增深加廣我們思考的深度與視野。

我們決心投入巨資，有計畫的系統梳選，成立「經典名著文庫」，

希望收入古今中外思想性的、充滿睿智與獨見的經典、名著。

這是一項理想性的、永續性的巨大出版工程。

不在意讀者的眾寡，只考慮它的學術價值，力求完整展現先哲思想的軌跡；

為知識界開啟一片智慧之窗，營造一座百花綻放的世界文明公園，

任君遨遊、取菁吸蜜、嘉惠學子！